Mark McGee
and the Valley of the
Shadow of Death

BILLY STANCIL

Mark McGee
and the Valley of the
Shadow of Death

Book 2

XULON PRESS

Xulon Press
2301 Lucien Way #415
Maitland, FL 32751
407.339.4217
www.xulonpress.com

Mark McGee and the Valley of the Shadow of Death
Book 2

Printed in the United States of America.

ISBN-13: 978-1-5456-7572-4

LETTER TO THE READER

D ear Reader, first of all, thank you for taking the time out of your busy life to walk with me, just briefly, down this crazy, winding path. My name is Billy Stancil, and I'm the author of the Mark McGee series. In this life, we are given by God, certain people who will guide us, encourage us, and shape us into the person that HE wants us to be. There are so many that I could name. My parents, Bill & Susie Stancil; my childhood pastor, Charles Lenn; great friends like Eric Osborne, Jason Green, Randy Scalise, and Bret Snyder...just to name a few. My wife Rachel and daughter Lesley were probably the biggest influences of my life. They both continue to amaze me everyday with their wisdom and talents.

I would have to say that my influences to become a writer, were my 11th grade English teacher, Ms. Harrell, who told me that I had quite an imagination and talent for writing; author Frank Peretti, who made spiritual warfare as exciting as an outer space fantasy; author JK Rowling, who transported millions of people happily into an amazing world that she created; and author Ted Dekker, who showed me that you can have action and adventure without foul language and crude content.

Mark McGee and the Valley of the Shadow of Death is the sequel to Mark McGee and the Gateway to God. My hope, as you join Mark and his friends in the adventure of their lives, is that you would get to know God in an exciting and personal way. Just as Mark, Scotty, and Gabi put their imperfect faith in a perfect God, may you come to realize that greater is He that is in you...

BOOK DEDICATION

For Susie Stancil, MOM. You were my biggest fan and ultimate hero. I miss you every day.

TABLE OF CONTENTS

Letter To The Reader v
Book Dedication vii
Introduction xi
A Day At The Beach 1
The Text 15
Todd 2.0. 32
Operation Vengeance 51
The Wheels On The Bus 69
Camp Ricochet 85
The Return Of The Dragon 105
The Fight For A Soul 123
Shadow Of The Almighty 140
Holding A Grudge 156
The Search 175
No Other Name 191
Heading Home 209
Death Comes 226
The Journey Begins 245
The Puppy 259
No Greater Love 273
The Shadow Of Death 283
The Welcome Home 300
Epilogue 309

MARK MCGEE AND THE VALLEY OF THE SHADOW OF DEATH

INTRODUCTION

Kevin could hardly breathe. The air was thick in this place. His heart rate had quickened, and his shirt was soaked with sweat. His face was streaked with tears and dirt. He'd screamed at the sky for what seemed like hours. He had nothing left to give or say. He was empty.

The ground was dry and cracked here. There was no breeze in this place. It was dark, but a different kind of dark. As if the sun was being darkened by black smoke; occasionally peeking through, but not enough to notice.

Kevin panted for water as he moved on, his thirst overwhelming. He had never been this thirsty. He had never been this dry. He had never been so alone. Still, he moved on.

He heard a clicking noise to his right and frantically turned. He was beginning to panic. He had sensed something following him for quite some time. "Who's there?" he screamed into the darkness. Behind him he heard it again. He screamed and turned. Nothing was there. Was there anywhere he could hide from these things of the night? It seemed now that they had always been there, just out of reach...tormenting him. He could hear their whispers, feel their claws, sense their presence. There was no hiding place.

From a distance the boulders had seemed large; a great place to hide. Though when he tried, it seemed they became smaller, as if he were in a dream. Some of the boulders became nothing more than large chunks of dirt that crumbled when he touched them.

So dry. So unbelievably dry. He could hardly breathe. His throat was so constricted. He fought for each breath.

There was another click and a loud screech. Kevin turned around in time to see the large arm just before it struck him in the chest. He flew back and hit the ground hard. He couldn't breathe. On hands and knees, he coughed and choked the dry air. Before he was able to move, he'd been hit again. This time to the stomach. He rolled across the ground and slammed into a boulder. "Please," was all he could manage as his attacker approached. Two strong hands lifted him up and tossed him like a rag doll. Dust flew into his mouth when he hit the ground. He tried to spit it out but seemed to swallow it.

He wasn't sure exactly what was attacking him. It was built like a large man. The face, or what he could make of it, was not human. Was it a dinosaur? A lizard? Its teeth were like razors. Its skin like an alligator. As it lifted him again, he noticed its eyes were like the eyes of a shark. Evil. The eyes of death.

This time it didn't throw him or hit him. This time it tossed him over its shoulder and carried him. It carried him on, away from the boulders. They began to head down a large embankment. Kevin tried to see where they were going but his head was behind the creature. He hadn't realized they had been on a hill or mountain. They just kept going down. He coughed and tried to breathe as the air seemed to get heavier and drier.

Out of the corner of his eye he saw something move. Blinking away the dust and sweat, he looked around. Terror filled his heart as he noticed that there were other creatures following them down the embankment. All of them were as terrible and unbelievable as the one carrying him. Surely his eyes were lying. Surely this was a nightmare. He saw a giant, deformed, bird-like creature. One had a body like a gorilla but the head of a cockroach. There was a lobster the size of a tractor trailer coming over the hill that let out a scream that made Kevin's blood turn to ice. What was this place? Now that his eyes were adjusting, he could make out hundreds of creatures...maybe thousands. They were all making horrible noises: clicking, screeching, screaming, growling, grunting. They began pressing in closer as they moved down the embankment. They began poking at him, grabbing his legs, arms and head. He tried to pull away but the creature carrying him had a death grip. He tried to scream but no sound came. His throat was so dry.

Further down they went. Kevin could no longer see the top of the hill or mountain or whatever this was. All hope was fading. He was gripped with fear and terror. He couldn't breathe. His lungs were on fire. This nightmare was more than he could stand.

Finally, the creature stopped and tossed Kevin to the ground. He hit hard with a thud. More dust in his mouth. He lay there panting, attempting to breathe. He closed his eyes tight, trying to will this all away. He could feel them all around him. Hear their grunts and growls.

"God, help me!" he screamed in his head. All at once, everything went quiet. In that moment, he remembered. It was as if a light had turned on. His past was played back to him like a movie. He was six, maybe seven years old. His Aunt Rebecca had taken him to church. He remembered that he hadn't wanted to go. He'd loved his Aunt Rebecca; she made the best butter cookies in the world; but church had sounded boring to a young boy with an attention disorder. Nothing about it had sounded fun. She had, however, promised him ice cream afterwards, so he had gone. It was nothing like he had expected. He'd absolutely loved the Sunday School class he'd gone to. His teacher had been so nice. They'd played games and had snacks and she'd told stories from the Bible. Children's church had been exciting also. There were fun songs to sing along with and hilarious puppets. The man that talked had made funny sounds with his mouth and tripped a lot. Kevin had laughed the whole time. He had loved it. Why had he never gone back? He should have gone back... oh yeah. His parents had divorced right after that and he and his father had moved away from Aunt Rebecca. His father who struggled with depression from that time on hated church and

God and anything that promised happiness. "It's all a lie!" his father had said to anyone that would listen. Kevin had never returned to church.

The memory faded as fast as it had come. Why had it come? Of all the memories of his thirty-two years, why had that been the one to pop into his mind?

All the noises of the creatures seemed to come flooding back. It was so loud he could barely think. He opened his eyes and saw that he was completely surrounded by what looked like thousands of foul creatures. The air was so thick. He fought for each breath.

Something grabbed Kevin under his arms and lifted him to his feet. His head was forced up. Through the smoke and fog he saw something coming toward him. It was quite large. It blotted out what little light shone through the clouds. The ground shook as it grew closer. All the horrible creatures began to back away. Kevin, however, was frozen in place. All he could do was watch. Then, it came into view. Kevin stepped back and choked out a scream. A scream that seemed to rip his head in half. A scream that caught in his throat and made no sound. What was this thing? It was every nightmare ever dreamed. It was fear, terror and horror all wrapped into one giant monster. It was staring right at Kevin.

"Come!" was all it said. Kevin trembled. Sweat poured from every pore in his body. The sunlight was gone. There was no more hope. The little light that he had glimpsed from his memory had been extinguished. He let out a sob and stepped forward. Darkness consumed him.

CHAPTER 1

A DAY AT THE BEACH

W as it possible that someone had unplugged the clock? Perhaps the power had gone out. No matter how long Mark ignored it, the crazy thing seemed to be frozen in place. So, there he sat with his black hair too long and covering his right eye, his surfer t-shirt and slip on shoes; waiting in gym class for the bell to ring.

Typically, Mark was excited to get out of his last period class on a Friday. Today, however, the excitement was even greater. This was no ordinary day for the students of Gateway Middle School. This was a magical day. You could cut the excitement with a knife. Today, was the last day of school.

It was the last day of the craziest school year of Mark McGee's life. He would never forget the seventh grade, no matter how old he lived to be. It wasn't because he'd had bad grades, his grades had been somewhat above average. It wasn't because of a specific class, though English had its memories. It wasn't even because of a girl, though he had lost a friend who happened to be a girl. No, it wasn't for any of the typical reasons that one looks fondly back on a school year that made this one special. It was, however, for a series of events that led to Mark making the greatest decision of his life.

He had moved to a new town. He had made new friends and even a few enemies. He had learned of an ancient secret that his new town held. He had curiously investigated this secret. He had hunted a dragon at the word of a boy he met in a dream. In turn, he had been hunted and captured by the same dragon. He had been held captive in a mysterious castle with several of his friends. One of those friends, the girl, her name was Angel, had died protecting him. Mark had faced creatures that he tried not to think about anymore. He had been sent on a fool's mission to find something that had been his for the taking all along – the Gateway to God, Jesus Christ. Jesus had died thousands of years ago to give Mark what he could never earn or deserve or find in a castle. Jesus had given him eternal life. Pretty sweet if you thought about it. Mark may not have any super-powers, but he was now immortal. Sure, his body would die, but he, Mark Evan McGee, would live forever.

Mark looked over at his best friend Scotty. Scotty was Mark's blonde double. Same long hair, clothes style and passion for skating. Scotty's mouth was silently moving to a countdown of seconds as he watched the clock. "Three-two-one," Scotty raised his hands in the air as the bell sounded. Shouts could be heard throughout the school.

Mark, Scotty, and Gabi walked across the gym floor and handed Coach Keys their papers. She had asked them to grade her performance as a teacher on the last day. She thanked them all and wished them a great summer. They couldn't get to the school bus fast enough.

On the ride home, Scotty asked if either of the others had any big plans for the summer.

"I plan on finally going to a Florida beach!" Mark replied.

"Dude, you haven't been to the beach?" Scotty asked.

"Scotty," Gabi said, "since he's been in Gateway, he's either been with us, on restriction, or in a castle!" They laughed.

Gabi was the more mature one in the group. She had long, straight blonde hair and wore glasses over her bright blue eyes. She may have been the smaller one but was definitely the most feared. She was also the one who had been a Christian the longest and had even been described as a Special Forces Christian.

"Well, I definitely plan on getting some surfing in this summer," Scotty said. "Feel free to join me, Mr. McGee."

"Scotty Morgan, you can hardly call what you do surfing," Gabi said. 'Besides, Florida beaches have no waves. We should all go to Australia."

"Australia?" Mark looked confused at this idea.

"She's always wanted to go there," Scotty replied. "And no, we're not going to Australia! I've dealt with enough deadly spiders and creatures for one lifetime thank you very much." Again, they all laughed. The castle had proven to be a breeding ground for all manner of foul creatures.

"So, what about you guys?" Scotty called back to Matt and Billy, who were sitting directly behind him, Mark and Gabi.

"My dad is making me help out with a reno on our house," Matt said. "He's totally remodeling our kitchen and bathrooms." Matt Ramsey was the older one in the group by a year. Having recently had a birthday, he was now fourteen. He was big for his age and already being sought by the local high school for playing football. Matt, however, hated sports and loved music. He was just a big teddy bear. His dad was a police officer in Gateway.

"Well, that doesn't sound fun at all," Scotty replied.

"No, but he's going to pay me. I'm saving up for a new guitar."

"And I have no plans," Billy said. "Though I do need to replace some loose boards in the treehouse." Billy's treehouse was the number one hangout place for the five friends. They would skate his halfpipe and chill out in the treehouse for hours. Billy Mumpower was a tall, lanky, nerdy-looking, freckle-faced boy with short, wavy, reddish-blonde hair. He lived just outside the neighborhood that the rest of the group lived in. His house was a small, rundown shack at best, but he had a larger yard with a halfpipe and a treehouse. It was just him and his Mom and sometimes her boyfriend Harold.

"What about you, Gabi?" Mark asked. "Do you have any specific plans for the summer?"

"Sort of," she replied, not looking up from her notebook she'd been writing in.

"Sort of?" Scotty asked. "What kind of…"

3

"Hey, can you two come with me to a short meeting after church this Sunday?" she asked, interrupting Scotty.

"What kind of meeting?" Mark asked.

"Yeah, you're scaring me," Scotty added.

"Church meetings should not scare you, Scotty Morgan!" Gabi replied, still not looking up.

"Yeah, Scotty," Billy said. "Not obeying Gabi should scare you too." He, Matt and Mark laughed.

"Church meetings don't scare me," Scotty replied to Gabi. "You wanting me to go to one without telling me why…now that scares me." Everyone laughed but Gabi.

After getting off the bus, Mark and Scotty walked Gabi home, even though both boys passed their own houses to do so. It was something they'd done since the castle incident. Even though Gabi was more feared by the neighborhood kids than Mark or Scotty, she loved that they acted as her protectors. The three of them had forged an inseparable bond. Something their pastor said happened when you go through an experience as they had. They each doubted, of course, that anyone had ever gone through an experience as they had. All Mark knew was, if anyone or anything messed with his friends, they would have to deal with him first. Of course, he also knew that they felt the same way. He and Scotty parted ways and agreed to meet up later.

Mark went straight to his bedroom when he got home. He knelt next to his bed and thanked God for another day. He also thanked Him for helping him make it through the seventh grade. His new English teacher hadn't been as friendly as Ms. Tyler… who happened to end up being a dragon intent on killing Mark and his little sister. He had passed English despite all the opposition. He stood and walked over to his bookshelf where he kept his skate magazines, video games and Bible. He picked up a small black bottle and held it in his hand. It had been given to Mark by someone he thought was a friend, only to find out later that he was the father of lies. When Mark had gotten home from the castle incident, he had discovered that the bottle was still in his pocket. He no longer believed that it contained the souls of hundreds of children, as he had originally been told. In fact, according to Mark's science teacher, it contained egg yolk and pond water. It was, however, a reminder to pray for the souls of the children in his school, neighborhood and town. What Satan had intended for evil, God had turned it to good. "I think that's in the Bible," Mark muttered to himself as he placed the bottle back on the shelf.

He walked down to his little sister's bedroom. Bethany was 7, but still loved all things pink. Her bedroom looked like the Barbie aisle at Walmart, only pinker. Her blonde hair was beginning to darken a bit but was still quite long. Bethany had gotten out of school a week earlier than Mark. She was lying on her bed coloring in a coloring book, she'd always loved to color. Mark knocked on her open door. "Hey little sis."

"Mark!" A smile spread across her face. "Yay, no more school!" she said excitedly.

He fell across the bed next to her. She was coloring a Disney princess. "So, are all princess dresses pink?" he asked.

"No, silly! Belle's is yellow."

"Oh, my bad," he said, kissing her on the side of the head. "You color really good." Mark had had no idea how close he had come to losing his little sister during the castle incident. She had gotten really sick and gone to the hospital with a rare heart condition during the time he was in the castle. He'd been attempting to escape the castle while she was fighting for her life. He had held her for fifteen minutes in a bear hug when they first got home. The whole family had cried. God had healed her that night. Something else to be thankful for.

"Here, you color the horsey, Mark." Bethany said. "And don't make him checkerboard." They laughed and colored together until their mom called them down to dinner. Mark carried Bethany down on his back, pretending to be the horse carrying the princess.

After dinner, Scotty called to tell him that they were all meeting at Billy's treehouse. Mark asked permission and headed that way on his skateboard.

As Mark got closer to Billy's house, he noticed Billy, Scotty and Gabi standing out at the road. They were facing the opposite direction where several police cars, a firetruck and a rescue squad were sitting in front of Billy's neighbor's house.

"What's going on?" Mark asked as he approached.

"We're not sure," Gabi replied.

"Here comes Matt now," Scotty said. "Maybe his dad told him something." Matt was walking back toward them from the neighbor's house.

"Who lives there, Billy?" Mark asked.

Billy shrugged. "A young couple rented the place a few months ago, but Mom said she heard that the wife left."

"Well?" Scotty said to Matt as he walked up.

"Well, apparently the guy killed himself," Matt said.

"What?!" Gabi gasped, putting her hand over her mouth.

"Dude, seriously?" Scotty asked.

"Oh wow," Billy said. "Do you know how?"

"Well, I'm assuming it was by hanging because I saw one of the officers carrying some rope. Nobody would tell me anything though. Well, except Mrs. Mullins. She said the poor guy had lost his job about a month ago and his pregnant wife had left him soon after. She went to live with her parents in Tampa."

"That is so sad," Gabi said. "I wonder how old he was."

"Not even thirty, according to Mrs. Mullins," Matt said.

About that time, the rescue squad went quietly past. They watched it go by. When they looked back, another car was coming toward them. It slowly pulled into Billy's driveway.

"Pastor Eric?" Gabi said.

His driver side window came down as he pulled in beside them. "Hey guys." Pastor Eric Osborne was the pastor of the church they all attended now; Lighthouse Christian Center. He had been a really big help during the castle incident. He had been there to comfort Mark's parents while Bethany was in the hospital and Mark was missing. He had also been used to lead Matt and Billy to Christ, after an angel sent them to him, of course.

"What happened, Pastor Eric?" Mark asked, approaching his car.

"Did any of you know Mr. Spiess?" Pastor Eric asked.

"I saw him a few times," Billy said. "Did he really kill himself?"

"I'm afraid so. It really is sad. He was so young."

"Did you know him, Pastor?" Gabi asked.

"No, I never met him, but apparently he called my office late last night. I guess he had no friends and wanted to make sure someone found him. I'd been out of town all day at a pastor's conference and didn't check my messages until about an hour ago. I called the police and met them here."

"Did he really hang himself?" Scotty asked.

Pastor Eric nodded slowly as if remembering what he'd seen. "Guys, no matter how bad things get, never give up. God always has a plan for your life."

They all nodded gravely.

Pastor Eric smiled suddenly. "So, school's out now?!"

"Yes sir!" they all said cheerfully.

"Well enjoy your summer break! Hey Gab, are you..."

"Yes!" she cut him off and glanced at Scotty. "Yes sir, I'll be there."

"Okay," Pastor Eric winked at her. "I'll see you guys Sunday, behave until then."

"Wait!" Scotty yelled, "so we can misbehave after then?"

Pastor Eric laughed.

"Scotty Morgan!" Gabi gave him a light shove. "Like you ever behave!"

Pastor Eric began backing out. "Remember to pray for Kevin's wife."

"Kevin who?" Matt asked, confused.

"Kevin Spiess." Pastor Eric pointed toward the neighbor's house. "I have to find his wife now and tell her the bad news." He backed out, waved and left.

"Oh wow," Gabi said, "she's going to be heartbroken."

"Why? She left him, didn't she?" Scotty replied.

"He had lost his job. She was probably just doing what was best for their unborn baby by going back to her parents," Gabi said. "This will probably crush her."

"Yeah, she'll blame herself," Matt added.

"Well, let's head to the treehouse," Billy said.

"Yeah, we can pray for her there," Mark said. "And Pastor Eric too. It can't be easy delivering that kind of news."

They gathered in a circle in Billy's treehouse and said a quick prayer for Kevin Spiess' wife, unborn baby and Pastor Eric.

After the prayer, they all found a place to sit. Nobody seemed to want to talk first, everybody was in deep thought over the death. Billy offered a pack of stale crackers, but Scotty was the only one to take any.

"Oh!" Scotty said, causing the others to jump. "What exactly are you planning, Gabi Motes?" Everybody looked at her.

"What do you mean?" she asked, picking up a nearby comic book and pretending to look at it. She wasn't making eye contact with anyone.

"Did you guys see how she cut Pastor Eric off when he went to ask her something?" Scotty said. "And she wants Mark and me to join her for a meeting Sunday after church." He tapped her shoe with his. "What are you planning?"

"Scotty Morgan," she said, giving him a death stare and setting the comic book down. "Nobody is making you do anything you don't want to do. Besides, I asked Matt and Billy to come also. Do you hear anybody else complaining?" All eyes were now on Scotty.

"First of all," Scotty replied, ignoring the smirks, "I'm not scared of you anymore. I have Jesus in my heart."

Her eyebrows went up and she shot out of her seat. Scotty let out a squeal and almost fell out of his chair. Mark, Billy and Matt burst out laughing. "Hmmm," Gabi said.

"Not scared, Scotty?" Matt said, still laughing.

"True bravery," Mark added. "You showed her, dude!" He smiled.

Gabi sat back down, still looking at Scotty. "You were saying?"

"Just tell us what the meeting is about. Why are you always so secretive?"

"Because," she said, giving Matt and Billy a slight grin. "I love driving you crazy." They laughed. Gabi stood to go. "And Scotty...I would really appreciate it if you were there." She climbed down the ladder and was gone.

Mark, Billy and Matt looked at Scotty, who sat with his mouth open, staring where Gabi had just been. "I am so going to marry that girl." They all laughed.

The guys spent the rest of their evening talking about their summer plans. Billy had invited them to go to the beach with his mother and him the next day and they'd all agreed. Mark asked his mom's permission when she called to tell him it was time to come home. She said he could go.

By mid-morning the next day, Scotty and Mark were taking turns riding some massive three-foot waves on Scotty's board. Matt and Billy were swimming nearby. Gabi had not come with them. She had mentioned something about an old friend coming to visit.

"So, any idea on who Gabi's long-lost friend is?" Mark asked Scotty.

"Her name is Brianna. Gabi used to talk about her all the time," Scotty replied. "They were best friends in first and second grade. I didn't know Gabi then. Brianna's family moved to California or something. They haven't seen each other since then, you know, except on Facebook and stuff."

"How long is she here for?"

"Most of the summer, I think. Gabi was excited when she found out last night. Their parents had planned the surprise for both of them. I don't think she's been that excited about someone since she met Topher." They both laughed.

Topher was an actual angel they'd met while on their castle adventure. He had first revealed himself to Gabi and then became a vital part of their mission. Topher was always excited and loved to celebrate at every salvation party the angels threw. They happened every time someone made a decision to become a Christian. Mark later learned that was actually in the Bible. He'd seen it in the book of Luke, where it said something like there being rejoicing in the presence of the angels of God over one sinner who repents.

Just then, a Frisbee landed in the water between Mark and Scotty. "Mark, over here!" Billy called, waving his hands. Mark tossed it to him.

After playing Frisbee and swimming for another half hour, Mark needed to go to the rest room. He and Scotty headed back up to the boardwalk. There were tons of people of all ages out enjoying the day. They were on benches, in chairs, on towels, and blankets. People walking, running and playing games. Mark loved the atmosphere of being at the beach. Everybody was happy at the beach. It was as if the sun had magical powers.

Scotty paused as they reached the men's room of the public bathrooms.

"Everything okay?" Mark asked, already knowing what Scotty was thinking.

"Yeah, just remembering," Scotty replied. Scotty had been abducted by a demon upon entering a public bathroom in Germany. That demon had taken him, kicking and screaming, into the castle.

Mark patted him on the back. Greater is He, dude, greater is He." They walked in. Greater is He had become their mantra ever since things had gotten normal again. They had quickly discovered that normal still came with problems and obstacles to overcome. Just because they had defeated the devil himself and a few thousand of his demons, didn't mean there wouldn't be temptations and other things to deal with each day. So, in order to encourage each other, they began quoting 1st John chapter 4 verse 4, where it says, "greater is He that is in you, than he that is in the world." God being the one that was in them meant no situation was too bleak to handle.

As the boys returned to the water, Mark was looking for where Matt and Billy had gotten to when Scotty grabbed his arm and stopped.

"Dude, look over there!" Scotty said, pointing to a thin blonde girl in jeans and t-shirt standing by herself near a blanket and chair with an umbrella set up.

"Yeah, so?" Mark replied. "Who is she?"

"She goes to our school...I think her name is Maria, and she's trouble."

She started digging through a large purse that had been hidden under a blanket under the chair. She was cautiously glancing around.

"Oh," Mark said. "I doubt that's her mom's purse."

"Dude," Scotty said. "She's robbing somebody." Just then, she stood up, slid something into her bag and walked away. "Shouldn't we do something?"

"Absolutely, come on!" Mark said. They ran towards her as she made her way back to the boardwalk at a fast pace. "Dude, call her name."

"I'm not sure..."

"Maria!" Mark yelled, cutting Scotty off. She turned around and stopped walking as they approached. She was prettier than Mark had first thought; a kind of natural beauty. She was too thin, and her long hair seemed to have been bleached more than it should, but her eyes were bluer than any Mark had ever seen. She made him think of a young clothing model.

She looked confused. "How do you know my name?" she asked, clearly not recognizing them.

"We go to your school," Mark said. "I'm Mark and this is Scotty."

She looked at them both closer. "Yeah, you're friends with little miss perfect, Gabi, aren't you? I don't..." She paused. "What do you want with me?"

"I guess we can't all be upstanding citizens like you, can we?" Scotty said, clearly defending Gabi. "What's in your purse there?"

"What are you talking about?" she asked in an irritated voice.

"You know good and well..." Scotty began.

"Mind your own business!" she turned to go.

11

"Maria, wait!" Mark began, but it was too late.

"Excuse me, ma'am." A police officer had come out of nowhere and grabbed Maria's arm. "I'm going to have to ask you to open your bag."

"You guys called the cops on me?" she turned and yelled at them.

"Not us." Mark said, raising his hands.

"So, what, you were just holding me up while they got here? You little snitches!" she yelled as she tried to pull away from the officer.

"Ma'am, we can do this here or downtown," the officer said.

Mark and Scotty walked away as they noticed a crowd gathering. "I guess we weren't the only ones who saw her," Scotty said as they headed back to the water.

"Probably the people she stole from," Mark said. He looked back in time to see Maria being led away in handcuffs. "That's so sad. What's her story?"

Scotty shrugged. "I think I heard that her dad left her and her mom a while back. They're real poor. She started hanging out with the wrong crowd. Trust me, this isn't her first arrest."

"Seriously? She's our age!" Mark said.

"She's in our grade, but a year older," Scotty said. "I heard she was caught shoplifting at a Walmart or something."

"Where've you guys been?" It was Billy. "We're trying to get some people together for a game of volleyball."

"Yeah, okay," Mark said. "Sounds fun." He watched as Maria disappeared behind the dunes, on her way to the police car. He'd have to remember to pray for her tonight.

The guys had an amazing day at the beach. Billy's mom had let them stay all day. They had surfed, swam, played Frisbee, volleyball, football, and surfed some more. Scotty and Matt had even attempted a sandcastle. It had looked more like a sand pancake in the end, though.

When Mark finally arrived home Saturday evening, he was exhausted. He ate dinner, showered and went straight to bed. As he faded into sleep, he remembered that he hadn't said his prayers. He hadn't prayed for his family or his friends. He hadn't thanked God for a fun day at the beach. He hadn't prayed for Maria. Amid all these thoughts, he fell fast asleep, having said no prayers.

Twenty something miles away, in the cold, dark room of a juvenile detention center, lay Maria Anne Lewis. She was fourteen years old and this was her second arrest. They had let her go with a warning last time and she did not expect that much leniency this go around. She may even get real time in this horrible place. Her mother would be heartbroken. Not because she cared about Maria, of course, but because she would have to take care of herself. Maria was tired. Sleepy tired, yes. Life tired, absolutely. More tired than a fourteen-year old should have to be.

Happiness and joy had vanished from her life the day her father had left her eight years ago. She could hardly blame him, though. Her mother was a horrible person, with her illegal substances and boyfriends she made no attempt to hide. Why though? Why had he left Maria? Why hadn't he taken her with him? She had been his baby girl, his little buddy. His pride and joy. He would read her bedtime stories every night. Her favorite had been the one about the little bird searching for its mother. She had loved bedtime stories. He would always do funny voices and tickle her at the silly parts. Then one morning she'd gone into the kitchen hearing her mother screaming into the phone angrily. She was told that evening that Daddy had left them and was never coming back. Maria had cried for days. She had only been six years old. The following eight years had been filled with every attempt possible to fill the void Daddy had left in her life. Boys, parties, alcohol, and every drug she could get her hands on. Then, in order to fund her addictions and her lazy mother, she'd began stealing. She'd stolen from her friend's parents at first, then moved up to shoplifting and swiping from the purses of distracted shoppers.

Maria sniffed and rolled over, angry at herself for the tears. She was so tired. Tired of her loser life. Not even a life. An existence. So tired.

As Maria slipped into a fitful sleep, she was quite aware of the six other girls in her room. Six troubled girls, who were there for various reasons; shoplifting, fighting, drugs, prostitution... mostly though, they were there because nobody cared.

What Maria was not aware of, however, were the seven creatures in the room. One stood next to the bed of each girl. These creatures were huge, scaly and shiny black. They had large, razor sharp teeth and the black eyes of death. Their long, sharp claws extended into the minds of each girl, sinking their souls further into a place of despair. A place they would most likely never escape.

CHAPTER 2

THE TEXT

Sunday morning Mark woke up even more exhausted than he'd been when he went to bed. What was always the deal with Sunday mornings? They seemed to be the most difficult days to get out of bed, regardless of what you'd done the previous day.

He checked his phone and had a text message from Scotty. "don't 4get mtg w Gab aftr chch! HELP ME JESUS!" Mark laughed and responded. "GR8ER IS HE..!"

He quickly showered and dressed and gave Bethany a horsey ride downstairs to breakfast. His mom and stepdad were already in the kitchen. They usually prepared a big breakfast on Sunday mornings. Mark was thankful that his family was closer now. It seemed that they did more things together since the castle incident. Mark, however, did not like to give the credit to the castle incident, but instead, to the God incident. His entire family had come to know God in a personal way during that time. He smiled as they all sat down to eat.

About two hours later, Mark was sitting on the second row at church between Scotty and Gabi, with Brianna on the other side of Gabi.

Brianna Bowers was even shorter than Gabi. She was very cute with her long dark hair and brown eyes. She was also very much like Gabi in personality, except for the fact that she was being nice to Scotty. She was a strong Christian with high standards and values. All it took Mark was being around her for five seconds to realize that.

Pastor Eric walked up to the podium after the offering had been collected. "Good morning!" he began.

"Good morning!" the crowd responded.

"First of all, I would like to thank our worship leader, Larry Motes, and the rest of our worship team, for an amazing time in the presence of the Lord this morning."

Amens, praise Gods and hallelujahs followed this proclamation along with a thunderous applause. Mark looked over as Mr. Motes only smiled and looked down at his feet.

Mark had barely known Gabi's dad, Larry, when he'd been pulled into their little adventure. He and his wife, Gae, had played a vital role in helping out. He had been a part of the Germany team that had been sent on a mission to find Mr. Hoffman, a missing link in the castle mystery. Mr. Hoffman had been one of the four people needed to complete a circle of prayer that destroyed the devil's castles. Gae had helped Mark's mom and stepdad deal with everything while Bethany was in the hospital. Gae had also been pregnant at the time. The funny thing was, she was pregnant now, though with a different baby. Eden Motes had been born shortly after the castle incident.

"Secondly," Pastor Eric said, "I would like to recognize Bret Snyder." He pointed toward the back where Mr. Bret, one of the ushers, stood smiling.

Mr. Bret was a tough looking guy that made Mark think of a stout biker. He wasn't very tall, but he was strong and mean looking with his bald head, broad chest and thick arms. To know him though, he was nothing like you would expect. Even though he attempted to act mean, he was nothing more than a big teddy bear that would give you the shirt off his back. He and his wife constantly opened their home up for the kids and teens to hang out. They lived in Mark's neighborhood.

"Bret will be putting together a team of leaders to take troubled teens to a summer camp that is set up to deal with the issues they face," Pastor Eric continued.

Gabi's Bible slipped out of her lap and Mark picked it up for her. "Thank you," she whispered.

"This is a ministry that is very much needed in this day and age, so let's all remember to pray for Bret and his team as they head to Camp Ricochet in North Georgia in just a couple of weeks."

Pastor Eric led them in a short prayer for Mr. Bret and his team and then had everyone turn to Job chapter 5, verse 7. "I would like to read this particular scripture from the New International Version this morning. It reads, "Yet man is born to trouble as surely as sparks fly upward." He paused and walked down to ground level. Pastor Eric loved being eye level with the congregation. "Not a very encouraging scripture, is it?" Some laughter. "Man is born to trouble!" he shouted. "I know I was", he smiled. More laughs and a few amens. "You are going to face trouble in this life. You see, basically the Bible promises us two things: mountains," he held his hand up high, "and valleys." He brought his hand down low. "And if you're walking this path called life, you're in one or the other. You might say, well Pastor, I'm in neither. I'm doing okay right now, no problems...but nothing great either. Not really a mountain or a valley. I would say this, you are on your way to one of them, so get ready. I heard a pastor one time that said you are basically in one of three places at any given time. You are either in a valley, on your way into a valley or on your way out of a valley." He walked down the aisle to the right of Mark and the group. "So, if valleys are such a major part of our lives, we should learn a little bit about them. What does the Bible have to say about valleys? Well, I'm glad you asked. Joshua talks about the Valley of Calamity. Psalm 84 talks about the Valley of Weeping. Hosea mentions the Valley of Trouble. Sound like places you want to schedule your next family vacation?" More laughter. "We even have a famous valley here in America called Death Valley." He turned and headed back up on stage. "This morning, however, we are going to discuss another valley." A scripture came up on the screen above and Pastor Eric turned to read it. "Psalm chapter 23, verse 4 says, Yea though I walk through the valley of the shadow of death," he turned and faced everyone. "The valley of the shadow of death. What is this place that David wrote about? You see, David was a shepherd before he was a king. He did a lot of wandering around in the desert and the wilderness and he probably knew a thing or two about valleys. You see, there is actually a place called the valley of the shadow of death or it is also known as the Kidron Valley. It is located between Jerusalem and the Mount of Olives. It's a steep valley; in fact, it is so steep that the sun only reaches the valley floor at noon." A picture of the valley came up on the screen. "As you can see, on one side, the Eastern side, there are tombs. Probably the reason it was called the valley of the SHADOW of death. The tombs, which were built into the walls, literally shadowed the valley. I would imagine that it was probably a dangerous place to wander into back in the days of David. A good place for robbers to hide and attack."

Just then, Mark's phone vibrated in his pocket. He pulled it out to check it and had a text from an unknown number. "Wassup McGee?" Quickly he replied, "In chch, who is this?" Gabi nudged him and gave him a dirty look for texting in church. A couple of seconds later, "look left." He looked over. There sitting at the other end of the church, on his same row against the wall, he saw a redheaded boy smiling at him. He looked to be around Mark's age but did not look familiar. He was sitting next to a man in an old looking brown suit with a scruffy beard and messy hair. Mark replied, "Sry, who r u?"

"Really?" Gabi whispered in his ear. "Stop texting in church."

"I don't know who this guy is," Mark replied and nodded towards the guy. Gabi looked over.

"What guy, Mark?" she whispered.

"The redheaded guy looking right at us," he replied with a worried look.

"Where? I don't see him," she said and couldn't stop the smile.

"So not funny," Mark said, blowing out a sigh. He remembered his friend David, who nobody could see but Mark. An invisible friend that turned out to be the devil himself.

18

Gabi started having a mini laughing fit right there, causing Scotty and Brianna to give them both a look.

"Do you know him?" Mark whispered. She shook her head no, still trying to stifle a laugh. Mark's phone vibrated again. "names rusty." Mark responded, "How do u no me?" Mark looked over at him again. The man next to the boy seemed to be stopping him from using his phone. Mark would have to wait for his response until after church. He couldn't imagine who the boy was or how he got his number.

"So, we can all agree," Pastor Eric was saying, "that valleys represent hard times in our lives. And let's face it; when we are in a valley or a hard or difficult situation, we feel like it's an impossible situation. Whether it be our finances, or our health, or our marriage, or our school grades, or whatever your problem is, it always feels hopeless." Again, he came down from the stage. "But allow me to tell you one last story of a truly impossible situation. You see, over two thousand years ago, a man named Jesus Christ was eating his last meal with some of his closest friends. He explained to them what had to take place and then he went out to pray. We all know the story. He was captured and led away to be tried, falsely convicted and crucified. Now, where the last supper took place and where the crucifixion took place, were on opposite sides of the Kidron Valley. You see, at some point between his last meal and the cross, Jesus Christ had to pass through the valley of the shadow of death. Keep in mind now, that he passed through it knowing he was actually going to be killed. Now, I've been in a lot of bad situations," he looked at Mark and winked. "But I've never knowingly gone to my death. You see, being dead takes bad situations to a whole new level." Some laughed, some said amen. "I mean you can't really have a more impossible situation than death. So, this man, Jesus, he passed through this horrible valley on his way to die. Are you feeling hopeless yet? Did he die?"

"Yes," came the murmur from the congregation.

"He did?" He stopped walking. "Wait, seriously? He died? So, the story's over?"

"No!" a few shouted.

"But you just said he died. That means it's over. What else is there?"

"He came back!" someone shouted from the back and several others shouted and clapped.

"Come on now!" Pastor Eric said. "You don't come back from the dead! That's impossible! Tell them Gabi," he looked at her. "Tell these crazy people it's impossible to come back from the dead. It's over!"

"It's not over, Pastor," she said calmly.

"What? But…"

"He rose from the dead," she said. "He's alive!" Cheers erupted across the sanctuary.

"Wait a minute!" Pastor Eric yelled, running back up on stage. "Order in the court! Are you telling me that this man Jesus is capable of overcoming THE most impossible situation there could ever be?"

"Yes!" the crowd shouted.

He stood there staring at them for a few seconds. "So," he paused. He CAN overcome your financial problems?

"Yes!"

He CAN heal cancer?"

"Yes!"

"He CAN fix a broken marriage?"

"Yes!"

"He CAN keep Mark McGee from texting in church even though Gabi can't?" Everyone laughed and Mark turned bright red. "I see everything, Mark," Pastor Eric said, laughing. "I'm only picking on Mark", he added. "I saw about sixteen other people texting or playing on their phones too."

Pastor Eric closed the service out with an altar call and prayer.

Scotty, Gabi and Brianna were laughing at Mark for getting called out. "Dude, you were totally busted," Scotty said.

"One of these days he is going to learn to listen to me," Gabi added.

"Yeah yeah, you always know best, Gabi," Mark said, trying to spot the guy who'd been texting him. He was nowhere to be seen. Mark pulled out his phone and texted him, "where did u go?"

Gabi tapped his arm. "Don't forget about our meeting. Meet me in the back in five minutes."

"Don't you mean in the vestibule?" Scotty asked, laughing.

Gabi rolled her eyes and walked away. Brianna followed her out.

"So, who WERE you texting, Mark?" Scotty asked. "I thought I was your only friend."

"Some redheaded guy named Rusty," Mark replied. "Sound familiar?" When Scotty looked confused, Mark continued, "He was sitting over there and texted me like I was supposed to know him."

"How old did he look?" Scotty asked.

"Our age, I guess, maybe older."

Scotty shook his head and started for the back. "Doesn't sound familiar. We better head to this mysterious meeting."

"I guess," Mark replied and followed him.

Five minutes later Mark, Scotty, Gabi, Matt, Billy, and Brianna were sitting in a small Sunday school room. Scotty and Billy were discussing their previous day at the beach, while Matt was telling Mark, Gabi and Brianna about how he had started the first song in this morning's service in the wrong key. Gabi assured him that nobody noticed.

"Why are we here, Gabi?" Scotty asked, "and why are we just sitting here?"

"You're here because you love Jesus," Brianna answered for her. "And you're sitting here to show him how patient you are." Gabi high-fived her. Everybody else laughed, except Scotty.

"Well, I do love Jesus," he retorted, "but..."

Just then the door swung open and Mr. Bret swept into the room. "Come on! Come on! Gather 'round, we don't have all day!" he yelled, and they all swung around to face the front.

"Okay," he said, clapping his hands together. "Does everyone know why they are here?"

"No!" Scotty answered. "Gabi wouldn't tell us anything!"

"She told me," Matt said.

"Me too," Billy added.

"I know why we're here," Brianna said.

"Really, Gabi?!" Scotty said, turning to her. "Really?"

"So apparently Scotty and I are the only ones clueless here," Mark said. He looked at Gabi. "We obviously aren't trustworthy."

Gabi only crossed her eyes and stuck her tongue out at the two of them.

"Well, that's actually my fault," Mr. Bret said. They all looked up at him. "I asked Gabi not to say anything to you until I spoke with your parents and I didn't get around to that until about," he looked at his watch, "two minutes ago." He smiled at Mark and Scotty. "So, tell Gabi you're sorry."

"Not a chance," Scotty said, sticking his tongue out at her.

"Anyway, I want to apologize to all of you for the short notice of this whole thing," Mr. Bret said. "I was just asked to do this on Thursday and was told I had one week to put a team together." It really looked funny seeing this tough looking, bulldog of a man standing up there smiling from ear to ear. They all loved and respected Mr. Bret. "So, as Pastor Eric said this morning, I am putting together a team of workers to take a group of troubled teens," he did air quotations on those last two words, "to Camp Ricochet in North Georgia. It's a week-long trip that starts this Saturday and ends the following Saturday. Your cost will be covered by the church." He handed Gabi a small stack of papers. She stood and passed them out. "That's a list of what you'll need and what will be expected of you. Listen, Pastor Eric and I hand-picked you guys, well, Gabi picked Brianna, and I trust Gabi, so...welcome aboard Brianna."

She smiled, "Thank you."

"You guys will be needed as assistant leaders. You will be staying in cabins with others your age, to basically help keep the peace when adults are not around. You will be expected to be examples and witnesses to these kids. Most of them have had a rough go at it and have no idea how to be anything but what they are. You won't be expected to fix them, just be there for them. Let God do the fixing." He smiled a big smile and continued, "You will also need to lead prayer and devotion in your cabins before bed. We will go over that this week."

Scotty raised his hand. Scotty was not big on speaking in front of people. He appeared to be in panic mode.

"I have been made aware of your fear of speaking, Scotty," Mr. Bret said. "Gabi and I will help you with that this week and I have complete faith in you. God is raising you up to be a leader and well, training is about to begin." Again, he smiled really big. "Now," he spoke to everyone. "We will be meeting right here each night this week for two hours to go over our battle plan and help get everyone prepared. Saturday morning, the van will be leaving the church at seven sharp."

Gabi raised her hand and Mr. Bret pointed at her. "Have you found out yet how many we're taking with us?"

"How many of what we're taking with us?" Scotty asked, clearly concerned.

"Yes," Mr. Bret said. "As of right now there are five on the list, but that could change."

"Five what on the list?" Scotty had his hand up now.

Mr. Bret smiled at him. "Five kids from this area that we will be taking to the camp."

"What? We're taking some of the troubled teens with us?" He was clearly not comfortable with this plan.

"Yes, Scotty, and you will have to sit with them and explain to them where they went wrong and how the Bible can change their lives," Gabi said. Everyone laughed except Scotty. He looked sick. "Scotty!" she continued. "It will be okay; we are all a TEAM in this."

"Do you know who the five are?" Billy asked.

"Kids from this area. I'm not sure if you guys know them or not," Mr. Bret said, looking through his papers. "Well, one of the girls goes to our church. Do you guys know Yvette Turner?" Everyone nodded except Brianna.

Yvette's family was really involved in the church, and Yvette had been a good kid until she got to middle school. She started hanging out with the wrong crowd and made some seriously bad choices. She still pretended to be the sweet, Christian girl when she was at church, but anyone who knew her outside the church, knew better.

"Okay," Mr. Bret said, clapping his hands together again. "Is everybody on board?" He looked from Scotty to Mark. They looked at each other and shrugged.

"Challenge accepted," Mark said.

"Awesome! I will see each of you right here tomorrow night at seven. Remind your parents that I need those permission slips as soon as possible. Have a great day!"

"I'm proud of you, Scotty," Gabi said. "I know this will be good for you."

"This will be good for all of us," Mark said. "It's really exciting."

"I know!" Brianna said. "I can't wait."

"It says here there will be swimming and boating and all kinds of fun things, Scotty," Matt said. "Should be a blast."

"Not to mention getting to see lives changed," Scotty said.

"Wow, Scotty!" Gabi said. "What a mature thing to say." Everyone looked shocked. Scotty smiled.

"Why does that surprise everybody?" Scotty asked. "I'm a mature person." They all laughed.

Samantha woke up lying in the dirt. She sat up slowly and looked around. Where was she? This place was horrible. She appeared to be at the bottom of an extremely large crater. The ground was dry and cracked and it seemed as if the air was just as dry. It was easy enough to breathe, but it didn't feel normal. She noticed that there was no vegetation in this place, not even a single blade of grass. The flat area where she was at seemed to extend on for miles in each direction. It gradually moved up what appeared to be a high mountain that surrounded her on every side. Samantha had no idea how she'd gotten here or where she was, but she did know one thing; she really needed to get up that mountain and out of this valley. She could feel it in her bones. She attempted to stand but immediately felt dizzy and had to bend over and put her hands on her knees. After a few seconds, she stood up straight and stretched. It was then that she noticed an even stranger thing about this place; the sky. It seemed to be a bright orange color, as if a fire were burning somewhere in the distance. The brightness of it, however, was blocked out by what appeared to be black smoke. The smoke moved like clouds on a windy day, but Samantha felt no breeze. She also could not smell smoke...or anything else for that matter. What was this place? Why was she here?

She tried to remember something, anything. She knew her name was Samantha. Samantha Gosset. She was forty-three years old, married to Albert Gosset and had two children; Bryce, who was twenty-four and Tiffany, twenty-one. She was madly in love with her husband of twenty-seven years and extremely proud of both of her children. Bryce loved to work with his hands and was moving up the ladder at the construction company he worked for. Tiffany was in high school, no, college. Samantha shook her head. Things were getting confusing. It was difficult to focus. Tiffany was in college. She was studying... something. What was Tiffany studying? Bryce was, what? Her son. Yes, Bryce was her son and Albert was her husband. She could never forget her sweet, loving, supportive husband... Albert, that was it. She just needed to focus and get to the top of that mountain. Albert and Bryce and Tiffany were waiting for her. They would be worried.

A clicking sound in the distance brought Samantha out of her thoughts. She looked in every direction and saw nothing. She needed to get moving. It really didn't seem to matter which way she went. Each direction looked just as treacherous as the other.

Dry ground, boulders and a really long walk. The clicking sound came again. What was that? She looked all around. Nothing.

She began walking. Where was this place? Why was she here? She tried again to remember. It was like trying to remember the details of a forgotten dream. Nothing came. She only knew that she had to get to the top of that mountain. Her family was looking for her. What were their names again? Why couldn't she remember?

The group had all been invited to the Morgan's house for pizza after church. The guys had all pigged out and went to Scotty's room to hang out. Gabi and Brianna had helped Mrs. Morgan clean up and then Gabi's mom had picked them up to go buy bathing suits in Jacksonville. Gateway didn't really have any good shopping places.

Scotty and Billy played video games while Matt crashed on Scotty's bed with Gameboy, Scotty's mutt dog, cuddled up behind him. They were both fast asleep. Mark attempted to watch Scotty and Billy's game, making comments on their lack of skills. His mind, however, kept drifting to Rusty. Who was he and how did he have Mark's number? Something just didn't feel right about it, although Mark hoped he was just being paranoid. Having gone through all that he had since coming to Gateway could do that to a person. He thought back to that first dream he'd had. How real it had seemed that he was actually staring down a dragon in the hallway outside his bedroom. Then the other dreams had come. David appearing like some creepy kid from a horror movie. Bethany being taken by the dragon. David introducing himself and then actually appearing to Mark while he was awake. Not to mention David telling him he had to kill someone at his school because they were actually the dragon in human form. Mark had put together several suspects and was ready to kill a few of them. He had never even suspected Ms. Tyler, his English teacher. She had been so nice, making him her assistant, giving him extra credit and not making him take tests or do homework. He'd really thought he had a good thing going. Not to mention how jealous Gabi had been. And then that fateful night he'd gone up to the school to help Ms. Tyler grade papers. She had given him a cup of cola that she'd drugged. He'd awoken in a tiny, pitch black cell in the center of the castle. His whole world had turned upside down after that.

Scotty yelled really loud, having defeated Billy at the game. It brought Mark out of his thoughts and woke up Matt and Gameboy. "Come on, man!" Matt said, rolling over. "People are sleeping."

"No, just you and that dog," Scotty replied. "And in my bed!" He threw a pillow at Matt. "Get up Goldilocks." Gameboy made a whimpering sound and put his head back down.

"Yeah, let's go to my house and hit the halfpipe!" Billy said.

"Sweet!" Scotty said, getting up and looking at Mark. "You've been quiet."

"Yeah," Mark replied, standing up. "I'm still tired from the beach yesterday."

"Yeah, Scotty," Matt added. "You guys have too much energy."

Scotty hit him with the pillow again. "Well come on, we're going to Billy's and if you stay here my mom will put you to work." They left and headed to Billy's.

Gabi and Brianna were at the mall with Gabi's little sister, Abi, the baby and their mom, Gae. Gabi and Brianna went shopping on their own. All they had to get were bathing suits, so they walked around slowly, enjoying themselves. They window shopped, people watched and played in the Disney® store. After finally finding the perfect bathing suits for their trip to the camp, they decided to treat themselves to ice cream. They got their cones and found a seat.

The song Crazy by the Newsboys let Gabi know she had a text. She checked her phone, expecting it to be her mom. She didn't recognize the number. "I'm watching you," was all it said. Gabi looked around, wondering who was playing a joke.

"What is it?" Brianna asked.

Gabi showed her the text.

"Well, that's just creepy. Do you know who it is?" When Gabi shook her head, Brianna looked around also. Everything seemed normal. Nobody stood out as acting suspicious. "Somebody messing around?"

"Probably," Gabi said. "I refuse to be as paranoid as Mark."

"Well, I suppose he does have good reason."

Gabi shrugged. "Greater is He." Just then, she received another text. "Curious?" She rolled her eyes and replied, "Show yourself or go away." She stood and gathered her things. "Come on, let's go find Mom."

As they turned to walk out into the mall, Brianna ran right into a big guy about her age. "Oh, excuse me," she said, stepping back to let him pass. He, however, stood right there with a smaller guy right beside him, grinning.

"Andy and Eddie?" Gabi said.

Andy and Eddie were two local bullies in Gateway. They'd had a run in with Mark just after he'd arrived in town. Their gang leader, Todd Johnson, had gone to the castle with Mark and had not been so lucky. He was never seen again. Andy and Eddie had continued to harass Mark until he'd managed to get them expelled from school. They'd been sent to a special school for troubled kids in Jacksonville. After Mark had become a Christian, he had sent them a letter apologizing for everything that had happened between them. They had never replied.

"Hello there, Gabi," Andy said, with a smirk on his face. "Who's your friend?"

"This is Brianna," Gabi replied. "Well, it was good seeing you guys, we're on our way to meet my mom."

"What's your hurry?" Eddie asked. "Something spook ya?" He laughed.

"How did you get my phone number, Eddie?" Gabi asked.

"Oh, it wasn't us," he grinned. "It was..." Before he could finish, Andy had elbowed him in the side.

"Tell McGee we're home for the summer," Andy said. "Looking forward to seeing him." He stepped aside and smiled at Brianna. "Very nice meeting you, Brianna."

She smiled and nodded as she walked past.

Gabi stopped and looked right at Andy. "Listen Andy, Mark has already apologized to you guys. Why don't you just let it go?" He shrugged. "Apology not accepted. We owe McGee." "Well, how's that worked out for you in the past?" she asked and walked away. Eddie mumbled something and both boys laughed.

After a couple of hours on the halfpipe, Mark and Scotty headed to Mark's house. Scotty, of course had gone straight to the video games. Mark, however, went to his bookshelf and grabbed his yearbook. He began looking for a Rusty. There was no sign of him.

"I wonder who he was," Mark said.

"Who?" Scotty asked.

"Rusty," Mark replied. "Don't you think it's strange that some guy I've never met starts texting me in church?"

"Dude, are you still on him? He was probably just some guy goofing around while bored in church."

"Okay, then how did he get my number?"

Scotty shrugged. "Don't worry about it."

"So, you think I'm just being paranoid?" Mark asked. "You know, after entertaining the devil himself."

"Fair enough," Scotty said, pausing his game. "Let's text him again."

Mark pulled out his phone and swiped it on. He scrolled for a few seconds. "Okay, this is strange." He stood up and looked at Scotty.

"What is it?" Scotty asked.

"It's gone! Dude, his number is gone!"

"Well, maybe you accidentally deleted it. I've done that before."

"No way!" Mark was panicking. "It was here! This is crazy!"
"Calm down, now didn't you say Gabi saw him too?"
"Yeah," Mark said. "I think so."
"Okay, so you aren't the only one that's seen him. That's good, right?"

Mark was already calling Gabi. He put it on speaker. "Hello?" There was talking and laughter in the background. "Hey, Gabi?" Mark said. "I have you on speaker. Scotty is with me." "Hold on," she said. Brianna was talking to her. The guys couldn't make out what she was saying. "Okay, what's up?" Gabi finally said. "Did you say you saw Rusty this morning?" "Who?" "Rusty, the guy that was texting me in church. Did you see him?" "I think so; I wasn't actually looking. I was trying to listen to Pastor Eric." "So, yes or no?" "Maybe, I couldn't identify him in a lineup if that's what you need." "He had red hair, Gabi! Don't you remember?" "I'm sorry, Mark. I really wasn't paying attention. What's going on?" "His number vanished from my phone and I just kind of freaked...crazy, huh?" "Not really, no. Listen, we're on our way back to Gateway. I have something sort of crazy to tell you. I'll have my mom drop us off at your house." "Okay, see you soon." "Bye Gabi," Scotty added, and Mark ended the call.

"Let's pray," Mark said. They sat on his bed and bowed their heads. "Father, we come to you in Jesus' name. First of all, we ask for your protection from the enemy. Both in our physical lives and in our minds. We pray that he is not allowed to get a foothold in our thoughts." Mark had heard Pastor Eric talk about that a few weeks earlier. "And, Father, please reveal to us the true identity of this Rusty person." Scotty snickered and Mark looked over at him. "Also, keep the Motes and Brianna safe on their drive home from Jacksonville. Amen."

"Amen," Scotty added. "And may I never be a rusty person." He grinned but Mark just shook his head.

Mark got up and put his yearbook away. "You wanna go sit outside until they get here?"

"Sure," Scotty said. They headed outside to wait for the girls.

After about fifteen minutes of skateboarding on Mark's driveway, they saw the Motes' van coming. Mrs. Motes pulled up to the curb and let the girls out. "Hey Mark and Scotty!" Abi yelled and her mom shushed her because the baby was apparently asleep. The boys waved.

They all walked up to Mark's porch and sat. "So," Gabi said. "We ran into your two best friends today." She proceeded to tell them the entire story.

"Wow," Scotty said. "Andy and Eddie are back. I really have missed them."

"So, they weren't actually the ones that texted you?" Mark asked.

Gabi shrugged. "It didn't sound like it, but you never know. Andy and Eddie aren't the most reliable sources."

"Do me a favor, Gabi," Mark said. "Check your phone. Show me that number."

She pulled her phone out of her purse and checked it. "Whoa," she said. "It's gone!"

"No way!" Scotty yelled.

Mark nodded. "That's what I figured."

"Let's not jump to conclusions," Brianna said. "Sometimes phones just do strange things."

"True," Mark replied. "But I still plan on jumping to conclusions. At least until this mystery is solved."

Mark and Scotty walked the girls home. After he and Scotty parted ways, Mark was walking home deep in thought. Just as he approached his driveway, his phone vibrated in his pocket. He stopped, took it out and couldn't believe his eyes. "Hey McGee! It's your buddy Rusty again."

CHAPTER 3

TODD 2.0

M ark stood there frozen in his driveway, staring at his phone. He didn't know what to do. Should he reply? Should he call Gabi? Should he throw his phone in the street?

It vibrated again and brought him out of his thoughts. "Sry if I freaked u out this mrng." Mark replied, "So who r u & how do u no me?" It almost immediately vibrated again. "LOL, I am a frnd of a frnd." Mark was done with the riddles and games. "OK, what frnd?" He walked up and sat on his front porch. It vibrated again. "Actually 2 frnds & u will b hearing from us soon. HAVE A GOOD NIGHT MCGEE!"

So, he was most definitely a friend of Andy and Eddie's. With Todd out of the picture, they'd probably found themselves a new gang leader. Probably some low life they'd met at that school for losers. Mark sighed. "I'm sorry God." He closed his eyes. "I shouldn't think like that. I pray that you would help me be a witness this summer to Andy and Eddie and this new guy, Rusty. Please Lord, teach me patience when it comes to dealing with bullies. Help me to remember that revenge is yours. Amen."

The front door opened. "Mark, honey?" It was his mom. "Who were you talking to?"

"David stopped by for tea, could you make us some please?" He smiled.

"Not funny," she replied with a smile of her own.

"Just praying, Mom. What's up?"

"Praying?" She walked over and sat next to him. "Is everything okay?"

"Yes ma'am. It's nothing God can't handle." He gave her a big cheesy smile.

"I'm so proud of you." She messed up his hair. "Are you hungry?"

"Very," he replied and stood to go in. "What do we have?"

"How does pizza and a movie sound?" she asked.

"Perfect." They went in.

The pizza was great, but it was Bethany's turn to pick the movie and Mark had watched that frozen princess so many times, he could practically recite it. A fact that Scotty could never know about. So, after hanging around long enough to hear the snowman sing about summer, he went to his room. He played a few video games and got ready for bed. After brushing his teeth and saying his prayers, he fell fast asleep. It had been a busy weekend.

"Mark, honey!" It was his mom. He opened his eyes. The sun was up, though it felt like he'd just closed his eyes. She stood in his open doorway. "Get up sleepy head. Scotty's been trying to reach you for an hour, and I can't hold him off any longer."

"What time is it?"

"Almost nine. Here's Scotty." She handed him the cordless.

"Geez, Dude, can't a guy sleep late on his summer break?" Mark said.

"Dude get up!" he seemed agitated. "You sleep too much."

"It's not even nine." Mark wiped the sleep from his eyes and sat up.

"Well, guess what!" Scotty said, clearly worked up. "My house and Gabi's house were robbed last night!"

"What?" Mark stood up. "Are you serious?"

"Yes! You may want to check your shed and garage too!" Scotty said frantically. "Dude, they took my surfboard! Along with my skateboard and some of my dad's tools. Gabi and Abi's bikes were taken from their garage."

Mark jumped up and put some shorts on. "Did you tell my mom?"

"No, I was hoping you would call me back sooner, then I just didn't think about it. Dude, my surfboard!"

Mark was downstairs and out the backdoor in a flash. His mother yelled something about the trash as he'd passed the kitchen. He got a sick feeling in his stomach when he saw his shed door wide open. He ran over and looked in. Bethany's bike was gone, along with his stepdad's lawnmower. "Aw, man!"

"What was taken?" Scotty asked, still on the phone.

"I didn't have anything out here, but they got Bethany's bike and the lawnmower. That's all I notice, anyway. Have you guys called the police?"

Yeah, they just got here, though. I'll let them know you got hit too."

"Thanks, Scotty. You know who did this."

"I have my suspicions," Scotty replied.

Mark proceeded to tell him about his text last night. "I guess I should've heeded his warning."

"So, you think this Rusty is the new Todd?" Scotty asked.

"Much worse. He's Todd 2.0. This guy seems smart." Mark headed back inside to tell his mom.

Two hours later, after the police left, Mark called Scotty and Gabi to schedule a meet up. They decided on Gabi's house. Mark had kept his skateboard in his room, so he, unlike Scotty, was able to ride his. Scotty had been busted for skateboarding in the house one time and was no longer allowed to bring it in. He had to walk to Gabi's house and was not in a good mood when he got there.

"Mark, we have to get our stuff back!" Scotty said, as he stepped into Gabi's room.

"Scotty Morgan, the police can handle this!" Gabi said. "Don't you dare go planting ideas in Mark's head! You'll both be in jail by the end of the day."

"She's right, Scotty," Mark said, and they both looked at him as if he'd just declared senility. "We told Matt's dad about our suspicions of Andy, Eddie and their new buddy. Let's just leave it in God's hands and the hands of the GPD."

"Wow, Mark," Gabi said. "I'm impressed. The old Mark would've already purchased the explosives." Brianna laughed.

"Dude, we can't just let them get away with this!" Scotty said, clearly not willing to let it go.

"They won't," Mark replied. "Besides, don't you think they're going to expect us to retaliate tonight? They'll probably wait up looking for us all night."

Scotty nodded. "Man, I hope they find our stuff."

"How did they get in your garage, Gabi?" Mark asked.

"The backdoor wasn't locked," she replied. "It rarely is if we were home. Abi and her friends use it when they play outside."

"This is so crazy," Scotty said. Brianna nodded her agreement. "I wonder if the police went to their houses yet."

"They said they would check it out," Gabi said.

"It's horrible to think about somebody being in your yard or house like that," Brianna said. "It's such a violation."

"Gabi!" It was her mom calling her from the kitchen.

"Yes, ma'am?" Gabi called.

Her mom came back to Gabi's room. "Hey guys, Officer Ramsey just called. He said they went to Andy and Eddie's houses and they didn't find anything there."

"What about Rusty?" Mark asked. "Did they find out anything about him?"

She shook her head. "He said both boys denied knowing anybody by that name."

"Oh, whatever!" Scotty exclaimed. "They're both nothing more than worthless liars!"

"So, what happens now?" Gabi asked.

Her mom shrugged. "They just wait and see if anything turns up."

"Wow," Scotty said. "I gotta go." He got up and walked out.

"I'll be back," Mark said, and he followed Scotty. He didn't catch up with him until he got to the street. "Dude, slow down." Scotty stopped. "Can you believe this? Those geniuses are going to get away with this!" He turned and began walking again.

Mark walked with him, carrying his board. They walked in silence for several minutes. "You know they won't get away with it," Mark finally said.

"Sure they will! By the time anybody figures out who Rusty is, he will have pawned all our stuff...and probably for chump change." Scotty was taking this a little too hard, there had to be more to it. "I want to go question them. We should..."

"Scotty," Mark said, grabbing Scotty's arm and stopping him. "What's up?"

Scotty looked down and kicked at a pebble. "It's just...that surfboard was a gift from my grandpa. He knew I really wanted one and my parents were never gonna fork over that much money for the one I really wanted. He was on a limited budget, but he did without...stuff he needed, to buy me that surfboard." He looked away.

"Dude, okay, I get it," Mark said.

"No, you don't get it!" Scotty said, looking back with tears in his eyes. "He died a week later. He died, Mark, because he didn't have his heart medication. He hadn't bought it. That's what he'd done without and then he had a heart attack." He started walking again.

"Dude, wow," was all Mark could say.

"Nobody ever said anything to me about it, but I overheard a few of my aunts talking about it at the funeral. They mentioned him having just made some extravagant purchase that caused him not to be able to afford his heart pills." They walked the rest of the way to Scotty's in silence. Mark had no idea what to say to his friend. They stopped at the end of Scotty's driveway. "So, you see why I want my board back so bad. It's the most important thing I own. I only kept in in the shed because my dad made a cool rack to hang it on. I'd have rather they taken my brother than that board."

Mark laughed. "Then we have to get it back."

"What? How?" Scotty asked.

"I'll think of something," Mark said. "Hopefully it'll be something that won't have us both in jail by the end of the day." He smiled and hopped on his board. "Keep your phone on." He texted Gabi and told her that Scotty was fine and not to worry about him. He also told her that he was heading home. He had chores to do…and a plan to forge.

After several hours of racking his brain to figure out how to get their stuff back without being vengeful or breaking any laws, Mark still had nothing. Everything he wanted to do was wrong. He couldn't take something of theirs and trade them. He couldn't threaten them. He couldn't destroy anything of theirs. Mark desperately wanted to please God in this situation, but he also wanted to get Scotty's board back.

Finally, he decided that in order to stay on track, he would need to pray. He knelt down next to his bed. "God, I really need your help here. I'm not going to bore you with the details that you obviously already know, but I will tell you that I don't care about getting any of that stuff back, except Scotty's surfboard. You know how important it is to him. Please give me wisdom to do this without taking revenge or breaking any laws or displeasing you. In Jesus' name I pray. Amen." As soon as he stood up, his phone vibrated with a text. It was Gabi. "Mark McGee, you have been too quiet today. You had better not be plotting anything! Romans 12:19 says DO NOT AVENGE YOURSELVES, but rather give place to wrath; for it is written, VENGEANCE IS MINE, I WILL REPAY, SAYS THE LORD! Don't make me hurt you! Love, Gabi." Mark laughed out loud. Then he read it again three times. That's when a thought entered his mind, He walked over to his bookshelf and picked it up.

After a few moments of pondering, he smiled. Mark had a plan. He texted the others to meet at Billy's treehouse. He would need some help with this one.

It had taken Mark a while to get everyone on board with his plan. They would be following through with it just before they had to be at their meeting at the church. Each of them had gone home to let their parents in on it.

At six o'clock, the plan was in place. They had decided it would be better to split into two groups. Mark, Billy and Brianna would take Andy; while Scotty, Gabi and Matt would get Eddie.

Mark's team slowly approached the front door of Andy's mobile home. Mark really hoped his plan would work. Vengeance was supposed to be God's but leaving it in His hands sure seemed silly to Mark.

Gabi led the way at Eddie's house. There was loud music playing inside, so they may not be heard. She looked back at Scotty. "You okay?" He nodded and Matt patted him on the back.

At almost the exact same time, Mark and Gabi knocked on their prospective doors. Gabi had to knock much louder because of the blaring music. Mark heard someone coming. Gabi heard a woman shouting.

The front door of the trailer opened. There stood Andy wearing gym shorts and an old t-shirt. Several looks registered on his face over the period of about three seconds. The first was shock, then fear, then confusion, followed by anger. "What do you want, McGee?"

At Eddie's house, a large sweaty woman slung the door open. She was wearing shorts and a tank top that were both about two sizes too small for her. Her hair appeared to have been colored so many times it didn't know what to do. "Yeah? Whatta ya want?" she shouted over the music. Before anyone could respond, she turned and shouted, "I said turn that off!" She was breathing heavy as if the walk to the door had been her monthly workout. "Eddie!" she shouted just as the music turned off, making her sound like a crazed lunatic. Gabi looked back at Scotty, who looked like he was about to cry.

"Hello, Andy," Mark replied, as Andy eyed him suspiciously. "We were on our way to church and wanted to bring your family this pie." He turned and Brianna stepped forward and held up a large, steaming apple pie.

"Good evening, ma'am, "Gabi said. "We're...acquaintances of Eddie's and we wanted to bring your family a pie we baked." Matt held it up to her.
"I ain't got no money!" she shouted, as if the music was still cranked.
"No ma'am, it's free," Gabi replied.
"Oh." She reached down and grabbed the pie out of Matt's hands and walked back in the house without another word. Gabi, Matt and Scotty just looked at each other. After a few awkward seconds, she yelled from inside the house, "Eddie! Your friends are at the door! And don't leave it open!"
"Wow," Gabi said quietly.
"Who is it, Mom?!" Eddie shouted. "Is it Andy or..." He'd appeared at the door and froze in place. "Whoa."

"Yeah, like I'm gonna eat a pie you guys baked," Andy said.
"I promise it's perfectly safe," Brianna said. "And delicious. We had one ourselves. Scotty's mom made them." They turned and waved at Scotty's mom sitting in the car. She waved back.
"So, why would you do this?" Andy asked.
Mark shrugged. "We thought you might want some pie, Andy."

Andy looked at each of them suspiciously. He reached down and took the pie. "If this is a joke, McGee."

"No joke, dude. Just good pie," he replied with a big smile.

"Well," Brianna said, "we have to get going." They all waved goodbye and turned. Brianna stopped and looked back. "Andy?"

"Yeah?" He looked at her.

"Jesus loves you." She turned and walked away as he stood there stunned.

"Hey...McGee!" he shouted from his door. Mark turned. "It won't work!"

"What won't work, Andy?" Mark asked, smiling.

Andy shook his head and walked inside.

"I said shut that door!" Eddie's mom yelled and he stepped outside.

"What's going on?" Eddie asked, standing on the top step looking down on them. He was wearing cutoff shorts and a black Megadeth t-shirt with the sleeves cut off.

"We brought you guys a pie," Gabi replied. "Your mom took it in."

"Oh-kay," he said it slowly as if he were trying to figure out their game. "Why?"

"Why not?" Gabi replied. "You like apple pie, don't you?"

"Yeah."

"Well, now you have one," Matt said. "It's legit, man. Scotty's mom made it. No strings attached. It's not poisoned. We had an extra pie and thought of you, that simple. Now we're on our way to church."

"Church?" Eddie said it as if he had caught them in a lie. "Yeah, right Matt! I've heard your views on church."

"A lot has changed since you left, Eddie," Matt said. "God got a hold of me. I would love to tell you about it sometime."

"I'm good," Eddie said. He still looked suspiciously at them. His eyes met Scotty's and Scotty didn't exactly look happy to be there. "So, you guys brought pie even though…I mean, I heard your houses got robbed."

Scotty stepped forward, but Gabi blocked him. "Listen, Eddie," she began. "You know me. If anybody were going to play a joke on you to harm you or get you in trouble, would it be me?"

He stared at her for a second. "No, I guess not. But it still doesn't make sense."

"Jesus loves you, Eddie," she said. "I hope you know that." She smiled and waved at him. "Enjoy your apple pie."

They each waved goodbye to a shocked and confused Eddie; and left.

They all met up at the church and discussed their experiences in the parking lot.

"Brilliant idea, Mark," Gabi said. "I am so proud of you. And thank you, Scotty for going along with it. I know you didn't want to."

Scotty nodded, but didn't say anything.

"Well," Mark began, "it was that scripture about vengeance that you texted me earlier that gave me the idea." He opened his Bible. "I went over and grabbed my Bible off my bookshelf to see if it gave any further instructions on the subject. Well, the next two verses in Romans chapter 12 explained everything." He read, "On the contrary: If your enemy is hungry, feed him; if he is thirsty, give him something to drink. In doing this, you will heap burning coals on his head. Do not be overcome by evil, but overcome evil with good." He closed his Bible.

"That says it all," Brianna said.

"Did you see Andy's face?" Billy asked. "There was definitely some coals being heaped on his head." He laughed.

"Yeah, Eddie too," Matt said.

"Well, just remember, it's more about the giving and loving than it is the satisfaction of their suffering," Gabi added. "Your heart has to remain pure in this, guys."

"Well, either way, it was still hilarious," Matt said. "Wasn't it, Scotty?"

Scotty shrugged and walked away. "I still don't have my board, do I?"

"These things take time, Scotty!" Gabi called after him.

Just then, Mark's phone vibrated with a text. It was Rusty. "Rumor has it that u guys had some trouble last night, McGee! Need any help finding the culprits, paying them back??? LOL!" Mark replied, "I'm sure u no all abt it." This guy was really making him mad.

"Something wrong, Mark?" Brianna asked, with a concerned look on her face.

"Yeah, Rusty," Mark replied. "Now he's taunting me. We really need to find this guy." He stared at his phone waiting for a response.

Gabi and Brianna shared a concerned look.

"Let's go!" Mr. Bret called to them from the front door of the church. "We have a lot to cover and no time to waste!" They all went in and joined Scotty in the classroom.

Mr. Bret opened in prayer and dove right into their game plan. They would be placed in cabins with their age groups and be in charge of keeping order, making sure everyone was where they needed to be, doing nightly prayer and devotions, and one-on-one ministry.

About thirty minutes into class, Mark felt his phone vibrate. He really wanted to check it but knew he couldn't in class. Come to think of it, he did need to use the restroom. He raised his hand and excused himself. He glanced at Gabi on his way by, attempting to communicate to her what he was doing. Once in the restroom, he checked his text. It was Rusty, "no but I will keep my eyes open. I am here if u need me tho." Mark replied, "who r u Rusty? Where do u live? Would love 2 meet u." Before Mark left the restroom, Rusty replied, "but u have met me, Mark." Mark shook his head. He was done playing games.

After their meeting, Mark told the group about Rusty's texts. They all agreed the guy was playing with Mark and needed to be found. When Mark got home, he made sure his shed and garage were locked, and nothing was left outside. Scotty hadn't said a word after the meeting. Mark said a prayer for his friend before he went to bed.

It felt as if Samantha had been walking for days, though looking back, she could still see the spot where she's started from. It had been quite slow going. The terrain was much rougher than it had first appeared. Samantha had already lost count of how many times she'd fallen. "It's not how many times you fall, but how often you get back up, that counts." Who used to say that all the time? Her father! Yes, her father had spoken those words so many times when she was growing up. She saw his face for just a second before it slipped away. "Daddy!"

That clicking sound again. She frantically looked around, with a growing feeling that something was stalking her. She saw nothing or no one. Only endless dry desert and mountains. "Hello!? Is anybody there?" For a moment she thought she saw something move from behind a large boulder. "Hello? It's okay, I won't hurt you!" She hoped they wouldn't hurt her either, who-ever it was. Nothing. "I just want to know where I am! Why am I here?" Her eyes teared up and she bent over with her hands on her knees. "Stay focused, Samantha," she told herself.

What was it she'd been thinking about? Her father. Daddy. It seemed she hadn't seen him in so long. Why was that? She couldn't remember. She had left home to go to college and then married right after that and moved far away to live in another state. It had been so sad moving away from her father. She remembered him fighting back the tears. They had only been able to visit him on Christmas. Then...no! He had died. A stroke. "Oh Daddy, I miss you so much." Suddenly, she was a little girl walking down the hallway in her nightgown. Her father's office door was open. It was late at night. He was sitting at his desk, working by the lamplight. He looked over at her and a big smile spread across his face. "Well, hello there, Pumpkin, what are you doing up?" She wiped the sleep from her eyes, and he held out his arms for her to come. She ran to him and jumped into his arms. He pulled her into a hug and set her on his lap. She'd always loved Daddy's lap. Being there made her feel special. For this busy, hard-working man to take time for her, meant everything. "I had a bad dream, Daddy." "Ahh, well, I bet your next dreams will be about cotton candy and butterflies," he said. She giggled and snuggled into his chest. "That's silly, Daddy," she said with a yawn. She looked down to see his open Bible and notebook. How many times had she found him just like that? His Bible and his notes. "Which story are you reading about, Daddy?" She could hear him smiling. "Do you remember the story of Lazarus?" She nodded excitedly. "I like the story of Larazusus, Daddy." "It's Laz-a-rus," he said, laughing. "And what do you remember about him?" "He died and Jesus raised him up from the dead." "Very good. Do you remember how many days he was dead?" She crinkled her little nose up in thought. "Three?" She held up three fingers. He reached over and lifted one more finger. "Four!" she shouted excitedly. "Yes!", he said just as excited. "Isn't that amazing? He had been dead for four whole days when Jesus raised him up." She nodded. Daddy loved talking about Jesus. "Never forget how amazing He is, Pumpkin. Never." "I won't, Daddy."

She found herself sitting on the dry ground again. Tears were rolling down her cheeks. "Oh, Daddy." Her heart ached for one more time in his lap. He'd been a truly good man. A good Christian man. A...pastor! Her father had been a pastor. She smiled at the fresh flood of memories. She had loved her father so much. He had truly been her hero. She had always dreamt of growing up and marrying a man just like him.

More clicking, and it seemed much closer. She jumped up and looked around. There was a loud roar that made the hairs on her neck stand up. She jumped back. Where had that come from? The clicking stopped. There was a loud screech as if something had been attacked. She still couldn't see anything or anyone. The mountain! She needed to get to the top of that mountain! It was the only thing she knew. Her family was waiting for her up there. She turned back to go the direction she'd been heading and screamed. A man was standing not five feet in front of her. "Hello, Samantha."

Mark woke up early Tuesday morning; well, eight-thirty was early for Mark. He knelt down and said his prayers, praying especially for Scotty. He wanted to do something special for his friend today. Scotty needed to be cheered up. He grabbed his phone and sent him a text, "Let's do something CRAZY today!"

He dressed and went downstairs to grab some breakfast. His stepdad was at work and Bethany typically slept later than Mark. His mom was sitting at their kitchen nook, drinking coffee and reading a book. "Good morning, Mom."

"Good morning, Mark," she said, smiling up at him. "I'm not cooking anything so just grab you a bowl of cereal."

"That's cool." He grabbed a bowl and spoon and headed for the pantry. "You wouldn't happen to be going into Jacksonville today, would you?"

"I do need to run some errands in town sometime this week, why?"

He shrugged. "Scotty's feeling down about his surfboard being stolen and I was wanting to take him somewhere fun. Just a thought."

"Well, where did you have in mind?" she asked.

"I don't even know what there is," he said.

"Let's see," she said, sliding her laptop over and pecking away at the keyboard. "Things to do in Jacks..oh, here we go. There's the zoo!"

"No, I don't think Scotty is quite ready to see large animals yet." Mark smiled.

"Okay, there's the Museum of Science and History, there's an art museum, there's a Riverwalk, the beach, several hiking trails." She looked up at him and nothing seemed to be what he was looking for. "Hold on a second, I heard one of the ladies at church talking about a new go-cart track opening up."

"Seriously?" She'd piqued his interest now.

"Yeah, you race them. Here it is! Autobahn Indoor Speedway®! It says here they go up to fifty miles an hour, wow, that's fast for a go-cart, Mark."

"Sounds perfect, Mom," Mark said. "Can we do it, please?"

She thought for a second, then shrugged. "Why not."

"Sweet!" He jumped up and hugged her. "I'll call Scotty now!" He called.

"Hello?" Scotty said sleepily.

"Dude," Mark said. "You got plans today?"

"Um, I don't know, why?"

"My mom offered to take us to this new go-cart track in Jacksonville! Dude, they go up to fifty miles per hour!" There was silence. "Scotty?"

"Yeah, I'm here. Are you talking about Autobahn?"

"Yep," Mark replied. "So, you've heard of it?"

"Yeah, I've been dying to go there. Everybody says that place is awesome!"

"Cool, ask your mom and text me back. My mom just said we can leave here around ten-thirty." As soon as he got off the phone with Scotty, his phone rang. It was Gabi. "Hello?"

"Hey Mark, can you come to my house real quick?" She sounded out of breath and very serious.

"Yeah, is everything okay?"

"Not really. Hurry Mark, and oh, don't tell Scotty," she said and hung up.

"Oh boy," Mark said to himself. This did not sound good at all. He finished his cereal and told his mom he would be back soon to get ready. He hopped on his skateboard and headed for Gabi's. It took him about three minutes to get to her road. He immediately noticed the police car in her driveway and his heart sank even lower. He ran up and rang the doorbell. Abi opened it.

"They destroyed Scotty's surfboard," she said.

"What? Who?" Mark asked, standing there in shock. "Is it here?" He stepped inside. Officer Ramsey, Mrs. Motes, Gabi, and Brianna were standing in the dining room. Brianna was holding the baby.

"There was other stuff too," Abi said quietly. "Pieces of Bethany's and Gabi's bikes."

"Pieces?" Mark asked.

She nodded and led Mark into the dining room where Officer Ramsey was talking quietly, apparently because the baby was asleep. He was explaining how they would try and get fingerprints.

Mark caught Gabi's eye. She got up and walked over to him. "Follow me," she said and led him into the garage. There was glass everywhere. "They already took the surfboard and bike pieces to try and get prints." She led him around the van and he could see where the side window of the house was completely busted out. "They tossed Scotty's board right through the window. Well, the two halves of it, anyway." She pointed to a large dent in the side of the van. "The bike parts were outside."

"This is crazy," Mark said. He noticed Brianna and Abi standing at the door. "Why did they hit your house?"

"Officer Ramsey thinks it's because of our location on the corner here. No neighbors on this side," Gabi said. "Dad saw the bike parts on the side of the house and texted Mom before he left for work."

"So, you guys didn't hear anything?" Mark asked.

"Not with this little thing crying all night," Brianna said. "Not to mention Gabi and I are on the other side of the house and Abi would sleep through a hurricane." Abi laughed.

"Neighbors?"

Gabi shook her head. "Nobody heard a sound."

"But Scotty's board," Mark said.

"It was just his surfboard though," Brianna said. "They didn't return everything."

"It was just the surfboard he cared about," Mark said. "This is not good."

"I know, Officer Ramsey was surprised they didn't try and pawn the surfboard," Gabi said. "Apparently it was quite valuable."

"You have no idea," Mark said. "Wow...just wow! This is going to kill Scotty."

"How do you want to tell him?" Gabi asked. "Do you want to do it together?"

Mark thought for a few seconds. "No, I'd better do it. I'll go over there now." He sighed.

"We'll pray for you, Mark," Brianna said.

"Thanks," he said as he walked past her and out of the house.

"Mark!" Gabi called to him as he reached the end of the driveway. He stopped and looked back. "What about Operation Vengeance?"

Mark smiled at her. "Tonight," he said. "We take them cake." He turned on his board to go and shouted, "this is God's fight!"

Ten minutes later, Mark was standing in Scotty's bedroom. He had walked right in and told him everything. Scotty was now sitting on his bed with his head in his hands. So far, he had not spoken a single word.

"Dude, I'm so sorry," Mark said. He sat down at Scotty's desk. Gameboy came in, tail wagging, and jumped on Scotty's bed. Ever since getting lost in the castle, Gameboy preferred to be an inside dog. Scotty liked having him inside too. Gameboy nudged Scotty's arm hoping for a good scratching.

"Go away!" Scotty pushed him off the bed. He looked up at Mark with glassy eyes. "I don't think I'll be riding go-carts today."

"That's cool," Mark replied. "We can postpone it."

"I also don't think I'll be going to camp, either."

"What? No, dude, you have to go!" Mark said. "We can't separate the dynamic duo!"

"Well, I'm not feeling very dynamic right now."

"Well," Mark responded. "Greater is He. It doesn't matter how you feel."

"Dude, I prayed and prayed that God would bring that board back to me...unharmed."

Mark walked over and sat on the bed next to his friend. "Dude, I know that surfboard meant a lot to you, and I'm really sorry it got destroyed. But it was just a surfboard." Scotty looked up like he was about to say something. Mark held up his hand. "I'm just saying; it's not like they killed a family member or a friend."

"But I trusted God, Mark!" Scotty stood and walked across the room. "I asked for one simple thing!"

"And all across the planet, every single person is asking God for one simple thing. Remember what Pastor Eric said? 'I used to complain about my shoes until I met a man with no feet,' Get your priorities in order. Besides, He's not a vending machine, dude! You know that. You can't just put in your order and expect it gift wrapped the next day. He is God. He knows best."

"So, why do we ask him for anything if He's just going to do what He wants anyway?" Scotty asked.

"We trust Him and we remember that this is His story... not ours."

Scotty shook his head. "Well, I don't know if I can trust Him anymore."

Mark stood up quickly. "Are you kidding me right now?" He walked right up to a shocked Scotty Morgan and poked him in the chest. "These words from the guy who stared down demons and evaporated them without blinking? This from the guy who took on all manner of foul creatures and lived to laugh about it? This from the guy who helped show me the power of the name of Jesus? The guy who, while ten feet tall and built like a beast, took out hundreds of demons with a sword? That same guy is going to let a couple of punks who stole one of his toys, defeat him? Nope! Not while I'm his best friend!" He had practically poked Scotty with every other word.

"Ow, dude!" Scotty said, rubbing his chest. "Chill out!"

"It's a surfboard, Scotty! You chill out!" Mark said, turning around and walking over to Scotty's wall that was covered with surfing posters. "When the police are done getting prints, we can hang one half of it here and the other half on that wall. It'll look totally cool. Then you can get a new board." He turned and faced Scotty and they stared at each other. Finally, Scotty smiled.

"Dude, you're intense."

"And you're going to camp."

Scotty nodded. "On one condition." Mark gave him a look. "If we can still go ride go-carts today." They fist bumped.

At that moment, Scotty got a text. He checked it and dropped onto his bed. He reached up and handed Mark the phone. "It's your buddy." The text read, "Hey Morgan, wanna go surfing? LOLOLOL!!!!

CHAPTER 4

OPERATION VENGEANCE

Having convinced Scotty to ignore the text, they sent Rusty's number to Officer Ramsey. Mark's mom took Mark and Scotty to Autobahn's for some serious go-cart racing. They had a blast. Scotty was almost back to his old self. He had actually liked Mark's idea about hanging his surfboard on the wall. After about two hours of intense racing and overall craziness, Mark's mom told them it was time to go. On their way to the door, Scotty grabbed Mark's arm and stopped him.

"Dude look!" he shouted and headed to the starting gate area. "Do you know who that is?"

"Who? Where?" Mark asked, trying to keep up. They were heading towards a group of people huddled together. "Who is it!?" He hadn't seen Scotty this excited since Gameboy returned from the castle.

Scotty ran up to the group. There was a tall, young, blonde man apparently signing autographs for fans. "Dude, it's him!" Scotty said. "Give me something to get signed." He picked up an Autobahn's pamphlet off the ground.

Mark's mom caught up with them. "What's going on, Mark?" she asked. Mark shrugged.

"Who is it, Scotty?"

"Are you guys serious?" Scotty said, clearly shocked. His poster is on my wall, Mark! That's Gabriel Butler! The new quarterback for the Jaguars. He's awesome! Dude is going to lead them to the next Superbowl!" He said that last part loud enough for everyone around them to hear. Some actually nodded their agreement. "I have to get his autograph." He got in line and told Mark to take his picture when he got up there.

It was all Scotty talked about on the way home. Gabriel Butler had played for the Gators, Scotty's favorite college team. He had won the Heisman trophy. He had thrown more touchdowns than any other quarterback in S.E.C. history. Scotty knew his statistics from as far back as when he played high school ball in Jacksonville. "He was the reason I started watching football!" He showed Mark his autograph again. He even called Gabi, Matt and Billy to tell them.

Mark was glad to see Scotty with a new thing to obsess over. He'd missed his hyper-energetic friend. They stopped for cake mix on the way home. Mark's mom had tonight's menu for Operation Vengeance.

Needless to say, Andy and Eddie were even more surprised to see them that night than they had been the night before. The teams, of course, had switched up. Mark, Billy and Brianna had Eddie. Gabi, Scotty and Matt had Andy. Neither guy said anything. They just took the cakes and gave the group really suspicious looks. Once again, they were told that Jesus loves them.

That night, before their class began, Mr. Bret called them to order. "Listen up!" he said. "Before we get started, I have a prayer request. Right as I was about to leave the house tonight, a friend of mine from Ohio called me. I went to school with him when I was your age. He's a pastor now. Anyway, his wife was in a car accident on her way home from the grocery store Sunday." He lowered his head and paused. They all waited quietly for him to begin. "He was my best friend for many years." He paused again and wiped his eyes. "His wife is in a coma and they don't give her much hope. He's with her now, in fact he said that while he was praying over her yesterday, she was actually crying. It really gave him some hope. Anyway, he asked me to pray for her and I figured since I had the crew of heaven at my disposal." He smiled at them and wiped his eyes again.

"Absolutely," Gabi said, standing and motioning for everyone to follow her up. They all gathered around Mr. Bret. "What's their names?" Gabi asked.

"Pastor Albert," Mr. Bret replied. "And his wife is Samantha."

When Mark got home that night, his mom informed him that Officer Ramsey had called. They would be having an officer driving through the neighborhood that night. He would be looking out for anything or anyone suspicious.

"Did he say anything about finding Rusty from the number we gave?" Mark asked.

"Yes. He said it was a burner phone and couldn't be traced by just the number."

"Really?" Mark asked, a little impressed with Rusty's tactics. This guy was smart.

"He said not to worry though, they would find him."

Mark went to his room and sat down to play video games. He couldn't stop thinking about Rusty. It was all so strange how nobody, but Mark, had seen him. Andy and Eddie hadn't even mentioned him. Gabi said Eddie almost said a name at the mall, but Andy had stopped him. It was also strange how Rusty had Mark, Gabi and Scotty's phone numbers. This guy was more than just a typical bully. It was like he had a purpose here. The way he had stolen their things and then destroyed them. Not even doing it for money, but for the pleasure he got out of taunting them. What kind of person did that to people he had never met? Of course, he could just be doing this to gain Andy and Eddie's trust, but somehow that theory didn't feel right. Their issues had been with Mark, not Scotty and Gabi. Andy and Eddie would have never dreamed of messing with Gabi. Even Todd had been scared of her. Mark had been the one to stand up to them. He had been the one to get them arrested and expelled. He had been the one that was with Todd when he was taken into the castle. Mark had been the reason Andy and Eddie were in a place for troubled kids. No, there was more to Rusty than bullying or even revenge. In fact, Mark's first suspicions may have been true. It was quite possible that Mark's new friend Rusty was not human at all.

Mark played video games for about a half an hour, but his heart was not in it. He got ready for bed and said his prayers. He especially prayed that God would reveal exactly who Rusty was.

At some point in the middle of the night, Mark woke up needing to use the bathroom. When he headed back to bed, something like a flicker of light caught his eye at the window. The more he looked in that direction, the brighter it got. He quickly walked over and looked out. He couldn't believe what he saw. The entire forest behind his house was on fire. "Mom!" he yelled as he slipped his shorts and t-shirt on. "There's a fire!" He ran out into the hall and yelled again as he ran downstairs. He heard his mother say something as he opened the door and ran into his backyard. It was far worse than he thought. Their neighbor's house along with the privacy fence between them was on fire. "Mom!" he screamed. "Call the fire department!" The blaze was so hot, Mark had to back away. He grabbed the water hose and began wetting the ground. He had heard one time that doing that would slow the fire and maybe keep it from spreading. He had to protect his house. He screamed again for his mother and stepdad as loud as he could. Maybe they were helping their neighbor, Mrs. Gray, get out of her house. Just then, Mark saw Mrs. Gray walking across her backyard in a robe. She was heading straight for the blazing forest. Mark thought, being she was quite old, she may be confused. "Mrs. Gray!" he yelled. "Come this way, Mrs. Gray!" He tried to run to her, but it was too hot. It felt like he was getting a horrible sunburn. "Mrs. Gray!" Then, to Mark's horror, she walked right into the burning forest and disappeared into the flames. Just then, a loud roar came from the forest. Mark stood stone still. What had made that sound? It had shaken the ground. "Mark McGee," a low rumble of a voice said from the forest. The hairs on Mark's arms stood up.

"Mark!" The voice was different. "Mark Evan McGee!" It was his mother. He sat up too quickly and squinted in the bright sunlight. His mother was standing over him in her robe, her hands on her hips. He was so confused.

"What on earth are you doing sleeping in the backyard?!" she asked.

He looked around. Mrs. Gray's house was still intact. The fence was not burnt. The forest was bright green. "Great!" Mark said. "Now I'm sleepwalking."

After showering and getting dressed, Mark called Gabi.

"Did you hear?" Gabi said as soon as she answered the phone.

"Oh no, what now?" Mark was almost afraid to ask.

"The park at the front of the neighborhood was vandalized. Also, some of our stolen things were left there, in pieces."

"Unbelievable!" Mark said. "And nobody saw anything?"

"Nope. The officer that was watching the neighborhood said it wasn't vandalized when he entered the neighborhood at three o'clock, but it was when he exited at three forty-five. This is really getting out of hand, Mark. Somebody has to find Rusty!"

"About that," Mark said. "I have a theory I want to run by you."

"Not the demon thing again?"

"Gabi, it makes perfect sense! Think about it."

"Mark, you're just suspicious because of David. You'll see, they will catch him and arrest him. He is a real person."

"Well, until then, I'm looking out for demons and dragons."

"Whatever!" Gabi said. "Hey, we're volunteering to go help clean up the park. Care to join us in about an hour, my fearless dragon slayer?"

"Yeah, sure," Mark said with a sigh. "Gabi, there's something else."

"What?" she asked.

He proceeded to tell her every detail of his dream and how he'd woke up in the backyard.

"Listen, Mark," Gabi said. "Don't jump to any conclusions. I mean, your dream really didn't have anything to do with Rusty. You dreamed about Mrs. Gray."

"I know, and I thought that was really weird," Mark replied. "Why would she be in my dream? I've hardly ever spoken to her." "Well, she IS your neighbor. Maybe you should speak to her. She may just need to hear what you have to say. She does live alone, after all. And she hardly ever goes anywhere. The love of Jesus and Mark McGee may be exactly what she needs."

"Yeah, she'll have to wait until after camp is over. I'm apparently going to be way too busy until then." He told her he would see her at the park in an hour and went downstairs to eat breakfast.

An hour later, Mark walked outside to head to the park. He looked over and saw Mrs. Gray working in her yard. She was watering her flowers. "Good morning, Mrs. Gray!" he called to her.

She smiled really big and waved. "Good morning, Mark! Lovely day, isn't it?"

"Yes, it is!" He threw his skateboard down and headed to the park. For some reason, he had a strange feeling that he'd forgotten to do something. Just then, he spotted Scotty up ahead, walking. He sped up to catch him. "Good morning, sir!" Mark said.

"This is so crazy," Scotty said, not even looking at Mark. "Look at that park...trashed."

Mark looked and his heart sank when he saw the damage. It was a war zone. The trash cans had been dumped out. The seats on the swings had been cut in half. Everything in the park had pretty much been spray painted. Most of it with words Mark didn't even want to read, let alone say. Gabi, Brianna and several others were already attempting to scrub out the bad words. Mark and Scotty grabbed some rubber gloves and started picking up the dumped trash.

After several hours of cleaning and scrubbing, Mark had a thought. Maybe if he could talk to Eddie alone, he could find out what Eddie knew about Rusty. He told his friends that he needed to take care of something, and he would see them later. He jumped on his skateboard and headed to Eddie's.

Eddie's mom told Mark that Eddie was around back somewhere. He found Eddie in a field behind his house mumbling something to himself and shooting cans and bottles with a pellet gun.

"Hello, Eddie," Mark said, keeping his distance. Eddie seemed upset.

Eddie swung around quickly and let out a breath. He looked relieved that it was Mark. "You scared me, McGee!" he said. "What do YOU want? Come to bring me some cookies?" He laughed.

"Not exactly, Eddie," Mark replied. "I just wanted to talk to you about something."

"Like what? Your precious new friend Jesus?" Eddie smiled in a mocking way.

"Well, no, unless you want to," Mark said seriously.

"Then what?" Eddie turned and took aim at a bottle. "Tell me how sorry you are for abandoning my friend and getting him killed?" He was, of course, talking about Todd. The bottle exploded when he shot it.

"Who is Rusty?"

Eddie spun around and froze. Mark actually saw fear in his eyes. "H..how do you..." He stopped himself. "Rusty who?" He turned back around and shot a beer can.

"Come on, Eddie!" Mark said. "Help me out here! Is he Todd's replacement or..."

Eddie jerked around and charged at Mark with his pellet gun aimed at him. He stopped about two feet in front of Mark. "Don't you ever say Todd's name again!" He spat the words out like a madman. "Do you hear me?" The gun was pointed right at Mark's chest.

Mark lifted his hands. "Okay, Eddie, I'm sorry Dude. Just put the gun down."

Eddie looked down as if he just realized what he was doing. He lowered the gun.

"Just answer me this," Mark said. "Are you helping Rusty trash our neighborhood or is he doing it by himself?"

Eddie just stared at him.

"I know you know who Rusty is, Eddie," Mark said as calmly as he could. "Are you scared of him?"

"It's time for you to leave, McGee," Eddie said. He turned around and began shooting at his targets again, as if Mark had never been there.

Mark was about to turn and leave but had an idea. "Hey Eddie, who is that red-headed guy coming this way?"

Eddie actually dropped his gun when he swung back around. He was looking in every direction. "What?"

"Talk to me, Eddie. I can help you. I know who this guy is."

"You don't know anything, McGee! Now get outta here before you get hurt!"

Mark backed away slowly. "I know you're scared, Eddie. I know Rusty is a punk and I need you to help me find him."

"You got my friend killed, McGee, why would I EVER trust you!!? Now LEAVE!!!" He turned around to pick up his gun.

Mark turned to leave. "Your friend was a big boy, Eddie," Mark said, making sure not to say Todd's name. "I tried to keep him from going with me! He kind of insisted!" A pellet hit the shed wall next to Mark.

"I won't miss again, McGee!" Eddie yelled. "Now GET!!!"

Mark walked about ten more feet and turned back around. Eddie was still watching him. "One more thing, Eddie!" he called out. "We'll be bringing brownies tonight!"

When Mark went past the park on his way home, he thought everyone had gone home. Then he spotted Gabi and Brianna talking to a girl at one of the picnic tables. The brown-haired girl looked vaguely familiar; probably went to their school. They appeared to be deep in conversation, so Mark was just going to go on by. Brianna spotted him and started waving for him to come over. He stopped skating and walked over. "Hello," he said.

"Mark," Gabi said. "Do you know Donna?"

"I've seen her at school, but no," Mark replied, holding out his hand to shake hers. She shook it. Donna was pretty and even though she was wearing shorts and a tank top, it was evident her family had money. She also had a very nice smile.

"Hi, Mark, nice to meet you." Her eyes looked like she'd been crying.

"So," Gabi said to Donna. "You wanna tell him, or should I?"

Donna smiled and wiped her nose with a tissue. She looked quite nervous. "I guess I will." She shrugged. "I just..." She looked at Gabi as if she had no idea what to say.

"She just became a Christian!" Brianna said and they laughed.

Donna wiped her eyes. "I'm going to cry again." She looked up at Mark and said, "I just asked Jesus into my heart." She broke down crying again and Brianna put her arm around her.

"Wow," Mark said. "That's so awesome, Donna! I bet Topher is REALLY excited right now."

Gabi and Brianna smiled and nodded.

"Who's Topher?" Donna asked.

"A crazy friend of ours who gets super excited when people get saved," Gabi said. She looked up at Mark. "Just think, we may have never had this opportunity to talk to Donna here today, if the park hadn't been trashed."

Donna nodded. "I'm leaving tomorrow for a two-week family vacation. I only came up here to see what all the fuss was about when I saw Gabi and Brianna."

"Well," Mark said. "I guess the devil has been defeated again. Congratulations, Donna, I will be praying for you." He smiled at her.

"Thank you, Mark," she said, smiling back and wiping her eyes again.

"Did Scotty go home?" Mark asked Gabi.

"The moment we started talking to Donna about Jesus!" Gabi said. "That boy has issues."

Mark laughed. "Well, I'll be sure to give him a hard time about it. See you guys later. Have a great vacation, Donna." He waved goodbye to them and headed for Scotty's house.

After making fun of Scotty for his fear of talking to people about serious things, Mark told him everything that happened at Eddie's.

"Dude, he shot at you? What were you thinking going by yourself?" Scotty was freaking out.

"I really think he's terrified of Rusty," Mark said. "Who I still believe is a demon or something."

"Well, if he is terrified of him," Scotty said, "he sure isn't going to talk."

Mark shrugged. "I tried. It's between him and God now," he said. "So, Billy's mom is baking tonight?"

Scotty nodded. "Dude, she makes the best brownies I have ever had. I can't wait."

"Remember, you have to save some for Andy and Billy," Mark said laughing. He got a text. "Well, I gotta go cut grass, I was just informed that the new mower is waiting for me."

Mark waved to Mrs. Gray again as he cut grass. Seeing her made him think of his horrible dream. It had felt like the whole world was ending. It had been so real; he could actually feel the heat. And that voice. "Mark McGee." It gave him chills just to think about it. The sleepwalking was something else to be concerned with also. He finished cutting grass, put the mower away and went to shower. After dinner, he headed to Billy's house.

Scotty had been right. Mrs. Mumpower's brownies were amazing. They all enjoyed a batch while she made a care package for Andy and Eddie's families. She then drove them all together to Andy's home. His mom told them he wasn't home and thanked them for the brownies. Gabi asked her if there was anything they could pray with her about. She smiled and asked that they remember her family. Next, they headed to Eddie's home. None of them were surprised when his mother told them that he wasn't home either. She then grabbed the plate of brownies and closed the door before any more questions could come. Not even a thank you or a good evening.

After class that night, Mark's mom picked up the group. She dropped off Billy first and then headed into the neighborhood.

Everyone panicked when they spotted a police car and a rescue squad near Mark's house. After getting a little closer they realized they were actually in front of Mrs. Gray's house. Matt's dad was in the yard talking to Mark's stepdad. They walked up to the van when they saw them drive up.

"What in the world happened?" Mark's mom asked. "Is Mrs. Gray alright?"

"No," Officer Ramsey said. "It appears that she suffered a massive heart attack. We're thinking she went instantly, never felt a thing." He said quietly. "Her son came by about a half hour ago to bring her some groceries when he found her."

"Oh, that is so sad," Mark's mom said. "She was such a sweet lady."

Mark felt sick as he remembered how he didn't have time to go see her. Had his dream been nothing more than a push from God to witness to her before it was too late? "Good morning, Mark! Lovely day, isn't it?" He could hear her saying just this morning. Little did she know it would be her last. He met Gabi's sad gaze and looked away.

It had taken Mark a long time to fall asleep, and he did not sleep well at all. He felt so guilty for not taking time to talk to Mrs. Gray. For not being a good neighbor. For not being a good Christian.

Early Thursday morning, his mom came in and woke him up. "Mark, sweetie?" She was sitting on the side of his bed. "Hey sleepy head," she said, pushing his hair out of his face. "I just got off the phone with Officer Ramsey, I swear that man is always working."

"What did he say, Mom?" Mark asked, sitting up. He was totally expecting to hear that there had been another theft or some kind of property damage.

"He said, that they found and arrested your friend, Rusty." She smiled. "Isn't that great?"

"Really?" Mark was totally confused. How did one arrest a demon? Had he been wrong? It had all made so much sense. "They actually found him? How? Where?"

"An anonymous tip last night led to his arrest. Don't know who, don't know where." She stood to go. "Anyway, thought you'd want to know."

"Yeah, thanks, Mom." He slid out of bed. This really was good news. Rusty was a real boy and did belong to God, after all. Mark texted the group. Of course, he was sure they already knew. Officer Ramsey would've called everyone involved and Matt would've told Billy. Mark still wondered who had called in the tip. If he had to guess, he would say Eddie. He had seemed so much more afraid than Andy. Ready to break. However, neither of them had been home last night when they'd taken the brownies. Had they acted together? Had Operation Vengeance really been a success? Well, he may never know the truth, but he sure was glad it was over. Gabi responded to his text. "How could they have caught a demon, Mark??? HMMM???" Sometimes he didn't like Gabi.

Gabi also mentioned that they should still continue Operation Vengeance tonight and tomorrow night.

As the day went on, Mark learned that Rusty's prints matched those found on the stolen items. They had also found the remaining items that he had stolen in the abandoned trailer he had been living in with some vagabond. He was definitely guilty.

Mark and Scotty had spent most of the day playing video games at Mark's house. Gabi and Brianna had gone to the movies with some other girls from the church.

They all met up at the Ramsey's house as Matt's mom made cupcakes for that night's Operation Vengeance. Once they each had a cupcake, they headed out together again.

They found Andy sitting on his front porch playing a game on his cell phone. "Well, if it isn't the goody two-shoes gang," he said without looking up.

"Hello to you too, Andy," Gabi said. They had voted her as the speaker of the group.

"You guys got me in all kinds of trouble," he said, putting his phone down and looking up at them.

"How?" Scotty asked. "Did you eat too many brownies?" Brianna nudged him. "No, I wanna know why he's blaming us for his troubles."

"By running your mouths," Andy replied. "I spent all morning at the police station."

"By run…" Scotty started to argue but Gabi cut him off.

"Well," she said. "I'm sorry you had a bad morning, Andy." She held out the cupcakes to him. "Maybe these will help."

He looked at Gabi with a death stare. "Why are you still bringing food? The culprit has been caught. You no longer need to love your enemy." He said those last three words sarcastically.

"Because Jesus still loves you, Andy." She smiled and set the plate down beside him. "And oh, let your mom know that she doesn't have to cook tomorrow night. We will be bringing a full dinner over about this time."

He shook his head and stood. "You guys are such losers." He turned and went inside, leaving the cupcakes on the porch.

"Can we eat them?" Scotty asked.

"No, Scotty," Brianna said. "He'll come get them after we leave."

Next was Eddie's house. His mother opened the door while calling Eddie. She grabbed the plate and was about to walk away.

"Excuse me, Ma'am," Gabi said.

She stopped and gave Gabi a look as if she were truly interrupting something important.

"I just wanted to let you know that we will be bringing a full meal tomorrow night about this time. So, you do not have to cook tomorrow evening." Gabi gave her a big smile.

"Really?" She actually smiled. "Well that is so sweet of you. There are four of us that live here." She walked away and Eddie came to the door.

"Hello, Eddie," Gabi said.

"Hey," he said, not making eye contact. "Um…thanks for the food." He glanced up at Mark and quickly looked away.

In that moment, Mark knew it had been Eddie that had called in the tip about Rusty. "And thank you, Eddie," Mark said.

Eddie gave Mark a stern look and closed the door.

"What did you thank him for," Scotty asked as they headed for the car.

"He knew why," Mark said.

"And," Matt added. "There are not four people living here. It's just Eddie and his mom."

That night after their meeting, Scotty spent the night with Mark. The boys had to agree to be quiet because Mark's stepdad had to work the next morning. They stayed up late playing video games and eating junk food. Sometime after midnight, they got ready for bed. Mark's mom had brought a cot in for Scotty to sleep on. They lay there in the dark talking for quite a while. Scotty did most of the talking. He'd started off with how he still found it hard to be around Andy and Eddie without getting mad and moved on from there to how cool it was to meet Gabriel Butler.

"Hey, if I can get tickets to some Jags games, would you want to go?" Scotty asked.

"Dude, I'm a Steeler fan...but yeah, definitely." Mark laughed.

"Hey, I think they play the Steelers this year!" Scotty said. "But I think it's in Pittsburgh."

"Jags are definitely going to lose that game," Mark said.

"No way!" Scotty said a little too loud.

"Dude, hush," Mark said. "Don't get us in trouble."

After several minutes of silence, Scotty said, "Did you hear that?"

"Hmm?" Mark asked, half asleep. "Hear what?"

"I could've sworn I heard a bus," Scotty said. "It sounded really close."

"I didn't hear anything, Dude," Mark said. "Are you sure you didn't dream it?"

"No, listen!" Scotty said.

Mark listened and heard absolutely nothing. "Nada, Dude," he said.

Just then a really loud truck horn blew. "Ha! I told you!" Scotty said.

"What's going on?" Mark asked. He got out of bed. "Let's go check." Scotty followed him downstairs. Mark looked out the front window. "Well, there's no bus, but what in the world?"

"Who are those people?" Scotty asked, looking out next to Mark. There were around a dozen people in Mark's front yard, just standing in random spots and staring right at Mark and Scotty.

"What's going on, Mark?" his mom asked from upstairs.

"I don't know, there's people standing in our front yard," he said, opening the front door. "And it's kinda creepy." He stepped out onto the front porch. They didn't move. They just stood there staring. "Is this a joke?" he asked and stepped out a little closer. He was already a little shocked to see all these people in his yard. He was even more shocked to see that Gabi, Brianna, Billy and Mr. Bret were there. But he would have to say that the most shocking thing of all, was seeing himself and Scotty standing there in his yard, staring at him. It was kind of strange staring into your own eyes, especially when those eyes revealed complete terror.

"Mark," Gabi said. He looked over at her to see that her clothes were completely saturated in blood. "Mark."

"What? What's happening, Gabi?!" he yelled.

"Mark!" Scotty's voice caused Mark to look at him. He almost didn't recognize him. Scotty's face was covered in blood. "Mark!"

"Scotty!" Mark screamed, running into the yard and noticing that they were all covered in blood. "Scotty! What happened?!"

"Mark!" Scotty yelled. 'Dude, get up!"

Mark sat up in bed, covered in sweat and breathing heavy. His sheets and blankets were on the floor. It was morning.

"Dude, you were freaking out in your sleep!" Scotty was standing next to Mark's bed. "David isn't back, is he?"

"Wow!" Mark said. "What was that about?" Once he calmed down, he told Scotty what had happened in the dream. "There were others there, but I never saw their faces."

"What do you think it meant?" Scotty asked.

"I have no idea."

"All I know is, you scared me good. You were writhing all over your bed saying mine and Gabi's names over and over."

Mark called Gabi and told her about the dream.

"Well," Gabi said. "That's just a little bit creepy."

"What do you think it means, Gabi?" he asked.

"I don't know," she said. "We're all covered in the blood of Jesus?" She laughed.

"Gabi!" Mark said, clearly not as amused as she was. "I dreamed about Mrs. Gray and she died the next day!"

"Pray about it, Mark," she said. "I have no idea what it meant.'

After breakfast, Mark and Scotty went over to Billy's to hangout. Matt was there, too. Mark told them about his dream as they sat in the treehouse. Neither Matt or Billy seemed to think too much about it, other than Matt joking about not being in it; so Mark decided to let it go. The guys skated, had a water gun fight and then decided that they needed to pack for their trip that started in the morning.

All five families met at the Motes house that night. They all brought a dish, ate and had a good time. Mark's mom drove the group to Andy and Eddie's homes.

They each stood there holding a covered dish when Andy opened his front door. He looked at them and shook his head. "Just so you know," he said. "I will be out of town for a while starting tomorrow."

"That's fine," Gabi said. "This is our last visit. For now, anyway."

He nodded, taking the food. "I still don't like you, McGee.'

"Well, you're not exactly my favorite person, Andy," Mark said. "But I think we can get along."

"Whatever." He closed the door.

"Well, we're making progress," Brianna said, laughing.

Next they went to Eddie's. His mom was actually waiting for them outside. She was sitting in a lawn chair, fanning herself. "Well, it's about time!" she said. "I'm about to starve." She grabbed all four dinners and headed inside.

"Is Eddie here?" Matt called before she vanished.

"He's on restriction in his bedroom!" She closed the door, leaving them standing there, speechless.

"Well then," Scotty finally said. "That was pleasant."

They headed to their last class. Once they were all settled into their seats, Mr. Bret opened up with prayer. When he had finished praying, he clapped his hands together so loud, they all jumped. "I have a praise report!" he said with a big cheesy grin. "Remember the other night when we prayed for my friend's wife, Samantha?" They all nodded. "Well, she's awake and doing great!"

"Praise God," Gabi said, and the others clapped. "That's amazing."

"Yeah, Pastor Albert said she has quite a testimony and I can't wait to hear it," Mr. Bet said.

"Well, be sure to share it with us when you hear it," Brianna said.

Two hours later, they dismissed after Mr. Bret reminded them of everything they could and could not bring. He wanted them to be there by eight o'clock in the morning, so they could get their bags packed into the bus.

Mark actually had a good dream-free night's sleep. He woke up earlier than he was used to and took his bags downstairs. His mom made him a big breakfast and drove him up to the church. Bethany had made him a card to take with him, so he didn't forget her. He kissed his mother goodbye and put his bags in the back of the bus. By the time he and the others had their bags put away and their seats picked out, Mr. Bret told them to come inside the church.

He led them into the sanctuary where seven teens were sitting on the front row with their backs to them. "Stand up and turn around as I introduce you!" Mr. Bret said. "Daisy Canard." A really pretty girl with sandy blonde hair stood and turned around. She did not look happy. "Yvette Turner." Mark recognized Yvette from church. She was a tall, pretty girl with dark hair. "Maria Lewis." Mark couldn't believe it. It was the girl from the beach. He exchanged a look with Scotty. Mark had forgotten all about her with all of the crazy events of the week. "Shadow Riley." A black haired, all black wearing, chubby Goth girl stood. It was quite possible that she had a pretty face, but she made it difficult to tell with all the makeup and piercings. Mark's heart broke as he thought of his friend, Angel.

"Cool name," Brianna said. "I like the name Shadow." Gabi nodded, but Shadow only rolled her eyes.

"Eddie Schumer," Mr. Bret said and each of them gasped to see Eddie stand up. "Andy Cruz." And there was Andy, a big smirk on his face, looking right at Mark. "And last, but not least," Mr. Bret said, motioning for the big red-headed kid to stand. "Rusty Staggerbush."

CHAPTER 5

THE WHEELS ON THE BUS...

"Nope!" Scotty said. "Nope, nope, nope." He turned around and headed out of the church.

Before Mark turned to go after him, he looked once more at Rusty, who met his gaze with a smile. It was more of a sinister smile than a friendly one. As Mark walked out the door to get Scotty, he wondered if his friend didn't have the right idea. The thought of a week-long trip with the guys who had stolen and vandalized their homes and neighborhood seemed downright cruel. Of course, it also seemed like just the kind of situation that God would orchestrate to show his love to Rusty, Andy and Eddie. Still, what kind of judge thought that summer camp was a good punishment for what Rusty was charged with doing? Mark stopped at the bottom of the front steps of the church and looked around for Scotty. Suddenly he had the odd feeling that maybe this was another dream. It had to be. That would perfectly explain how Rusty...whatever his last name is, was here. Mark half expected to look over and see a dragon peeking around from behind the bus. What he did see, however, was Scotty on the bus, looking for his bags. "Scotty!" Mark ran onto the bus.

"Don't try and talk me out of this, Mark!" Scotty said. "There is no way I am going on this trip with any of those three!"

"Yeah, I'm in shock myself, Dude. I thought I was having another nightmare," Mark said. "So, I totally understand."

"Well, here's one of your bags," Scotty said, holding it out for Mark. "We could hang out at my house today. Maybe my mom could take us to the beach."

Mark gave it some serious thought for about ten seconds and then shook his head. "No."

"Your loss." Scotty grabbed his own bags and headed towards Mark, who was blocking his path.

Mark held up his hand to stop him. "Would you agree or disagree that this has all the makings of another God adventure?" Mark asked him.

"Dude, I already didn't want to go! You know that! You know I hate confrontations! You know I hate speaking! You know I hate praying out loud…and I absolutely hate the thought of being stuck in some cabin with those three criminal slash bullies in there for a whole week! You also know they're only going to taunt us and do nothing but make trouble!"

"Yeah," Mark replied. "So, you're just going to leave the rest of us to deal with it?"

Scotty stared at him for a few seconds. "You've got each other." He tried to get around Mark.

Mark didn't budge. Their eyes met. "We're a team, Dude," Mark said. "I would be dead right now if you hadn't stepped up and stopped those demons after Angel died. I need you."

"For what?!" Scotty asked. "This isn't demons and dragons, Mark! This is real life, Dude!" He paused and stepped back. "And that's much scarier to me! Listen, I'm sorry." He pushed past Mark and got off the bus.

"I'll have your back, Dude!" Mark called after him. "I'll pray when it's your turn. I'll do your devotions! I'll do my best to keep you from any…embarrassing situations."

"If you're willing to do all that for me, then why do I need to go?" Scotty asked.

"To be my friend." Mark said, shrugging.

Scotty hung his head. "Dude, you'll have Gabi. You'll have Matt, you'll h…"

"I won't have my BEST friend!" Mark interrupted him. He felt his phone vibrate. "Come on, Dude! You don't want us coming back with stories of some epic adventure that you weren't a part of, do you?" Scotty gave him a weak smile. "Not to mention, me and Gabi might start dating," Mark added.

Scotty laughed at that. "Yeah, right! That's my wife you're talking about."

"Well, that's also your wife you're talking about abandoning." He pointed to the church. "To the wolves, no less."

Scotty gave him a long look. "Okay...I'll go, but you're keeping your promises." They fist bumped as Scotty walked back onto the bus.

Mark checked his phone. It was Gabi. "Did u stop him from leaving?" Mark replied, "Yes but nvr ask me how."

After going over all the rules, Mr. Bret had the group enter the bus. It wasn't a full-sized bus, so the luggage took up quite a bit of space. There were only eight available seats for sitting. Rusty claimed a seat by himself as far back as he could get. Andy and Eddie sat in the seat across from him with Eddie against the window. Shadow sat by herself in the seat in front of them. Across from her and in front of Rusty, was Yvette and Daisy with Yvette at the window. Matt and Billy sat in front of them with Billy at the window. Across from them and in front of Shadow, was Mark and Scotty with Scotty at the window. Gabi and Brianna were in front of them and right behind the door with Brianna at the window. Directly behind the driver, Mr. Bret, sat Maria.

It was fairly quiet on the bus for the first fifteen minutes. Some talked quietly among themselves and others were texting, playing games or listening to music. As soon as they got on the interstate, Mr. Bret said, "Okay, Maria! Why don't you get us started?"

"Really? Pick somebody else to go first!" she said, clearly shaken.

"I'm picking you," Mr. Bret said. "Just get it over with."

Maria shook her head and sighed. Reluctantly, she sat up on her knees in the seat and faced the others. "I'm Maria," she said, rolling her eyes. "I'm fourteen years old and was recently arrested for stealing." She gave Mark and Scotty a death stare. "It wasn't my first arrest, so I was sentenced to probation and this stupid…" She glanced back at Mr. Bret. "I have to go to this camp for rehabilitation, by orders of the judge." She plopped back down in her seat.

"Now see!" Mr. Bret said. "That wasn't so bad. Yvette, you're up!"

Yvette stood up and set her things in her seat next to Daisy. "I'm Yvette. Fourteen, almost fifteen. My parents think I need to come to this camp to get my life straight." She laughed, but nobody else did. Rusty smirked from behind her. "Anyway, anything that gets me away from them for a week, can't be that bad." She grabbed her things and sat back down.

"Daisy!" Mr. Bret said.

Daisy stood up, handing her things to Yvette. "My name is Daisy Canard. I'm…"

"Canard?" Rusty said, laughing. "Isn't a canard a duck?" He laughed again. "That makes you…"

"Yes!" she said, interrupting him. "Thank you, Rusty! My parents thought it was cute. Anyway," she continued, "I'm thirteen. The reason I'm on this trip is because my stupid parents…"

"Daisy!" Mr. Bret stopped her.

"Sorry," she said, smiling a cheesy smile at him. "My parents think I need to get out and enjoy nature and do…stuff."

"Too much time on your computer?" Rusty asked, smiling at her.

She sat back down and took her things back from Yvette.

"Wow!" Maria said. "What a couple of spoiled brats!"

"Excuse me?!" Yvette said.

"I'm just saying, if I had parents that cared enough to send me to a place like this, I wouldn't be here," Maria said. "And here you two are moaning about it. Poor babies!" She poked out her bottom lip.

"Okay!" Mr. Bret said. "Let's keep it civil! Shadow, you're next!"

Shadow took her earbuds out and stayed seated. "My name is Shadow. Fourteen. My parents hate me and just want me out of the house." She put her earbuds back in.

"Eddie!" Mr. Bret said.

He stayed seated. "My name is Eddie, I'm thirteen and the court ordered me to be here." Rusty laughed out loud. Eddie looked over at him nervously.

"And I'm Andy. Fourteen. Court ordered." Andy waved and smiled.

"Yeah!" Rusty yelled, causing Yvette and Daisy to jump. "I just want to say that I am SO excited about this trip. Getting to know each of you on a personal level." He winked at Daisy, who had turned around when he yelled. "My name is Rusty Staggerbush and I'm fifteen. I did some really bad things and a judge thought that sending me to a camp full of juvenile delinquents was a good idea." He smiled real big. "This is going to be so much fun."

"Okay, that was our guests!" Mr. Bret said. "Now for our hosts. Gabi?"

"I'm sorry!" Rusty yelled. "First can we sing, The Wheels on the Bus Go Round and Round?" Andy and Maria laughed. "I've always wanted to sing that song."

"Maybe later!" Mr. Bret said. "Go ahead, Gabi."

Gabi raised up on her knees. "Hi, everyone! I'm Gabi. I recently turned thirteen. Like Rusty, I'm really excited to get to know each of you better. I really hope that we can all be friends by the end of this trip."

"Highly unlikely," Maria muttered.

"Anyway," Gabi continued. "I really believe that if you guys let Him, God can change your lives over this next week." She smiled and sat down.

Brianna sat up on her knees and smiled really big. "I'm Brianna. Thirteen also. I actually live in California and am staying with Gabi for the summer. We were elementary school friends. I agree with what she just said about God. I gave my heart to Jesus about..."

"You're not going to preach, are you?" Rusty asked.

"Rusty!" Mr. Bret said. "Stop interrupting."

"As I was saying, I was saved about two years ago at a youth camp in Northern California. I've never been the same." She smiled at Rusty and sat back down.

"I'm sure you were SAVED from a horrible life of sin!" Maria said, looking over at Brianna. "Drugs? Alcohol? Prostitution?" Rusty and Andy laughed.

"You too, Maria!" Mr. Bret said. "Try and get along. Go ahead, Billy."

Billy sat up and leaned against the window. "I'm Billy, thirteen. I like skateboarding and long walks on the beach." Matt moaned and Mark and Scotty laughed. "Just trying to lighten the mood, sorry. I look forward to getting to know all you guys and I also look forward to swimming in that huge lake." He sat down.

Matt turned, facing the aisle. "I'm Matt. Fourteen. I love music and will be running the sound system at camp. Oh, just because I'm big, don't pick me to be on your team in any sports. I'm not really any good." He smiled and turned back around.

Mark quickly stood up. "I'm Mark and I actually turn thirteen this Wednesday," he said. "Which makes me the youngest one on the bus. Anyway, I look forward to getting to know you all, and then beating you at every sport."

"Whatever!" Gabi said.

"Hi, Mark," Daisy said, smiling up at him. He smiled back.

"And this," Mark said, putting his hand on Scotty's shoulder. "Is my best friend, Scotty. He is also thirteen."

"Hi, Scotty," Daisy said, smiling at Scotty.

"Why can't he speak for himself?" Rusty asked. "Cat got his tongue?" Andy and Eddie laughed.

"Rusty?" Mr. Bret said. "Really?"

"I'm just asking!" Rusty said. "Everybody else had to talk."

Scotty turned around in his seat. "I'm Scotty." He cleared his throat. "I'm thirteen and I hate speaking in front of people." He gave Rusty a big smile. "Nice to meet you all." He turned back around.

"Okay," Mr. Bret said. "This is a seven-hour trip! Everybody play nice! We'll stop for lunch when we get to Macon!"

'Hey, McGee!" Rusty said. "Why don't you come sit with me?" He slid over and patted his seat. "Let's get to know each other." Andy laughed, Mark walked back and sat next to him. Rusty fist bumped him. "Sorry for all the trouble I've caused you and your friends, McGee. I sometimes have trouble with my social skills."

"Well," Mark said. "I can't imagine why." They both laughed. "I'm sure we can work through everything this week."

"Not planning on getting me saved are you, McGee?" Rusty smiled. "Cause that ain't gonna happen."

"I don't know, Rusty," Mark replied. "Stranger things have happened."

"No." Rusty shook his head. "No, they haven't." Andy and Eddie were whispering something, and Andy laughed.

Mark noticed Daisy get up and sit next to Scotty.

"So, McGee," Rusty said. "Tell me the story about how you got Todd Johnson killed." He smiled at Mark.

"Yeah, McGee," Andy said. "I wouldn't mind hearing it first-hand myself."

"Andy," Mark replied. "Todd was what, six foot two? He weighed at least two hundred pounds. How exactly do you think I made him go with me to that castle?"

"I never said you made him do anything," Andy said. "I said you abandoned him."

"To go get help," Mark said. "Don't you think someone big enough to grab Todd, was probably too big for me to fight? Listen, he insisted on going with me, against my wishes."

Rusty laughed. "So, you escaped the clutches of the old groundskeeper and ran for help, huh?"

"Yeah," Mark said, nodding. "Once we realized that Old Man Willoughby was onto us, we knew that he could only catch one of us. So, whoever escaped would bring help."

"Well," Rusty said, looking over at Andy and Eddie. "I think it took guts for McGee here to go to that castle at night; with or without a six-foot two bodyguard." He patted Mark on the arm. "Respect, McGee."

"Nah, it was stupid," Mark said. "There was no excuse for doing something so stupid."

"Yeah," Andy said. "And it was that stupid idea that got Todd killed."

"So, is it true that you guys ended up going into the castle later?' Rusty asked, nodding toward Scotty and Gabi.

Mark was taken aback. They had never told their story to anyone other than the families involved. "Where did you hear that, Rusty?"

Rusty shrugged. "Is it true?"

"I'd rather not talk about it, if that's okay," Mark said.

"Why not, McGee?" Rusty asked. "Seems to me that a story like that would be worth talking about."

Mark shrugged. "Perhaps."

"Well, here's what I think," Rusty said. Andy leaned over to listen. "You move to Gateway. You hear about this mysterious castle that you can't help but be curious about. I mean, it was right behind your house. So, one night you sneak out to go see what you can find. Only, you run into Todd along the way and he insists on going with you. He ends up getting caught and taken. You, however, get away and report it to the cops. They, of course, don't buy your story. Not to mention, they were already terrified of that castle. Now, your story is a little fuzzy after that. All I really know is that a teacher's body was found, and you disappeared the same night. Gone for a few days, weren't you?"

Mark just stared straight ahead, unsure of what to say.

"And then there was the mysterious death of that loser Goth girl. What was her name?"

"Her name was Angel, and she was my friend," Mark said.

"Okay, I'm sorry," Rusty said. "They never did find her body though, did they?"

Mark just looked at him.

"And what about that quack reporter that showed up talking about how her life had been changed and she'd found God?" Rusty asked. "All right after her cameraman had been found dead. Sounds to me like the makings of quite a conspiracy."

"Yeah," Andy added. "It all sounds kinda fishy to me." Eddie just watched Mark's reactions.

"So, why don't you fill in the blanks, McGee," Rusty said. 'Because, here's the thing. I don't trust you. You or your friends over there. You all say you want to get to know us. Well, first you need to come clean. How do we know you didn't kill Angel... and that teacher?"

"And Todd," Andy said.

'True," Rusty said. "Where'd you hide the bodies, McGee? Are they in that forest?"

Mark smiled at Rusty. "Well, Rusty, I guess once I find out exactly who YOU are, and what YOUR story is, I'll be more willing to 'fill in' your blanks." He patted Rusty on the leg and got up.

Daisy slid closer to Scotty when she saw that Mark wanted his seat back. "Hi, Mark," she said with a giggle. "Have a seat."

Mark sat down on the edge of the seat. "Hello, Daisy," he said with a smile. "How are you?"

"I'm good," she answered. "So, Scotty was just telling me how you and him have made some kind of pact to not have girl-friends." She giggled again. "I think that is so cute."

Mark glanced at Scotty who just shrugged. "Well, that's us...cute."

"Yes, you are." She laughed. "I just don't understand why you would do that," she said. "I mean, come on, live a little."

Mark smiled. "That's what we're doing, Daisy. See, while everybody else is freaking out about who likes them or who doesn't like them, Scotty and I are over here like, 'you wanna go skateboard?' We're actually living a little."

She nodded. "I guess that makes sense, but..."

"But nothing," Mark said. "There's plenty of time for all that silliness later. We're still young."

"But what if the girl you're supposed to be with, ends up with somebody else, because you waited?" she asked.

Mark shrugged. "Then she wasn't the girl I was supposed to be with. The girl I'm supposed to be with is worth the wait... and so am I."

"Yeah," Scotty said, and Daisy looked at over at him. "What he said."

"Hmm, you Christians sure have a funny way of doing things," she said with a sigh.

"Actually," Mark said. "I made that decision long before I was a Christian. After watching one of my friends lose his mind after getting a girlfriend, I decided to enjoy being a kid a little longer."

"So, it's not a Christian thing?" Daisy asked.

"No," Mark replied. "But it IS a smart thing."

"Well, it's just too bad," she said. "You guys are missing out on a lot of fun." She stood, slid out into the aisle and looked back at them. "Let me know if you change your mind."

Mark and Scotty fist bumped. "Heart breakers," Mark said.

"You know it," Scotty replied.

Gabi and Brianna both turned around after obviously listening in to the whole conversation. "Well put, Mr. McGee," Gabi said.

"Yeah," Brianna added. "I'm proud of you guys, because Daisy's a pretty girl."

"Really?" Scotty said. "We hadn't noticed." They all laughed.

Billy leaned forward and tapped Maria on the shoulder. "Hi," he said awkwardly. "Um, so did you pass seventh grade?"

"Um," she replied mockingly. "No, I failed every class. What do you think?" She didn't even look up from her book.

He nodded even though she couldn't see him. He was trying to think of what to say next.

"Besides, I'm done with school," she said. "What's the point?"

"Well, there's the tater tots," Billy replied. "They're pretty awesome."

She only shook her head, but he actually saw a smile.

"So, what are you reading?" He asked. "And please don't say a book."

She shrugged. "It's nothing. One of the girls in jail gave it to me." She showed him the cover. Daddy's Girl was the title. "Just some stupid novel to pass time."

"Okay, well, enjoy," Billy said, and sat back.

"Hey, Billy!" Rusty yelled. "Did you get her digits?" He and Andy laughed.

"Just being friendly, Rusty!" Billy yelled back. "Try it sometime!"

"Yeah, 'cause you know you don't have a shot with Maria!" He laughed.

Gabi got up, walked back and sat down next to Rusty.

"Whoa!" Rusty said. "Come to give me YOUR digits?" He laughed.

"Dream on," Gabi said.

"Seriously then, what do you want?" Rusty asked.

She turned to face him. "To find out what your problem is."

"But I don't have a problem." He smiled a big fake smile at her.

"So, you're just that guy that needs to laugh at everybody else in order to feel big?" she asked. "Just so you know, it may make you FEEL big, but it makes you LOOK small."

Rusty looked up and saw Brianna, Mark and Scotty watching them. "Why don't you just go back up there and sit with your freaky friends? I don't trust you any more than I do McGee. You probably had something to do with those deaths too."

She smiled at him. "Jesus loves you, Rusty."

"OH MY GOD!" he shouted, making everybody jump. "You gonna baptize me now?!"

"No, not yet," Gabi said calmly. "But I will be praying for you." She smiled at him one last time and went back to her seat.

"You're wasting your time!" he called after her, with a laugh.

About fifteen minutes later, Brianna went back and sat down beside Shadow. Shadow still had her earbuds in, and her head pressed against the window. Brianna tapped her on the arm.

"Go away," Shadow said without even looking over.

"Hey, Brianna!" Rusty said. "You can come sit with me."

"Yeah, me too," Andy said, laughing.

"Can I come sit with you?" Mr. Bret asked. "Be respectful!"

Brianna ignored both of them. She just sat there beside Shadow, writing something on a notepad.

Rusty leaned up next to her. "You don't have to write me a love note," he whispered. "Just tell me what you're thinking."

"You know what, Rusty?" Brianna said, without looking up from her notepad. "Ew." Mark, Scotty, Matt, and Billy all busted out laughing. She tore her note out, folded it and slid it into Shadow's hand. She stood up and faced Rusty. "If only everyone enjoyed the sound of your voice as much as you do." She went back to her seat.

Rusty mumbled something only Andy could hear. Andy laughed.

A few minutes later, Shadow opened the note. "Hello Shadow, I know you want to be left alone, so I will respect that. I would love to be your friend or at least someone you can hang out with. I promise not to preach to you unless you ask me to. Brianna." She read it again and then folded it up and slid it in her pocket.

"So, can we sing The Wheels on the Bus Go Round and Round now?" Rusty yelled

"Start it!" Gabi yelled back.

He did and a few of them sang along, including Mr. Bret.

An hour and a half later, they pulled into a gas station in Macon, Georgia. Mr. Bret told them all to use the restroom and to meet him inside the restaurant that was in the gas station. He was, after all, paying for their food.

About an hour later, they were back on the road, heading to Camp Ricochet. Everybody seemed tired after having filled up on burgers and fries. Most were attempting to sleep; the others were either reading or listening to music.

Mark had noticed at lunch how Eddie didn't seem too comfortable around Rusty. He wondered if Rusty knew it was Eddie that had ratted him out. Mark would have to try and connect with Eddie and get him out of that circle. Meanwhile, he could barely keep his eyes open. He put his knees up on the seat in front of him and put a towel behind his head. He looked over at Scotty, who was already drooling.

Glen checked the address one more time and kept walking. He slid the crumpled piece of paper back into his pocket and adjusted his backpack. It was heavier than it had been in a long time, thanks to the church he'd passed earlier. That Pastor Joshua sure was a talker, though the canned goods he'd handed out were appreciated. If memory served him well, his destination was about a mile away and the sun had already set. He needed to hurry. He passed the local middle school.

Glen sure hoped this place was better than the last one. Of course, the last one was a dump. Literally. It had been an old trailer that someone had left sitting next to a landfill. The smell had been horrible. In fact, the only perk it had, was a roof. A roof that leaked, but a roof. Not to mention all of his roommates. He had to laugh. There had been quite a few, if you included the ants, roaches, spiders, rats, mice and an occasional family of possum. He'd also had a human roommate, but for the life of him, couldn't remember the guy. Try as he might, he couldn't remember the guy's face...or name. They hadn't lived together long, but the guy was super nice. He was always sharing his alcohol and drugs with Glen. He laughed again. That might have something to do with why he couldn't remember him. Then one day, the guy just up and disappeared. All he'd left behind was a half empty bottle of whisky, a bag full of useless junk and a note. "Glen my friend, sorry I had to leave. You better go too. The police may come snooping around. I think you will find the address at the bottom is much more suitable for you. Trust me. Maybe I'll see you soon." He hadn't even written his name.

As he passed by the houses with their lights on and the families inside together eating dinner and watching television, he couldn't help but wonder how he'd gotten here. Fifty-eight years old and homeless. His mama sure would be ashamed. It hadn't always been like this, though. Not that many years ago, he'd had a wife, a job, a mortgage, and even a dog. He, Glen Joseph Jones, had had a life. What had happened? What or who exactly was to blame for his present state of being? Surely it wasn't him. It had nothing at all to do with his love for the bottle. It would also be useless to point your finger at his obsession with the dog tracks or the internet cafés. What about his need for other things on the internet? No, when Sharon left him, it was because she was weak and couldn't handle a little bit of a struggle. Wasn't it supposed to be for better or for worse? Again, he laughed. "No, Glen!" he said out loud. "It was you!"

He wondered what kind of place this would be. An old abandoned house or trailer? Maybe he would get lucky and there would be running water. He was rarely that lucky, though he really could use a shower. He sniffed his shirt. A change of clothes wouldn't hurt either. He hoped more than anything that the place was well hidden. He didn't need nosy neighbors snooping around and calling the cops. The cops. They had come…just like the note had warned him. They'd confiscated that bag of useless junk and evicted Glen from the place he'd called home for over a year. Again, he had to laugh.

It was getting late and the streetlights seemed to be getting further apart. Still, he walked on. He hated being this far from local businesses. There were always treasures to be found in their dumpsters at night that were much fresher than anything he'd been able to get out of the landfill. Being this far away may cause him to have to set traps for food. He'd done it before, but it wasn't the best plan. Catching your food meant cooking it and fires could give away your hiding place. Especially in this rural area.

The road he'd been walking on was about to dead end into the road he was looking for. There were no streetlights on the corner, and he had no idea which way to go. He stood at the corner and looked both ways. There was a dark driveway about fifty feet to his left. He would go there and see if there was an address he could work off of. There was a full moon out tonight, but it mostly stayed hidden behind the clouds. He approached the driveway and saw an iron post that had at one time held a mailbox. There were numbers on the post, and he turned it to where he could read them. "No way!" he yelled a little too loud. Could he really be this lucky? This was the place. He looked up to see a circular driveway with a large mound of dirt and overgrown weeds in the center. He walked around it. On the other side, to his surprise, was a large iron gate with one side hanging off the hinges. There were Do Not Enter signs posted everywhere and Glen hoped everybody else was obedient. He stepped past the hanging gate onto an old stone driveway that had been overtaken with weeds. The driveway may have been wide enough for a car at one time, but the forest on both sides was now closing in. Thank goodness for the little bit of light that the moon was casting, because this was quite scary. After several minutes of climbing over fallen trees, walking through spider webs, and tripping over loose stones, he came to a clearing. He stopped to let his eyes adjust.

To Glen's right were the remains of an old shack that had fallen over and been claimed by the forest. Hopefully that wasn't where he was supposed to live. To his left, amidst tall weeds and overgrown shrubbery, were piles of what looked like black rock. He walked over and bent down for a closer look. It appeared to be stone or marble, as if a statue had once been there. Interesting. What kind of place had this been? He walked back over to the stone driveway, which was barely visible in here. He looked ahead and was once again surprised by what he saw. A wooden bridge that curved up and over. Did that mean there was a creek? That would be good. He walked up to the bridge and slowly crossed it. Looking over the side he saw that there was nothing but a dried-up creek bed. Oh well. On the other side of the bridge, the driveway ended. There was nothing but forest around him. No house. No trailer. No...wait. There was a light in the forest ahead of him. He tried to get a better look, but it was too thick. It almost seemed like the light was coming up out of the ground. He set his pack on the bridge and searched for a way to check out this strange phenomenon.

Glen found an entry point into the forest that wasn't so thick and made his way in. He got caught up in several bushes and limbs that cut him, but he pressed on. It almost looked as if a spotlight had been buried in the dirt and left on, just shining into the night sky. As he got closer, it looked as if something large had come out of the ground and a mound of dirt and forest had formed around it. He walked to the other side and found where the light was coming from. There was a wide opening in the mound. He stepped closer for a better view and was pleasantly surprised to find a set of ancient stone steps leading down. What was causing the light, though? Was there someone down there? "Hello!?" he yelled into the hole. Not even an echo replied. "Well," he said to himself. "At least there's a light." He stepped inside and made his way down the wide steps. Two things Glen had expected upon entering the hole: One, that it would only go down about ten feet or so; just enough to be the height of a regular room. And two, that he would immediately find the source of that light. Neither seemed to be true. The steps spiraled down further and further with no sign of a light source. It was almost as if the light were moving just ahead of him. Just out of sight. After walking down the steps at a good pace for at least fifteen minutes with no sign of the bottom, Glen stopped. He turned around and looked back up. It was like looking up into a pit of darkness. Just then, he heard something move from below him. He turned to look, and the light went out. Something grabbed him by his ankles and snatched his feet out from under him. As he was being drug down the steps on his back screaming at the top of his lungs, he had an odd thought. Rusty. That had been his roommates name. Rusty.

CHAPTER 6

CAMP RICOCHET

Mark jumped awake when Scotty nudged him. He squinted in the sunlight and had no idea where he was. Oh yeah, bus. Summer camp. He'd been having a crazy dream, but it quickly slipped away from his memory. Given his dream history, that was a good thing. He looked around and saw open fields on the left of the bus and thick forest on the right. They seemed to be driving on a back, country road. He checked his phone to see that it was fifteen minutes after five.

"We're almost there, Dude." Scotty said, pointing to a sign up ahead on the right. It was a large chocolate brown, wooden sign that read CAMP RICOCHET in large light blue letters, and below that it said, John 3:17 in smaller green letters.

"I thought John 3:16 was the big verse," Billy said. "Gabi, what's John 3:17 say?"

"For God did not send His Son into the world to condemn the world, but to save the world through Him." She looked back at Billy. "Had to learn it for children's church, won a bag of Skittles®."

They turned onto a dirt road just after the sign. Mark looked back to see that everyone was awake and looking around except Rusty, who was laying on his back with his feet in the aisle. It didn't take but a few seconds for the darkness of the forest to cover them. The road was quite bumpy, and Mr. Bret attempted to swerve and miss as many holes and bumps as he could.

"Oh look!" Billy said. "A nature trail." He pointed out his window.

"Remember it," Maria said. "It may be an escape route." Andy laughed.

"There will be no escaping," Mr. Bret said. "You'll be having too much fun." He smiled at Maria in the mirror.

"I'm sure," she said.

"There will be plenty of opportunities to have fun, Maria," Gabi said with a smile. "The choice is yours."

"Wow!" Maria said. "Do you even realize how much you sound like a fortune cookie?"

Rusty busted out laughing and sat up. "That was epic!" he yelled. "And un-fortune-ate for you, Gabi." Andy and Maria laughed.

"So clever, Rusty," Gabi said.

Slowly they drove deeper and deeper into the forest. There were occasional trails, but it was mostly dark, thick forest.

"How far back is it?" Brianna asked.

"Three miles," Mr. Bret answered as he swerved to miss a large hole. "But at this speed, that could take a half hour."

"Three miles into the woods," Rusty said in an ominous whisper. "So, no one can hear our screams." They all looked at him. "MWAHAHAHA!" He and Andy laughed.

"Screams of laughter and shouts of joy!" Brianna said.

"Well, either way!" Rusty replied. "The adventure begins."

"Yes, it does," Mark said, meeting Rusty's eye. "Yes, it does."

After about five more minutes of bouncing over ruts, roots and car-sized potholes, they came into a clearing. To the left was a field that was being used as a parking lot. There were several church vans and busses lined up in rows. To the right were small, gray cabins slightly greened with a mossy covering. The cabins seemed to be scattered randomly throughout the forest, each with a blue number painted next to the door. Straight ahead were three much larger buildings that were supposed to look like big log cabins but were more like metal buildings painted brown. Each one had a large porch with rocking chairs and benches. Beyond the larger buildings and to the right was a large sitting area with log benches set up in a circle around a large fire pit. There were several rows of benches. This was most likely where the campfire services were held. Further back was a large lake with several docks and a small floating island about twenty feet out.

"Oh yeah!" Billy said excitedly. "Come to papa!"

"Can we swim today?" Yvette asked. "That's so beautiful!"

"I think there will be free time tomorrow after Sunday service," Gabi replied.

As Mr. Bret pulled into the parking area, they saw what looked like an obstacle course with bales of hay, large oil drums and small sections of wooden fences placed randomly. All covered in brightly colored paint.

"Dude!" Scotty yelled. "Paintball!"

"Yes!" Mark replied and they fist bumped. "It's on!"

"You guys try not to wet you're your pants, now," Andy said. Rusty and Eddie laughed.

"All I know is," Mark said. "I've seen Eddie shoot, and he's on my team." He saw a flash of surprise cross Eddie's face before he looked away to stare back out the window.

"There's supposed to be archery too," Matt said. "Never tried it, but I want to."

"Everyone remain in your seats until I tell you otherwise!" Mr. Bret said, as he parked the bus. "I need to talk to you first!" He shut it off, unbuckled his seatbelt and stood up. He reached under the driver's seat and pulled out a plastic bin about the size of a shoebox. "Okay! As we discussed, I will now be collecting all of your electronic devices. Go ahead and turn them off and hand them over. Cellphones, games, music devices, i-thingys, or whatever you have." He walked down the aisle, and everyone placed their things in the bin. "If you are found in possession of any form of electronic devices once you exit this bus, those of you who are guests," he looked at Eddie, "will receive a personal chaperone for everywhere you go and everything you do. Your own babysitter." After collecting them all, he headed back to the front. "And that goes for breaking any rules at all. You will be trusted until you show us you can't be. Then you will not be trusted again. Am I clear?" Nods and yes sirs followed. He locked the bin in an overhead compartment above the driver's seat and opened the door. "All the ladies may gather their purses and exit the bus. The gentlemen will then gather the luggage and set it outside for everyone to collect. Gabi, please make sure all the ladies stay together next to the bus."

Rusty raised his hand before anyone moved. "You said ladies. What about Maria?" He and Andy laughed.

"Shut up, moron!" Maria said.

Mr. Bret put his hand on her shoulder to calm her down and looked at Rusty. "What she said." Everyone else laughed.

The girls got off the bus and stood next to it while the guys formed an assembly line removing the luggage and equipment.

By the time they had had finished unloading, a young man who appeared to be in his early twenties walked up. He was tall, well built, had a dark tan, and blonde hair cut short. His arms were covered with tattoos. He wore khaki shorts and a tank top. "Hello and welcome!" he said to everyone and shook Mr. Bret's hand. "I'm Dean, camp counselor in charge of games."

"Hi Dean!" Daisy said, with a big smile on her face. "I'm Daisy."

"Games, huh?" Scotty said. "Lead the way."

Dean laughed. "Not so fast! That won't start up until after lunch tomorrow. First we need to get you guys settled and fed." He saw the church name and location on the side of the bus. "Gateway, Florida? Where exactly is that?"

"Near Jacksonville," Mr. Bret said.

"So, you guys have been on the road for a while," Dean replied. He whistled really loud to a couple of guys sitting on the front porch of one of the larger buildings and waved them over to help with the luggage. He took the permission slips and check from Mr. Bret and led them towards the cabins. "The ones closest to the road are for the girls. Guys, we'll have to go a little further into the woods." He stopped walking when he reached the first cabin and checked his clipboard. "Okay, we have Gabi and Brianna as hosts?" He looked up and they waved at him. "Great," he said. "And Shadow, Daisy, Yvette and Maria as guests?" They all nodded except Daisy, who was busy talking to the teenage boys that were helping with the luggage.

"Daisy!" Mr. Bret yelled, making her jump. "Focus!"

"Okay," Dean said. "Gabi and Brianna, we have way more guests this year than hosts. Especially with the girls. There will be a total of ten girls in your room and you will be the only hosts." He looked up at them. "Can you handle that?"

They both nodded. "Yes, sir," Gabi said.

"Oh, they can handle it!" Scotty said, and all the other hosts laughed.

"Perfect," Dean said. "You girls are in cabin number three... this way." He led them over to the small porch. "Here's the information on the other girls staying with you." He handed Gabi a sheet of paper and the key to the cabin. "If you have any problems, the women counselors are in cabin number one." Gabi nodded. "As soon as you are settled in, head on over to the first main building there." He pointed to the closest of the large buildings. "That's the Mess Hall, as the kids like to call it."

"Okay, thank you," Gabi said, and she led the girls into the cabin.

"Alright!" Dean said, "Onward men!" He led them past all of the cabins that they could see, to a boardwalk that led them deeper into the forest.

"This is so cool!" Billy said.

"Yes, it is!" Mark agreed, looking over at Scotty, who was grinning. "Glad you came?"

"So far so good," Scotty said.

After walking for about a hundred or so yards into the forest, the boardwalk ended into a clearing with eleven cabins scattered randomly about. "Okay, Bret," Dean said. "You will be in cabin twelve here." He pointed to the cabin closest to the boardwalk. "There will be four other counselors sharing it with you. We put you guys here so anybody trying to sneak out, has to pass your cabin."

"Well, my guys won't be sneaking out," Mr. Bret said, looking at them all. "Right boys?"

They all nodded. He set his things on the porch and walked with them to their cabin.

"You guys got lucky," Dean said. "You get a cabin all to your-selves. Cabin twenty-two." He led them to the very last cabin and checked his clipboard. "Matt, Billy, Scotty, and Mark?" They each waved to him. "More hosts than guests, this should be my most well behaved cabin." He smiled at them. "And Andy, Eddie and Rusty are our guests." They nodded. "Get settled in boys," he said. "Then head on down to the Mess Hall." He handed Matt the key to the cabin and he and Mr. Bret headed back toward the boardwalk, leaving them standing there.

Matt unlocked the door and led them inside. There were five bunkbeds and five small dressers set up in the main room. Two on the right-hand side, two on the left-hand side and one on the back wall. There were several pictures of nature on the walls. To the right of the back wall was a door that led to the bathroom, where there were three shower stalls separated by curtains.

Rusty and Andy quickly claimed the back-wall bunkbeds. Mark and Scotty took the back bunks on the left and Eddie took the back bunk on the right. Billy took the front left and Matt took the front right.

Mark noticed how Eddie seemed quiet and nervous. He was keeping his distance from Rusty.

"Okay guys," Matt said. "I don't know about you, but I'm starving." He walked toward the door. "Let's go ahead and hit the Mess Hall, we can unpack later."

"Um," Rusty said. "I have to use the bathroom." He put his hand on his stomach. "I'll catch up in a bit."

Matt paused at the door and looked at him. "We should prob-ably stay together."

"Dude, I don't need a babysitter!" Rusty said. "What hap-pened to trusting until there's a reason not to.?"

"Says the guy who demolished our neighborhood," Mark said, still sitting on his bottom bunk.

Rusty glared at him for a quick second and then relaxed. "Listen, this place is my last chance. I do real time if I mess this up, okay? I'm not stupid."

"Please don't ask me to comment on that," Scotty said, jumping off the top bunk and heading out the door.

"Well, there goes a loving example of a true Christian," Rusty said and Andy laughed.

"That surfboard you split in half had sentimental value," Mark said. "I wouldn't exactly be looking for him to send you a Christmas card this year."

Rusty shrugged and headed for the bathroom. "Hang around if you want. I hope you brought air freshener."

Andy laughed. "I'm outta here." He and Eddie headed for the door.

"You guys go," Mark said. "I'll wait for him." He looked towards the bathroom. "Actually, I'll wait for him on the front porch." They all laughed.

Ten minutes later, Mark and Rusty showed up in the Mess Hall. Inside, it was one large room with rows of picnic tables lined up throughout. There was a counter in the far corner that separated the kitchen from the dining area. Several people were busy preparing and serving food. Tonight's meal was barbecue chicken, corn on the cob, baked beans, and cornbread. Mark and Rusty got their plates and joined the others.

"This is so good," Matt said, his mouth covered in barbecue sauce already.

Mark looked around. The place was pretty full. "Wow," he said. "There has to be at least 200 people here."

"208 to be exact!" came a booming voice from behind him. A large, well dressed black man had walked up to their table. Mark thought he looked odd dressed in a tie at summer camp. "Hello kids!" he said with a big smile. "Name's Pastor Jenkins, but everybody just calls me Moses!"

"Well, nice to meet you, Moses!" Gabi replied.

"And it's nice to meet all of you! I look forward to getting to know you." He smiled and was about to move on to the next table when his gaze fell on Rusty. He stopped and pointed at him. "What's your name, son?"

"Rusty, sir," he replied, taking a bite of baked beans.

Moses just squinted down at Rusty for a few seconds like he was thinking of what to say. Finally, he just nodded. "God's got something in store for you, Rusty." He smiled and nodded. "Yes, sir. God's got something for you." He walked on to the next table.

Rusty smiled at the rest of them who were now staring at him. "Not me, he don't."

A few minutes later, Moses walked up to the podium and picked up the microphone. He tapped it to make sure it was on, causing several people to jump. "Good evening!" he said with a big smile.

"Good evening!" most everyone said back to him.

"Moses! I love you!" someone yelled from the back and everyone laughed.

"I love you too, Jasper!" Moses said with a hearty laugh to the camp counselor. "I am Pastor Jenkins, but please, feel free to call me Moses," he continued. "First of all, I would like to welcome you all to Camp Ricochet!" He paused while everyone cheered and clapped. "For those of you that are here to ...grow; I encourage you to let go this week. Let go and let God, as I like to say! Let go of the old self, the old habits, the old problems, the old...you. Let God have it all...including you." He flashed a big smile and continued. "For those of you that are here voluntarily, I thank you! I thank you from the bottom of my heart." He paused and placed both hands over his heart. "Now, we're going to have fun this week, I promise you! But...we're also going to dig into God's word and let Him start a new work in us!" Several people shouted amen. "Between your room prayers and devotions, the workshops, Sunday morning's service, and our nightly campfire meetings, you won't be able to miss God!" He checked his watch. "You will get to experience several different

speakers this week, but tonight ya'll are stuck with ol' Moses."
More clapping and cheering. "I will also be closing out the week
with Friday night's message." He said. "Now, why don't everybody take about an hour to get to know each other, maybe go
exploring, or just hang out in here and enjoy another helping
of Miss Dot's famous banana pudding. We'll all meet up at the
campfire at seven-thirty. Thank you!" Everyone clapped and
began to get up.

Scotty leaned over to Mark. "You want to go check out
the lake?"

"Yeah, you guys in?" Mark asked the rest of the table.

"I have to help set up the sound for the service," Matt replied,
and went to throw away his plate.

"We were going to check out the paintball area," Rusty said.
"Come on, Eddie.'

"Hey Eddie, you can go with us if you want to," Mark said.

"Nah," Rusty replied. "He's with us, McGee." He patted a
scared looking Eddie on the back. "Right, Eddie?"

"Yeah, right Rusty," Eddie replied. "Coming."

"What was that about?" Scotty asked Mark.

"We need to try and get Eddie away from those two,"
Mark replied. "Have you noticed how uncomfortable he is
around Rusty?"

"I have," Gabi said. "He seems downright terrified."

They headed outside onto the back patio. There were several
benches and chairs set up out there. Most everyone had gone
toward the lake, so Gabi suggested that they hang back for a
second. Brianna and Shadow walked over and sat on a bench.
They were laughing about something.

"Looks like you lost your BFF, Gabi," Scotty said.

"That's fine," Gabi said. "I can't believe how Shadow took
to her after that note Brianna gave her. She even asked if they
could share a bunkbed."

"What a view," Billy said, gazing toward the lake. Most of
the crowd had moved down onto the docks, to sit, play and hang
out. "It's a really big lake."

To their left was a big sand pit with a volleyball net set up. There was a place to play horseshoes, a small putt-putt area, a bean bag toss, and a large swing set that had already been claimed by a group of girls. To their right was the campfire service area.

"Come on," Scotty said. "There's a trail that circles the lake." He started walking that way.

"We can't go far, Scotty," Gabi said, and turned to the others. "Is everyone coming?" Everyone but Brianna and Shadow, followed them.

"This place is lame," Yvette said. "Can't we go to a mall?"

"I know," Daisy added. "We're going to get ticks. And it's so hot out here; my hair."

"Speaking of lame," Maria said. "Can't you two whining brats even hear yourselves?"

"Yeah," Billy said. "This is amazing! I love the outdoors."

They walked the trail that circled close to the lake's edge for about twenty minutes before Gabi insisted they turn around and head back. They saw Mr. Bret looking for them when they got back to the main area.

"Rusty, Andy and Eddie?" he asked with his arms out.

"They were going to check out the paintball area," Mark said.

"Those guys do not need to be left alone!" Mr. Bret said. "Come on Mark, Scotty and Billy! Help me find them!" They headed past the Mess Hall towards the paintball area just as Rusty, Andy and Eddie came walking out of the parking area. Rusty was smiling from ear to ear.

"Mr. Bret, can you let me in the bus, please?" Andy asked. "I can't find my wallet."

"What do you need your wallet for, Andy?" Mr. Bret asked. "You guys can't be wandering off. Come on, let's go get a seat." They headed over for the campfire service.

The worship band was really good. Dean was the singer and that counselor from dinner, named Jasper, was on the drums. The others were all teens. Moses preached a passionate message and several kids went down to the altar. Mark saw Brianna talking quietly to Shadow, who was wiping her eyes.

It was dark by the time they headed back to their cabins and all the counselors were using flashlights to lead the kids back to their cabins. The only lights in the forest, other than the flashlights, were the front porch lights on the cabins. In order to help keep the kids inside at night, they weren't allowed to have flashlights.

Back at their cabin, the boys all changed for bed and Matt did a short devotion and asked for prayer requests. He had Billy close in prayer and told them to hang out for a bit; but lights out in thirty minutes.

As Mark was about to sit down on his bed, he noticed something move under the blankets on Eddie's bed. Eddie was standing next to Rusty and Eddie's bed, with them. "Um, Eddie?" Mark asked. "Did you bring a pet?" He walked over and pulled back Eddie's blankets. A huge rattlesnake lunged out at him, hissing and quite angry. "Whoa!"

"Dude, look out!" Scotty yelled. Everyone jumped back. "Matt, go get Mr. Bret!"

Mark noticed that Rusty was the only one unaffected by the snake's appearance. He just stood there grinning. "Friend of yours, Rusty?" he asked.

Rusty looked at Mark and his smile faded. "No, McGee, just enjoying watching all you girls freaking out. What are you suggesting anyway?"

Mark shrugged. "If Eddie had waited until lights out to go to bed, he wouldn't have seen it." He met Eddie's eye.

"And what has that got to do with me?" Rusty asked.

"You tell me, you're the one that was in here alone earlier. Not to mention, you're the one standing there grinning about all this."

Rusty walked over and stood right in front of Mark. He was practically a head taller. "If I had put a snake in somebody's bed, McGee, it wouldn't have been Eddie's."

Just then, Matt came in with Mr. Bret and another counselor. The snake was still curled up on Eddie's bed. The other counselor told the boys to get out of the room while they captured the snake. A few minutes later, they came out with it in a pillowcase. They all checked the entire room for any more critters. Eddie didn't say anything for the rest of the evening. If he didn't seem scared before, he definitely did now. Matt suggested he move to the top bunk.

"Whoa! That was close!" Caleb screamed. He was panting and his heart was about to explode in his chest. That dump truck had nearly hit them. Caleb had borrowed his dad's truck to pick Megan up for their date. They had just eaten at her favorite Italian restaurant and were on their way to the movies. He was so shaken up he couldn't even remember which movie. He just sat there with his head in his hands trying to shake the fog from his brain.

"Uh...Caleb," Megan said softly.

He shook his head and looked over at her. "Wait...what?" He quickly jumped up and looked around. Instead of being in his dad's truck sitting on the side of the road, they were in some...desert? "Megan! Where are we?!" As far as he could see, there was nothing but sand and boulders with mountains in the distance.

"Caleb?" she moaned again and began to cry.

Caleb knelt down beside her. "Megan, are you okay, baby?" Her face was ghostly white, and she wasn't responding. "Megan! Stay with me!" He lifted her head onto his lap and stroked her hair. "Megan! Baby, wake up!"

Caleb and Megan had known each other for as long as either could remember. Their parents had met in college and became best friends; even moving into neighboring houses. They had started liking each other around the age of thirteen and been a couple now for over four years. Megan was the head cheerleader at their school and had a 4.0 grade point average. Caleb was the star pitcher for their baseball team and also had a 4.0 GPA. They had just graduated and were about to go to college together. Both had been accepted at NC State. They were enjoying their last summer at home.

"Baby!" He rubbed her face. "Please stay with me!" He looked around. "Is anybody here?!" he screamed. "Somebody, help us!" Where was this place? What had happened? It was then that he noticed the eerie sky. It was a dark orange color that was hidden behind what appeared to be black smoke. "Where are we, baby?" He shook his head. This didn't make any sense. Had the truck actually hit them? Were they dead? Unconscious? Was this a dream?

"Caleb," Megan moaned again. Her breathing was raspy.

"Megan, I'm here." He said, stroking her hair again. "Stay with me, Megan! It's going to be okay."

There was a loud clicking from behind him and he jumped. "Is somebody there?!" he called and gently set her head on the ground. He stood up and looked around. "Please, is somebody there? My girlfriend is hurt!" He walked over to the closest boulder. "Hello?" He walked around it and when he got to the other side, he saw a large creature standing over Megan. "Hey!" he screamed, but the creature didn't budge. "Get away from her!" From the back it had the build of an extremely tall man. Maybe more than nine feet. He was totally black and scaly, as if he were wearing a snake costume. He just stood there staring down at Megan. "Hey! I'm talking to you!" Caleb walked up closer to him. "What are you..." Caleb gasped when it turned its head and looked at him. Its face was straight out of a horror movie. Black, dead eyes that seemed to see into Caleb's soul. It didn't have a nose, and the mouth was massive with large razor-sharp teeth. It made a biting motion with its mouth and Caleb heard that clicking sound again. Then, it raised its head and looked past Caleb. It was then that Caleb heard sounds from behind him and spun around. He screamed. What was this place? There were hundreds, maybe thousands of creatures coming towards him. They were even more horrifying than the one next to Megan. Megan? He had to get her. He spun back around just as the creature picked her up and threw her over its shoulder like a sack. "No!" he screamed. Please no!" He ran up to the creature and tried to reach for Megan. The creature swung its powerful arm and hit Caleb square in the chest, knocking him to the ground several feet away. By the time he was able to look up, the creature was already walking away with Megan.

There was a loud roar behind Caleb and he quickly jumped up and spun around. The creatures were upon him and he was immediately knocked to the ground. They passed by him as he lay there. Giant spiders, half crab-half dogs, scorpions of all sizes, a lobster as big as an elephant, lizards as long as cars, and hundreds of foul creatures beyond description. There were even more of the tall, black, scaly creatures. A loud scream came to his left and he looked over to see an enormous caterpillar the size of a jumbo jet: its thousands of legs leading it forward. Caleb could only lie there, frozen with terror. The monsters, however, payed him no attention. They seemed to be following the creature that had Megan.

"Megan!" Caleb screamed and jumped up. He had to find her. "Megan! I'm coming, baby!" He took a deep breath of dry, hot air and mustered every ounce of strength and courage he had left. He ran as fast as he could, passing the creatures, monsters and beasts of all sizes. Some of them attempted to block his path, some of them succeeded in knocking him down. He would get right back up and find a way around them. "Megan!" he screamed. "God help me find her!"

The monsters seemed to be coming from every direction now. Everywhere he looked, there were more. Hundreds, thousands, maybe millions. They all seemed to be heading to one central location though. That had to be where Megan was. He made his way in that direction, screaming her name. The smell was horrible. The heat, unbearable. Was this a nightmare? Was this hell?

Caleb had never believed in hell. He'd never had time for any of that nonsense. He was too intelligent to be sucked into that scam. That kind of thinking was for losers. People without lives. People who had to believe in a God because they couldn't handle life by themselves. The 'God loves me, Jesus died for me' crowd. Yeah, losers.

"Megan!" he screamed, feeling like he should be close to the place she was at. The sky began to blacken. Caleb started to panic. What if he never found her? "Megan!"

"Caleb!" he heard her scream. "What's HAPPENING!!! Caleb, where are you!!?" she screamed.

Then he saw her as the creature tossed her to the ground like a doll. She hit hard but tried to slide away. "Megan!" he screamed, and she looked his way, terror in her eyes. Just then, a hand grabbed Caleb by the arm and gripped it like a vice. He turned to see it was another of the big, black, scaly creatures. "Let me go!!!" He tried to pull away, but the grip didn't budge.

The sky continued to blacken. Caleb looked up. It almost looked as if the sky was alive and moving. As if darkness itself had taken form. The creatures began to move back. Megan screamed. The creatures were moving away from her, but she was looking up. That's when Caleb saw it. The eyes. What at first could be mistaken as two giant red moons in a sky of blackness, were actually eyes. Fear seized Caleb like he'd never imagined. The creatures continued to move back, leaving Megan alone in the center.

She lay on her back, no longer able to scream. She sobbed and tried calling out to Caleb. "Please help me, Caleb!" She coughed and began choking, turning her head toward the ground.

"Megan!" he called. "Megan! Come to me, baby!" He tried again to get free from the hand that gripped him like a vice and was cutting off his circulation. "Megan! Over here!"

"What is this place, Caleb?! Where are we?" She tried to crawl towards him, sobbing and coughing. One of the creatures kicked her back into the center and she screamed. She lay there sobbing. There was nothing Caleb could do, but watch.

There was a loud groan from the blackness of sky. A hot wind began to blow, and Caleb had to cover his eyes. He heard

Megan scream and looked toward her. She was attempting to crawl away from something. "NO!" she screamed. "Please no!" The darkness seemed to just gather around her like a pitch-black blanket. "Caleb!!" she screamed. "Help me Caleb!!! I'm burning!!! NOOO!" The darkness lifted and Megan was gone.

Mark awoke Sunday morning to the sound of bells chiming over a loudspeaker. He opened his eyes to see that the sun was barely up. The others were stirring.

"Rise and shine, ladies!" Matt said coming out of the bathroom, showered and dressed. "Who's next? The water's great! Billy? Mark? Scotty?"

"Where am I?" Scotty asked. "Uhh, so that wasn't a nightmare."

"Sshh!" Billy said. "People are sleeping."

"For real," Andy added. "What time is it?"

"Time to get ready and go to breakfast," Matt said as he sprayed on some cologne and checked his hair in a small mirror. "I have to go down early because I'm running sound for the Sunday service, so you guys need to get a move on!" He saw that Mark had sat up. "You got this, Mark?"

"Yep, we're good," Mark said. "Come on, Scotty! Get up!"

"Don't forget you have devotions tonight," Matt said to Mark as he headed out the door. "See you guys later."

"So, what's the agenda for today?" Rusty asked. "Do we really have to go to church?"

"Yes, we do," Mark replied as he gathered his shower supplies. "And you won't even be able to text." He smiled at Rusty on his way by.

An hour later, they all headed to the Mess Hall for breakfast. They could smell the bacon frying from the boardwalk. "Oh wow," Scotty said. "I'm hungry now."

"Good morning, Mark! Good morning, Scotty!" Daisy yelled from the front porch of her cabin as the boys passed by. They looked over to see her and Yvette sitting in rocking chairs waiting for the others. Daisy jumped up and opened the door. "Gabi, can we go to breakfast with Mark and Scotty and the others?" Gabi said something the guys couldn't hear. "Okay, see you in the Mess Hall!" They ran to catch up.

"Good morning, Daisy," Mark said. "Yvette."

"Hey, Mark," Yvette said.

Mark looked back to see Maria come out and head their way. He stopped to wait for her. "Good morning, Maria."

"What do you want?" she said, not looking too happy to see Mark.

"Listen," he said. "We got off on the wrong foot and I want you to know that Scotty and I did not call the police on you at the beach that day."

"Okay," she said, stopping in front of him. "You feel better now?"

"It's just...you accused us of ratting you out," Mark said. "I wanted you to know that we didn't."

"So, if you hadn't been sticking your nose where it didn't belong, I wouldn't have gotten caught," she said. "Did you ever think of that?"

"Well, you did steal."

"Good-bye," she said, rolling her eyes and trying to get around him.

He blocked her path. "Listen, I'm not trying to be your best friend here, just...don't hate me."

"Okay, I don't hate you," she said. "Happy?"

He smiled real big. "Very."

"Good, now can I please go eat?"

"On one condition," he replied. "Promise me you won't smile all day."

She huffed and walked past him. "Loser."

"Come on, Maria!" he called after her. "That always works on my kid sister!"

Scotty was waiting on Mark at the door. "Hey, check it out," he said. "You see those guys over there?" He nodded toward five large, older boys sitting together and being loud. They definitely looked like trouble.

"Yeah, why?" Mark asked.

"The big blonde one just shoved Rusty and made him drop his tray," Scotty said, sounding a little too happy about it.

"So, what is he, your hero now?" Mark asked, giving Scotty a disappointed look.

"The guy busted my surfboard!" Scotty said.

"Let it go, Dude!" Mark replied. "Besides, those guys probably busted somebody else's surfboard." Mark looked over and Rusty and Andy were eyeing those guys. "So, what happened?"

"Rusty bumped into him and the guy shoved him," Scotty said.

"No, I mean after that," Mark replied. "What did Rusty do?"

"That's just it, Dude!" Scotty said. "He didn't do anything. He just let them laugh at him, while he got back in line and got more food."

"Hmm," Mark said. "We should probably keep an eye on Rusty then"

"What are you saying?" Scotty asked as they got in line.

"I'm saying that Mr. Rusty is quite conniving." He looked back at Scotty. "I know he put that snake in Eddie's bed. He's capable of anything. And I'm still wondering what he was actually up to in the parking lot yesterday."

"Yeah, but you don't think he would do anything to those guys do you?" Scotty asked. "They're huge."

Mark shrugged. "We'll see." They got their food and headed over to the table with the rest of the group. Rusty was still looking over at the guys. "You alright, Rusty?" Mark asked.

Rusty jumped as if being shaken from a trance. "Yeah, McGee, I'm good. How are you? You sleep good?"

"Don't let those guys get you in trouble, Dude," Mark said. "They're just bullies."

"Get to me?" Rusty laughed and shook his head. "There's only one person in this room that gets to me, McGee!" He paused and took a breath as Gabi walked up to the table staring. "And it sure ain't any of those idiots!" He paused and looked back over there. "Besides, he'll get what's coming to him."

No sooner were the words out of Rusty's mouth, when the blonde guy began to choke. At first his friends were laughing, but then he started turning bright red. A girl screamed as he tried to stand up. Dean ran over and told people to back off as he performed the Heimlich maneuver on him. Several other counselors ran over.

Rusty caught Mark's eye. He was smiling. "Karma, McGee, what goes around...comes around."

Blonde guy seemed fine but was led out to see the nurse.

After breakfast, they all headed to building three for Sunday service. It was the same size as the Mess Hall but set up like a church. There was a stage with a podium, a drum set, keyboard, and several guitars. Facing the stage were about three hundred green cushioned chairs.

Mr. Bret came over to make sure the group was together. "Where's Daisy?" he asked Gabi.

"Wherever the most boys are at," she said, looking around.

"Daisy!" Mr. Bret had spotted her heading up front with two boys. She looked back, mortified that he had yelled her name. "Get over here! Stay with your group!"

"You're terrible," Gabi said to him.

He smiled. "If I embarrass her enough, maybe she'll be too scared to do anything bad."

Brianna and Shadow led the group down an aisle they could all fit on.

"Hey, Maria!" Mr. Bret yelled a little too loud as she passed him, causing her to jump. "You okay?"

"Yes," she said, giving him a harsh look.

"Okay," he said. "Quit complaining and go sit down."

"I didn't comp..." She saw him smiling and realized he was kidding. She shook her head. "You people are whack."

Once everyone had settled down, Jasper walked up to the microphone. Mark had found out that not only was Jasper the drummer for the worship band, he was also the director of activities. He was in his early thirties with long, bushy hair and a full beard. He made Mark think of one of those nature loving hippies.

"Good morning," Jasper said. "Can I please have your attention?" He paused for a moment and looked down. "Last night after the bonfire, Moses left to go to his house, which is just a few miles away. Anyway, he was in an accident." There was quite a bit of commotion and Jasper held up his hand. "He's okay! A couple of broken bones...but it could've been a lot worse. God really protected him." Several people yelled amen and praise God. "He called me this morning from the hospital to ask for our prayers. He hopes to be able to come back and speak on Friday night." Jasper bowed his head. "Guys, I saw his car last night. It was totaled. It was a complete miracle that Moses lived through that accident. The crazy thing was, the police said his brakes were cut."

CHAPTER 7

THE RETURN OF THE DRAGON

Sundays were typically slow days around Gateway. The perfect time to play catch up if you were behind on paperwork. Officer Ramsey had just plopped down at his desk to tackle a mountain of it, when the call came in.

"Ramsey! Line two!" his sergeant called to him.

"This is Officer Ramsey, how…"

"Nathan!" It was his wife and by the sound of her voice, something was wrong.

"What is it, Patricia?" he asked. His mind immediately went to his son, Matt, who had volunteered to help out at a summer camp for troubled teens. "Is Matt okay?"

"It's Rick." Rick was his older brother, a police detective in Charlotte, North Carolina. His stomach tightened as he braced for the worst. "Megan's been in an accident!" She began to cry. Megan was Rick's teenage daughter. "Nathan, she died."

He was speechless. They had just gone to Megan's graduation ceremony a few weeks ago. She had graduated with honors. She had even gotten a scholarship to North Carolina State where she wanted to study law. This couldn't really be happening. She was so young. So beautiful. So full of life.

"Nathan, are you there?" Patricia asked, through her sobs.

"I'm here." He managed to say, fighting back his own tears. "What happened?"

"Apparently her and Caleb were on a date in his father's truck. A dump truck ran a stop light and hit them." She stopped talking, obviously blowing her nose. "Megan was dead at the scene. Caleb is still in surgery, but..." She cried. "They don't think he'll make it." Caleb was Megan's long-time boyfriend. He was a really good kid who'd also graduated with honors. He planned to go into law enforcement like his dad.

"Dear God," Officer Ramsey said. "Not Megan...Rick must be devastated."

"Nathan, we have to go up," Patricia said. "I'm going to start packing. We'll need to go get Matt from camp too."

"Yeah," he replied, trying to gather his thoughts. "Yeah, let me talk to Sergeant Butler." He hung up and sat there for a minute. Megan Ramsey was dead. He just couldn't grasp that reality. So alive one second and gone the next. We really aren't promised tomorrow.

Mark and Scotty took their lunches outside and sat at a picnic table in the shade of a large oak tree. Everyone seemed to want to sit inside where there was air conditioning, so it was the only place they could be alone. Mark had told Scotty that he needed to talk to him.

"So, what do you think?" Mark asked him.

"About what?"

"About Moses' brakes getting cut on the same night that Rusty and his gang were found wandering around in the parking lot."

"I thought about that too," Scotty said. "But why would Rusty go after Moses?"

"I don't know." Mark replied. "When Moses saw Rusty for the first time, he knew something was wrong with Rusty. Didn't you see the way he looked at him? And Rusty looked nervous."

"Maybe, but that still doesn't give Rusty a reason to try and kill him. Rusty is a troublemaker, yes. But a killer?"

"Listen," Mark said, leaning in close and whispering. "I wonder if I wasn't right about Rusty in the beginning."

"Come on, Mark," Scotty replied. "You're too paranoid. He's nothing more than a jerk."

Mark continued. "Eddie squeals on him and gets a snake in his bed. Blonde bully guy knocks him over at breakfast and almost chokes to death a few minutes later. Moses knows something is wrong with him and his brakes get cut. Think about it, Dude!"

Scotty nodded, having taken a big bite of his cheeseburger. "I'll admit…" he chewed and swallowed. "It's all strange. But none of it points to him being a demon. Any deviant can cut a brake line and put a snake in somebody's bed."

"What about the choking? It was like he knew it was going to happen!"

"Hey, Mark!" It was Rusty, who'd come up behind him and made him and Scotty jump. "When you girls are done eating, come on over to the paintball area! We're gonna pick teams in about twenty minutes!" Mark nodded to him.

"I don't know, dude," Scotty said, watching Rusty walk away. "Maybe you should talk to Gabi."

"Nah," Mark said. "Between Daisy and Maria, Gabi has her hands full."

"Yeah, boy-crazy Daisy!" Scotty said with a snort. "I think that girl has flirted with every guy at camp."

Two hours later, totally exhausted and covered in paint splotches all the guys headed for the lake. A quick swim out to the floating dock and back, totally rejuvenated them. They spent another forty-five minutes dunking each other and fighting over the inner tubes.

Gabi had spent quite a bit of her day attempting to connect with Yvette, who had quickly tired of all Daisy's boy craziness. Gabi really felt like she was getting somewhere with Yvette as they randomly wandered the property. She was quite spoiled and shallow but understood the basics of Theology. Gabi was trying to help her see that being a Christian could be fun, while at the same time, a necessity. "Trust me, girl," Gabi said. "When you do it right, there's rarely a dull moment."

Brianna and Shadow had spent the day in the cabin, just hanging out. Brianna was reading some of Shadow's dark poetry and basically just trying to be a friend. A friend was something Shadow had not had many of in her life. She was really enjoying having someone to listen to her problems without judging her.

Mr. Bret had threatened Daisy with kitchen duty for every meal if he caught her hanging out with one more boy. She was now lying near the lake on a towel all alone and pouting. Apparently, all the girls hated her, because she had flirted with all the guys. And all the guys were warned to stay away from her by either their counselors or their girlfriends.

Maria just sat under a tree reading her book. She'd given a lot of thought to her conversation with Mark. She knew that he and Scotty were good guys, but she desperately needed someone to blame for her troubles. It sure wasn't her fault. Perhaps she would eventually forgive them and try and be nice. She looked up just as both of them did a cannonball and screamed like a couple of idiots. She shook her head. Maybe she wouldn't forgive them.

Everyone was told, via an intercom announcement, that they needed to clean up and get ready for dinner and the campfire service. They all headed to their cabins to shower and change clothes.

"Dude," Scotty said to whoever was listening. "I may not be able to stay awake for the service tonight. I'm exhausted." He was lying across his top bunk after getting dressed.

"Yeah, I think we've already lost Eddie," Mark said, pointing to Eddie's bed, where he was out like a light. He had been one of the first to shower and change.

"Let him sleep," Rusty said, with a smile that gave Mark a chill down his spine.

"Eddie?" Mark yelled and walked over to his bunk. Eddie didn't move. "Eddie! Let's go man!" He shook Eddie's arm.

"Dude!" Eddie said grumpily. "I'm tired!"

Rusty laughed. "What is it, McGee!? Did you think I killed him?"

"Come on, Eddie!" Matt said. "Let's go to dinner! We're all tired, Dude!"

"Ugh!" he grumbled and sat up. "I could sleep until morning."

"Well, at least you got a power nap!" Billy said. "I for one, am starving."

"Let's go!" Matt said and opened the door. They all headed to the Mess Hall.

As they stood in line waiting to get their fried pork chops, mashed potatoes and green beans, Mark saw Rusty watching the blonde boy who had choked that morning. Mark hadn't seen the boy all day.

"Matthew Ramsey?!" a woman called from the back door. "Matt Ramsey?!"

"Yes ma'am?" Matt replied and raised his hand. He had just received his pile of mashed potatoes.

"I need you to come with me, Honey!" she said in a sweet Southern accent. Several people made comments about Matt being in trouble. Matt looked a little aggravated to be denied his meal but went with her anyway.

About ten minutes later, Matt returned with his head down. The group had all claimed a table and were busy eating. Billy had been allowed to finish loading Matt's plate. "Hey, Matt! I have your plate over here!" Billy called. "Dude, are you okay?"

"What's going on, Matt?" Gabi asked. "Is everything alright?"

"Not really." He looked up and it was evident that he'd been crying. "I have to leave."

"What?!" Billy got up and stood next to him. "Dude, what's going on?"

"My parents are here," Matt said. "My cousin Megan," he looked at Billy, "the one who just graduated."

"Yeah, she wants to be a lawyer!" Billy said.

"Well...she was killed in a car accident last night." Matt looked away.

Gabi gasped and put her hand over her mouth. "I'm so sorry, Matt." She stood and gave him a hug.

"No way!" Billy said. "Oh man." He clearly had no idea what to say.

"She was only seventeen," Matt said. "Straight A's and about to go to college." He wiped his eyes. "Her life was just getting started."

Mark stood and shook Matt's hand. "Sorry Bro, we will all be praying for your family."

"Yes, we will," Brianna added, standing to give him a hug. "Are you okay?"

Matt nodded. "I guess. Listen, I'll see you guys back home next week." He turned to go and then stopped. "Oh, Mark, you're in charge of the room. Billy's too nice and Scotty's... well, Scotty."

Scotty smiled. "Take care, Matt. Sorry, Dude."

The rest of the night went by in a haze for the group. None of them really said much. They had all somehow managed to stay awake through the campfire service. Jasper had been the speaker and turned out to be hilarious.

Mr. Bret came over to the group after the service. He needed two of the guys to volunteer to help clean up. Mark raised his hand and picked Eddie to help him. The two of them and four other guys picked up trash, dumped bags into the dumpster and made sure the fire was out.

On their way back to the cabin, Mark said a quiet prayer for Eddie. "Hey, Dude," Mark said, patting him on the arm. "Can we talk?"

"You're the boss, McGee," Eddie said. "Just don't try and save my soul."

Mark laughed. "I'll leave that to Jesus. Listen, I just want you to know that you can hang out with us. Scotty, Billy and me...if you want."

"What are you talking about, McGee? Why would I possibly want to hang out with you guys?" He was trying to act tough.

"It's just...I know Rusty is kind of rough." They walked on in silence. When they got close to the cabin, Eddie stopped and looked down.

"He scares me, Dude," Eddie said without looking up. "He's not normal."

Mark looked at him. "What do you mean?"

"I mean, he's psychotic!" He looked toward the cabin and lowered his voice. "Todd was crazy. Andy and I had fun with him. You know, we got in trouble, but it was never too much. There was a line we never crossed." He met Mark's eye. "But Rusty...he has no line. He scares me, Dude."

"Well, the offer still stands," Mark said. He followed Eddie into the cabin.

Billy was just finishing up with the devotion. "Scotty, will you close us in prayer?" Scotty looked up in horror.

"Hey Billy," Mark said. "Can I pray?" Billy nodded and Mark prayed; remembering to especially pray for Matt's family.

"We decided to go ahead and do devotion so we could go to bed," Billy said to Mark. "You can do devo tomorrow night."

Mark saw Rusty grab Eddie's arm and pull him away from everyone. He was whispering something in his ear.

"Everything okay, Rusty?" Mark asked.

"Yeah, McGee," Rusty replied, not bothering to turn around. "Don't worry about me."

Mark laughed. "You're about the only one I am worried about." Rusty turned around and gave him a death stare on his way to the bathroom. Mark only smiled at him.

"Wow," Billy said. "What was that about?"

"No idea," Mark replied. They all got ready for bed.

Mark was awakened at some time in the middle of the night by someone knocking on the door. He looked around and nobody else was stirring. Either he had dreamed it or the others were hoping somebody else answered it. He lay there for a few more seconds and they knocked again. "It's okay guys," he said out loud. "I'll get it." Luckily Billy had plugged a night light in near the front door, so that nobody would break their necks in the night. He stumbled to the door in his boxers, cracked it open and peeked out. Nobody was there. He opened it a little more. "Hello?" Was somebody playing a joke? "Not funny!" He couldn't see or hear anything outside. He decided to close the door and stand there in case they knocked again. After just a few seconds, they did, and Mark swung the door open immediately. To his complete surprise, nobody was there. He pinched his arm to make sure he wasn't dreaming. "Ouch!" He stepped out on the porch and closed the door. "Who's out here?" he called into the night. All he could hear were bugs, frogs and the wind blowing through the trees. He walked down the steps and looked around the corners of the cabin. Nobody there. "Okay! One more knock and I wake the counselors! They'll do a bed check!" He listened for any sound. Nothing. "Okay!" He turned to go back up the steps and jumped back.

"Whoa!" he yelled in unbelief. There, standing in front of the door and facing Mark, was a huge demon. He was the biggest one Mark had ever seen, having to bend over to keep from bumping the porch ceiling. It smiled its razor-sharp teeth at Mark and made a clicking sound. With lightning fast speed, it was off the porch and slamming Mark to the ground. He landed on his back about five feet away, unable to catch his breath. Before he could move, the demon was on top of him. Grabbing Mark by the ankle, it swung him around and tossed him into some bushes. Badly scratched up and bleeding, Mark tried to get out of the bushes before the demon could get to him. A huge vice-like hand grabbed him by the arm, pulled him out and slammed him against a tree. Mark hit the ground struggling to breathe. He knew he needed to pray but had to get away first. Before he could stand up, the demon had lifted him up and tossed him over his shoulder. He began to walk into the forest, Mark's legs getting scratched up by tree branches as they went. He had no fight left in him. He was barely hanging on to consciousness as it was. "God...need..." The last thing he remembered was the sound of the leaves and twigs crunching under the demon's feet and the smell of pine.

Mark had no idea how long he'd been out or where in the forest he was. He was awakened, however, after being thrown to the ground in a small clearing. His legs were cut and bleeding, his head was pounding, and it hurt to breathe. He looked around and saw that the demon had backed away into the trees. "Ugh,"

Mark moaned, feeling the pain of moving. "Wh..." That's when he heard it. At first, he thought it was thunder, but when he looked up, he saw something move in front of him. Then he heard the sound again and realized it wasn't thunder at all. It was the low rumbling laughter of his old enemy. The laughter grew louder as Mark's eyes adjusted to the darkness. It was so dark he could barely make out the features. The long snout. The huge teeth. The long, shiny, black body. There, in the forest, larger than Mark had remembered, eyes glowing red, teeth bared, head raised in pride, stood the dragon.

"We meet again, Mark McGee!" He laughed and the ground seemed to tremble. "Of course, I am always with you, Mark! You and your family will never be rid of me!" More ground shaking laughter.

Mark rolled over on his stomach slowly, hoping to be able to stand. He slid his knees underneath him.

"That's right, Mark McGee, kneel before me!" This time his laughter was so loud, the trees shook, and Mark heard birds and other forest creatures scurrying away.

With every ounce of strength that he could muster, Mark managed to stand. Every bone, nerve and muscle in his body seemed to be on fire. Still, he faced the dragon.

"And there is nothing that you, your family, your friends, or your pitiful god can do about it!" He laughed again.

Mark simply smiled up at the dragon and bowed his head. "Father, this is your enemy and your battle. I turn it completely over to you in Jesus' name. Amen." When he opened his eyes he noticed that the dragon was staring at him with actual fear in his eyes. Then Mark looked down to see that he was about ten feet tall and in full battle gear. Sword in one hand and shield in the other. With one swift motion, he swung around and split the demon behind him in half. It didn't even have time to scream. Mark then turned back to face the dragon, who took a step back. "Be strong in the Lord and in His mighty power!" Mark said.

"Shut up!" the dragon roared.

"Put on the full armor of God so that you can take your stand against the devil's schemes!"

Balls of light began to fall from the sky and become brightly lit angels that surrounded the dragon on every side. Swords of fire were drawn. The dragon lashed about in an attempt to escape.

"For our struggle is not against flesh and blood, but against the rulers, against the authorities, against the powers of this dark world and against the spiritual forces of evil in the heavenly realms!" The dragon roared and spun around.

The angels closed in on him and he raised up to strike at them. "Soon Mark McGee!" he roared. "Soon, you will have no help!" And he vanished into the darkness. The angels instantly became balls of light and made chase of the dragon.

Everything went dark again. Mark looked around. He stood alone in the forest. Normal size. In his boxers. "Really?" he yelled to the forest. "I have NO idea where I am!" He began to feel weak and sore again. Everything began to spin. He reached for the nearest tree, but saw the ground getting closer.

Gabi lay her head back down. "That was crazy intense," she said to Brianna, who had jumped awake at the exact same moment as her.

"Yes, it was," Brianna replied, leaning over from the top bunk. "Do you think he's okay?" They'd both known that they had to pray for Mark immediately.

"I think so," Gabi replied. "The urgency to pray has passed. I wish I could text him."

"What do you think happened?" Brianna whispered.

"With Mark McGee there is no telling," Gabi said. "He could've been dealing with Rusty or the devil." They both laughed.

"What's going on?" Maria asked, clearly aggravated at having been woken up.

"Nothing," Gabi said. "Sorry."

Mark woke up with a very bright light shining in his eyes. His first thought was that someone had a flashlight. "What's going on?" he asked, covering his eyes.

"Be well, Mark McGee," someone said from close by. The light went out and Mark opened his eyes. He was lying in a bed of leaves right outside his cabin. Nobody else was around. Sitting up quickly, he realized he wasn't sore anymore. It was still dark out. He stood up and checked himself. Bruised and scratched, but no worse for the wear. He looked up to the sky. "Thank you!" he yelled to whatever angel had transported him, and quietly went back inside. He headed for the bathroom to rinse off.

"Where you been, McGee?" Rusty asked quietly as Mark passed his bed. "Out for a stroll in your underwear?"

"Thought I heard a noise," Mark replied.

Rusty sat up and looked at him. "You sure got awful dirty and cut up hearing a noise."

"Well, I guess I chased it into the woods."

"Chased what?"

"The noise," Mark said. "Go back to sleep, Rusty." He went in the bathroom and rinsed off.

Considering everything that had happened to him, Mark couldn't believe how fast he had fallen asleep. When he awoke the next morning to the sound of chiming bells, he couldn't wait to tell Scotty and Gabi everything that had happened.

However, the morning turned out to be busier and crazier than any of them had planned. It was almost impossible to get the guys up and moving. Mark almost had to go get Mr. Bret to get Rusty and Andy out of bed. Gabi had to deal with an actual fight between Maria and Daisy. Daisy had taken too long to do her hair and Maria had made a comment about why Daisy needed to look pretty. Daisy had responded with a comment about Maria being unable to look pretty. Things had gone downhill from there. Gabi spent half of her breakfast time sitting in a meeting listening to a camp counselor explain to Maria and Daisy why fighting was never the answer. After breakfast, Scotty was picked to help clean up the Mess Hall and Mark had to help gather all the guys for a quick meeting at the campfire area. Apparently, some of the boys needed to be reminded about how to conduct themselves around girls. The meeting was followed by two hours of Bible workshops, where they learned how to read and understand the scriptures.

Mark noticed Rusty giving Eddie a hard time all morning and decided to invite Eddie to hang out with Scotty and him during a short break between workshops. They went for a walk down by the lake.

"I'll probably get beat up for hanging out with you guys," Eddie said.

"Yeah, well we're totally worth it," Scotty replied, causing Eddie to smile.

"I noticed Rusty hassling you all morning," Mark said. "I figured you could use a change of pace."

"Hey, I can take care of myself," Eddie said. "I don't need you protecting me, McGee."

"I didn't say you did, Eddie," Mark replied. "But there's no sense in being miserable the entire week either."

Eddie was quiet for several minutes and then stopped to stare out at the lake. "I have no idea how he found out I ratted him out."

"So, he knows?" Mark asked.

Eddie nodded and replied, "Andy tried to talk me out of it that night. He told me that Rusty was not someone to cross." He paused for a few seconds. "We had never argued like we did that night. Andy is terrified of Rusty. He only befriended him at school for the protection he offered."

"You don't think Andy told him, do you?" Scotty asked.

"No way, he swore he wouldn't. I mean, he told me I was on my own if I talked to the cops. But he promised he would never tell Rusty."

Maybe Rusty just figured it had to be you," Scotty said. "With Andy being so loyal and all."

"Maybe," Eddie replied. "Doesn't really matter now, does it? He's just going to keep tormenting me and making me do things for him."

"Like what?" Mark asked.

Eddie looked at Mark and shook his head. "Nothing."

"Like cutting Moses' brake line?" Mark asked and he saw fear in Eddie's eyes for a brief second.

"We should probably get to the next workshop," Eddie said, walking away.

"Eddie!" Mark called to him. "Do you think Rusty put that snake in your bed?"

Eddie stopped and looked back, smiling. "I can take care of myself, McGee."

"We can help you, Eddie," Mark said, catching up to him. "You don't have to face him alone."

Eddie laughed. "No offense, but what are you two going to do? You have a gun in your pocket, McGee?"

"No, Eddie," Mark replied. "But I have Jesus in my heart."

"Not interested, McGee!" Eddie said. "Sorry, but I'm not exactly into God."

"Well, maybe it's time you got into him, Dude," Mark said. "Because He's real! Trust me on that."

"There you are!" Billy called from the end of the trail. "I was hoping I didn't have to walk around the lake to find you. It's time to go back in."

They had an archery class after their workshops. Although hardly anybody was able to hit a single target, they had a blast trying.

Mark was finally able to get Scotty and Gabi alone at lunch. They had gone outside to the picnic table under the tree. He told them his entire story.

"And you're sure it wasn't a dream?" Gabi asked.

Mark showed her the back of his legs. "Pretty sure."

"Well, that explains why Brianna and I were awakened at the same time to pray for you. Thank God you're okay, but I can't believe you didn't put that demon in his place sooner."

"He was so fast," Mark said. "He caught me by surprise."

"I don't understand what he was up to," Scotty said. "The dragon. Why did he do that? What was his plan, meeting you in the forest?"

Mark shrugged. "To remind me he was still here, I guess."

"But why?" Scotty was confused. "Wouldn't he be more likely to defeat you if you let your guard down? If you forgot about him?"

"He said he would always be after my family," Mark said. "Maybe he just wants me to be afraid."

"Why does the devil ever attack Christians?" Gabi said. "He hates us. He hates us because we belong to God and he really hates God." She turned to Scotty. "When Mark got saved, Scotty, it broke the dragon's curse on him. He's not just going to take that lying down. He is going to do everything he can to get Mark back."

"The devil comes to steal, kill and destroy," Mark said.

"Exactly!" Gabi said. "It's all he does! And by the way, Mark McGee, I'm really impressed with your scripture quoting."

Mark smiled. "Yeah, when that dragon started talking smack, all I could think of was my favorite scripture, Ephesians 6:10-18. Topher told me to memorize it after our mountain experience."

Gabi looked over at Brianna and Shadow sitting on a blanket near the lake. They were reading the Bible. "Speaking of a mountain experience," she said, pointing at them. "Shadow asked Jesus into her heart last night."

"Really?" Mark said. "That's awesome!"

"Brianna did the devotion in our room. When she asked if anybody had a prayer request, we noticed that Shadow was crying. Brianna went over and prayed with her and she said she'd never believed in God until Brianna became her friend. She said that she could see Him in Brianna's eyes, and she wanted that."

"Wow," Scotty said. "That is so cool."

"How's it going with Yvette?" Mark asked.

Gabi sighed. "Yvette is a little more difficult to get through to," she said. "She's grown up in church and knows the basics. She's never had a relationship with Jesus, though, so church bores her."

"So, she needs a Holy Spirit kick in the pants," Mark said.

"Yeah!" Gabi said, laughing. "Something like that."

"What she needs," Scotty added, "is a castle experience." Mark and Gabi both looked at him. "Hey, all I'm saying is, that's what it took to wake me up!" Gabi smiled at him.

"Yeah," Mark said. "Scotty was a beast in that castle!" They fist bumped.

"Hey! Maybe you could talk to Yvette, Scotty!" Gabi said.

"Maybe not," Scotty said. "You know I can't do that, Gabi."

"No, I don't, demon slayer!" she replied. "I don't doubt your ability to do anything, Scotty Morgan." With that, she stood to leave. "I guess we should go check on everybody. I need to make sure Daisy is behaving."

"Fat chance there," Scotty said. "Talk about someone needing a kick in the pants."

Mark saw Eddie heading toward the trail around the lake. "Hey Eddie!" he called. "Can we join you?"

Eddie shrugged. "Free country, McGee!"

He and Scotty dumped their trays and ran to catch up with Eddie. "How's it going, Dude?" Mark asked.

"Not too bad," Eddie said. "Other than having these two guys that keep stalking me." He smiled at them.

"Oh, you mean us?" Scotty said. "I thought we were best friends now!" Scotty laughed.

"You wish, Morgan!' Eddie replied. "You have to be cool to hang out with me." He pulled a berry off a tree and tossed it at Scotty.

"Oh, is that how it is?" Scotty started picking a bunch of them and Eddie started running away. They spent the next half hour throwing berries at each other and seeing who could skip rocks the best.

About halfway around the lake, they saw three of the guys from the group that had messed with Rusty. The blonde guy that had choked was one of them. They were carving their names into a tree when they noticed Mark, Scotty and Eddie. They stopped what they were doing and walked over to meet them. The blonde guy, Mark had heard that his name was Chris, was apparently the leader. He was followed by a tall, heavyset kid with a face as smooth as a baby. The other guy, who moved around behind Mark and them, was a short, black boy who appeared much younger than the other two.

"Hey Chris, is this the kid?" baby face asked, pointing at Eddie. "What's your name, kid?"

"What's it to ya?" Eddie asked.

"Don't get smart, Punk!" the black kid said from behind them. "Just answer the question."

"Or what, little man, you gonna beat me up?" Eddie laughed.

"Maybe I will," baby face said. "Answer my question."

"Listen guys," Mark said. "Scotty and I are hosts and…"

Chris stepped up face to face with Mark. "Is that supposed to scare us?" he asked, looking down at Mark.

"I'm just saying," Mark said. "We're not looking for trouble."

"And here you done found it," the black kid said.

Baby face stepped up to Eddie and pointed his finger into Eddie's chest. "Is your name Eddie?" he asked menacingly.

Eddie looked at him suspiciously. "Yeah, why?"

"Because we were told you were responsible for trashing our cabin earlier today," Chris said. "Is that true, Eddie?"

"Who exactly told you that?" Mark asked.

"A little birdie told us," baby face said. "Even gave us your description. Blonde, greasy headed punk." The three of them laughed.

"Eddie's been with us all morning," Mark said. "He didn't do it."

"Maybe you helped him, Host," the black kid said with a laugh.

"Your little birdie wouldn't happen to have been a red bird, would he?" Mark asked Chris.

Chris smiled at him. "Doesn't really matter does it, because Eddie here is going to pay for the damage he did to our room."

"I'm telling you, he didn't do it," Mark said. "You were lied to...probably by the guy who actually did it."

Baby face shoved Eddie back and Mark stepped between them. "Dude, chill out!" Mark yelled, and Scotty stepped in behind Mark.

"Oh, I'll take all three of you!" baby face said.

"How about all four of us?" someone said from behind Chris. They all looked that way to see a big black guy walking toward them. He was tall, muscular and looked to be in his early twenties.

"This doesn't concern you!" Chris said. "Just keep walking!"

"Yeah, this little punk trashed our cabin," baby face said.

"Well then," the new kid said. "Let's report him to a counselor."

"I didn't do it!" Eddie said. "You were lied to!"

"A likely story," Chris said, and was about to move around to Eddie when the new guy grabbed his arm and spun him around face to face. The new guy was as much taller than Chris as Chris was to Mark.

"I don't think so," the new guy said in a calm voice. "It's time you boys left."

Chris stared him down for several seconds before backing away. He looked back at Eddie and pointed at him. "Watch yourself, punk! Come on Terry and Marcus, let's leave these losers alone." They walked away laughing.

"Wow, Dude!" Mark said to their new friend. "You're a life saver!" Mark shook his hand. "I'm Mark, this is Scotty and Eddie."

"Name's Charles." He smiled real big. "I'm just glad I decided to take a walk." He laughed.

"Yeah, me too," Scotty said, shaking Charles' hand. "I was about to have to put a few karate moves on those guys." He smiled real big and Charles laughed again.

"Thanks," Eddie said, also shaking his hand.

"Will you be our new friend?" Scotty asked.

"Yes, I will," Charles smiled. "In fact, having just arrived this afternoon, I've been added to you boys' cabin!" He laughed again. "A Mr. Bret told me I might find you back here while I was exploring"

"Wait," Mark said. "You're a kid?"

"Seventeen years old!" he said, backing up and doing a turn in place. "All six foot five inches and two hundred and twenty pounds." He let out a hearty laugh, causing the three boys to smile.

"Unbelievable," Scotty said.

"I'll be eighteen in a few weeks, though," Charles said. They started walking.

"So, what's your story Charles?" Mark asked. "Why are you here?"

"A pastor recommended it,' he said with a laugh. "Decided to check it out!"

"That pastor wouldn't happen to be Moses, would it?" Scotty asked.

"Why, yes it would!" Charles laughed. "In fact, that's why I'm late getting here. His accident and all."

"Hey Mark," Eddie said, pulling him to the side while Charles and Scotty kept going.

"What's up, Eddie?" Mark asked.

"I just, you know, just wanted to say thanks," Eddie said.

"Sure Eddie," Mark said, patting him on the back. "I told you we would look out for you."

"That really took guts, Dude," Eddie added. "Two of those guys were pretty big."

"Well, I was going to let you and Scotty have those two," Mark smiled at him. "But seriously, we've got your back. And now with Charles in our room, we can keep Rusty on his toes."

Eddie nodded. "Yeah, until something bad happens to Charles."

CHAPTER 8

THE FIGHT FOR A SOUL

After recovering from the shock of Megan vanishing before his eyes, Caleb had run. He had run past all of the monsters, creatures and foul beasts that had surrounded him. Oddly enough, none of the creatures had tried to stop him. Nor had they attempted to follow him. Once he'd finally gotten past them all he had continued to run. The mountains in the distance were now his destination. Perhaps he could figure out where he was from the top of a mountain. It seemed as if he'd been running for hours when he finally stopped for a quick rest. He looked back to see that he had gone far enough that the creatures could no longer be seen. He bent over with his hands on his knees, trying to catch his breath. He could still hear Megan's screams in his mind. Why couldn't he wake up from this nightmare?

This place was so dry and desolate. There wasn't a single sign of greenery or any other form of life here. Just endless sand and rocks with an occasional hot breeze. This truly was a land of death and despair. He looked back again to make sure he wasn't being followed. When he didn't see anything, he continued on.

It almost seemed like those horrible creatures had only wanted Megan. The thought of her caused him to sob again. His tears were dried up, but he still cried. Megan. His sweet, sweet Megan. Where had she gone to? He hoped beyond hope that he would wake up any second and find that this entire thing was just a nightmare. Megan would be fine, and they would laugh about his silly dream over coffee and dessert tonight. "Oh God, please let this be a dream," he said out loud and then scolded himself. He would not be a hypocrite. "You can't pray to what doesn't exist, Caleb!" he said with a laugh. "The situation is bad enough without offering yourself false hope!" He almost tripped over a rock he hadn't noticed. "Belief in God is the ultimate sign of a weak mind! And you do not have a weak mind!"

Suddenly, everything changed. Caleb stopped walking and looked around. What was happening? Was he in a park now? Yes, it was the park near Megan's house. How had he gotten here? It was a beautiful sunny day. "Oh wow," he sighed. "It WAS just a nightmare." It was then that he heard voices behind him. Someone was coming up the path near the baseball field. He turned around and saw…wait, what was happening? He took a step back. It was Megan and himself that he saw. They were walking hand in hand and laughing out loud about something. "Hello?" he said to them…himself and her. They apparently couldn't see or hear him. He was wearing cargo shorts and a polo shirt. Megan had on her yellow sundress that he absolutely loved. She looked so good with her hair pulled back and her dark tan. Just as they passed the spot where he stood, someone called to them.

"Caleb!? Megan!?" a guy about their age approached from behind them. Wait…it was Dustin. He remembered this. It had been just a month ago. He couldn't stand Dustin. Always preaching Jesus to everybody and trying to save their souls. He was tall and lanky and wore a cheap pair of blue jeans and a white t-shirt with a logo from his youth group. They had stopped to look back. "Beautiful day, isn't it?" He panted as he approached.

"Yes, it is, Dustin," the other Caleb said. "Please tell me you didn't run this whole way just to tell us that it's a beautiful day. Because we could've figured that out."

Megan laughed but gave him a gentle shove. "Be nice."

Dustin smiled and held out a pamphlet. Megan took it from him and held it up.

"I wanted to invite you guys to a youth service tonight at my church!" He said, still catching his breath. "There will be several bands there and food and games also. It'll be a blast and..."

"Dustin," Caleb interrupted him.

"this really amazing speaker named..."

"Dustin!" Caleb repeated. "We're not going."

"Okay, well...you're still invited. I hope you change your mind. It starts at six." He turned to walk away.

"Thank you for the invitation, Dustin!" Megan said. He waved over his shoulder.

"Hey Dustin!" Caleb called to him and he turned around.

"Be nice," Megan said quietly to Caleb.

"You do realize," Caleb said to Dustin, "that only crippled people need a crutch, right?"

"Excuse me?" Dustin said, looking confused.

"A crutch," Caleb said. "You know what a crutch is, right?" Dustin nodded. "Crippled people use them for assistance in walking, correct?" Again, Dustin nodded. "Well, God is a crutch, Dustin." Dustin still looked as if he didn't understand where Caleb was going with this. "For mentally crippled people." He tapped the side of his head.

"Caleb, stop," Megan said, nudging him. "I told you to be nice."

"I'm just saying," Caleb added. "Man invented God as some kind of crutch to lean on. Some kind of false hope in his time of need." He tapped the side of his head again. "A strong mind, Dustin...doesn't need to invent a god to lean on." Dustin just stared at him. "Exactly," Caleb said, pointing at him. "You're proving my point." He was about to turn and go.

"Trusting in yourself, Caleb?" Dustin said, causing Caleb to pause. "That's false hope."

Caleb smiled at him. "Would you like to put that to a test, Dustin? Let's meet up right here in five years. We'll see exactly whose life looks better. Yours with the help of your Jesus, or mine with the help of my brain." He smiled big as Dustin just stared at him. "Didn't think so." Caleb laughed.

"What about a hundred years?" Dustin blurted out. Caleb and Megan both laughed this time.

"Chances are, we'll all be dead in a hundred years, Dustin," Caleb said. "How convenient for you."

"Exactly!" Dustin said, walking towards them. "Let's see who's better off then."

Everything faded and Caleb was back in the desert, lying on the dry ground. He coughed and rolled over on his back. What had just happened? Of all the memories to have pop into his head...that was an odd one. He stood up and started walking again. "What a moron," he said out loud. "What about a hundred years?" Caleb laughed.

There was a clicking noise from behind him.

Mark, Scotty and Eddie took Charles to the cabin to help him get settled in. He took Matt's bed and put his things away in the dresser. Charles really seemed like a super nice guy. They were excited to have him in their room.

"Well," Scotty said. "We have about an hour and a half before dinner. What do you guys want to do?"

"What exactly is there to do?" Charles asked.

"Why don't we give Charles a tour?" Mark suggested.

"I like that idea," Charles said with a laugh. "Lead on!" He Mark and Scotty headed for the door.

"Coming, Eddie?" Mark asked.

"Nah, I'm kinda tired," Eddie said. "I'm going to lay down."

"Okay, Dude!" Mark replied. "We'll see you at dinner." Eddie nodded.

They took Charles for a full tour of the grounds. He seemed to be so full of joy, laughing at everything they said and did. He absolutely loved the idea of the paintball arena, having never played. The tour ended up back at the lake where Charles confessed that he'd never been swimming.

"Dude!" Scotty exclaimed. "I could totally teach you! I taught my brother!"

"Alright, alright!" Charles laughed. "We'll see what happens."

"It's so easy! I could teach you in like ten minutes."

The announcement came that it was dinnertime, so they made their way to the Mess Hall. As Mark held the door open for a group of girls, he noticed Maria standing at the corner of the building. She appeared to be having a heated discussion with someone that Mark couldn't see. He decided to hang around and make sure she was okay. Whoever she was talking to was on the other side of the building, just out of sight. She went to walk away, and they grabbed her arm. "Let go of me!" she yelled.

"Maria!" Mark called and she looked his way. "Is everything okay?"

Just then, Rusty stepped out from behind the building. "Why can't you ever mind your own business, McGee?" He walked toward Mark.

"I should've known it was you, Rusty," Mark said. "By the way, thanks for siccing those goons on Eddie!" Mark stepped right in front of him. "That was sweet of you!" They stood toe to toe with Eddie quite a bit taller. "Not to mention you're out here harassing girls." Maria just walked past Mark and headed inside without a word.

"What are you talking about, McGee?" Rusty replied. "What goons? Eddie is my friend! Why do you keep accusing me of things?"

"Maybe because you keep doing things, Rusty!"

"You must really hate me, McGee!" Rusty was right in Mark's face now. "I thought you Christians believed in forgiveness! Not Mark McGee! He just can't let go, no sir! Just keeps on accusing people of doing things with absolutely no proof whatsoever!"

Mark smiled up at him and took a step back. "Jesus loves you, Rusty."

"WOW, McGee!" Rusty said, pushing past him. "You really need to get a life!"

Mark laughed. "Jesus IS my life, Rusty!"

"Just shut up, okay!" Rusty stopped and spun back around. "Your God and everything about him offends me, okay!" He pointed right at Mark. "So, you can just stop your stupid preaching!" He turned and went inside.

A small crowd had gathered by the door. Some followed Rusty inside and others just stood there staring at Mark with their mouths open. That's when he noticed Eddie walk up with his head down. "Hey, Eddie!"

"Not now, Mark," Eddie said, covering his face with his hand and going inside.

"Well," Mark said to those who remained outside. "At least I learned how to get rid of Rusty."

For dinner they had a choice between tacos and pizza, and it seemed like almost everyone had chosen both. By the time Mark made it to the table, Scotty had already introduced the group to Charles, who sat between Billy and Andy with a big smile on his face eating a taco. Mark had to laugh when he noticed that Gabi had strategically arranged it so that Scotty was sitting next to Yvette. He caught Gabi's eye and she just gave him the duck face.

"So, Scotty," Gabi said, leaning over. "Have you shared your testimony with Yvette yet?"

Scotty gave her an evil look and Yvette asked him to tell her everything. Gabi smiled and winked at Mark.

Mark sat down next to Eddie and looked over at him before he could turn away. That's when he noticed the black eye. He nudged Eddie. "Dude, what the heck?"

"It's nothing," Eddie replied. "I fell off the top bunk."

Mark gave him that 'yeah right' look and pressed on. "Did you run into our friends from the trail?"

Eddie shrugged. "Don't worry about it, Mark...seriously. I can take care of myself."

"Well, did you?" Mark asked. "Dude, if they jumped you, we can..."

"Just let it go!" Eddie snapped. "I'm fine."

"McGee can't let anything go, Eddie," Rusty said from behind them at a different table. "He apparently can't protect his friends either."

"I don't need protecting, Rusty," Eddie said. "I'm fine."

"Don't worry, Dude," Rusty said. "I got your back."

After dinner, they all made their way to the campfire service. The buzz among the camp counselors was that whoever was speaking tonight was really good.

As soon as worship ended, Dean got up and gave a few announcements. "Okay guys, are you ready for the Word tonight?" There was an eruption of clapping and cheering. "Well, I am very excited to introduce a man that I've heard a lot about but have never had the privilege to hear. He comes to us all the way from Jacksonville, Florida by special invitation. He is one of the coolest guys you will ever meet…he gave me five dollars to say that." Several people laughed. "Please give it up for Pastor Jason Masters!" Another eruption of screams and cheers. Pastor Jason was a young-looking guy that was probably in his early thirties. He had short, sandy blonde hair and tattoos down one arm. He wore cargo shorts and a t-shirt that said, 'Stay Anchored In His Presence.' He walked up to the microphone with a big smile on his face and totally full of energy.

Mark looked over and noticed that Rusty was leaning forward and saying something to Maria. Her eyes were closed, and Mark couldn't tell if she was attempting to ignore Rusty or trying to concentrate on what he was saying. Mark looked to the back and got Mr. Bret's attention. He nodded toward Rusty. Mr. Bret walked right up behind Rusty and pulled him back. He put his finger to his lips to shush him and walked away. Mark noticed that Maria kept her eyes closed and appeared like she could be crying. Rusty looked over at Mark and smiled. When Mark looked away, he noticed that Charles was also watching Rusty.

Everybody laughed at something Pastor Jason had said and brought Mark out of his thoughts. He looked over and Gabi was watching him. She sat in the row in front of him about 3 seats over. "What's wrong?" she mouthed to him.

Mark just shook his head. There was no way to convey everything that he thought was wrong right now. He had a really bad feeling about what Rusty was up to. He gave Gabi the 'we'll talk later' nod.

"Submit yourselves, then, to God," Pastor Jason said, reading from James chapter 4. "Resist the devil, and he will flee from you! Then it goes on to say in verse 8," he smiled excitedly, "and this is my favorite part! Come near to God and He will come near to you." He walked right up and stood in front of the first row. "So, you've already learned how to become a Christian. Now you know how to stay one! Right?" Several people nodded. "I'm not convinced!" He smiled. "You see, just because you ask Jesus into your heart, doesn't mean that you will stop being tempted to sin. Guys! If checking out a hot girl is an issue today and you get saved tonight…guess what!? You'll still struggle with it tomorrow! Ladies! If you have trouble with gossiping today and get saved tonight…guess what!? It's going to be a problem tomorrow!" He walked up the aisle. "You will have to RESIST the temptation!" he said with a big smile. "You see, as a Christian, you will want to please God! And not sinning is one of the best ways to do that! Resist the devil, and he will flee from you! Come near to God and he will come near to you! WOW! Sounds easy doesn't it!?" He ran back down to the podium. "Well! It's not!" Everyone laughed. "In fact, sometimes it feels like it's impossible. Let's face it, one of the easiest things in the world is giving in to temptation. Am I right?" Everyone nodded. "If I'm on a diet and you take me out to dinner to Dairy Queen…how easy would it be for me to eat ice cream? How difficult would it be to just sit there and watch you eat ice cream in front of me?" There was some laughing and talking. "However, the more you resist, the more you put this into practice, the more you do without your sin and draw near to God, the easier it will be to resist temptation the next time. Just like on a diet…if I'm seeing results, and I'm starting to look good in my Speedos!" Everyone burst out laughing. "What? Ask my wife… never mind, don't ask her." More laughter. "But if I'm seeing results, it will be easier to say no to that ice cream than it was when I first started. You see, when you give your life to Jesus, the devil is going to come to you a few days later. He's going to whisper in your ear that you didn't really get saved. He's going to say, 'if you were really saved, you wouldn't be having those thoughts about that girl or that boy. If you were really saved, you wouldn't be wanting to get high with your friends tonight. If you were really saved, you wouldn't have lied to your mom about not putting the cat in the dryer'." More laughter. "But be encouraged! The longer you resist him, the easier those things will be to overcome. The more you 'come near to God' and He 'comes near to you,' the stronger you will become in your faith. Amen?" Almost everyone shouted amen. He walked over and sat down on the front row, making some girls scoot over. "Yeah, Pastor Jason! That's awesome! Keep preaching!" he screamed, and everybody laughed. He stood back up. "Now! If you're here tonight and you have yet to give your heart and life to Jesus Christ!" He paused as he stood right in front of Brianna and looked down at her. "This girl has Jesus in her heart!" He smiled at her. "I can see Him in her eyes!" Brianna teared up and nodded. Shadow patted her on the back, and they cried together. "The altars are open for those of you who don't have Jesus in your heart! Come on! Don't do the easy thing and stay in your seat! Get down here!" He walked back to the podium and several people went down to pray.

To Mark's surprise, Scotty stood up and made his way down their row. He stopped, however, right in front of Yvette and knelt down. As soon as he did, she began to cry. Charles was watching and shouted out, "Praise God!" Mark noticed that Gabi was also watching with her hand over her mouth. Scotty had overcome his fear. He stood up and led Yvette down to the altar. Brianna and Shadow went down and knelt behind them to pray for Yvette.

Mark looked over at Eddie who sat stone faced between Andy and Rusty. It almost looked as if he were afraid to blink. Andy sat there with his arms crossed and a defiant look on his face. Rusty was…wow! Rusty was sitting there with his elbows on his knees and his fingers in his ears. Mark couldn't help but find it amusing. Instead of resisting the devil, Rusty was resisting God.

There was such an excitement after the service. Twelve kids had given their hearts to Christ. In fact, the counselors were so excited, they decided to let everyone go for a late-night swim. Dean turned on the flood lights that were on the docks and told everybody to go suit up. It was a fun evening of celebration.

When they got back to their room and cleaned up, Mark had them gather around for a quick devotion.

"Wow," Rusty commented. "Haven't we had enough church for one day? I mean, we get it."

"Obviously you don't, Rusty," Mark replied. "If you did, you wouldn't be complaining." He smiled as Rusty sat down on the edge of his bed giving Mark another death stare.

"Whoa!" Charles yelled out scaring everybody. "If looks could kill…ol' Rusty woulda just put three caps in you, Mark!" He laughed, not taking his eyes off of Rusty.

"Yeah, well nobody asked you," Rusty said, looking away.

Mark recapped what Pastor Jason had talked about and closed them in prayer. Everyone was so tired they all went straight to bed.

Scotty fist bumped Mark before he climbed onto the top bunk. "Is it okay if I do the devotion tomorrow night?" he asked.

"Wait! What?" Mark asked with a laugh. "Who are you and what have you done with my best friend?"

Scotty laughed. "Greater is He, Dude! Greater is He!"

Maria lay in her bottom bunk, below some girl from Atlanta, named Connie. She had been lying there staring at the top bunk for hours. She was so numb she could no longer feel the pain that was her life. She had absolutely no more tears to cry. This morning, she had tossed her book in the dumpster and concluded that this was as good as it gets. Yeah, all these Christians seemed to be happy and worry free, but Maria was way past any help that their God could offer. She had considered, for a brief second, going down to that altar tonight. Bending her knees, crying her tears, receiving the love and hugs that came with it...but then what? Would her mother miraculously sober up and get a job? Would her father come driving up that three-mile driveway and sweep her into his arms? No. God would only offer her another empty promise. There really was only one way to escape this madness. Even Rusty had said as much. "You know you can escape the pain, Maria," he had said. "If it really is as bad as you say, I mean." Then he had handed her the shiny silver razor blade. "There's no shame in it, you know." She had tried to maintain some sense of pride by arguing with him. Mark had walked up at that point, thinking he was defending her. Mark. She would love to have what he had. That peace that she could see in his eyes. All of them. She hated to admit it, but Scotty, Gabi, Brianna, Billy, Matt...even Mr. Bret, they all had such a peace about them. That had to be so much more than God, though. That had to be family, friends, love...so much more than she could ever hope for. Then she thought about Mr. Bret. He reminded her of her father. Always trying to be so serious, but just a playful teddy-bear underneath. A tear slid down her cheek. "Why did you leave me, Daddy?"

"Because you're not worth loving," the large, black, scaly demon whispered in her ear. "You were not worth staying with. You never really made him happy."

She choked out a sob as she remembered what Rusty had whispered in her ear at the campfire service. "Perfect peace awaits you, Maria. It won't even hurt...you'll just fall asleep, and then, nothing." Nothing sounded good right now. Nothing sounded just perfect.

Maria sat up and lifted her pillow. There lay the razor blade. She picked it up and stared at it in her palm. So small. Someone in the room coughed and startled her. She looked around and decided that she couldn't do it here in the room. Where then? Not the bathroom. She wanted to go somewhere peaceful. The lake...yeah, she would sneak out and walk down to the dock. It would be so quiet and peaceful there.

"Do it now," the demon whispered. "Be brave. Free yourself once and for all."

She quietly slipped on a pair of shorts and picked up her flip flops. With the razor in her hand, she walked to the door, quietly opened it and slipped out. She stepped into her flip flops and made her way to the lake.

Brianna opened her eyes, being a light sleeper, she could've sworn she'd heard a slight click. She sat up and looked around. Nobody seemed to be up. She rolled over to go back to sleep, but realized she needed to go to the bathroom. She got up and quietly made her way by the light of her small reading light. On her way back out, she noticed that Maria's pillow was in the middle of her bed. She walked over for a closer look and saw that Maria was not there. She looked around and whispered, "Maria!" No answer came. Brianna went back into the bathroom to check all the stalls. Nothing. Back out in the main room, she went to Gabi's bed and shook her arm. "Gabi?" she whispered. There was no sense in waking everyone up. "Gabi."

Gabi began to stir. "Huh...what's wrong?" Gabi asked in a groggy voice.

"Gabi, Maria is gone," Brianna whispered. "She's not in the cabin."

"Huh?" She raised up onto her elbow and wiped the sleep from her eyes. "You checked the bathroom?"

Brianna nodded, "Yes."

Gabi sat up. "Okay," she said while yawning. "We can go look for her together." She grabbed her shoes from under her bed. "Get your shoes." They both tiptoed out of the cabin in their pajamas and sat down on the steps to put their shoes on.

"It's so quiet out," Brianna said. "Where do you think she went?"

Gabi shrugged. "Mark seemed concerned with her last night, but I never got to talk to him about it. She seemed okay when we got back to the room."

"She's so quiet," Brianna said. "It's hard to tell what's going on with her."

"Unless you make her mad," Gabi said, remembering how Maria had attacked Daisy. She got up and walked over to the side of the cabin and called Maria's name. Brianna did the same thing on the other side.

"Should we get a counselor up?" Brianna asked.

"Not yet, I don't want to get her into trouble unless it's necessary," Gabi replied. "And we'll get Mr. Bret before we get anybody."

Maria sat down on the edge of the dock. It was beautiful out here. The water was so smooth. The moon's reflection from behind the clouds gave off just enough light. She leaned back on her hands and looked up. There were no stars out, but the sky was still beautiful. It was so peaceful with the only sounds coming from the frogs and the crickets. She heard an owl from somewhere in the distance. She smiled. What a perfect scenario to end her imperfect life. It was almost so perfect that she didn't want to go through with it. Almost. She had set the blade down on the dock, taken her flip flops off and set them beside her and dipped her feet into the cool water. She sighed really loud. "It really is the only way, girl," she said aloud and looked across the lake.

"Yes," whispered the demon who stood over her, his claws buried into her mind. "The only way." He was joined on the dock now by several other demons and foul creatures who had come to stand guard and watch. Being directly in the enemy's camp meant you couldn't be too careful. They each smiled as they waited for victory to come. Another soul snatched from the enemy's hands. "Rest now," he whispered. "Rest." Maria reached down and picked up the razor blade.

"Wait," Gabi said, grabbing Brianna's arm. They had looked everywhere from the boardwalk to the parking lot.

"What is it?" Brianna asked.

"Father, we lift up Maria to you right now!" Gabi said. "She is your child and you love her! I pray that wherever she is, you would protect her...protect her from the enemy as well as from herself. And please help us to find her. Amen."

"Amen," Brianna said. "I felt it too, she's in trouble."

As the demon held Maria's hand steady, bringing the blade to her wrist, he whispered encouragement into her ear. "Such a perfect place. Such a perfect time. Such a perfect ending."

The other demons had gathered behind him, drooling with anticipation. "Yes! Do it now!" they sneered. "Another win for the Master!"

Just then, one of the demons standing guard to the right of Maria, let out a scream. "Nooo! Hurry! Do it now!!! The enemy comes!" The other demons looked up just as several balls of light shot through the air above the lake.

The demon with Maria lifted his head and screamed, "Go you FOOLS! Stop them!" Each of the demons took flight, meeting the angels with a roar and a sword.

"This is our victory, Daniel!" one of the demons swore. "You cannot have her now!" He screamed as Daniel sent him to the abyss with one swipe of his fiery sword.

Brandon, the large angel closest to Daniel, laughed. "What is that foul stench?" He swung his sword and split two demons at once. "Behind you, Captain!" he yelled, and Daniel spun to disintegrate a charging demon. Several more angels and demons appeared.

Maria held the blade to her wrist and paused. Suddenly she was having second thoughts. What if these Christians were right? What if there really was a heaven and a hell?

"Come on, my sweets," the demon whispered, watching the battle. Hundreds of demons and angels continued to appear all around the camp. The battle for his Maria's soul was on. He would not lose her. Holding her hand steady, he whispered, "Daddy never loved you. He couldn't wait to leave you. He is so much happier now."

Maria pressed the corner of the blade into her skin. A droplet of blood appeared. "I can do this," she said aloud, a tear rolling down her cheek.

"Yes, you can," the demon hissed. "Just a little more." He gripped her hand tighter. It began to slide across her wrist.

"Maria!" Gabi yelled from behind her. "What are you doing?"

Maria jumped at the sound of her name. She turned to see Gabi walking toward her. "I'm okay!" she yelled. "I'll be back up in a minute!"

"Yes!" the demon screamed in her ear. "Get rid of that meddling prissy!"

"Well, I can't leave you out here," Gabi said. "Can we talk?"

"No! Go away, Gabi!" she screamed. "Leave me alone you meddling prissy! I don't want to talk!" She brought the blade back to her wrist. The blood was already running onto her leg.

"Yessss!" the demon screamed. "Do it!"

"Maria!" Gabi said. "I really think you need to hear this!"

"Go away!" Maria screamed. She was shaking violently with rage now. "Leave me alone!" she spit the words out like venom.

"Jesus loves you so much, Maria," Gabi said calmly.

"Do it, Maria!" the demon screamed into her ear. "End it now, right in front of that little goodie two-shoes!" Just then something tapped his shoulder and he jumped up and spun around. Towering in front of him was heaven's largest and most deadly angelic warrior. He stood several feet taller than the demon and was almost as thick with muscles. His wings fanned out over the water. The demon gasped as Adam's sword pierced his throat and lifted him off the ground. Adam smiled at him as he kicked his legs out for traction. "You lose." With one twist of his sword, the demon exploded before him and was gone.

"Maria!" Mr. Bret yelled from up at the cabins. It scared her to hear his voice and she jumped, causing the blade to slip from her fingers and fall into the water. "Maria!" He was running to her with Brianna right behind him. Gabi had gotten to her first and gasped when she saw the blood. "What are you doing, girl!?" Mr. Bret asked as he approached.

Maria began to tremble as she looked down and saw the blood on her arm and leg. She let out a sob. She had almost killed herself.

Mr. Bret ran up and took in the situation. As soon as he saw her arm, he knew what had happened. He knelt and scooped her into his arms. He lifted Maria up as if she weighed nothing. Draped across his arms, she put her cut arm around his neck and cried into his chest. Gabi and Brianna prayed silently beside them.

Above the lake, smiling down on them, Daniel and Adam fist bumped. "She'll be okay," a nearby angel said.

"Yes, she will, Chaz!" Adam replied. "Now back to your posts everyone. She's just fine!"

"Absolutely," Daniel replied. "Her story is about to begin." His eyes fell on Gabi, who had just looked up. It was almost as if she could see them.

Gabi smiled as she looked up into the sky above the lake. There sure were a lot of stars out tonight.

The next morning at breakfast, Gabi quietly told Mark and Scotty what had happened. She and Brianna had gone to find bandages while Mr. Bret had held Maria just like that for two whole hours. Jasper had been the only one they'd told, and he had recommended pastoral counseling for Maria. Mr. Bret had driven her to Moses' house this morning.

"Wow," Scotty said. "You just never know what somebody is dealing with."

"I just know that Rusty had something to do with this," Mark said. "I caught him and Maria arguing about something yesterday and then he was whispering something to her during the service. I had completely forgotten about it after the service with all the excitement and celebrating going on."

"All I know is," Brianna said. "Mr. Bret was like a daddy bear protecting his cub when I woke him up. You would've thought she was his daughter."

"Well, I thought it was sweet the way he just held her and let her cry and bleed all over him," Gabi said. Brianna nodded. "It was probably the first time she'd been held since she was a little girl. She actually fell asleep in his arms."

"Hey Gabi!" Rusty called from across the table. "I hear Maria chickened out from offing herself!" He laughed. "What a loser!"

Gabi stood up and reached across the table so fast that Rusty dropped his drink in his lap trying to jump back. She put her finger right in his face before he had time to blink. "Rusty Staggerbush!" she yelled so loud, everyone turned to look. "You need Jesus Christ in your life!"

At that Rusty came out of his seat and screamed, "Don't you ever put your finger in my face!" His hand came around in a swing, but before he could connect with Gabi's face, Scotty had launched himself over the table and took Rusty to the ground.

The entire place erupted with yells and screams. Several guys tried to pull Scotty and Rusty apart while each of them delivered blows to each other. Charles finally managed to hold Rusty down long enough for two other guys to pull Scotty away kicking and screaming something about his wife.

"What did he say?" Gabi asked Mark.

"I have no idea," Mark said, still sitting there in shock at how fast Scotty had attacked Rusty.

Dean led the two boys out of the Mess Hall.

"Come to camp, they said," Billy yelled. "It'll be relaxing, they said!" Everyone around him laughed.

They were all then told to head on over to the sanctuary for the first workshop of the day.

"So," Brianna said, leaning in close to Gabi. "Somebody has a personal bodyguard."

Gabi blushed bright red and told Brianna to shut up.

CHAPTER 9

SHADOW OF THE ALMIGHTY

Mark didn't see Scotty again until after the first workshop Tuesday morning. He was waiting outside the sanctuary on a bench, looking quite upset. Mark, Gabi and Brianna approached him with grins on their faces. "What's up, you beast?" Mark asked with a laugh.

Scotty tried to hide a smile. "Dude, I got dishes duty for the rest of the week!"

"What did Rusty get," Brianna asked, looking around for him.

Scotty shrugged. "He's still being talked to by Jasper." Scotty shook his head. "Can you believe that guy?"

"You're the guy we can't believe!" Gabi said. "What were you thinking?"

"What?! Are you kidding me?" Scotty asked. "He was about to hit you!"

Brianna laughed out loud. "Come on, Gabi! He was defending you!" she said, and Gabi shot her a look. "I'm just saying, the guy DID look like he was about to slap you...he'll think twice about it next time!" Again, she laughed.

"Anyway," an exasperated Gabi said. "Thank you for defending me, Scotty." She sighed and sat down next to him. "But next time you don't have to go all psycho." She smiled at him.

"Yeah, sorry. I guess I had a little pent-up anger towards that..." he glanced at Gabi. "Wonderful boy." He smiled. "They put me on notice. They called it behavior unbecoming of a camp host."

140

"I'll say," Gabi said, shoving him. "But he DID deserve it. I couldn't believe what he said about Maria."

"Are you kidding me?!" Mr. Bret said, walking up. "I'm gone for five minutes and you get in a fight?"

"How's Maria?" Gabi asked him.

"Better." He shrugged. "We have to notify her mother to see what she wants to do."

"She'll just want her to come home," Gabi replied. "For selfish reasons, of course. Maria takes care of her."

"Where is she at?" Brianna asked.

"Mess Hall," Mr. Bret replied. "She was starving."

"Oh, I bet," Gabi said. "Can we go see her?" He nodded and she and Brianna headed that way.

Mr. Bret kicked at the bench next to Scotty. "Talk to me!"

It wasn't until lunch that Rusty made his first appearance. He walked straight over to their table. Billy nudged Scotty when he saw him coming.

"Hey Rusty!" Andy called. "I saved you a seat."

Rusty walked right up beside Scotty and held out his hand to shake. Scotty looked up at him. "You got a good right cross, Morgan." Rusty smiled. Scotty shook his hand but didn't say a word. Rusty walked away to get his food.

Mark leaned over to Gabi, "So, is Maria sitting with Mr. Bret by choice or does he have to keep an eye on her?"

Gabi shrugged. "They couldn't get a hold of her mom. I would imagine she's embarrassed and is more comfortable over there."

Rusty came back with his food and sat down. "Ugh, this place sucks," he said.

"How much trouble did you get in?" Andy asked him.

"Trash detail all week," he replied. "Jasper said they would be watching me, though. Said he was giving me enough rope to hang myself with. A little morbid, all things considered." He looked at Gabi. "I'll be fine though."

"Hey Eddie!" someone yelled across the room. They all looked over to see Chris, the blonde bully kid. He and his baby-faced sidekick Terry were grinning at Eddie. "What happened to your face, Eddie?" Eddie looked away red faced.

"Hey Chris!" Rusty yelled back to him, putting his arm around Eddie. "What happened to your other girlfriend? Marcus, isn't it?" Chris looked around and said something to Terry. They both walked out. Rusty smiled at Mark. "Gotta keep jerks like that on their toes."

"What did happen to Marcus, Rusty?" Mark asked.

Rusty just shrugged and continued to eat. "Not my day to watch him, McGee."

There was an announcement that anyone interested in playing paintball was to meet at the arena in twenty minutes. All the guys scrambled to go get ready. Scotty had to stay behind to do the dishes. On their way to the arena, they found out that Marcus had been attacked by hornets and had to be rushed to the hospital.

Rusty and Andy laughed out loud. "Yeah!" Rusty said. "That's what happens when you mess with my boy!" He pulled Eddie in for a hug. "See, dude! I told you they would pay!"

Scotty nudged Mark. "I have to admit it, that's a little strange."

Mark looked at Eddie, who looked scared to death walking with Rusty. "Hey Eddie!" Mark said. "You okay?"

"Yeah, I'm okay, McGee," Eddie mumbled, keeping his head down. Mark noticed he was back to being McGee again now that Eddie was with Rusty.

"Why wouldn't he be okay, McGee?" Rusty asked. "His true friends know how to defend him."

"Controlling hornets now, Rusty?" Mark asked. Rusty just smiled.

Upon hearing the clicking sound, Caleb had run like never before. He didn't even look back. He just ran as fast as he could, putting as much distance as he could between himself and whatever monster was trailing him. His legs were beginning to burn now. He desperately needed to stop and rest. He chanced a look back and didn't see anything. Slowing down to a gradual stop, he plopped down onto the dry ground, panting.

Looking ahead, Caleb saw that he was much closer to the mountains now. Another few hours and he should be there. Somehow, he just knew that he would be okay if he could just get to the top of that mountain. A famous quote by John Muir came to mind at that thought: "Thousands of tired, nerve-shaken, over-civilized people are beginning to find out that going to the mountains is going home…" Caleb was so tired. He lay back in the dirt and closed his eyes. Perhaps a quick power nap would revive him.

"Hey, silly, are you sleeping?" He lifted his head at the sound of Megan's voice. He was in the school library. He looked over at the table next to the one he sat at. There was himself and Megan again. She stood beside his seat, holding a stack of books. The other Caleb lifted his head and gave her an impatient look.

"Are you ready to go yet? We've practically spent our entire lunch period in here," the other Caleb said, looking at his watch.

"Almost," Megan replied. "Hold on, I need one more book." She turned to go and a tiny book fell from her stack of books onto Caleb's arm.

"What is this?" he picked it up. "Is this a Christian tract? Where'd you get this?"

"Oh," Megan said, looking as though she'd been caught cheating on a test. "It's nothing. Trina asked me to read it."

"Give me a break!" Caleb replied, tossing it over to the table that he was now sitting at watching them. "That junk is poison!" Several people shushed him, and he continued in a whisper. "Why do you hang out with her?"

"I don't know, Caleb. She's really nice." Megan replied. "Just because you disagree with someone doesn't mean they can't be your friend."

"Our friends are our influences, Megan," he replied. "And Trina is a bad influence on you."

"Yeah, okay Caleb," she said, laughing. "That whole love your enemy thing is really dangerous."

"No, but that whole, 'you need Jesus because you're too stupid to make it on your own' thing, is." He gathered his books and stood. "Listen, I have to go to my locker, I'll see you in Calculus."

The Caleb that was watching, saw himself walk away, and then watched Megan as she disappeared down one of the aisles. He looked down at the tract and suddenly, he remembered this entire conversation. The title of the tract read, "Don't Go to Hell."

He jumped awake in the dirt wondering how long he'd been asleep. He stretched his back and was about to stand when he heard the crackling of a fire. He quickly looked around. There, not ten feet behind him, sat an old man next to a small campfire. His back was to Caleb and he appeared to be cooking something. There was a large pouch sitting on the ground beside him. "Um, hello?" Caleb said, standing up.

"Caleb!" the old man exclaimed, turning and looking at Caleb with a big smile on his face. "Come! Sit down and eat!"

Keeping his distance, Caleb walked around to the other side of the fire. "How do you know my name?" he asked.

"Oh, my boy!" the old man said. "I know so much more than your name." He held up a small plate with some form of meat on it. It smelled absolutely delicious. "You should eat."

Taking the plate and looking at the unrecognizable cooked carcass on it, he said, "Thank you, but…"

"It is nourishment, my friend! Eat up!"

"So, it's probably better to not know." Caleb smiled and sat across from the old man. Taking a bite of the delicious nourishment caused him to forget what kind of animal his teeth were ripping into. "Oh my, thank you so much! This is amazing!"

"Water?" the old man held up a canteen for Caleb. He graciously accepted it and almost choked on the cool refreshing water.

"Careful!" the old man said, with a laugh. "It would be a shame for you to come so far only to drown in a desert!"

Wiping his mouth and setting the canteen down, Caleb only now looked at the old man. He looked like someone that would have lived hundreds of years ago in the desert, with his unkempt hair and beard. His face was weathered and dry and his eyes were almost completely white. His smile seemed genuine and his food delicious, but Caleb was still skeptical. "I'm sorry, you know my name, but…"

"Torheit, my boy!" My name is Torheit!" He laughed and took a swig from his own canteen.

"Torheit? What exactly is that?" Caleb asked.

"Why, it is my name," he replied with a wide smile.

"Well, Torheit, may I please ask you where, in the world we are?"

"You may indeed," he replied and looked curiously at Caleb.

After waiting several seconds, Caleb gave a frustrated grunt and asked again, "So, where in the world, are we?"

Torheit smiled and poked at the fire with a small stick. "My dear boy, we are nowhere in the world."

Caleb watched him. This was a game to the old man. Well, Caleb could play games too. He decided to switch gears and come back to the location question later. "Where exactly did you find all these sticks for the fire, Torheit?" Caleb looked around. "Because I've been out here for hours and haven't seen the first one."

Again, Torheit smiled at Caleb. "Excellent observation, my boy," Torheit said and he held a small stick up in the air. It immediately became a beautifully colored bird and flew away, screeching.

Caleb blinked at this apparent magic trick and leaned back onto his hands to stare at Torheit. "So… what?" Caleb asked. "You're a magician?"

Torheit smiled. "I am many things, my friend. Many things. I am a man with many talents."

"Except for being able to give a straight answer." Caleb smiled now.

The old man pondered Caleb for several minutes and answered. "When a person is born, a path is laid before them. Some are given a short path. Some are given a long path. Some a path with many obstacles. Some a path with few obstacles. ALL are given the task of reaching the end of their path."

Caleb squinted at him and waited for more. When it didn't come, he replied, "Well, that was helpful!" in as sarcastic a tone as he could conjure.

"This place," Torheit said, looking Caleb straight in the eyes. "Is part of your path."

"But where is this place?!" Caleb yelled, quickly becoming impatient. If he could find out where this place was maybe he could figure out where Megan was.

Torheit looked up as if in deep thought. "I suppose in your tongue it could be considered as a waiting room."

"A waiting room?" Caleb was so confused. "What are you talking about? A waiting room for what? What exactly am I waiting for?"

"For death, my dear boy," Torheit replied with a smile. "For death."

"The rest of Tuesday had gone by rather smoothly. No fights. No suicide attempts. No insect or reptile attacks. In fact, there were no near-death experiences at all. Dean had spoken at the campfire service and done a great job. Yvette had attempted to get Daisy to go to the altar at the end of the service, but Daisy had assured her that she was okay.

Back in their cabin, Scotty had given a short devotion quite nervously. Rusty had attempted to mock him, but Charles had kindly asked him to let Scotty finish speaking. Oddly enough, Rusty had sat back on his bed and shut up.

In Gabi's room, Shadow asked if she could say something after their devotion. It took her a few minutes to get it out, because she had teared up. "I'm sorry," she said.

"Take your time, Shadow," Brianna said, smiling at her. "This is the reason we are here." The change that had come over this rebellious Goth girl was overwhelming. It was like she had become a different person since getting saved.

"My whole life," she started, "it was like there was a dark cloud over me. I always thought my parents had named me perfectly. Shadow. I mean, what kind of name is that?"

Gabi began flipping through her Bible as Shadow spoke.

"I've never been successful at anything. I've never had many friends. My parents basically ignore me." She wiped away a tear and Brianna walked over and sat beside her on the bed. They hugged each other. "So many times, I have considered," she looked at Maria, "ending it all. I totally understand where you are, Maria." Maria looked away. "But, thanks to Brianna, and Gabi, and so many others here at the camp, I've been able to experience the love of God." Again, she wiped her eyes. "Now," she sighed. "I almost feel ashamed of my name. I hate that I'm so full of light and love and my name is Shadow." She smiled at Brianna and then looked at each girl. "So, I thought, I want to change it." She wiped her nose with a tissue. "You know how a shadow is basically a reflection of darkness?" They all smiled and nodded. "Well, I thought about a mirror, and how it is a reflection of light...I know it sounds silly, but I want to change my name to Mirror. Mirror Riley." She looked around for comments or even facial expressions.

"Um." Gabi cleared her throat. "Shadow, I personally think your name is perfect." Brianna nodded in agreement. "Listen to what it says in Psalm 91:1." And she read, "He who dwells in the shelter of the Most High will rest in the shadow of the Almighty." She looked back up at Shadow. "Did you hear it? The SHADOW of the Almighty. That could be your personal verse. People can find rest just being in your presence, Shadow."

"That's awesome, Gabi!" Brianna said.

"I love it!" Yvette added. "The Shadow of the Almighty! Wow!"

Shadow nodded. "That IS beautiful!" She wiped her eyes. "Thank you, Gabi!"

"Well," Gabi said. "I'm just glad you like it. Because Mirror was just dumb." They all laughed.

Just as Mark went to shut off the lights for bedtime, there was a knock at the door. He opened it to find Mr. Bret standing there. "Hey!" Mark said, surprised to see him.

"Got spiders?" Mr. Bret asked, with a smile.

"Um." Mark was confused. "Do what?"

"We need to check your cabin for black widow spiders," he said, walking in.

Scotty immediately jumped out of bed and began frantically checking himself. "Are you serious?"

"What's going on?" Billy asked, laughing at Scotty.

"One of the other cabins was crawling with black widows," Mr. Bret said. "I mean, they were everywhere. Two boys were bitten and had to be taken to the ER." He began moving things around and searching. "Come on, look everywhere, strip your beds down."

Mark noticed that Rusty and Andy were the only ones not looking.

"I REALLY hate spiders," Scotty said.

"Billy, Eddie, go check the bathroom," Mr. Bret said. "Pay special attention to any holes in the wall and the corners."

"Black widows can kill you!" Scotty said.

"You sure would think so hearing that Terry boy screaming," Mr. Bret said.

"Wait!" Mark said, glancing at Rusty. "Did you say Terry? Who else was bitten?"

"That blonde kid that almost choked," Mr. Bret replied. "Some people aren't meant for the outdoors, I guess. Of course, one could argue that cabin being cursed too. Same cabin the hornets' nest was found this morning. Well, you guys seem fine. I'm outta here!" He headed for the door. "Good night."

Mark looked right at Rusty. "Cursed indeed."

"Oh, wow, McGee!" Rusty exclaimed. "Now I have control over hornets and spiders? Dude, you really need to chill out. We're in the woods, these things happen!"

"They just seem to happen a little more to people you don't like, Rusty!" Mark replied.

"I don't know, McGee," Rusty said, stepping towards Mark. "Nothing's happened to you yet."

"Okay, boys!" Charles said, standing up and towering over the both of them. "Ain't nothing gonna get settled by arguing all night."

Rusty stared Charles down for several seconds and then looked at Mark. "You better listen to your bodyguard, McGee. There's no sense in anybody else going to the hospital tonight."

Everybody finally got calmed down and settled in for the night. Mark lay in his bed pondering all the things that had happened this week. Moses' brake line cut. A snake in Eddie's bed. A kid almost choking. Mark's visit by the dragon. Matt having to leave because of a death in the family. Maria attempting suicide. Three kids either bitten or stung and having to go to the hospital. Almost all of them could be blamed on Rusty, given Mark's logic. The guy was definitely evil.

Of course, there were also a few good things that had happened this week. Shadow had gotten saved. Scotty had overcome his fears of talking to people and speaking. Yvette had gotten saved as a result of that. Maria's suicide attempt had failed, and she was being counseled. Mark and Scotty had befriended Eddie.

Considering that it was only Tuesday evening, it had been quite an eventful trip. Much more exciting than he would have expected. As he was about to fall asleep, another thought occurred to him. Tomorrow was his thirteenth birthday.

Matt woke up early on Wednesday morning with a sense of dread. Today was Megan's funeral. He still couldn't believe it. His cousin, Megan Ramsey, was dead. She would never go to college. Never get married. Never have children. Never get to grow old. She was gone forever. So young. Too young.

He sat up and looked around. He had slept in the basement at Uncle Nathan's house. He loved it down here. It was set up as Uncle Nathan's man cave, with a huge screen television and the most comfortable leather furniture Matt had ever experienced. Being the only cousin on Dad's side of the family, Matt always had the basement to himself when they visited. This visit had been even more lonely. In the past, Megan would come down and watch movies with him. In fact, just last summer, they had sat on this very couch and watched the entire collection of Star Wars®. They'd eaten pizza, popcorn and potato chips and drank root beer. It had been so fun. Caleb had joined them somewhere in the middle of Episode IV.

He really liked Caleb. He and Megan had been friends forever and were perfect for each other. He said a quick prayer for him. They had visited the hospital where he was at yesterday. Not being family, they hadn't been allowed to see him. He was in ICU and still in critical condition. Matt's dad had said that the doctors were hopeful that he would make a comeback. He was already showing signs of improvement. As good as that news had been, it didn't seem to lift the spirits of anyone in this household.

Matt's aunt and uncle were basket cases. Neither one of them were handling the entire situation very well. His aunt pretty much stayed in her bedroom crying. His uncle couldn't even stay focused on the planning of the funeral. Matt's parents were basically taking care of everything. The fact that his aunt and uncle weren't believers didn't help either. Matt couldn't imagine the hopelessness they felt.

He stood up and gathered his things to go shower. It was going to be a really long day.

Mark was awakened by the sound of someone banging on the door just minutes before the morning chimes were set to get them up.

"What in the world?" Andy mumbled into his pillow.

"Who's banging on the door?" Billy asked, groggily.

"Seriously?" Scotty added, looking at the clock. "We still have ten minutes!"

After all the complaining was over, Mark looked up to see if anyone had made a move to answer the door. Of course, nobody had. "It's okay guys!" he said. "Let me get it! It's only my birthday!" He headed for the door.

"Happy birthday, Mark!" Scotty mumbled.

"Yeah, yeah, yeah, whatever," he said as he opened the door and found nothing there except a small package that read, To Mark, From Gabi and Brianna! Happy Birthday! He looked around. They were long gone. Smiling, he grabbed the package and took it to his bed. He quickly opened it to find another even smaller box. Opening that one he found two more boxes. The first one had Gabi's name on it. He opened it to find a really cool black, leather, beaded necklace that she must've made in her crafts class. The second box had Brianna's name on it and contained a matching bracelet. "Sweet," he said to himself. He would definitely be wearing them today.

After breakfast that morning, Charles pulled Mark aside. "Good morning, Mark. Happy birthday?" He had a concerned look on his face.

"Thanks, Charles...what's up?"

"It's Daisy, Mark," he said in a serious tone. "Have you talked to her about Jesus?"

Mark immediately felt guilty. "Actually no, we've all been so busy keeping her away from boys that I don't think anybody has had a one-on-one sit down with her about Jesus yet. Wait, I think Yvette was talking to her after service last night."

"Well, I know it isn't my place, but I really think you need to talk to her, Mark," Charles said. "Just call it instinct."

Just then, Rusty, Andy and Eddie walked past them and Rusty bumped into Charles without saying anything. Charles just watched him as they walked away.

"Watch yourself with that guy," Mark said. "Bad things seem to happen to people he doesn't like."

"I'm not worried about Ol' Rusty!" Charles said with a laugh. "He needs to be worried about me." He turned to look at Mark again. "What about Andy and Eddie?"

"What about them?" Mark asked.

"They need Jesus too," he said with a grim look, before walking away.

Mark watched Charles go and thought he'd been acting a bit strange lately. What did Mark know though, he'd only known the guy for a few days, maybe this was normal for him.

"Hey, Mark!" Daisy said as she walked by. "You need to stop daydreaming and come to workshop." She gave him a big smile.

"Oh yeah!" Mark laughed. "Hey, Daisy!" He walked with her.

"So, rumor has it that today is your birthday," she said with a laugh.

"Yep, I'm officially a teenager today," he replied.

"Happy birthday," she said.

"Thank you very much."

"Would it be okay if I sat with the birthday boy in workshop?" she asked.

"Absolutely, Daisy," Mark said with a big smile. "I would be honored." She smiled real big as he held the door open for her.

Of course, Mark received some strange looks from his friends when he and Daisy walked in and sat down beside each other. He was intently listening to a story she told him about something funny that had happened to her last night, which kept him from having to make eye contact with Scotty or Gabi. Daisy really did seem to be as nice as she was pretty. Mark wondered where her need for boy attention came from. Mark leaned over to her before class began. "Can we talk after class?"

She smiled and nodded. "I really think we're too young to get married, though." His eyes got as big as saucers and she laughed so loud she snorted. "I'm kidding," she said, giving him a light shove.

He looked over and Scotty, Gabi and Brianna were all watching him with confused looks. He crossed his eyes and stuck his tongue out at them.

After class, before anyone could question him, he led Daisy around to the bleachers at the paintball arena. They sat down as she finished telling him a story about what her parents did for her on her last birthday. Mark laughed. "Wow, that is so cool."

"So," she said. "What does the mysterious Mark McGee want to talk with little old me about?"

"Oh, I'm not mysterious, Daisy," he replied. "I think confused is a better word." He gave her a big smile and she laughed. "Speaking of mysterious, there's something I can't figure out about you."

"Okay," she seemed intrigued. "And what would that be?"

"First of all, I'm not the best communicator, so promise me you won't get mad at me if I say this wrong."

She laughed. "No boy is ever a good communicator."

"Fair enough," Mark said. "Okay, here's the mystery: when a person first sees or meets Daisy Canard, cool name, by the way." She smiled. "They see an extremely pretty girl." She smiled even bigger.

"Thank you, Mark!" she replied, but he held up his hand for her to let him finish.

"Then," he continued. "Once they talk to you, they find an extremely nice girl who has an amazing personality and a great sense of humor."

"Wow, Mark McGee!" she replied, blushing. "You know what they say about flattery!"

"Hold on now," he said. "Here's where the mystery part comes in." He paused as if thinking of the right words to say. "I guess I just don't understand how a girl so pretty and sweet has to be so boy crazy." She looked away and he hoped he hadn't lost her. "It's just, that scares guys away, you know. The nice ones anyway. I mean, a girl as amazing as you should just sit back and wait for them to come to you. They would literally line up." He laughed, but she still wouldn't look at him.

She was quiet for a few minutes and Mark desperately hoped he hadn't hurt her feelings.

"Listen, what I'm trying to say is that you are way too pretty to be chasing boys. You should totally be making them pursue you, because I know for a fact that they will!" She looked at him with tears in her eyes and smiled. "I'm serious."

She laughed. "Mark McGee, you CAN communicate. Thank you, you are very sweet." She sighed really big and wiped her eyes. "I suppose I do reek of desperation. I just..."

"You don't have to explain anything, Daisy," Mark said. "It's all just my opinion."

She smiled at him. "Well, you're very sweet, Mark McGee. You're going to make some girl very happy one day."

"Well, I don't know about that," he said, and she stood up to go. "Hold on, one more thing." She sat back down. "What about Jesus?"

"Jesus?" she asked, looking confused.

"He's actually a guy you need to be pursuing," Mark said.

"There you are, McGee!" Rusty had walked up behind them. "I've been looking for you!" He looked right at Daisy. "Whoa, way to go, McGee! I didn't think you had it in ya!"

"We're just talking, Rusty," Mark replied. "What do you want?"

"I'll let you guys talk," Daisy said and before Mark could protest, she had walked away.

Rusty gave him a wicked smile. "Too bad, McGee."

"What do you want, Rusty?" Mark asked in a frustrated tone.

"Easy, McGee, I just wanted to wish you a Happy Birthday!" Rusty held out his hand to shake.

Mark shook his hand. "Rusty, if I didn't know any better, I would think you interrupted us to keep me from talking to Daisy about Jesus."

"Wow, McGee, are you serious?" Rusty said with a laugh. "You bring a pretty girl like Daisy over to the bleachers to talk about God? Wow, and they say I'm a loser!" He walked away laughing.

Up above them, all around the camp, angels were gathering one by one. They were being posted in strategic spots. Some were even assigned to specific people.

"They're still arriving, Captain," Brandon said to Daniel as he stood atop the sanctuary looking over the camp. "Have you determined the enemies plan yet, sir?"

"To steal, kill and destroy is all we really need to know, Brandon," Daniel said with a concerned look on his face. "We must be prepared for whatever they bring."

"Do you suppose it has something to do with Mark McGee and his friends?" Brandon asked.

"I believe it has everything to do with them," Daniel answered. "But we must not take our eyes off of ANY of God's children."

An extremely large angel appeared just above them with his sword drawn. "The enemy's troops are gathering on the other side of the lake, my Captain!" Adam said. "With your permission I would very much enjoy attacking them."

Daniel smiled knowing that Adam would likely destroy them all single handedly. "Not yet, Adam! We must await the General's orders. For now, we stay alert!"

CHAPTER 10

HOLDING A GRUDGE

"Death?" Caleb asked. "What is that supposed to mean? A waiting room for death?"

Torheit gave him a grim look. "You were in an accident."

Caleb shook his head. "No! We missed that dump truck! Don't you think I would remember hitting a dump truck?!" He stood up. "There has to be another explanation! Tell me!" He walked around the fire and stood over Torheit.

"My boy," Torheit said. "I have told you. At this very moment your body is lying in an Intensive Care Unit with tubes and needles sticking out of it."

Caleb stood there staring down at him. It didn't make any sense, he thought, looking down at himself. How could his body be in a hospital? It was right here. He was right here...in this strange place. This, sort of hellish place that he'd never heard of...because it didn't really exist, on Earth. Maybe it did make sense, now that he thought about it. Maybe he really was in some kind of after life or between life place. "Wait!" he said, stepping back. "What about Megan? She's not here! Does that mean that she survived?" Hope began to rise up inside of him. If he could just make it to the top of the mountain, he could be with her.

Torheit took another bite of the mystery meat and did not look up.

"Torheit! Answer me!" Caleb screamed. "Is Megan okay?"

"I am sorry to have to tell you this, Caleb." He finished chewing and looked up. "But Megan is dead."

Caleb just stared at him for several seconds. "No!" He shook his head, turned around and walked back around the fire. "NO NO NO!!" he screamed to the sky. "You can't know that for sure!"

"You witnessed it, my boy," Torheit said. "You witnessed death himself consuming her."

"Wait!" Caleb said, turning to face the old man. "That black shadow thing that covered the sky…and sort of wrapped itself around her…that was…"

"Death." Torheit continued for him.

Caleb began to pace. "No, this is crazy! This is not how it all works! There's no such thing as monsters!" He stopped and looked back at Torheit. "Is this all inside my head? Is this all just being created by my brain as some sort of coping mechanism?"

Torheit shook his head. "No, Caleb. This is all very much real."

"Why didn't I know about this?" Caleb asked. "Why didn't anybody ever tell me about this place?"

Torheit shrugged. "Perhaps they tried."

"No!" Caleb shouted. "Nobody ever…"

"Would you have listened?" Torheit, using a cane that Caleb had not previously noticed, stood up. "My dear boy, you have to admit," he said, breathing hard from the effort of standing. "You have never been a very open-minded person."

Caleb stared at him and nodded. "That's true, but what you call being open minded I call being stupid. I have always made decisions with my brain and not my heart."

"I know, Caleb." The old man smiled. "Trust me, my boy. I know."

"But still!" Caleb continued. "Nobody ever mentioned monsters!"

"How about demons?" Torheit asked, reaching down to pick up his things.

"Excuse me?" Caleb said, standing stone still.

"Demons, my boy!" Torheit repeated, motioning for Caleb to follow him.

"Demons?" Caleb asked with a laugh. "You mean like from the Bible?"

"Bingo!" Torheit said. "Now, come with me and I will show you the way out of this wretched place."

"Are you telling me that the Bible is true?!" Caleb asked. He stood there frozen to his spot. There was just no way that all that 'Jesus died for my sins' junk was true. Torheit continued to walk away. "Torheit! Tell me! Is the Bible true?"

"What do you believe, my boy?" Torheit called over his shoulder.

"Well, I have always prided myself in never following any of that folly."

"Good! Very good, Caleb!" Torheit said. "Now come!"

Caleb began to follow him and stopped. "Hold on, Torheit! You're going the wrong way! That's the direction I just came from! The mountains are closer this way." He pointed behind them.

"Trust me, my boy!" Torheit said. "This is the way out."

"But..."

"Come!" the old man yelled. "There is no time to waste."

Caleb followed him.

Mark looked over at Eddie during lunch and could tell he was miserable. He was sandwiched between Rusty and Andy and being as quiet as he could. Nudging Scotty to look at him he leaned over and whispered, "Dude, we need to rescue Eddie."

Scotty looked over just in time to meet Eddie's eye. Eddie quickly looked away. "You're right, he looks scared to death. What should we do?"

"Hold on, I have an idea," Mark said and leaned across the table. "Hey Andy! Can I talk to you after lunch?"

"No way, McGee!" Andy replied. "I have nothing to say to you."

Rusty laughed. "Be careful, Andy! He might bake you a cake!" They both laughed.

"Yeah," Mark replied. "I guess you wouldn't know what to do without daddy Rusty there to tell you." Scotty almost spit his drink out snorting. "Wouldn't want to confuse you."

"I don't need Rusty to tell me anything, McGee!" Andy protested.

"Sure you don't, Andy," Mark replied. "You've practically sat on his lap this entire week." Mark smiled at Rusty, who looked furious. "Besides, I won't take up much of your precious time."

Andy stared at him for several seconds. "Alright, McGee. I'll give you five minutes." Rusty rolled his eyes and shook his head.

Mark nodded. "That's all I need."

Scotty leaned over. "What are you up to?"

"As my friend, wouldn't you do about anything to help me out of a jam?" Mark asked him.

"Of course, but what does...Ohhh! I see what you're doing." Scotty nodded. "But we are talking about Andy here."

"Pray for me," Mark said, standing up and leading Andy outside toward the lake.

"Don't ask me to hold your hand, McGee," Andy said.

Mark turned to face him. "What's the deal, Andy?"

"Whoa, what are you talking about?"

"I thought Eddie was your friend," Mark said, pointing up to the Mess Hall. "Dude, everybody can see how miserable he is around Rusty!"

"There's nothing..."

Mark held up his hand to silence Andy's defense. "This is MY five minutes, so just listen. Don't even think about defending Rusty! He's a snake and you know it! He's way more trouble than you and Eddie need, and I don't know about you, but Eddie knows it! Haven't you even noticed that everyone that crosses him ends up in the hospital?"

"Come on, McGee!" Andy said with a laugh. "It's all just a big coincidence!"

"Please tell me you're not that stupid, Andy!" Mark replied. He leaned in and whispered, "The guy is evil." He saw a shadow pass over Andy's eyes. "Yeah, you know it. Now listen, your friend in there, Eddie...he wants out. Because of you, though, he won't say anything." Mark poked him in the chest with his finger to get his attention. "If you don't care about yourself, you at least need to be a good friend and get Eddie away from Rusty. I'm begging you!" Mark stepped back and looked at him. "He's manipulating him, and Eddie isn't as strong as you are."

"Relax, McGee," Andy said, softening up. "I'm not going to let anything bad happen to him."

"Oh yeah?" Mark stepped back up to him. "Who cut Moses' brake line, Andy?" Andy blinked and stepped back. "Yeah, Rusty made Eddie do it, didn't he? And now he's using it as leverage. Not going to let anything bad happen to him, huh?"

"I don't know what you think you know, McGee," Andy said "But..."

"Save it, Andy!" Mark said. "If you're any kind of friend to Eddie, you need to protect him! Get him away from Rusty!" Mark turned and began to walk away.

"McGee! Hold on!" Andy said with a sigh. "Let's talk."

Gabi and Brianna went back to their cabin after lunch to put away their Bibles. They walked in laughing about Brianna's broken sandal that Gabi had just noticed, when they saw Maria sitting on her bed writing in a small notebook.

"Hey Maria!" Brianna said, walking over and sitting down beside her. She wrapped her arm around her and gave her a hug. Gabi sat down on Maria's other side and did the same.

"Hey," she replied, closing her notebook and sliding it under her pillow. "You guys are crazy."

"You know you don't have to write us a letter thanking us for being such amazing roommates," Brianna said with a laugh.

"That is exactly what I'm doing," Maria replied sarcastically. "How did you know?"

"Is that your diary?" Gabi asked.

Maria nodded. "I just started it this morning. Moses told me to keep track of all the positive things that happens throughout the day so I can go back and read them when I'm feeling down."

"Great idea!" Brianna said excitedly. "Will my hug be in there?"

Maria smiled at her and grabbed her notebook. "Absolutely."

"So how is Moses doing?" Gabi asked.

"He's good," Maria responded. "He has to stay off his feet, so he hates that. But he's in good spirits." She jotted something into her book.

"Well," Gabi said. "I can't imagine Moses not being in good spirits." She patted Maria on the hand. "And how are you doing?"

"I'm okay," Maria said. "Thank you for asking. You guys are so nice to me. I really don't deserve it."

"Well," Brianna said. "Gabi doesn't deserve to have me as her best friend, but God's kindness is extended to her as well." She laughed and jumped up as Gabi tried to swat her leg. Maria laughed at them.

"So," Gabi said, looking at the schedule. "Which event do you guys want to go to? Crafts, archery, rowing, or volleyball? And please don't say archery."

They decided on rowing and headed down to the lake. Once down there, they realized that it was only two to a boat. Brianna insisted that Gabi and Maria go together.

"I'll find some unlucky partner," she said, as someone tapped her on the shoulder.

"Hey Brianna." She turned to find Andy standing there looking quite awkward. "Um, if you need a partner, so do I."

"Well...okay, Andy," she said with a smile. "But try not to slow me down."

"Oh, okay, I'll do my best," he said. They picked their boat and slid it into the water. Andy held it still while she climbed in and moved to the front. He climbed into the back, sat down and shoved them away from the shore.

Dean stood on the shore calling out instructions to them all. They were to cross the lake and return. No racing or horse play. He then climbed into a boat with an older kid and followed. Gabi and Maria were way ahead of Brianna and Andy.

"So," Andy said. "How long are you in Florida?"

"I'm not in Florida, Andy," she said, turning around with a grin. "This is Georgia."

"Oh…yeah, right," he said, obviously embarrassed. "I just…"

She laughed. "I'm visiting Gabi for another month. I fly back home at the end of July." He nodded. "So, where's Rusty and Eddie?"

He shrugged. "I'm taking a break from them right now."

"Oh really?" Brianna said. "That is very interesting." When she saw his confused look, she said, "you guys just seem inseparable."

"It was actually Mark's idea," he replied. "An effort to protect Eddie."

"Wow! Sounds like a story worth hearing," she said, turning back around and rowing.

"Eddie is…not very comfortable around Rusty…for many reasons," Andy said, and Brianna nodded. "Actually, he's terrified of him. I get it, the guy is seriously intense." Andy shrugged. "He even scares me a little." He paused and looked out over the lake. "Anyway, Mark and I devised a plan to get them apart. Rusty is quite possessive of the both of us, so it wasn't easy. I actually had to pick a fight with Eddie, without his knowing what I was up to." He shrugged again. "I told him I was done with him and he needed to get lost."

Brianna smiled back at Andy. "Dude, you actually picked a fight with your best friend to save him from being scared and miserable?" He nodded. "That has got to be one of the sweetest things I have ever heard, Andy! Good for you!"

"Well, don't tell anyone," he said. "I have a reputation."

"What did Rusty do?" Brianna asked.

"I didn't give him a chance to do anything," Andy said. "I told him I wanted to be alone and went out to the boats."

"Well, I'm proud of you!" she said.

"Yeah, Mark is supposed to explain the whole thing to Eddie. We'll just kind of stay away from each other for the rest of the week."

"So, tell me something, Andy," Brianna said. "Now that you are an independent man and all, how do you feel about all this God stuff?"

He laughed. "I wondered how long it would take you to bring that up. Yeah, it's not for me."

"It's kinda for everyone, Andy. Everybody needs Jesus. The Bible says, 'For ALL have sinned and fall short of the glory of God.'"

"Yeah," he replied, nodding. "I guess I'm just not that concerned about all that right now." He shrugged. "I'm still young."

"Well," Brianna said, pausing to think before she spoke. "Your friend Todd was young too." She looked over her shoulder at him.

He glanced at her and quickly looked away.

"I'm just saying, we're not promised tomorrow," Brianna said, knowing she'd hit a nerve. "This boat could flip over and you could hit your head and drown in the next five minutes."

He looked at her for several seconds. "Listen, no offense, Brianna...but I've already sat through enough altar calls without having to endure another one while I'm trying to enjoy myself."

"Okay, Andy," she replied. "God's gift is free. He doesn't force it on you and neither will I." She gave him a big, sincere smile.

"Great, now can we talk about something else?" Andy asked.
"Like what?"

"Like, maybe...you and me going on a date when we get back to Gateway?"

She continued rowing for several seconds before responding. "Well, thank you for the sweet offer."

"But..." he said.

"But I don't date yet. And even if I did, Andy...I would never date a nonbeliever."

"Hey! Isn't that racist or something?" He protested.

She laughed. "No! It's actually in the Bible."

"Well," he said, "that darn Bible keeps ruining all my plans."

Mark and Scotty had been on their way to archery when Eddie came towards them. "Can we do something else?" he asked. "Rusty and Andy are back there." He seemed extremely upset.

"Of course, man! What happened?" Mark asked, already aware of what he was going to say.

"Andy is what's wrong!" he said, kicking a nearby trash can. "He just started messing with me! Out of nowhere, calling me a crybaby and a wimp!" He looked like he wanted to punch something.

"It's probably best that you left archery," Scotty said.

"Can you believe that guy?!" Eddie said. "We've been friends like forever! And he calls me a wimp because I don't like hanging out with Rusty!" He was pacing now. "He told me to get lost!"

"Eddie!" Mark said, grabbing his arm and stopping him. "Dude, hold on!" He waited for him to chill out and look at him. Mark looked around and lowered his voice. "I asked Andy to do that."

"What?" Eddie asked, looking real confused. "Why? What are you talking about, Mark?"

"Do you remember when I asked Andy if I could talk to him earlier?" Mark asked and Eddie nodded. "Well, we both agreed that you were miserable around Rusty but there was no easy way to get you away from him." Mark held up his hands. "And now you are."

Eddie stared at him for several seconds, before he smiled. "Are you telling me that was all an act?" Mark nodded. "I'm free from Rusty?" Again, Mark nodded.

"Yeah," Scotty said. "As long as Rusty bought it."

"Well, he looked as shocked as I did," Eddie said. "He even tried to calm Andy down."

"So," Mark said. "How does volleyball sound?"

"I can't believe that punk!" Eddie said, as they headed towards the volleyball court. "He was quite convincing, though."

"Yeah, well you two have to stay mad at each other for the rest of the week, for it to work," Mark said.

"So maybe I'll slug him later," Eddie said with a laugh.

They arrived just as the captains were picking teams. "I'll take Eddie!" Charles yelled. "You guys can have Mark and Scotty!" He laughed.

"Wow, thanks, Charles!" Mark said. "We love you too!"

"Sorry you have to be on the losing team, Eddie!" Scotty said.

"Whatever, guys!" Charles said with a hearty laugh. "I am never on the losing team!"

"The enemy remains quiet, my Captain!" the warrior angel, Brandon, said. Having just made his rounds in the camp, he met Daniel and two others in the sky above. "Other than a few exceptions, they remain across the lake."

"Yes," Daniel replied. "Our presence may have thwarted their plans." He turned to gaze across the large body of water. "We must, however, remain vigilant. There are two things I am certain of, Brandon: They will attack, and they will do so without mercy." He turned to face his warrior. "How many are we?"

"We are ten thousand strong and ready, sir!" Brandon replied. "Nothing will be made easy for our enemy, I can assure you, Captain."

Daniel smiled. "And Adam?"

"It was a brilliant plan to have him as the personal guard of Gabi and Brianna, sir. They are perhaps the safest children on Earth, at the present time." Brandon smiled and they both glanced down to see Adam standing on the water between both girl's boats. He glanced back and forth, his hand gripping the hilt of his sheathed sword.

"He is, with no doubt, a warrior among warriors," Daniel admitted. "And speaking of mighty warriors, has there been any word from Chaz?"

"He has assured me that all is well with the McGee cabin. Though the enemy has made his presence known, he is not foolish enough to strike with Chaz so close."

"That would be foolish indeed, Brandon," Daniel replied, scanning the camp. His eyes fell on the volleyball game near the lake, where Charles had just spiked the ball on Scotty and laughed loudly as he helped his friend up. "Foolish indeed."

That evening at the campfire service, the worship team started off by singing Happy Birthday to Mark. Scotty, Gabi, Brianna, Billy, and Eddie all laughed at him as he stood there embarrassed.

Maria was sitting between Gabi and Brianna and had seemed to be in deep thought ever since her long talk with Gabi in the boat earlier. Gabi had answered all of her questions about becoming and being a Christian. She hadn't been ready to make a decision, but Gabi felt like she was close.

Mark looked over at Daisy, who sat on the row in front of him. She had pretty much avoided him like the plague ever since their earlier conversation. He wasn't sure if it was because she had hoped he'd liked her, he'd hurt her feelings, or because he had tried to talk about God. He had mentioned it to Gabi and hoped that she would get a chance to talk to Daisy. Perhaps Daisy would be more open to listen to Gabi. It did appear, however, that one good thing had come from his talk with Daisy. He had not seen her flirting with a single boy all day.

One of the female counselors, Mindy, was that night's speaker. She was hilarious as she told stories of previous year's camp experiences.

During the altar call, Gabi leaned forward and tapped Daisy's shoulder. "I'd be willing to walk down with you if you want to go to the altar."

"Nope," Daisy said. "I'm good...but thank you."

"Yep," Gabi said, patting her arm and leaning back. She gave Mark a glance and shook her head.

Brianna walked over and slid between Rusty and Andy. "Hey," she said in Andy's ear.

"Um...hey," Andy replied, clearly confused.

"Will you go to the altar with me?" Brianna asked, seeing him look over at Rusty.

"I told you, Brianna. That stuff's not for me."

"Wow!" Rusty whispered as loud as he could, over the music. "You guys are relentless! The boy said no!"

Brianna turned her attention to Rusty. "How about you, Rusty?" she asked. "Would you like to accept Jesus Christ as your personal..."

"Not in this lifetime!" Rusty yelled this time. People began to look over at them. He stood up and pointed back toward her seat. "Just stop harassing us!"

Brianna looked back at Andy. "Don't let him continue to control you, Andy."

"Hey!" Rusty grabbed her arm and within a second Charles had grabbed him by the shoulder and spun him around.

"Is there a problem?" Charles asked, leaning in close to Rusty.

"Nope," Rusty said. "Not unless you want there to be."

"It's okay, Charles," Brianna said, standing up next to the two boys. "Rusty, just sit down. I'm going back to my seat."

Rusty looked over at her and smiled. "Good idea." He looked back at Charles and sat down. Brianna pulled Charles away and they both took their seats.

Mr. Bret appeared at the end of the row and motioned for Rusty to join him. Rusty let out a loud groan and obeyed.

Maria leaned over to Brianna. "What in the world?" Brianna only smiled at her. "Well, you sure did something to ruffle ol' Rusty's feathers." She looked down to see Mr. Bret giving him a good talking to. She looked over at Gabi. "Listen, don't be offended because I haven't, you know, gotten saved. It's just...I don't trust so easily." Gabi smiled and nodded. "Just give me a little more time."

Gabi put her arm around her. "Of course, we will, and remember that we are here for you. Don't hesitate to ask me or

Brianna anything." She pulled Maria into a hug. "Can I pray for you?" Maria nodded and Gabi could tell she was crying. "Father, I lift up Maria to you right now. I pray that you would give her a clear mind. That you would completely and totally reveal yourself to her. Show her your love for her, God. I pray your blessings over her life. Give her a peace that passes all understanding and wisdom like she's never known. She is your child, God. Wrap your arms of love around her in Jesus' name...Amen."

Maria looked up with tear stained eyes and smiled at Gabi. "He's already showing me His love." They hugged again.

As the campers were dismissed and told to head back to their cabins, little did they know what lurked in the shadows beyond. Under the cover of night and hidden behind the thickness of the forest, they were watched by evil eyes. Plans were being made to snare them. To deceive them. To seduce, entice and steal their souls forever.

"Hold your ground," a large demon said to the hordes of hell under his command. Each of them possessed a blood lust for these children that could not be contained. Their goal for tonight was to cause nightmares, to remind failures, to reveal weaknesses, to take back what the enemy had stolen this week. Their swords and bows were at the ready. They also desired blood. Not just any blood, though any blood would satisfy them. There was one...one they wanted more than the others. "The enemy is aware of our presence," the large demon said. "We must strike as swift as hammer to nail."

"Mark!" Mr. Bret called. "Scotty, Gabi, Billy, Brianna!" They all looked back from the trek to their cabins. "We need to have a quick meeting!" He called from the front of the Mess Hall. Each of them headed over. "Is everybody okay?" he asked. They all nodded. "Any problems in your rooms?"

"Girl cabin is good!" Gabi said.

"Boys too!" Scotty added. "As long as Brianna stops harassing Andy and Rusty!" Everybody laughed.

"Hey!" Brianna yelled.

"Okay, great!" Mr. Bret said. "I just wanted to check in. Don't hesitate to let me know of any problems."

"Yes, sir," they all said.

"And make your devotions count," he said. "Most of them won't have this kind of stability when they get home. Mark, let me know if Rusty gets out of line. Okay, good night." He waved them off and headed into the Mess Hall for a sponsors meeting.

"So, Gabi, what did Daisy say?" Mark asked as they headed back toward the cabins.

Just then, a brilliant flash of light appeared right in front of them. They each stopped and covered their eyes wondering who could've done that. All the other campers had already gone inside. There was nobody out except them and...

"Topher!?" Scotty yelled, being the first to look up. There stood their angelic friend in jean shorts, a polo shirt and sandals. They all ran to hug him...except Brianna, who had immediately dropped to her knees and began to praise Jesus.

"She's cool!" Topher said. "I really like her."

"Topher!" Billy said. "What are you doing here?"

"This is so awesome!" Scotty said. "I never thought we'd see you again!" Gabi was hugging him tight and crying into his shirt. Mark just stood there smiling, wondering what kind of craziness could have possibly brought Topher back into their lives.

"Hello, Mark McGee!" Topher said, with a big smile on his face. "Christ be praised!"

"Christ be praised!" Mark replied with a quizzical expression on his face.

"You are concerned by my appearance," Topher said. It was a statement, not a question. Mark nodded.

"Extremely," Mark replied. "Angels rarely show up to discuss the weather."

Topher smiled. "Try telling Noah that."

"Wait!" Billy said. "There's going to be a flood?"

Topher laughed and gave Gabi another squeeze. She backed away and wiped her eyes. "No floods tonight!"

"So, what?" Scotty asked. "Do we have another mission?"

"You always have a mission, Scotty Morgan!" Topher replied. "Every morning you wake up, you take on the responsibility of a new mission." Scotty smiled at him. "But quickly!" Topher said, motioning for each of them to come close. "Everyone, gather around!" He looked up and turned in a circle as if watching something in the sky. They all stepped closer with Brianna in the center. Topher locked eyes with her and smiled really big. "Hello, Brianna Bowers, I've heard big things about you."

"What?" She looked totally shocked. "What kinds of things?"

"BIG things," he said with an air of excitement. "The Father speaks of you often when He converses with the devil."

"Wait…WHAT?!" Brianna said, stepping forward.

Topher held his hand up and looked to the sky.

"He does this often," Scotty whispered to Brianna.

"You must each remain alert," Topher said, looking directly at Mark. "The enemy is planning an attack."

"An attack?" Mark asked. "What…"

"I do not know many details," Topher said. "Only that there is a strong demonic presence around this camp."

"So…what do we do?" Billy asked.

"We pray," Gabi said. "Like never before."

"Yes!" Topher shouted. "And be encouraged! There are more than just demons in your midst! You are not alone!" He stepped back, away from the group.

"Wait, don't leave us, Topher!" Scotty said.

Topher smiled at him and then turned his attention to Mark, with a concerned look. "Do you remember your last dream, Mark McGee?"

"The one where Scotty was with me?" Mark asked, as he remembered the gory details of seeing himself and his friends all covered in blood.

Topher nodded. "Pray!" And he was gone.

Two hours later, everyone was tucked into their beds and sound asleep. All was quiet at Camp Ricochet. Not a frog was croaking. Not a cricket was chirping. It was eerily quiet. Unless of course, you could hear the approaching army of demons on a mission of destruction. Thousands approached and circled the tiny cabins that sat deep in the North Georgia forest. Their targets were two cabins in particular, but for most of the demonic horde, blood was blood. They approached in complete silence. Swords drawn. Arrows set to bows.

Charles had insisted that the guys pray one more time before bed, despite the grumblings of Rusty and Andy. Mark, Scotty and Billy had taken turns praying over the camp and the kids within it.

Gabi, Brianna, Shadow, Yvette and two other girls had gone out onto the porch to pray before bed. Gabi and Brianna had remained another hour after the other girls had gone to bed. They too had eventually succumbed to sleep.

The demons pressed in. Some were to cause confusion. Some were to bring strife and anger. Some were to bring division and hatred. Others bore the flaming arrows that were to burn two of the cabins to the ground.

The demon captain's hand was raised to signal them to hold their ground. The eyes of each demon moved to the sky. All was clear. Though they were aware of the presence of a few warrior angels, it would not be enough to slow their attack. Over ten thousand demons had been dispatched for this battle. The dragon would have his revenge. The captain's hand remained high. He scanned the trees.

Scotty snored loudly as he lay on his back. Billy kicked off his covers and they fell off the bed. Gabi sighed in the midst of a peaceful rest. Shadow drooled onto her pillow as she lay on her stomach.

The hand dropped. At that instance, a horn blasted that was heard throughout every corner of the universe in the spirit realm. As the demonic forces took their first steps to attack, the entire sky lit up with the flashes of brilliantly bright angels and their flaming swords. They had been hiding behind the clouds, the trees and even within the walls of the cabins.

Adam stood in the center of the room in Gabi's cabin, prepared to destroy any demon that entered the room. Chaz stood guard, sword in hand, in the center of Mark's room.

The demons paused only for a second. The battle began. Like ants descending on their prey, they came from every direction. They were met, however, with extreme resistance. Instead of children, the only thing they saw were swords and shields. Several demons did manage to make it through the walls of the cabins...it was the last thing they did.

Mark, still asleep, rolled over against the wall. Eddie grunted and spoke an unintelligible word. Brianna, though curled up in a ball at the head of her bed, was sound asleep. Maria moaned and pulled her covers up over her shoulder. All around them, demons were being sliced into pieces. Swords clanged, arrows flew, shields blocked.

Just then, there was a ground shaking roar that caused every angel and demon to take notice. Then, from within Mark's cabin, with liquid fire pouring from his mouth, rose the dragon. With fury in his eyes and destruction in his heart, he stood to full height. His head was higher than the nearby trees as he roared into the night, giving boldness to every demon. He let out a burst of fire that singed several passing angels. From within the cabin, he felt the piercing blade of Chaz's sword as over and over he stabbed his legs and belly. The giant angel turned his full attack onto the dragon. As he did, hundreds of demons moved in for the kill. To their dismay, however, they were met by the blades of Daniel and Brandon's swords. The demons were no match for these two mighty angelic warriors as they were sliced before they could touch the children. Another burst of fire into the forest and the dragon moved away from the cabin and Chaz's sword. Chaz, however, gave chase along with several hundred angels that had descended upon the dragon.

In Gabi's cabin, Adam proceed to help hundreds of demons find their way back to hell. Daniel joined him in a flash. "How are you doing, my brother?!" Daniel called to him as he joined the fight.

"Never better!" Adam replied, splitting several demons at once.

"The enemy has begun his retreat!" Daniel said.

"Defeated again!" Adam cried.

A demon appeared through the wall above Gabi and reached for her. "You belong to me, my princess!" Before his claws could touch her, he'd been sliced into three pieces.

"Not on my watch, filth!" Adam screamed.

"I'm assuming you've got this!" Daniel called.

"You know I do, Captain!" Adam replied, removing the head from a passing demon that was reaching for Shadow.

"To VICTORY!" Daniel yelled and flew through the walls to join the battle in the forest.

The demons couldn't retreat fast enough. They scattered into the forest, the sky, across the lake, and even into the ground.

The angels gathered in the sky and circled the camp.

"They have retreated, my Captain!" Brandon said, turning in a circle and looking in every direction

"We have fought well tonight!" Daniel called out to the host of angels. "The prayers of the saints have strengthened us!"

"Have you determined their plan, sir?" Brandon asked. "Why were there so many? What exactly were they after?"

"Revenge," Daniel replied. "The dragon failed to stop Mark McGee from destroying the castles." He looked out beyond the horizon. "It appears that he wants to destroy the boy and his friends who defeated him. It appears that our foe, Anansi, the dragon pet of Satan," Daniel said with a smile. "Is holding a grudge."

A loud clanking sound awoke Mark from a deep sleep. He jumped up and looked around, dazed and confused.

"Sorry to wake you, Mark," Charles whispered. "Just heading to the bathroom."

CHAPTER 11

THE SEARCH

"Mark!" Scotty was shaking Mark awake on Thursday morning. "Dude, we have a problem."

Mark sat up and wiped the sleep from his eyes. "Huh? What's wrong?"

"Rusty's gone." Scotty pointed towards Rusty's bed. "At first we thought he was in the bathroom, but he isn't."

"He's flown the coop!" Charles said.

"So, are we sure this is a bad thing?" Billy asked.

"Any ideas, Andy?" Mark asked, noticing Andy sitting up in his bed. "Did he say anything?"

"Like I just told the others, he never said anything to me," Andy replied.

"Would you tell us if he had?" Scotty asked.

"Probably not, but he didn't." Andy got up and headed for the bathroom. "Besides, if I'd known he was leaving, I'd have gone with him."

"And nobody heard anything?" Mark asked. "Charles? You were up last night."

"Half asleep too," Charles replied.

"Dude!" Scotty said. "I don't think I've ever slept that hard."

"Me too!" Billy replied. "I don't think I even rolled over once." He stretched his back. "I'm so stiff."

"Scotty, since you're already dressed, will you go inform Mr. Bret about Rusty, please?" Mark asked. Just then the wake-up alarm sounded over the intercom. Everyone would be getting up now.

"Yeah, no problem," Scotty said, heading for the door. "You don't think he would've left the camp, do you?"

Charles laughed. "No telling with that one!"

"Well, let's all get ready for breakfast," Mark said. "We'll let the counselors worry about Rusty."

Thirty minutes later they all headed out for breakfast only to be stopped at the boardwalk by Mr. Bret and two other counselors. "We're going to need you boys to help us look for Rusty!" Mr. Bret said. "Andy, Eddie and Mark can come with me in the bus. We'll check nearby houses and stores. If we don't find him soon, we'll have to notify the local police."

"Aw, come on!" Eddie said. "I couldn't care less if you find him! Let us go to breakfast! I say good riddance!"

"Well, I don't remember asking for your opinion," Mr. Bret said. "Scotty, Billy and Charles can go walk around the lake trail and report back to these guys." He pointed to the two counselors that were with him.

"Yes, sir!" Charles said. They all nodded and headed that way.

Mark, Andy and Eddie followed Mr. Bret to the bus.

"I hope he realizes that this is going to be reported to the judge," Mr. Bret said. "He'll probably get real jail time now."

"He doesn't care," Andy said. "It's not like he has a home to go back to." He and Eddie shared a glance. "We cool?" Eddie nodded and they fist bumped.

Fifteen minutes later, they were standing in front of the store clerk at a nearby gas station. The guy told them he hadn't seen any red-headed boys or any other headed boys all morning, though they'd only been open for a few hours. Mr. Bret drove them slowly for about ten miles in each direction from the camp. They stopped at every store and house along the way. The boys would take turns running up and asking if anyone had seen a red-headed teenage boy. After three hours and no sign of Rusty, they headed back.

"Well, if nobody has found him back at camp, we are going to have to notify the police," Mr. Bret said.

"So, what happens in a case like this," Mark asked, "where there are no parents to notify?"

Mr. Bret shrugged. "I have no idea, but I assume we'll be finding out. I should probably call Pastor Eric and inform him."

They got back to find Dean and Jasper in the parking lot splitting up all the kids into groups for search parties. Apparently, this was how their Thursday at camp was going to be spent.

Gabi and Scotty walked over to Mark as he got off the bus. "No luck?" Scotty asked.

Mark shook his head. "No sign of him."

"This is crazy," Gabi said. "Could this have something to do with Topher's warning?"

Mark shrugged. "Rusty wasn't in my dream that night."

"Brianna and I have been praying all morning," Gabi said.

"Well, don't stop," Mark said. "I've got a funny feeling about all this."

"What do you mean?" Scotty asked.

"I don't know," Mark replied. "But we ARE talking about Rusty."

Daniel stood on the bank of the lake on the opposite side from the camp. With his hands on his hips, he gazed across the water to see Brandon flying toward him.

"My Captain!" Brandon said, hovering over the water. "There are none."

"None?!" Daniel asked, quite surprised.

"Not a single demon can be found in or around the entire camp. It's really strange. Do you suppose they've given up?"

"Absolutely not," Daniel replied. "Something strange is definitely going on. Have everyone remain in place. Adam and Chaz are to keep their posts."

"Yes, sir!" Brandon said and turned to go.

"Brandon!" Daniel called and he turned back. "Be on your guard." Brandon nodded with a somber look and was gone.

Daniel remained, gazing over the waters. "What are you up to, Anansi?"

Caleb continued to follow Torheit. They'd been walking for hours and Caleb needed a rest. He was so tired and discouraged. The knowledge that Megan was actually dead had drained his will to go on. He didn't want to believe it but found it difficult to argue. His only hope was that all of this was a dream. He could hardly bear the thought of never seeing her again. They'd been together for so long. Made so many plans. He would be lost without her.

"Keep up, Caleb!" the old man called from several yards ahead. "We must not delay."

"I'm exhausted!" Caleb yelled. "Can't we stop?"

"It's all in your head," Torheit said. "Keep moving."

Looking around, Caleb realized that they were probably getting close to the place where he'd started. The mountains were equally as far away on each side. "Where exactly are we going, Torheit? If this is all in my head, what difference does it make which direction we take to the mountains?"

"Who said anything about going to the mountains, my boy?" Torheit asked. "I promised you a way out."

Caleb stopped walking. "But I thought... we have to get to the top of the mountains!"

Torheit also stopped walking. He turned around to face Caleb, leaning onto his staff. "My dear boy, imagine where you could be, had you not dedicated your entire life, to following Folly." He gave Caleb a big smile and vanished.

"What?!" Caleb yelled and ran forward. "Torheit!?" He turned looking in every direction. "What do you mean?! Torheit?" He was gone. Caleb was left standing in the very place he'd started. The very place where Megan had been taken by Death. He dropped to the ground, exhausted. He began to weep. Caleb was so far from where he needed to be, and he was too weak to move. Too weak to go on. Instead he lay back on the dry ground and began to sob. He desperately needed sleep. Perhaps just a few hours of rest. He closed his eyes and began to drift away. The last thing that he heard was a clicking sound in the distance.

Mark, Scotty and Eddie ended up in the same search party along with Charles, Daisy, Yvette and Jasper. Each of the search parties had been given a specific area to search. Their party had gone into the forest behind the paintball area. It was somewhat thick and difficult to maneuver, so they moved slowly.

"This is crazy," Daisy said, "Why would Rusty have come this way?"

"We have to check everywhere," Jasper said. "Wouldn't you want us to look everywhere if it were you?"

"NO!" Daisy replied. "Not if I had run away! I would want you to leave me alone."

"Well, we don't know that he ran away, Daisy," Jasper said. "At this point, we can't assume anything."

"You don't actually think someone would have taken him, do you?" Scotty asked. "Cause, he was the furthest one from the door, and next to Charles, he was the biggest guy in the room."

"Not to mention, they would have quickly realized their mistake and returned him as soon as possible," Yvette added, with a laugh.

"Okay, most likely he has run away," Jasper said. "We still have to look everywhere."

Mark made his way as close to Daisy as he could. "Hey, Daisy," he said quietly, so only she could hear.

"Hey, Mark!" she replied, a little too loud. "How are you doing?"

"I'm good, Daisy," he said. "And yourself?"

"Just dandy," she said, wiping her brow. "Spending one of my last days at camp trekking through the woods looking for some loser that probably doesn't even want to be found." She stopped abruptly. "Agghh! Are you serious right now!?"

"What is it?" Mark asked and stepped closer. The others stopped to look at her.

"My shirt just ripped on this stupid thorn bush! OH! MY!..."

"Daisy!" Jasper said and she looked over at him. "Focus!"

She rolled her eyes. "This sucks," she mumbled and then noticed Mark standing right beside her. "Do you need something?"

"Nope. Just making sure you're okay."

"Why, Mark? Do you want to pray for me? Get me saved?" She stomped away.

Mark looked over to see Scotty and Charles looking at him and chuckling.

"Rusty!" Jasper yelled and everyone jumped. "Let's all try and stay focused on the task at hand, please."

Gabi, Brianna, Shadow, Andy, Billy, Maria, and Dean were all in a group together. They had headed out in the direction behind the cabins and toward the main road. They were randomly calling Rusty's name.

"I'm telling you guys," Andy said. "If Rusty ran away, he's in another state by now. The guy is quite resourceful."

"Yeah, well it's still our job to look for him," Dean replied.

"It's not my job," Andy said. "We're just wasting our time... of course, this entire week has been a waste of My time."

"What are we keeping you from, Andy?" Billy asked. "Bullying small children? Trashing neighborhoods? Stealing bicycles or skateboards?"

"Whatever, I'm just saying... we're not going to find Rusty. Besides, aren't you guys supposed to feed us? We didn't even have breakfast."

"We're meeting back up at the Mess Hall at one for lunch," Dean said. "I don't think you'll starve, dude."

"I just find it difficult to believe that Rusty never said anything about running off to the one guy he's been hanging out with all week," Billy said, looking at Andy.

"Hey!" Andy said, holding his hands up. "I was just as shocked as everyone else. He never even hinted that he was leaving. Trust me, if he had, I'd have helped him plan it...and gone with him."

"Gone where, Andy?" Brianna asked. "You guys don't have any money or any place to stay. You're an entire state away from home."

"Gone away from this stupid place," Andy replied.

"This stupid place that is trying to help you?" Gabi asked.

"By shoving their beliefs down my throat!" Andy stopped walking and looked at her. "It's a stupid place with stupid beliefs in a stupid God!"

"Okay, Andy," Dean said, as calmly as he could. "We get the point. Now, let's keep moving."

"Dude, that was beautiful!" Billy said to Andy. "You really should write poetry."

"I'm so done here!" Andy said. "Sorry, Dean, but I'm heading back! We're never going to find Rusty and honestly I couldn't care less if he was dead!" He turned around and headed back in the direction they'd just come from.

"Andy!" Dean called after him. "We have to stay together!"

"Not my problem!

"You DO realize that I'm the one that will be writing up your report to give to the judge, don't you?" Dean asked.

Andy stopped and turned around. "We're NOT going to find him, Dean!"

"So, what do you suggest, Andy? We not search for kids when they go missing? We just assume we'll never find them? I'm sure the authorities and parents of all the kids here will like that!" He walked back to where Andy stood. "Listen, I know that you're upset that your friend left without telling you, but we HAVE to look for him and we HAVE to stay together."

"ALL of my friends leave!" Andy replied. "And they NEVER come back!" Andy replied. "First Todd and now Rusty!" He hung his head and sighed. "Whatever, let's just get this over with."

Dean looked at Gabi and she just nodded. "Thank you, Andy." They began walking again.

"Can we sing a song?" Billy asked.

"No!" the rest of them said in unison.

"How far do we have to go?" Eddie asked after they'd been trekking through the thick forest for over an hour.

"All the way to the property line," Jasper answered. "There should be a fence up here somewhere."

"I spent five days trying to get away from this jerk and now you have me hiking through the woods looking for him," Eddie said, causing Scotty to laugh.

"Andy is probably the only one searching that actually wants to find him," Yvette said.

"Rusty!" Jasper called, cupping his hands over his mouth. "Rusty!" He looked back at the group. "Anyone know his last name?"

"Staggerbush," Eddie replied. "What a name."

"Yeah, I thought Billy's last name was bad enough," Scotty added. "Mumpower."

"Are you serious?" Jasper asked with a laugh. "The guy's actual name is Rusty Staggerbush?"

"Yep," Eddie replied. "Sad but true."

"That's actually a tree," Jasper said, continuing to walk. "It was named after its crooked trunk."

"That's Rusty," Scotty replied with a laugh. "Quite crooked." Mark laughed with him.

"It's also called Tree Lyonia," Jasper said.

"Lyonia?" Yvette asked. "What does that mean?"

Jasper shrugged. "It's a flowering plant. A specific species. They can be trees or bushes, mostly evergreen."

"Well, Rusty definitely is not a flowering plant," Scotty said.

"No, he isn't," Eddie replied. "Quite the opposite."

"Well, another name for the Rusty Staggerbush plant is the Dragon Tree," Jasper said. "Rusty!" he yelled into the forest. "Rusty Staggerbush!"

Mark and Scotty stopped walking and looked at each other. "Did he say Dragon Tree?" Mark asked.

Everyone had arrived back at the Mess Hall by one thirty. Having skipped breakfast, they were all quite hungry. They each had stories to tell of their search in the woods, though nobody had spotted a trace of the missing boy.

Gabi and Brianna told their story about Andy's meltdown.

"Wow," Scotty said. "He really said that he hoped Rusty was dead?"

Gabi nodded. "I think his anger was a mixture of both Rusty and Todd abandoning him."

"Well," Brianna added. "He probably didn't tell him because he knew Andy would want to go with him. And let's face it, Andy has more to lose by running away than Rusty does."

"Yeah, I'm sure Rusty was thinking about the well-being of others," Mark said, giving Scotty a glance. "Him having such a moral compass and all." Scotty nodded.

"What?" Gabi asked.

"Well, you know how I have had my suspicions about Rusty from the beginning?" Gabi nodded with a skeptical look on her face. "So, the guy has no family, no home, no...anything. He just appears out of nowhere causing chaos for all around him. He commits some fairly serious crimes and even admits to them; yet gets sent to summer camp as his punishment."

"Get to the point, Mark," Gabi said.

"Isn't that all a little strange, Gabi?" Mark asked. He looked at Scotty. "And then there's his name."

"This is crazy," Scotty said, nodding for Mark to continue.

"What about his name?" Brianna asked.

"Rusty Staggerbush is actually a tree," Mark said.

"A crooked tree," Scotty added.

"Well," Gabi said nodding to Brianna. "That settles it! His name means crooked tree! He's a demon!" They both laughed. "Come on, guys!"

"The tree has another name, Gabi!" Mark exclaimed.

"What?" Gabi asked with a grin. "The I am a Demon Tree?" Brianna almost spit her drink out laughing.

"No!" Scotty replied. "The Dragon Tree!"

Gabi and Brianna both stared at the boys.

"Don't you see?" Mark asked. "He's..."

"No, Mark!" Gabi said. "I don't see!"

"Then you need to open your eyes!" Scotty said, causing several people to look their way. "I think Mark's right about him."

"I'm sorry, Scotty Morgan," Gabi said, leaning in close to Scotty and talking quietly. "But you need just a little more evidence than that to accuse someone of being a demon or a dragon or the devil himself. Don't you remember how Mark was ready to stab several people last year," She glanced at Mark, "because he thought they were a dragon? He was prepared to kill them!" She whispered the last sentence loudly.

"Wow, guys," Brianna said. "Imagination much?" Both boys sat back and shook their heads.

"Listen, Mark," Gabi said. "I know you've seen some stuff. So, have I. But I'm going to need a little more than Dragon Tree to start planning an exorcism."

"It's different this time, Gabi," Mark said. "I can feel it. He's not normal. Don't you remember how you felt when we met Lucius Willoughby? Rusty is not...normal."

"Well, Mark, God puts people in our path all the time that aren't what we think is normal," Gabi replied. "That doesn't make them demons or dragons or even bad people. The reason they cross our path could be as much for our benefit as theirs. Maybe God is attempting to see if we'll show His love to everyone."

"I agree with you, Gabi," Mark said. "We should absolutely show His love to everyone we meet. Rusty Staggerbush, however..."

"What are you guys talking about?" Maria asked, sliding up next to Gabi.

"Just wondering about Rusty," Scotty said.

"Yeah, here's my theory," Maria said. "He made it out of camp last night and hitched a ride to Atlanta. A guy like Rusty could work himself right into the system in a big city."

"Yeah," Scotty replied. "The prison system"

"So, how are you doing, Maria?" Gabi asked, attempting to change the subject.

Maria shrugged. "I'm good. Actually, I think all this searching for Rusty and stuff is pretty cool. It's helped to take my mind off of MY problems."

"Good," Gabi said. "You were so quiet when we were out there, I kept forgetting that you were there."

"That's me, forgettable!" Maria said with a big smile.

"Never!" Brianna said. "We could never forget you...ummm, what's your name?" They all laughed.

"Excuse me, everybody!" It was Dean at the microphone. There was a police officer standing just behind him. "First of all, I want to thank everyone for helping to search for Rusty this morning. Unfortunately, we still haven't found him. That said, we are now going to be turning the search over to the professionals." He pointed over to the officer who nodded and stepped up to the podium.

"Good afternoon! I'm Officer Daryl Highsmith with the Georgia State Police. We have set up a fifty-mile perimeter and are checking all bus and train stations. We at the Georgia State Police will be doing everything in our power to return Mr. Staggerbush to his friends as soon as possible."

"Friends?" Scotty said a little too loud and caught Andy's eye. "Sorry, dude."

"If I may," continued Officer Highsmith. "I would like to meet with each of the boys who shared a cabin with Mr.

Staggerbush. Now, that would be," he checked a notepad in front of him, "Mark McGee, Scotty Morgan, Billy Mumpower, Eddie Schumer, and Andy Cruz...oh, and you too Charles." If you boys would, see me over in the sanctuary building in ten minutes, please. Thank you."

"Why does he want to see us?" Billy asked.

"You were the last ones to see him," Gabi replied. "He'll just question you to find out what you know."

"But we don't know anything," Scotty said.

"Then tell him that," Brianna said with a smile.

"Everyone is dismissed," Dean said. "You can have the rest of the day through dinner as free time. Please, no wandering off! All guests must remain in the presence of a host or counselor. Thank you!"

"Cool!" Shadow exclaimed. "Anybody for a swim?"

"You don't have to ask me twice," Brianna said.

Mark, Scotty, Billy, Eddie, and Andy each headed next door for a meeting with Dean and Officer Highsmith.

Matt was sitting in the living room of his uncle's house. The funeral had been yesterday and there was still a sense of sadness in the air. Several friends and family members were there, mingling about. So much food had been brought that it would take a year to eat it all. Matt's half eaten plate of chicken and rice sat in his lap as he listened to a couple of women discuss how his aunt had fainted at the funeral. It had shocked everyone when she just collapsed while standing over the casket. He looked around. People all around him were standing in groups whispering or crying. He could hardly take anymore. His heart and head were suffocating under the depression. He went outside and found his dad in the garage with his uncle. They were keeping busy by sanding down an old chair that needed repairing.

"Hey, Dad," Matt said. "I'm going to go for a walk."

"Okay, Matt, don't go too far buddy," he said, smiling affectionately at him. He knew his dad was thinking about how horrible it would be to lose a child. All week, both of his parents had been treating him like he was made of glass.

"Yes, sir," Matt said. "I'm just going to head over to the park." He weaved his way past all the cars and onto the sidewalk. His aunt and uncle lived in a quiet and beautiful neighborhood. Matt had always loved how the oak trees hung over the road. As he walked on, the trees made him think about camp. He wondered how all of his friends were doing and wished he could call them. They were probably swimming or playing paintball or hanging out and laughing about something crazy that had happened. He really wished he was still there. Anything would be better than the depressing situation he was presently in.

He sighed really loud and looked up past the trees to the blue sky above. "Why, God? Why did you have to take her? She was so young and full of life." He stopped walking and placed his hand on a nearby oak tree while he fought back the tears. "She wasn't even a Christian." He sobbed into his arm as he leaned against the old tree.

Three blocks later, Matt crossed the street and entered Harrill Park. He absolutely loved this park. The giant oak trees, the flowers, the water fountains, the nature trails. It was all so beautiful. His sadness seemed to melt as he took it all in. There weren't very many people in the park as Matt headed toward the big fountain that he always loved to visit. He saw an older couple walking hand in hand down one of the trails. There was a woman with a stroller beside her, sitting on a bench in the shade, reading a book. A young man in shorts and a t-shirt was sitting beside the fountain staring right at Matt as he approached. Matt tried to look away but found it difficult because of the big grin on the guy's face. "Topher?!" Matt exclaimed and ran over to embrace his angelic friend.

"In the flesh!" Topher said, wrapping his arms around Matt and pulling him into a big hug.

Matt began to cry uncontrollably into Topher's shoulder. "I'm so sorry about your cousin, Matthew."

After several minutes, Matt backed away and they walked over and sat on a nearby bench. "How are you holding up?" Topher asked, placing his hand on Matt's shoulder.

Matt sniffed and wiped his eyes with the back of his hand. "I'm okay...just really sad."

Topher smiled and nodded. "He heard you, you know?"

"Who?" Matt asked. "Heard what?"

"God," Topher replied. "What you asked him a while ago."

Matt nodded feeling a little embarrassed. "And does He have an answer?"

"Of course, He does."

"But I probably don't want to hear it, do I?"

Topher shrugged. "You have to understand something, Matthew. The Father loves all of His children madly. They are all He ever thinks about."

"Yeah? Then why do bad things have to happen to them?" Matt asked before he could stop himself.

"Because of sin," Topher replied as a matter of fact. "His children live in a world that is consumed by sin."

"Then why doesn't He stop it, Topher?" Matt said, standing up and facing the angel. "He's God! Why doesn't He stop the bad stuff?"

Topher smiled up at him. "If I were to give you the choice right now between being a millionaire for the rest of your life but having your parents die in the next few seconds or keeping your parents alive and living a normal life, which would you choose?"

"All the money in the world couldn't replace my parents," Matt replied. "Their love and support for me is...priceless."

Topher nodded. "That's how God wants His children to feel about Him. To choose Him over their pleasures, over their desires, over sin." Topher stood up now. "Don't you see, Matthew? Removing the bad stuff would be removing the sin, which would in turn, remove the choice. That ability to choose Him over the pleasure of the world is what separates you from the angels. We cannot choose to love Him. We were created to serve Him. You!" Topher said, poking him gently in the chest, "have the ability to show Him love...by choosing Him."

"But if there was no bad stuff, wouldn't it be easier to choose Him?" Matt asked.

Topher shook his head. "Ask yourself, Matthew...if you had everything you needed and lived a problem free life, would you really need God?"

"I guess you have a point," Matt said. "I suppose I wouldn't need faith if I never had problems."

"Exactly!" Topher said. "And faith is the signature of your love for God!"

"Wow," Matt said, sitting back down. "Thanks, Topher, I really needed this." Topher sat down beside him and smiled. Matt looked down and sighed. "But can I ask you one more question?"

"Of course, you can," Topher replied.

"Is Megan in hell?"

Topher sat up straight and looked Matt right in the eyes. "In Megan's short life, she was given one hundred and seventeen opportunities to choose Christ." Matt looked surprised. "You were actually one of those opportunities just a few weeks ago, Matthew. You obeyed God by sharing your testimony with Megan and asking her if she wanted to accept Christ into her heart."

"She told me that she respected my decision, but it wasn't for her." Matt looked at the ground. "Not at this point in her life, anyway. Maybe one day, she said." A tear rolled down his face.

"One day never came," Topher said, placing his hand on Matt's back. "Nobody is ever promised tomorrow."

Matt nodded and wiped his eyes. "Can you tell me what hell is like, Topher?"

Topher looked away and thought for a few moments. "It's a terrible place that is totally void of the presence of God," he finally said. "You can't even imagine what that is like, Matthew. There is NO love. There is NO mercy. There is NO hope...ever."

"What about..."

"Matthew Allen Ramsey!" Topher instantly stood over Matt in all of his angelic glory. His wings over ten feet high, pointing to the sky. The light shining from him was too bright for Matt to look at. Sliding from the bench and onto his knees, he let out a sob. Topher reached down and lifted him up. "Thank God that you will never stare into the fires of hell, my friend...Praise Him!" He set Matt back down to where his feet were on the ground. "Think on Him, Matthew. Think on the goodness of God. Use this horrible loss to His glory."

Matt fell back onto the bench and opened his eyes. Topher was gone. He looked around to see that he was all alone in the park. Heading back to his aunt and uncle's house, he determined in his heart to remain positive. To be a witness for Christ. On the way, he prayed for God to give Him the strength.

As he walked into the yard, he noticed his mother was sitting on the porch crying, with the cordless phone in her hand. "Mom?" She looked up at him. "What is it?"

"It's Caleb," she said through her sobs. "He died."

CHAPTER 12

NO OTHER NAME

M ark and Scotty had decided to take a walk around the lake. Things had been so crazy all week; they just needed to get away. They'd slipped out during dinner and figured they could make it back before the bonfire service.

"We won't need a flashlight, will we?" Scotty asked.

Mark looked up. The sun was still above the trees to the left. "Nah, we should be fine."

"So, what do you think will happen if Rusty doesn't turn up?" Scotty asked. "Will we just go back to Gateway without him?"

"I guess," Mark shrugged. "At least he doesn't have any family to freak out about it."

"Yeah," Scotty replied. "So, do you really think he's not human?"

"I honestly don't know what to think," Mark said. "When it comes to Rusty, nothing makes sense."

They walked on in silence for several minutes. Both boys seemed to be in deep thought. Other than the sound of their footsteps, the wind in the trees was the only thing that could be heard. Mark was desperately trying to make sense of the mysteries that surrounded Rusty Staggerbush. He had, if nothing else, made the trip more interesting. A twig snapped behind them and both boys swung around to look.

"You heard that, right?" Mark asked.

Staring at the empty trail behind them and scanning the thick forest next to them, Scotty nodded. "Probably a raccoon or something."

"So," Mark said as they turned and started walking again. "Are you glad that you came?"

"Absolutely! Scotty replied. "All things considered; this has been a pretty fun trip. I've even managed to overcome a few of my fears."

Mark laughed. "Well, I'm definitely glad you came." Mark patted him on the back. "Thanks again."

They came up to a large opening where there were no trees or bushes blocking their view of the lake. The ground was quite sandy and had the feel of a small beach. They walked up to the edge of the water and stared out over the lake.

"It's so peaceful here," Mark said. "I think I want to live on a lake when I grow up. Wouldn't that be so cool?" When Scotty didn't reply, Mark looked over to see him staring wide-eyed in the water to his right. "What is it?"

"Do you see that?" Scotty pointed to something light colored and large just below the surface. "Is that a…" At that moment, the water bubbled, and the object rose to the surface. First, they saw the hands and arms, then the head with eyes staring right at them. They both stepped back as the body of a very pale, red-headed boy began to float toward them. "Whoa!" Scotty exclaimed, backing away even more.

"Scotty, go get Mr. Bret!" Mark said. "Hurry!"

"What are you going to do?" Scotty asked, looking at Mark like he was crazy. "Dude, there might be a murderer in these woods!"

"I'll be fine! Just hurry! I'll try and get the body on shore."

"You're crazy!" Scotty said as he began running down the trail in the direction they'd just come from. Mark watched him go until he was out of sight.

"I suppose I am," Mark said to himself. He began looking around for a stick big enough to help him pull the body up close to shore. He found one at the edge of the woods and walked back over to the water's edge. "What?!" Mark scanned the area to the right and left. "Where did it go?" Rusty's body was gone. He poked the stick into the water. "No way! Are you kidding me?" There was no trace of it. Had it sunk again? He stepped up to the edge of the water and looked both ways along the shoreline. "This is crazy!"

"What are you doing, McGee?" someone said from behind Mark, causing him to jump and slip right into the water. He fell back with a splash and then stood up almost as fast as he'd fallen. There, standing on the shore with a great big smile on his face, was Rusty. Mark stood frozen to that spot, unsure of what to do or say. Rusty walked up to the edge and held out his hand. "Give me your hand, McGee," he said with a chuckle. "I didn't mean to scare you."

Noticing that not only was Rusty Staggerbush standing in front of him very much alive, but that he was also quite dry, gave Mark enough reasons to not take the boy's hand. "I'm fine."

"Okay," Rusty said, looking in the water past Mark. "What were you looking for?"

"Oh, nothing," Mark said, walking cautiously out of the water and onto the shore. "Thought I saw something in the water." Rusty nodded with a smile. "So, where you been Rusty?"

"Yeah," Rusty said. "I'd had about enough of all that God stuff."

Mark nodded. "I'm sure you did. You had everybody worried. We spent most of the day looking for you; in fact, the police are searching for you right now."

"Listen, Mark," Rusty said, taking a step closer. "I know you don't trust me...or like me for that matter."

"What's not to like, Rusty?"

"It's just, I've had a rough life and..."

"Save it, Rusty!" Mark said, interrupting him. "I really don't want to hear anything you have to say." He saw a shadow pass over Rusty's face and heard another twig snap behind him. This one much louder than the last one. Mark turned to look, hoping it was Scotty, Mr. Bret and half the camp. Instead, there was nobody there. When he turned back around, Rusty was gone. "Rusty!?" he yelled. "I know what you are!" He ran up the trail a short distance, but there was no trace of him.

"Maaark!!!" Scotty screamed from far away. It wasn't the kind of yell where you were just calling someone, but rather a terrified scream. Mark took off running toward the camp as fast as he could. He hadn't noticed how dark it had gotten. It was as if the sun had suddenly vanished. How long had they been on the trail? Surely the campfire service had already begun. As he rounded the last bend in the trail, he saw Scotty just ahead. He was leaning back against a tree facing the camp, with a terrified expression on his face.

"Scotty!" Mark yelled as he approached cautiously. "Scotty, what's wrong?" Scotty was breathing heavy and staring toward the Mess Hall wide-eyed. Mark placed his hand on his friend's shoulder. "Scotty?"

"Dead," Scotty mumbled. "All dead."

"What?" Mark asked, looking toward the extremely quiet Mess Hall. "Who's dead?"

Scotty looked at him with terror in his eyes. "Everybody."

"What? What are you talking about, Scotty?" Mark shook him. "Scotty! What's going on?" Scotty seemed as if he were in a trance.

"They're all dead, Mark!" Scotty said, sliding down the tree and sitting on the ground. "Everybody is dead."

There wasn't a single sound coming from the Mess Hall or any other part of the camp. It was eerily quiet as Mark slowly began walking toward the place where he'd recently left around two hundred kids and their counselors. There were no birds chirping, no insect noises, no laughing, talking, no sounds at all.

"Everybody's dead," Scotty mumbled from behind him, still sitting on the ground.

"No, it's not possible," Mark said, stopping at the base of the steps and staring at the door. With a determination to prove Scotty wrong, he climbed the steps and crossed the back porch to the door. He reached for the handle, fully expecting to swing open the door and find everyone with their heads bowed in prayer. Praying for Rusty or Moses or their last day of camp. Instead, he opened the door slowly to reveal a dark room with only shadows beyond his line of sight. He reached to his right against the wall and flipped the light switch. He jumped back in horror when he saw what the light revealed. There were bodies lying everywhere. On the floor, across the tables, on the benches, some had just dropped their heads right into their plates of food. "Hey!" Mark yelled hoping beyond hope that they were still alive. "Wake up!" He reached for the closest body to him, a boy lying on the floor near the back door. As soon as he touched him, he knew he was dead. The body was already cold. "Oh God," Mark whispered. "No." He spotted what looked like Gabi and Brianna lying side by side near their table. Mark jumped up and ran toward them. "No!" he screamed. "Gabi! No!!" He fell to the floor and shook her. "Gabi! Wake up!" Nothing. Like the boy, her body was cold to the touch. Brianna also. He saw Billy and Eddie hunched over in their seats where he had last seen them eating. Andy was on the floor behind them lying next to Yvette and Shadow. They were all dead, just as Scotty had said. He saw Mr. Bret and Jasper lying on the floor next to the front door. "What is happening," he mumbled to himself. "God, what is happening?" Standing up, he stumbled back to the door where he'd come in. It was now totally dark outside. He could barely make out Scotty still sitting beneath the tree. He choked out a sob as he walked toward his friend. They were the only ones alive in the entire camp. What was going on? "Oh God, Scotty!" Mark cried out. "What is happening?" He fell to his knees in front of Scotty, crying. "We need to get out of here. Find the police." Scotty only stared at him unblinking. "Come on, we need to... Scotty!" He reached out and touched his friend's face and Scotty fell over, still staring straight ahead. "Noooo!" Mark screamed. "No, God, noooo!!!" He grabbed Scotty and shook him, but it was too late. He was already ice cold. "Scotty! Nooo!"

195

"Nooo!!!" Mark screamed, sitting up in bed covered in sweat. There was a sudden flash of light that caused him to cover his eyes. "What?" he panted, looking around. "What's happening?"

"What's going on?!" It was Charles standing in the middle of the dark cabin.

"What in the world?!" Billy yelled. "Who was screaming?"

"Dude, are you okay?" Scotty hung over the top bunk to look down at Mark.

Looking around and seeing everyone alive actually made Mark start laughing. "Wow!" He said through his laughter. "Wow!"

"Bad dream?" Charles asked, kneeling next to his bed. Mark nodded and rubbed his face with his hands. Charles patted his back. "You gave us quite a scare."

Mark was still breathing heavy. "It was so real." He looked around; his eyes having adjusted to the dark. Eddie was sitting on the edge of his bed rubbing his eyes. Andy was raised up on his elbow, shaking his head. Billy was standing next to Charles, and Scotty was still leaning over the top bunk. "Sorry guys," Mark said. "Go back to sleep."

"Man," Andy mumbled, getting up to head to the bathroom. "This place is like an insane asylum. Always something..." He disappeared through the door.

"So, what was the dream?" Eddie asked.

Mark glanced at Scotty with a concerned look, then at Eddie. "Just a crazy dream."

"Mark's right," Charles said, standing up. "We still have a few hours to sleep. Let's not waste them over a silly dream." He looked down at Mark and smiled. "Good night, everybody."

Within five minutes the room was filled with heavy breathing and snores. Everyone was apparently asleep but Mark. After going over the dream several times in his mind, he began to pray for his friends and everyone else at Camp Ricochet. There was just something strange about that dream that he couldn't shake. Seeing all your friends lying dead would probably do that to a person. Mark really felt like the enemy was cooking up something and prayer was his best defense.

Not far away, in the girl's cabin, Gabi woke up knowing that she had to pray. She also knew that Brianna needed to join her. She quietly awoke Brianna and the two girls slipped outside onto the front porch. Sitting down on the steps, they began to pray for God's protection over the camp, its leaders, and each individual camper that they could think of.

Adam could feel the strength of their prayers as he stood guard next to them, his eyes scanning the camp.

What neither he nor anyone else realized, was that right behind him in the cabin, a demon henchman had entered the room. Quietly and patiently he'd slipped through the wall and crossed the room to his victim. Standing over her bed, he slid his claws into the unprotected mind of Maria Lewis.

Maria was back home in her trailer. She sat on the couch watching some stupid show about who was whose baby daddy eating a bag of chips, when she heard her mother getting out of bed. She looked at the clock and saw that it was a quarter after one in the afternoon. That was actually early for her mother, who tended to sleep away the days and spend her evenings drinking and doing God knows what.

Good morning, Mother," she said in a cheerful voice as her mother stumbled into the room looking dazed.

"What are you doing home?" her mother asked. "Aren't you supposed to be at school or something?"

"No, ma'am, it's summer break," Maria replied. She had made up her mind that she would attempt to have a better attitude with her mother. If nothing else, camp had taught her that attitude was everything. This was her life...she needed to accept it and appreciate it for what it was, whatever that meant.

"Ma'am?" her mother said it as if the word was acid on her tongue. "Don't call me ma'am!" She began looking through the kitchen cabinets. After mumbling a few swear words under her breath, she slammed a cabinet door shut and turned on Maria.

"You need to get a job! Instead of mooching off of me every day! We need food! Go on! Get out of here! Go find a job!"

"Shut up that hollerin'!" her mother's latest boyfriend, John, screamed from the bedroom. "I'm tryin' to sleep!"

"Why don't you make HIM get a job?!" Maria asked, pointing toward the bedroom. "He's the mooch!"

"He is presently between jobs," her mother replied. "And he at least does things around here! Unlike you...you leech!"

"What exactly does he do around here, Mama? Besides bringing his friends over to have their way with ME?!" So much for a good attitude.

"You shut your mouth, girl!" Her mama put her finger in Maria's face. "That is a good man in there!" She snatched the bag of chips from Maria's lap.

"Yeah, keep telling yourself that, old woman!" Maria screamed, standing up now. "You'll never sober up long enough to know better anyway!"

"I said shut up!" John screamed, slapping the wood paneling wall with his hand.

"Get out of here!" her mother said to her, pointing at the door. "And don't come back until you have some money! And I don't care how you get it!"

She stood right in front of her mother. "I know you don't, Mama," Maria said calmly. "You don't care about anything but getting drunk and getting high."

"You little ingrate!" Her mother slapped her face hard. "Don't act so innocent little princess, you get high just as much as I do! Now get out!" She started pushing Maria toward the door.

"SHUT UP!" John was coming down the hall in his boxer shorts. He tripped over a box of pictures that Maria had taken out to look at her daddy. Letting out a stream of profanity, he threw one of the dining room chairs against the refrigerator. "Your mama said for you to get out! Now GO!" He grabbed her by the upper arm with one hand, opened the front door and shoved her out. Before she could even protest, he had slammed the door and locked it. She could hear them laughing as the chain lock slid into place.

It was a fight she'd had a thousand times, though it never hurt any less to be thrown out of your house by your own mother. She stood there rubbing her burning cheek and holding back the tears for several minutes before walking down the steps and leaving their tiny yard. As she left the extremely trashy trailer park where they lived, she had no idea where she was heading. There was only one thing that Maria knew for sure; there was only one thing that a fourteen-year old girl could do to make money in this part of town. The thought made her sick to her stomach.

A light flashed in her mind. She was back standing in the kitchen of the small trailer. John lay passed out on the couch. Her mother was leaning over the sink, barely able to stand. "What are you telling me, Maria? Are you seriously telling me that you're bringing another mouth to feed into this family?" Her mother's words were slurred but the meaning behind them was clear.

"Mama, I'm sorry! She cried, looking down at her large belly. "I didn't plan it, Mama! I tried to be careful!" Tears and snot were running down her face. "I'm sorry, Mama!"

"Sorry don't cut it, girl!" Her mother turned and faced her. "You need to get rid of that thing!"

"No, Mama!" she sobbed. "It's my baby! It's not a thing!"

Her mama grabbed her by the arm. "You are not bringing no baby into this house for me to take care of!" She pulled Maria to the front door. "Now you go find you a doctor to take care of it!"

"Mama, no! It's too late! I have to keep it!" Her mother wouldn't listen as she pushed Maria out the door. "Mama! They won't abort it now!"

"That's not my problem!" her mother spat. "And don't come back until you've gotten rid of it!" Again, the door was slammed in Maria's face as she stood on the front steps crying.

"I wish I would've killed myself at camp!" she screamed. "I was going to you know!"

"Too bad you didn't!" her mother yelled from inside. "Then I'd be rid of you!"

Maria awoke in a cold sweat as depression settled over her mind. As good as it might seem here at camp, there really was no hope in her life back home. She began to cry as she lay there contemplating whether or not she would kill herself.

The demon stood over her, twisting his claws through her mind. He had her this time. Maria Anne Lewis would not be making the return trip to Gateway, Florida.

It was the last full day of camp and there was a mixture of sadness and excitement in the air. All the Bible workshops would be wrapping up today with everyone having been taught the purpose of God's word and the way of salvation. Projects in crafts would be finished; some having made baskets, some artwork for their parents or themselves, some even attempting to make vases or bowls from clay. The final paintball battle would even be fought today, which had most of the boys extremely excited. Awards would be given out for excellence in many different areas.

Moses had made an appearance at breakfast. He'd been taken around in his wheelchair by his wife to talk to the kids as they ate their eggs and bacon. He had even announced to the camp that his very best friend would be speaking at the closing ceremony that night and he was super excited.

Gabi had noticed that Maria had been kind of mopey all morning, so she approached her as they walked to their first workshop. Sliding her arm around Maria's shoulder, she gave her a slight squeeze. "How are you doing?"

Maria shrugged and looked away. "I'm okay."

"Pants on fire," Gabi said with a chuckle. "Don't lie to me. What's wrong? Wait! I know! You're sad that our time together is almost over and you want a camp do-over!"

Maria gave her a slight grin. "Nailed it," she said and rolled her eyes.

"Admit it, girl," Gabi said. "The thought of not seeing me every day has really got you down. Trust me, there are a lot of people suffering from that very same thing." There was a counselor standing near the door talking to a boy who looked extremely upset. "See that guy?" Gabi pointed at the boy. "He's got it bad."

Maria smiled. "You're crazy."

"What's going on?" Brianna asked, walking up next to Gabi.

"I was just explaining to Maria how she is not the only person at camp that is totally devastated that their time with me is almost up," Gabi said.

"It's true, Maria," Brianna added. "Camp counselors are working overtime this morning. They're calling it NoGabiphobia, or the fear of no more Gabi...it's a thing." They both smiled at Maria who just shook her head.

"Regardless of all that, though," Gabi said, stepping in front of Maria and stopping her. "I want you to know that I care about you and want to be your friend." She gripped Maria's arm. "Especially when we get back to Gateway." Maria's eyes teared up and she looked away. "AND!" Gabi added with an extra squeeze of Maria's arm. "Once we finally get rid of Brianna at the end of summer, you and I can be besties."

"Wait...what?" Brianna asked, smiling at Gabi.

Before Gabi had time for a comeback, Maria embraced her in a tight hug. She held her close and sobbed into Gabi's shoulder. Brianna rubbed her back and began to pray for her. They stood there like that with people walking past staring at them. Gabi looked over and saw Mr. Bret watching them with a concerned look on his face. Gabi smiled at him and could've sworn she saw him wipe a tear away as he turned to go inside. After several minutes, Maria backed away and wiped her eyes. "I'm sorry."

"Don't be," Gabi replied, rubbing Maria's arm. "I'm here for you, Maria."

Maria sniffed and smiled at her. "I'm really going to need a friend when we get back home. I don't have any real ones."

"Not true anymore," Brianna said. "We can even keep in touch when I go back to California."

Maria smiled at her. "I'd like that." She gave Brianna a big hug also. "You guys are exactly what I need, she said with another sniff. "I am not looking forward to going back home."

Before heading into workshop, Scotty pulled Mark aside. "Dude, what happened last night? I'm hoping that was a dream. One never knows with Mark McGee."

"It was," Mark replied. "And boy was it the mother of all nightmares."

"What happened?"

"Let's just say, everybody at camp was dead," Mark said, noticing that they were about to be late. He saw that Gabi, Brianna and Maria were the last ones going through the door.

"What!?" Scotty exclaimed.

"Come on," Mark said, heading for class. "I'll tell you later."

The day went by quick and was quite uneventful. At lunch, Mark told Scotty, Gabi and Brianna about his dream and how he couldn't go back to sleep. Gabi assumed that was why she had felt the urge to pray.

"Honestly," Scotty said. "I don't know how you ever fall asleep. If I had half the dreams you've had, I would never sleep."

Maria walked over to where they were sitting and stood next to their table holding her tray.

"Hey girl!" Gabi said. "Would you care to join us?" She slid over to make room. Maria just stood there staring at her as if she were trying to think of what to say. "Is everything okay?"

"I had a REALLY horrible dream last night," she blurted out and Mark and Scotty looked at each other.

"Okay," Gabi replied. "Would you like to talk about it?"

Maria shook her head. "No, it was about my life, basically... and how hopeless it is."

"Maria…" Gabi began but Maria cut her off.

"I was going to kill myself today, Gabi," she said as a tear rolled down her cheek. She set her tray down and wiped it away. "I didn't want to cry." She stood up straight and sighed. "My life is hopeless and depressing and I really don't want to go back to it." She glanced at each of them and knew she had their full attention. "My father, who I loved with all my heart, left me when I was young. He left me with a drug addicted mother that I have to take care of while her many boyfriends try and make sport of me with their friends." Again, she wiped a tear. "I'm fourteen years old and I have to take care of my mother, who tells me every day how useless I am." The tears flowed freely now. "I hate my life, Gabi…and I don't see any hope of it getting any better."

Gabi stood and reached her hand out. Maria took it into her hand and squeezed it, smiling at Gabi through her tears. "I had it all planned out. Like Rusty, I was going to vanish…only, you guys would've found me." She looked at each of them again. "And then Gabi had to come and ruin it this morning," she let out a slight laugh. "All begging me to be her best friend and all." Gabi and Brianna laughed through their tears as well. "Anyway, I just went and talked with Mr. Bret and he prayed with me." She squeezed Gabi's hand even harder. "I asked Jesus into my life!" They all stood up and hugged her.

"That is so amazing, Maria!" Gabi said. "Wow, thank you, Jesus!"

"I think Mr. Bret is still crying," Maria said with a laugh and giving Gabi a big hug. "Thank you so much!"

The paintball war had been an epic battle. Almost everybody had shown up to play, including most of the girls. They'd all been divided into four teams and no mercy had been shown. In the end, Billy's team, Those Who Must Not Be Named, came out victorious. Eddie had been on the same team but had been shot halfway through the battle.

"Dude!" Scotty said to Mark. "Your dream must've been a prophecy of this game, because we ALL got killed."

After dinner that evening, they all gathered around the campfire for their very last service as a group. After an amazing time in worship, Moses was led up to the podium in his wheelchair. "Praise God! I want to thank everyone that has made this week possible!" He went down a list of counselors, sponsors, volunteers, and speakers. "I am truly sorry to have missed most of it, but I know that you have all been in good hands." Everyone clapped. "I know that one of the flock has gone missing and from the last word I received from the State Police, Rusty has not yet been located. Let us all remember to keep him in our prayers...Now!" Moses shouted the last word with a big smile on his face. "I told you this morning that my very best friend in the world was going to be speaking tonight! Well, my lovely wife got onto me bad for saying that. She informed me that she was supposed to be my very best friend and she was not the one speaking tonight." Everyone laughed as his wife yelled out an Amen. "Well, Baby, you are my very best friend, and NOBODY can compare!" More laughter as Moses blew his wife a big kiss. "So, to my friend that is speaking tonight, I have to apologize! You will have to settle for second place." He turned and smiled at someone off stage that the kids couldn't see yet. "Now, without any further delay, would you all please welcome a man so full of the Holy Ghost, he could probably float up onto this stage! All the way from Atlanta, Georgia...my second-best friend in the world...Pastor Randy Scalise!"

Mark, Scotty, Gabi, and Billy came out of their seats screaming as Pastor Randy walked up onto the stage with a big smile on his face. It was the first time they had seen him since the whole castle incident. He paused before speaking and just stared at the four of them. He almost looked like he was about to cry.

Turning toward Moses, Pastor Randy gave his friend a big hug and they shared a laugh at something nobody else could hear. As Moses was helped off the stage, Pastor Randy went over to the microphone. "Brother Moses, I am honored to be your second-best friend!" Moses gave him a thumbs up. "Coming in second place to a woman as lovely as your beautiful bride, is especially an honor." Taking the microphone out of its stand, he walked around in front of the podium. "Good evening!"

"Good evening!" came the reply from the crowd.

"I love you, Pastor Randy!" Scotty yelled.

"I love you too, Scotty!" Pastor Randy replied. "Let me just say something really quick before we get started tonight." He jumped off of the small stage and walked over to the four of them. "You guys stand up...is Matt not here?" He looked around.

"He had to leave because of a death in the family," Scotty said.

Pastor Randy nodded and continued. "These kids right here," he began and had to pause because he was already getting choked up. "I had quite an adventure with these kids right here...especially Gabi and Scotty." He smiled at the two of them, remembering them standing in his church after having just been dropped off by an angel. Remembering their adventure in Germany. "I saw God use these kids right here like I've never seen Him use anybody. In fact," he turned around, wiping his eyes. "You guys can sit down. In fact, taught me more about faith and the power of prayer than any professor or pastor I've ever known or heard." Everybody was staring at the four of them. "Not to mention, Mark, Scotty, and Gabi have practically been to the very gates of Hell!" He smiled at them. "But that is a story for another time."

Scotty nudged Mark. "Dude, we're famous."

Having stepped back up to the podium, Pastor Randy opened his notebook. "It says in the book of Hebrews, chapter 1, verses 3 and 4, 'The Son is the radiance of God's glory and the exact representation of his being, sustaining all things by his powerful word. After he had provided purification for sins, he sat down at the right hand of the Majesty in heaven. So, he became as much superior to the angels as the name he has inherited is superior to theirs.'" He walked over to the edge of the stage. "The name He has inherited! The name! What is His name?"

"Jesus!" several people shouted.

"I can't hear you!"

"Jesus!" everyone shouted.

"Okay, let's make the demons hiding on the other side of the lake hear you!"

"JESUS!" they all shouted quite loud.

He smiled and nodded. "Throughout the New Testament, demons were driven out by that very name. So, let me just give notice right now to every demon within the sound of my voice! It is about to get really uncomfortable for you tonight!"

Everyone cheered. Adam, standing at the back with his arms crossed smiled at Chaz, who had looked back and nodded. They both looked around at the army of angels that surrounded the camp.

"A few years ago," Pastor Randy continued. "Back when I had a real job." Several people laughed. "I had a boss named Todd. My first day on the job Todd told me that I was to go to each department supervisor and inform them of what they needed to do each day...no problem, right? The new guy, who doesn't know anything about the business, going up to the bosses of each department and telling them what to do." Everyone laughed. "Yeah, I was laughed at, yelled at, made fun of, ridiculed. Not one of those guys took me serious." He stepped off the stage and walked out to where the kids were sitting. "Then one day, I saw my boss walk up to the department heads and as he did, each one of those guys took notice. It was 'yes, sir, this and yes, sir, that!' They were literally running into each other trying to do what he wanted." He walked into the crowd. "Are you guys getting this?" Several people nodded. "Well, after witnessing that, I decided to try something different. The next day, I walked up to each department supervisor with my list of expectations. But this time, instead of telling them what I wanted, I said, 'Todd wants you to do this, this, and this.' Do you know what happened? They didn't smile or laugh or mock. They simply nodded, took the list, and did the job." Pastor Randy ran back up onto the stage. "That simple! You see, that was the day that I learned that there is definite power in a name. In that company, the name Todd had respect! It had authority! It had power! It came with fear even! If I don't do what Todd says I might lose my job!" He walked across the stage. "Did you hear me? There is POWER in a name! And I'm not here tonight to preach the gospel of Todd, but to tell you about the name above ALL names, the King of kings and the Lord of lords! His name is JESUS!" Everyone erupted in applause. "Ephesians 1:19 through 23 says, 'That power is like the working of his mighty strength, which he exerted in Christ when he raised him from the dead and seated him at his right hand in the heavenly realms, far above all rule and authority, power and dominion, and every title that can be given, not only in the present age but also in the one to come. And God placed all things under his feet and appointed him to be head over everything for the church, which is the body, the fullness of him who fills everything in every way.' Philippians 2:9 through 11 says, 'Therefore God exalted him (Jesus) to the highest place and gave him the name that is above every name, that at the name of Jesus every knee should bow, in heaven and on earth and under the earth, and every tongue confess that Jesus Christ is Lord, to the glory of God the Father!' Are you excited yet?" Several people were already on their feet clapping. "What about Colossians 2:10 where it says, 'and you have been given fullness in Christ, who is the head over every power and authority.' Just like me under Todd, we as believers have full authority under the name of Jesus!"

Mark was clapping along with everybody else when a flash of light in the forest behind the stage caught his attention. When he looked, he saw people in the forest running toward him. They seemed to be running scared, as if something were chasing them. Then he realized that it was him and his friends that were running. They were dodging trees and tripping over limbs in order to escape some foe that was apparently behind them. He, Scotty, and Gabi cleared the forest followed by Brianna, Yvette and Eddie. Just as it looked like everyone was about to make it out, the dragon appeared from nowhere and grabbed Daisy in his powerful jaws. She screamed a gurgling sound and was pulled back into the forest. Mark stood and screamed, "NO!!! LOOK OUT!!!" and pointed to the forest behind the stage. Pastor Randy fell silent and looked behind him. There was nothing and no one. Everyone looked at Mark who stood panting.

After an awkward moment of silence and a knowing nod from Pastor Randy, Mark apologizes and sat down. Gabi and Scotty were staring at him with looks of concern.

"Usually when people don't like my preaching, they just go to sleep," Pastor Randy said, attempting to make light of the situation. Everybody laughed.

Gabi got up from her seat and slid between Mark and Scotty. "Are you okay?" she asked Mark.

"I don't know what's going on," Mark replied, still breathing heavy. "I'm either being warned or threatened, but something big is about to happen."

Pastor Randy paused and looked at Mark, Gabi, and Scotty. "I really feel like we should move into our altar time now," he said, closing his notebook. "Let me just say this one last thing before we do, though. For those of you that have somehow managed to hold out and not surrender to Christ yet. Maybe you're waiting on a better deal. Maybe you want to have a little more "fun" before you give yourself to Him. Acts 4:12 says, 'Salvation is found in no one else, for there is no other name under heaven given to men by which we must be saved.' JESUS! No other name!"

CHAPTER 13

HEADING HOME

"What is the plan for the day, Captain?" Brandon asked Daniel as they stood on the bank of the lake in the early morning light.

"Keeping these children safe," Daniel replied. "There will be two angels posted over each van and bus that leaves here today."

"I would like to volunteer to go with the Gateway bus, sir," Brandon said, standing up straight. "I believe I am fully prepared for a mission of such magnitude."

Daniel looked over the young warrior that stood before him. New to the ranks of Daniel's command, Brandon was brave and true. As fierce a fighter as Daniel had ever known. "This is perhaps the most dangerous of missions today, Brandon. Do you not think it wiser for me to place Adam and Chaz, the more experienced warriors, to this task?"

"I beg of you, Captain! Give me the honor of this mission. I will not let you down."

Daniel smiled. "I'm sure you will not disappoint me, my friend. Send Adam to me."

Brandon beamed with a smile that shined through the morning fog. "Thank you, sir!" And he was gone.

Seconds later Adam appeared next to Daniel. "You wish to see me, Captain?"

"Yes, Adam, you will remain with me today. Brandon will accompany Chaz back to Gateway." Adam nodded. "Brandon is a fierce warrior. Young and inexperienced, but fierce."

Daniel smiled, noting Adam's concern. "Do not worry my friend. You and I will be keeping a watchful eye on them." He scanned the forest around them. "The enemy has been too quiet. Something big awaits us this day."

Matt sat in the backseat of his parent's SUV with his headphones on listening to TobyMac. They were heading back home and had been on the road now for about two hours. He had been so relieved when his father announced that he had to get back to work. There was absolutely no way that he could handle another funeral right now. The entire family had practically crumbled at the news of Caleb's passing. Never before had a young couple been so destined for success, only to have their lives snuffed out in one evening. Like Topher had said though, nobody is promised tomorrow.

He thought about his friends at camp and how they would be packing up to leave this morning. He sent Billy a quick text, 'Dude, let me know when you have your phone back.' Matt desperately needed his friends right now. Both of his parents were in a dark place and were pretty much not saying a lot. After his mother had given him the news about Caleb, he had attempted to take Topher's advice and be more helpful and cheerful. He'd tried without success to keep everyone's spirits lifted. It had been so draining that he was now mentally exhausted.

As TobyMac sang, "I can't stop, I can't quit, it's in my heart, it's on my lips!" Matt determined in his heart that he was going to find the light in this darkness… "Til the day I die."

Mark awoke to the sound of their final wake up alarm over the intercom. He sat up in bed and wiped his eyes. He started thinking of all he needed to do. Shower, dress, pack his things, make sure the room isn't a disaster…

"Dude, where's Charles?" Billy asked, pointing at Charles' made up bed. "All his things are gone."

"No idea," Mark replied. "Did he say anything to you guys?"

Scotty climbed off the top bunk. "I wonder if his group left early."

"Still, you'd think he would say goodbye," Billy said.

"He wasn't with a group," Mark said. "He lives in the area. He said he knows Moses."

"Great, you lost another one, McGee," Andy said. "You're quite the leader."

"I'm heading to the shower," Eddie said.

"Yeah, me too," Andy said. "Before McGee misplaces me."

Mark stared at Charles' empty bed for a few seconds. "Let's just get ready, I'll ask Dean about Charles at breakfast."

Forty-five minutes later, and still no word on Charles, the guys headed to breakfast carrying their bags. The plan was to leave directly after they ate. "We have a long trip ahead of us," Mr. Bret had said last night before they'd all gone to their cabins. He'd told the girls to leave their bags on their front porch since their cabin was so much closer to the bus.

As they entered the Mess Hall, Mark made his way over to the table where Dean and Jasper were sitting. "Good morning, guys!" he said.

"Well, if it isn't the legendary Mark McGee!" Dean said with a big smile. "Pastor Randy told us a little bit about your adventures. Hit me here!" Dean held up his fist and Mark pounded it. "Keep the faith, my friend!" Jasper just looked at Mark with a big grin.

"Listen," Mark said. "Do you guys know where Charles is? His bed was made, and he was gone this morning without a word."

"You didn't lose another camper, did you, Mark?" Jasper asked with a concerned look on his face.

Mark shrugged. "I..."

"Just kidding," Jasper said with a laugh. "Actually, he had to go in to work. We got a call early this morning. He said he didn't want to wake you guys but to tell you that he would be in touch."

"Oh good," Mark said. "As long as everything is okay."

"Charles is good people, isn't he?" Dean said.

"Yes, he is," Mark replied. "Well, thanks guys." He went over and joined the others in the food line.

After breakfast, Mr. Bret had Mark, Scotty, and Eddie load the luggage onto the bus. Everyone else was told to use the restroom and say their goodbyes. He then proceeded to hustle them onto the bus. They all reclaimed their same seats with Andy and Billy now having one to themselves.

Instead of taking his place in the driver's seat, Mr. Bret plopped down next to Maria. "How are you doing?"

She shrugged. "Okay, I guess. Not looking forward to going home. I suppose this is where trusting God begins." She gave him a weak smile.

"It'll all work out. You have new friends now." He looked over and winked at Gabi, who was watching him. "And I'm only a phone call away." He handed her a piece of paper with his phone number on it. "Put this in your phone." He stood up. "Which reminds me!" He took out the bin and asked Brianna to hand out the electronic devices. He looked down at Maria, who still looked like she was about to be sick. "I promise you; God has everything under control."

"I know," she said with a smile. "I just wish things could stay like they've been all week."

Mr. Bret nodded and took his seat. "Okay, everybody!" he said as he started the bus. "Keep your hands and feet inside the bus at all times!"

"Very funny!" Gabi replied.

"But seriously," Mr. Bret added. "I hope you guys had a great week. I know it was interesting at times, but all in all, I think it went well."

"Yeah!" Andy yelled a little too loud. "We only lost one kid! Sounds pretty awesome to me!"

"He'll turn up!" Mr. Bret said. "And we didn't lose Rusty. He ran away."

"Andy's just mad because Rusty didn't invite him to go with him," Billy said.

"No! Andy's mad because he had to spend a week at this place having religion shoved down his throat!" Andy replied.

"Okay," Mr. Bret said. "Let's be nice." He started down the long, bumpy drive to the main road.

"I don't even want to listen to my old music anymore," Shadow said. "Gabi, you guys will have to hook me up with some good Christian music."

"Absolutely," Gabi said, going back to Shadow's seat. "Here, check this out." She handed Shadow her ear buds. She put them in and smiled.

"Oh wow, that's really good!" Shadow said a little too loud. "Who is this?"

"His name is Phil Whickam," Gabi said. "There are plenty of artists on there that you will love." She handed Shadow her iPod. "Keep it for the trip."

"Wow, thank you so much!" Shadow gave her a hug. "You guys are so awesome!"

Gabi smiled at her. "But I'm more awesome than Brianna though, right?" They laughed and Gabi went back to her seat.

"So, dude," Scotty whispered so only Mark could hear him. "What do you think will be done about Rusty? I mean, if he really is what you think he is, he'll probably never turn back up."

Mark shrugged. "I wanted to talk to Pastor Randy about it but never got the chance to get him alone. Rusty's disappearance was just as strange as his first appearance. As much trouble as he was, I really believe that being at a Christian camp surrounded by Christians and their angels, kept him from being as evil as he would've liked." Mark paused to think for a few seconds. "Somehow though, I don't think we've seen the last of Rusty Staggerbush."

Chaz and Brandon flew on different sides of the bus. Each remaining on full alert with their eyes wide open and ready for an attack at any second.

213

"What does the captain think the enemy has planned, Chaz?" Brandon asked without losing focus.

"He believes that we will surely be hit," Chaz replied. "That this quiet is the calm before the storm. Stay on your guard, for the lion prowls!"

"And what about that foul dragon, Anansi? Has he been found?"

"He has not been seen since our battle at the cabins," Chaz replied. "I am concerned that he will return more dogged than before."

"He has been a thorn in the side of the McGee family long enough!" Brandon said, drawing his sword. "It is time his neck was introduced to my blade!"

"Be cautious, my friend!" Chaz said. "It is not Anansi's strength in battle that makes him dangerous, but his cunningness! So again, my friend...be on your guard!"

"Hey! I have a few texts on my phone from Matt!" Billy announced. "Aw man! Megan's boyfriend, Caleb, died."

"Oh, that's so sad," Brianna said, and Gabi nodded.

"How's Matt?" Gabi asked.

"He's okay. He should be home when we get to Gateway," Billy said and leaned over close so only Mark, Scotty, Gabi, and Brianna could hear him. "He says Topher visited him."

"What?!" Scotty said in a too loud whisper. "Are you serious?"

"Why?" Mark asked.

"Apparently to encourage him," Billy replied. "He says the family is taking it all pretty hard."

"Well," Gabi said, looking at each of them. "Tell Matt we're all praying for him and we love him."

"And remind him," Brianna said. "That in all things God works for the good of those who love Him!"

"We should all meet up at the treehouse tonight," Scotty said.

"Agreed," Mark replied. "I really feel like something big is brewing."

"So, do I," Gabi said, giving Mark a concerned look. "You guys be praying.

It was a beautiful day in Northwest Georgia. The sun was out with very few clouds in the sky. Three hours into their trip, they were just past Macon on Interstate 16. The kids, either sleeping, playing games on their phones, or reading a book, were being rather quiet. Mr. Bret would randomly ask Maria a question concerning her home life or plans for the summer; but mostly he just read the road signs and hummed quietly a song that was stuck in his head. On either side of the bus flew angels. Their eyes moving to the left and to the right, ready for any form of demonic attack. Unknown to these two warrior angels and several miles above them, were two other warrior angels. Daniel and Adam were also keeping watch over the little bus that was heading to Gateway, Florida.

"You feel strongly that Anansi will attack, Captain," Adam said.

"There is no doubt in my mind, Adam," Daniel replied. "Anansi is rarely bested. His vengeance will be unmerciful. We must remain vigilant, my friend! Not since Job, has he been denied his prey."

"So, he is the one who Lucifer sent to destroy Job?" Adam asked. "I was not aware of that."

"Anansi destroyed all of Job's family, his servants, and his fortune," Daniel said, remembering it as if it were yesterday. "We were not allowed to intervene. Only to protect Job and his wife from harm as their world crumbled around them." He looked over at Adam. "I can tell you, my friend, that Anansi was not too happy about that either. He begged Lucifer to allow him a surprise attack after Job's life was restored."

"So that is why you suspect one now," Adam said.

"It is," Daniel replied. "Even though Mark is a Christian now, Anansi will still want to end the McGee line. It has been his task for centuries, and he will not likely stop when he is so close."

"I am assuming that Bethany McGee is being protected," Adam said.

Daniel laughed. "A thousand angels are presently surrounding her. Even Anansi isn't foolish enough to attempt anything with her. Besides, the McGee name ends with Mark. When Bethany marries, she will take another. For now, the dragon's bloodlust is Mark, I am sure of it."

"Why do you not have a thousand angels guarding Mark, Captain?" Adam asked. "If that is where you believe the attack will be."

Daniel looked over at his friend with a smile and snapped his fingers. Immediately the sky split open above them and tens of thousands of angels appeared, swords and shields in hand. "Chinua!" Daniel called.

"Yes, my Captain!?" a large, dark skinned angel in the front replied.

"Are we ready for that putrid dragon?"

Chinua smiled. "That we are, Captain...that we are!" The army then vanished as fast as they had appeared.

"Whoa!" Scotty said, looking up at the sky. "Did the sun just get brighter? Did you guys see that?"

"It did seem to get brighter for a moment there," Yvette said. "Was the sun behind a cloud?"

"There are no clouds!" Scotty replied. "Seriously, it was like a burst of light."

"Would you guys please shut up?" Andy said. "Some of us are trying to sleep!"

Mark, who also had been asleep, got up and walked back to Eddie's seat. Eddie was leaning against the window just staring out. "How's it going?" Mark asked, patting Eddie on the chest as he sat down.

Eddie shrugged and glanced at Mark. "I'm alright."

"You look like you're in deep thought," Mark said. "What's up?"

"Just wondering how things will be when we get back home. I mean, now that I don't hate you guys so much anymore." He gave Mark a slight grin.

"Well, you're more than welcome to hang out with us as much as you want." He noticed that Eddie glanced over at Andy. "So can Mr. Grumpy Pants over there," Mark said with a smile. "Though he probably won't want to."

"I just have this fear that Rusty is going to show back up and start some more trouble," Eddie said. "Andy would probably join him," he added in a whisper.

"Well," Mark replied. "I have a feeling that if Rusty shows up, the judge is going to want to talk to him."

Eddie nodded and appeared to be in deep thought. "Yeah, though the judge will also probably die an unexpected death."

Mark stared at his new friend for a second. "God's got this, dude." It was all he could say for now. Once Eddie became a believer, he might tell him how he suspects his old friend is a demon from hell. It seemed like Eddie suspected as much already. "So, stop worrying about it and think about some of the things you learned at camp." Eddie glanced over at him with a confused look on his face. "Like how Jesus died for your sins." He punched Eddie's leg lightly and went to sit next to Billy, who appeared to be trying to sleep. Leaning forward, Mark tapped Daisy on the shoulder. She had been sitting quietly, listening to her music. Pulling her earbuds out, she turned to see who it was. Disappointment washed over her face at the sight of Mark. "How are you doing?" Mark asked.

"I'm good," Daisy replied, turning to put her earbuds back in.

"Hold on," Mark said, stopping her right hand before it reached her ear. "Can't we be friends?"

"What does it matter, Mark?" Daisy asked, turning to face him. "We weren't friends before this trip. I don't see why anything should change. Besides, I have plenty of friends back home. I never should have listened to Rusty in the first place...I don't need you," she paused as if about to cry, "or anybody else from this horrible trip, thank you very much."

"Wait," Mark said. "Listened to Rusty about what? What did he tell you?"

"It doesn't really matter now, does it?" She turned around, sliding down low in her seat and put her earbuds in.

"Daisy?" He looked around the seat but she had put her hair to the side so he couldn't see her face. Yvette gave him an awkward smile and he looked over to see Gabi and Brianna looking at him. He slid into his seat next to Scotty, which was also right across from Daisy. He looked over to see her wiping her eyes. "Well, that went well."

Gabi motioned for him to lean forward. "Just got this text from Yvette," she whispered to Mark and showed him her phone. 'Apparently Rusty told Daisy that Mark liked her a lot. When Mark asked her if they could talk, she thought he wanted to be her boyfriend. That's why she is upset.' Mark looked over at Yvette, who was now looking at a magazine.

"More of Rusty's lies," Gabi said. "You want me to talk to her?"

"No," Mark replied, trying to decide the best way to handle this. "Do you have Daisy's number?" When Gabi nodded, Mark asked her for it.

"The good news," Gabi said, "is that she didn't flirt with anymore boys after your talk."

"The bad news," Brianna added, "is that she hardly spoke to anyone at all."

As soon as Mark got her number, he typed, 'Hey Daisy, I just found out what Rusty told u. I'm sorry he lied to u. I nvr told him that. Now, while I think u r a very pretty grl, I am not doing the boyfrnd-grlfrnd thing. I really do wnt 2 b ur frnd tho. Mark ☺.' He read it again and hit send.

"Greater is He, dude," Scotty said.

Looking out of the corner of his eye, Mark saw her check her message. "Greater is He," Mark mumbled, hoping he hadn't done more harm. "This is one of the reasons I don't want to date. Too much drama."

Scotty nodded with a big grin. "But us hot guys still have to break hearts, though." Gabi and Brianna looked back and rolled their eyes.

Mark's heart lurched when he noticed Daisy typing. A few minutes later, his phone vibrated with a text from her. 'I am sorry Rusty said it 2. Then u were being so nice 2 me and it made me think u did like me. I got so mad when I realized u jst wanted 2 tlk abt god. Thk u 4 saying I am pretty and do not need 2 chase boys. It has made me think. I will try 2 do better. Maybe we can b friends someday. I jst need time. U R A SWEET GUY MARK MCGEE!!! ;).' Mark looked over and she was smiling at him. He nodded and smiled.

"Hey everybody!" Mr. Bret said. "We'll be stopping at the Cracker Barrel in Dublin in about thirty minutes!"

"Dublin, Ireland?" Gabi asked. "I think you took a wrong turn somewhere!" Her and Brianna laughed.

"There's always one," Mr. Bret said. "It's just not usually you, Gabi."

Thirty minutes later, as the bus pulled into the parking lot of Cracker Barrel, Daniel was posting angels in every nook and cranny. There would be no surprise attacks here. Adam, Chaz, and Brandon were told to stay with the kids while Daniel and several other angels guarded the roof. So far, no demons had been spotted; something Daniel found quite odd indeed.

"What are your thoughts, Adam?" Chaz asked as they stood next to the table where the twelve were seated. "Do you agree that it is way too quiet?"

"I do," Adam said, his eyes scanning back and forth. "Not a single demon spotted all day. How often does that happen?"

"Not too often," Chaz replied. "Considering that hell takes no time off." He also scanned the room for any sign of demonic activity. "I almost wish the captain would allow us transport them straight to Gateway."

"I agree," Adam said. "But the enemy can just as easily attack them in Gateway as he can here."

"Well, I just wish they would show themselves," Brandon said from across the room. "I'm ready to send them to hell where they belong!" His hand was on his sword.

"Soon, Brandon," Adam said, continuing to glance in every direction. "Soon."

"So, Andy," Mark said from across the table. "What kind of plans do you have for the rest of the summer?"

"What do you care, McGee?" Andy snapped, causing everyone to look at him. "I mean seriously...what do you care?"

"Just making polite conversation, dude."

"Yeah, Andy," Eddie said. "Cut him some slack, man!" Andy shot Eddie a look. "After all you've done to Mark, you can at least be polite."

"So what? You and McGee BFF's now, Eddie?" Andy asked. "You doing each other's nails?"

"Or you could keep being a jerk," Eddie said.

"Chill out, Andy!" Mr. Bret said from the other end of the table. "Or you can come sit next to me."

Andy looked at Mark. "Just mind your own business, McGee. We're not friends and we never will be."

"Dang," Mark replied. "And I was going to get your name tattooed on my shoulder." Gabi nudged him.

"Hey, Brianna," Shadow asked from beside her. "Do you think we could hang out any before you go back to California?"

"Absolutely," Brianna said. "How far from Gabi do you live?"

Shadow shrugged and said, "I live on Church Road. How far is that from you, Gabi?"

"A couple of miles, not too far," Gabi replied. "I'll get my mom to come and get you one day and we can hang out. Maybe we can get Maria, Yvette, and Daisy to come over too. Have a sleepover." She saw Daisy look up, surprised that she'd been included. They smiled at each other. Gabi looked over and noticed that Mr. Bret and Maria were having a serious conversation. Maria looked like she was about to cry.

"Hey everybody!" Billy said, holding up his phone. "I just texted my mom and asked her if we could have a cookout. She said yes and we are going to try and plan it for next Saturday! All of you are invited.'

"We can all bring something!" Gabi said, knowing that Billy's mom didn't have a lot of money. "Sounds like fun!"

"Awww!" Brianna said. "That was sweet of you, Billy! A great idea too!"

"You can come too, Mr. Grumpy Pants," Gabi said to Andy. "Billy has a halfpipe, you know."

"I don't skateboard," Andy replied without looking up. "Not to mention..."

"He'll be there," Eddie said, interrupting him. "Or I'll tell his mom he learned so much at camp that he is just dying to have her give him more chores." Andy fixed him with a death stare. "Chill out dude, it won't kill you."

"I may kill you," Andy replied.

"Wow, he IS a grumpy pants," Brianna said. "Smile, Andy; you're starting to act like you've been away at summer camp against your will." She gave him a big smile and tapped his leg with her foot.

Andy just rolled his eyes and looked away. "You guys are so lame."

The waitress came with their food and everyone got quiet as they received their plates. Mr. Bret prayed the blessing and they all dove in. After several minutes of forks scraping plates and ice clinking in glasses, Brianna noticed Andy was looking at her with a mixture of anger and sadness.

"Listen," Andy said, not breaking his stare. Everyone looked over at him. "I'm sorry for being so...grumpy. I just...with Rusty leaving and all. I'm just confused." He took a big bite of mashed potatoes and looked away.

"It is kind of strange," Yvette said. "How they never found him. They should've found him by now."

Maria nodded. "Yeah, they haven't even found a trace of evidence. No footprints, nobody saw him at any of the gas stations or even walking down the road. It's like he just vanished." Mark looked over at Scotty.

"You don't think he was abducted, do you?" Shadow asked.

Eddie laughed out loud. "If somebody abducted Rusty, they would turn themselves in within the hour, and vow to never commit crime again." They all laughed. Even Andy smiled at that.

"What do you think happened to him, Mr. Bret?" Maria asked.

Mr. Bret shrugged. "He'll turn up."

"Like I told Scotty," Mark said, and everyone looked at him. "We have not seen the last of Rusty Staggerbush."

As the bus pulled back onto the highway, Daniel sent several angels ahead to scout for any traps the enemy may have set. He also had Adam join Chaz and Brandon with the bus. Daniel himself remained high above them with an eagle's eye view. He just couldn't shake the odd feeling of a coming storm.

"Hey, as a tribute to Rusty, we should all sing the Wheels on the Bus song!" Billy suggested.

"No!" Andy yelled. "Please, no!"

"I'm afraid I'm with Andy on this one!" Scotty said. "Just say NO!"

"Aww, come on, guys!" Brianna said with a laugh. "I'll lead!" She turned and got on her knees in the seat. "The wheels on the bus go round and round!" To her surprise, everyone actually joined in. Well, everyone except Andy, who just sat there shaking his head. "The wheels on the bus go round and round! All 'round the town!"

Daniel saw a bright flash of light ahead in the distance. "Adam!"

"On it!" Adam vanished.

"Be alert! Daniel called to Chaz and Brandon. Snapping his fingers, a thousand angels appeared behind him in the sky.

"The wipers on the bus go swish, swish, swish! Swish, swish, swish! Swish, swish, swish! The wipers on the bus go swish, swish, swish! All 'round the town!" Brianna, Shadow, and Yvette were waving their hands back and forth.

"It's an ambush, Captain!" An angel appeared before Daniel. "Adam sent me to report to you. About fifty miles ahead, there are tens of thousands of them!"

"Go!" Daniel ordered his army. They were all gone in a brilliant flash of light. Daniel swooped down to the roof of the bus with his sword in hand. Chaz and Brandon remained on either side with their swords drawn as well.

"The driver on the bus goes 'Move on back! Move on back!'" Mr. Bret waved his fist in the air and laughed. "The driver on the bus goes 'Move on back,' all 'round the town!" They were all using their thumbs to motion behind them. Andy did his best to ignore them as he listened to his music.

More angels poured in as Adam stood his ground in the median of Interstate 16. Traffic zoomed past on both sides, unaware of the spiritual battle being fought all around them. Thousands of angels and demons were fighting a bloodthirsty battle for the lives of twelve people on a small bus heading their way.

"The people on the bus go up and down. Up and down. Up and down!" They were all bouncing in their seats. "The people on the bus go up and down! All 'round the town!" Mark and Scotty were having way too much fun bouncing up really high. Even Daisy was laughing at them.

"Captain, we are greatly outnumbered!" An angel appearing above Daniel reported and then vanished to go back to the fight.

"Go, Captain!" Chaz called to Daniel. "We've got this!" Daniel nodded and vanished.

When he appeared in the median next to Adam, there were demons coming from every direction. Adam was swinging two swords and cutting them down as fast as they could appear. "To the pit with you!"

"Adam, my friend!" Daniel called.

"My Captain!" Adam said as six demons screamed, having met his sword. "It is worse than we imagined!"

"The horn on the bus goes beep, beep, beep!" Mr. Bret blew the horn, causing everyone to laugh. Andy just rolled his eyes. "Beep, beep, beep! Beep, beep, beep!" They were all pushing on the seat in front of them as if it were a horn. "The horn on the bus goes beep, beep, beep! All 'round the town!"

Chaz flew above the bus, spinning around to check every direction.

"We're getting closer to the battle, Chaz!" Brandon yelled, seeing the flashes of light and black smoke in the distance. They were about thirty miles away. "I could give the bus a flat tire!"

"Not yet!" Chaz replied. "We will wait for word from our captain! Stay alert and ready to fight!"

"One more time!" Brianna yelled. "The wheels on the bus go round and round!" Scotty got up on his knees to help her direct. "Round and round! Round and round!" Andy lay back in his seat and turned up his music.

Anything moving caught Chaz's eye. A lone bird flew toward a tree to the north. A family of racoons moved hastily through the brush in the forest to their right. Traffic moved along west bound on the other side of the expressway. A black rig bobtailing behind them, was about to pass on their left. A family in an SUV was approximately seventy-five feet in front of them. In the distance, he could hear the clang of sword on sword.

"Behind you, FOOL!!!" Came a voice from behind the two angels along with the flapping of the mighty dragon's wings.

"The wipers on the bus go swish, swish, swish!" All the kids were moving their hands side to side now, laughing. "Swish, swish..."

"Pow!" An extremely loud pop came from behind the bus. Someone screamed as the bus was hit with a loud crash. It was sent into a spin that caused it to roll and flip into the air crashing down onto its roof, rolling several times before coming to an abrupt stop in the middle of the highway. There was the sound of squealing tires as the big black semi-truck slammed into the bus once more before it flipped over into the forest next to the expressway. Everything went quiet.

CHAPTER 14

DEATH COMES

B rianna felt as light as a feather. It was as if she were floating to the ground without a care in the world. Where was she? What had happened? What was going on? One second they were all singing and laughing and then…there was a loud noise. How long ago was that? Years or seconds? She attempted to open her eyes but the bright, piercing light was too blinding. She squeezed her eyes shut and turned her head.

"Do not be afraid, Brianna Bowers," a smooth, deep voice like a flowing creek, said to her. "For God is with you…beware though, of the evil one."

Suddenly she felt the grass beneath her as if she'd just been set down. She looked up into the face of a mighty warrior angel and gasped. She immediately bowed her head and praised Jesus. When she looked back up, he was gone. "No! Come back!" A sob escaped her lips. Looking down she saw that her jeans and t-shirt were ripped. She quickly checked herself and found that there was no blood. She made a mental note to text Gabi and tell her that she'd just seen an angel of God. "Wait! Gabi!" Brianna screamed and jumped up. Looking around, she caught a brief glance of a bright light setting another person gently onto the ground. She ran in that direction as the light vanished. "Don't leave!" She saw that it was Yvette that had been set down and ran to her. "Yvette," she screamed as she knelt on the ground next to her. "Yvette!" Her eyes fluttered open. "Oh, thank God!"

"What happened?" Yvette asked, clearly confused. "Where are we?"

"Are you hurt?" Brianna asked her, checking for any sign of blood. She seemed fine.

"I don't think so," Yvette replied. "Why am I in the grass?" She tried to sit up but became dizzy and put her head back down.

"The bus crashed," Brianna said. "You stay here, I'm going to go check on the others." She stood and turned around to face the highway for the first time. She couldn't believe the scene before her. The small bus they'd been on was a twisted mess. There was glass and metal everywhere. She then noticed the tire marks that led into the woods where a large semi-truck had crashed. She also noticed that several people were stopped and getting out of their vehicles.

"There's someone over there!" A young twenty-something looking man was walking toward her. "Are you alright?"

"Yes, check my friend here," Brianna said, pointing to Yvette. She headed for the bus.

"Are you okay, honey?" An older woman asked Brianna, stepping in front of her. "Jack, there's a young lady over here!" She gave Brianna a concerned look. "My son is a nurse." A tall, thin man with a well-trimmed beard came running over.

"I really need to check on my friends!" Brianna said. "They're still in the bus!" Panic was beginning to settle in. "There's twelve of us in all!"

"We've called 911, honey," the woman said. "We should let the professionals deal with the ones still in the bus."

"There's one over here!" a man called out and Brianna looked over to see an older man kneeling in the grass in the median. "Need some help over here!" Brianna and the nurse, Jack, ran over.

"Don't move him!" Jack said.

At first, Brianna couldn't tell who it was, other than the fact that it was one of the boys. He was completely covered in dirt and blood. His right arm looked like it had been caught in a blender. She moved in for a closer look and noticed the short blonde hair of Eddie. Yes, Eddie had been wearing that light blue shirt. "God, please help Eddie," she whispered.

"We need to get these people out of this bus!" There was a woman standing beside it, looking over the side into the bus. "Nobody in there seems to be moving!"

"Oh God!" Brianna screamed and bolted for the bus. The woman tried to stop her again, but Brianna escaped her grasp. "Gabi! No! Shadow! Mark! No, Jesus, please!" Two older men grabbed her and held her back. "My friends are in there!" she screamed, spit flying. "Let me go! I have to help them!"

"Young lady, it is very dangerous!" one of the men holding her back said. "For you and them! Listen to me!" he said as Brianna struggled. "If you touch them right now, it could do more damage! Rescue workers are on the way." He said the last part in a much calmer voice. Brianna made eye contact with him and he seemed like a sweet old man. She nodded.

"Can I just look?" Brianna asked. Just then, they all heard sirens in the distance. "I just want to look." The old man let loose his grip on her arm and she pulled away and eased over to the bus. Looking over the side of the mangled bus, she saw the bloodied and broken bodies of her friends. She couldn't hardly tell who was who, because of all the luggage and metal and broken seats. It appeared that Scotty's body was draped over Mark's, and Maria was twisted into a strange position. Daisy's head was out of sight because of luggage but her clothes were almost completely soaked in blood. Gabi looked as if she were sleeping with her head propped up on one of the seat cushions. Andy appeared to be wedged under the bottom part of the bus, which was actually the side of the bus. None of them, however, looked like they were alive. Brianna let out a wail of grief and her legs gave away. The old man caught her as she dropped and pulled her away from the bus.

"I'm losing him!" Jack yelled out from where he worked on Eddie. "Quick, tilt his head back!" Brianna heard him say before the loud sirens drowned out his voice. Was this truly happening?

Were all her friends indeed dead? She sobbed and tried to call out to God, though no words came.

Mark woke up coughing and fighting for each breath. He could hear the sounds of his friends doing the same. Attempting to open his eyes, it felt as if there was sand in them. After blinking several times, he opened them and looked around in total confusion. He had expected to find himself on the inside of a crashed bus, with luggage and debris all around him. Instead, it appeared that he was lying on a dry desert ground. How was that possible? His mind was spinning a million miles an hour trying to put it all together. They'd been in the bus heading home. They'd been singing and laughing and...then there had been a loud crash. He turned over and sat up. Looking around he saw that he was indeed in the middle of a desert. Everything was dry and dusty with no signs of life or civilization for miles. The sky was a dark orange with what seemed to be clouds of darkness. In the distance, he could see mountains. They almost seemed to be green with life and Mark instantly felt compelled to go to them.

"Where in the world, are we?" Andy said from behind him. He was clearly as confused as Mark.

"Whoa!" Scotty exclaimed. "What happened?"

Mark looked over to see Shadow, Eddie, and Scotty to his right. To his left, Billy was just standing up and Maria seemed to be in a daze.

"Daisy!" It was Gabi from behind him. "Daisy! Are you okay?!" Everyone was making their way over to her. She looked totally pale and lifeless. Gabi was checking her for a pulse. "It's weak." She looked up at Mark. "Where are we?"

Shrugging, Mark replied, "I was hoping that you knew."

"Dude!" Eddie said and stumbled backwards. Falling on his rear, he looked up at the others in shock. "What's happening to me!?"

"What's wrong?!" Andy cried out and ran to him just as Eddie vanished into thin air. "What happened?! EDDIE!!!" He looked at Mark. "What's going on, McGee? Where is this place? Are we dead?!!"

"Hey! Are we?" Billy asked. "Brianna and Yvette aren't here!" He turned in place to make sure.

"Yeah, Mr. Bret isn't here either," Shadow added.

"Calm down everybody!" Gabi said. "We need to make sure Daisy is okay!"

"If we're already dead, then it hardly matters!" Andy yelled, turning on Gabi. "So tell us, Ms. Know-it-all! Are we dead?" Every eye was on her.

Looking around at each of them, Gabi let out a sigh. "I honestly have no idea where we are or what is going on."

"We've got him!" Jack yelled from where he was administering CPR on Eddie. "We've got him back!" Several people clapped and a few paramedics headed toward them.

"Is anyone alive in there?!" Brianna screamed to the rescue workers who were cautiously climbing into the overturned bus.

"Sweetie, what's your name?" A middle-aged woman that had come over to comfort Brianna, asked her. Brianna noticed that she had a very pretty smile.

"Brianna..." she replied, with a sob. "Is anyone on the bus alive?"

"They're checking on them now," she said. "Listen, my name is Rhonda." She tried to get Brianna to focus on her. "Is there somebody we can call? Your parents? A pastor?"

Brianna gasped. "Yes!" She slid her cell phone out of her back pocket, where she'd put it when she'd sat up to sing. That seemed like a lifetime ago. "I should call Gabi's parents!"

"Is Gabi on the bus?" Brianna nodded and wiped her nose. "Yes," she said, choking out a sob. "She's my best friend." She searched for the number in her phone. "Will you please check on everyone while I call?" The woman nodded and walked toward the bus. Brianna called Gabi's dad.

"Hello, Brianna! How are you?" Larry said in a cheerful voice as he worked in his studio behind his house. Being the worship leader at their church, he was preparing for tomorrow's service.

"Mr. Larry..." she said, almost crying into the phone. Attempting to control herself caused her to break into a coughing fit.

"Brianna?" He stood from his seat and set his guitar down. "What's wrong?"

"Mr. Larry, we've been in a very bad accident," she managed to say through the coughing and crying. "The police are here and the paramedics," she sobbed.

"Brianna, is everyone alright?" Larry asked, trying to stay calm.

"I don't know," she said, wiping her eyes. "Yvette is okay, and they just revived Eddie, but I don't know about the others." She looked over to see a police officer leading Yvette toward an ambulance.

"Do you have any idea where you're at?" Larry asked, his mind spinning. "Can you ask someone?"

"We're in Georgia I know, um...we stopped for lunch a little while ago in Dublin." She began to cry again, remembering how they'd all been having such a good time.

"Brianna! Is there someone that you can give the phone to?" Larry asked. "I need to find out what hospital they're taking you guys to."

"Yes, sir," she said, and looked for Rhonda, who was heading back toward her. There was an awful lot of commotion going on behind her at the bus. Rhonda looked sad and Brianna was afraid to ask her anything. She just held the phone up to her. "It's Gabi's dad."

"Are you seriously telling me there's something that Gabi Motes doesn't know?" Andy said with a laugh.

"Look around you, Andy!" Mark said. "One minute we're all singing a song on the interstate in the middle of Georgia and the next we're lying in a desert in the middle of nowhere. I mean, did that accident knock us all the way to the Mojave Desert?"

"But Gabi always knows everything!" Andy replied, pointing at Gabi as she leaned over Daisy. "I'm just shocked that she hasn't quoted something from the book of Hezekiah!"

"There is no book of Hezekiah!" Gabi yelled back at him. "Daisy! Please wake up!" She patted Daisy's arm. "And none of this makes sense, Andy! I don't know where we are."

"Well then," Andy said with a smile. "Maybe you were wrong this whole time. Maybe your God of the Bible is all a lie!" He walked toward her. "Ha! You wasted your whole life, little Ms. Perfect! I love it!"

"The Bible is not a lie, Andy," Gabi replied calmly. "And I've never even pretended to know everything OR be perfect."

"Did you guys hear that?" Scotty asked. "It was a strange clicking sound."

"I heard it too," Shadow said. "Guys, I'm scared."

"Don't be," Mark said. "Greater is He!"

"There it was again!" Scotty said, turning in place and trying to pinpoint the sound. He caught Mark's 'stop freaking everybody out' look and added, "maybe someone is coming to help us."

"I heard it that time," Billy said. "I think it came from that direction." He pointed to his right.

"I don't see anything," Scotty said.

"You guys are hearing things," Andy said with a snort. "You're just trying to scare everybody. Typical Christians! What's next, the altar call?" He laughed.

"Yeah well, if you'd shut up for five seconds, you might hear it too!" Scotty said and Andy turned to face him.

"How about I punch you in the mouth, Morgan?"

"Guys?" Maria said in a dreamy kind of voice.

"Chill out, Andy!" Mark said, stepping between him and Scotty. "Let's figure out where we are and what we need to do before we go punching mouths."

"Guys!?" Maria said again.

Andy shoved Mark back. "How about you stay out of my face, McGee! Before I..."

"Guys!!!" Maria screamed and they all turned to look at her. She was staring in the opposite direction from where Billy had pointed.

"Whoa!" Scotty exclaimed.

"No way!" Billy said.

"What in the world?" Andy added.

"Now can I be scared?" Shadow asked, backing away.

There were hundreds, maybe thousands of disgusting looking creatures and monsters heading in their direction. Some were as big as tractor trailers, some as small as a cat. All of them were as foul looking as the next.

"Gabi?" Mark asked. "Where are we?"

"Guys, Daisy is waking up!" Gabi said and Daisy began coughing. "It's okay, sweetie." Gabi rubbed her face and helped her to sit up. "It's okay."

"Um, there coming from every direction," Shadow said. "What's happening, Gabi?"

Gabi looked around. "I have no idea," she said, and stood up. "But if they're demons, we know what to do."

"Yeah we do!" Scotty said, and he, Mark, and Gabi began walking toward the ones that were closest.

"No guys!" Shadow said. "Stay here!"

"Spread out guys," Gabi said, and lifted her hands toward the oncoming creatures. "Stop in the name of Jesus!" The creatures stopped walking and looked thoroughly confused at this change of events. Mark and Scotty went in separate directions and did the same. "Billy! You, Shadow, and Maria have this authority in Jesus' name! Use it!"

"Yeah guys!" Scotty added. "Demons tremble at that name!"

Billy and Shadow took their places and rebuked the demons. Shadow giggled with excitement when the foul creatures came to a stop at the sound of Jesus' name. Maria continued to stand in her spot and was now staring at the sky.

"I feel like we're in some kind of sci-fi movie!" Andy said. "I sure hope I wake up soon."

"Do you see now, Andy?" Scotty asked. "Jesus is real!"

"Have you guys noticed the sky?" Shadow asked, having looked up at what Maria was staring at. "It seems to be getting dark awfully fast."

"Gabi?" Daisy said, having just noticed the situation they were in. "Gabi!? What's going on? Mark? Are you here?!"

"It's okay, Daisy!" Mark called to her. "Jesus is in control!"

"Yeah, McGee!" Andy scoffed. "Everything is just peachy! We're surrounded by all of hell here and he says it's okay!"

"Make yourself useful, Andy!" Gabi said. "Help Daisy! See if she can get up."

There was a low rumble of thunder across the sky that almost sounded like laughter.

"Um, did the sky just laugh at us?" Shadow asked.

"What's the plan, Gabi?" Mark asked. "We need to get out of here, and I'm thinking those mountains need to be our destination!"

"I agree!" Gabi said, looking around.

More thundering laughter from the sky caused everyone to look up. A shape was forming out of the darkness.

"What's happening?!" Andy yelled, leaving Daisy's side and backing away.

The shape of darkness seemed to be forming directly above them. The creatures grew restless and began to roar and grunt and make that awful clicking sound. Flashes of lightning began to strike the ground in the distance and the thundering laughter grew louder.

"Andy!" Gabi called. "You need to help Daisy up!"

Mark saw that Andy wasn't budging as the shadow seemed to descend just above Daisy. He ran to her as she began to scream. "Come on Andy! Help me!" Andy just continued to back away slowly. Just as Mark was about to bend down and lift her up, a bolt of lightning struck the ground beside him and knocked him backwards several feet. Shadow screamed.

"I am the god of this place!" A deep voice said from the darkness. "Bow before me or perish!" More thundering laughter that shook the ground this time. Andy dropped to his knees. Daisy began to scream and attempted to crawl away. Lighting struck all around her causing her to curl up into a ball, shaking.

"We bow to Christ alone!" Mark screamed at the sky. Another bolt of lightning knocked him back again. This time Gabi screamed and ran to his side.

The ground began to shake as the thunder grew louder. Even the demons and foul creatures were backing away quietly.

"PRAY!!!" Gabi screamed to the group. She looked at Daisy, who remained in a tight ball, crying and shaking. "Daisy! Listen to me! You need to pray! Ask Jesus into..." A lightning bolt knocked Gabi several yards away where she crumbled to the ground.

"No!" Scotty screamed and he and Shadow ran to Gabi.

The darkness descended and a strong, hot wind began to blow. Daisy screamed as if she were being tortured. Mark attempted to run to her, but the wind was too strong. "NOOO!!!" Daisy screamed. "Oh God!!! I'm burning!!! Nooo!!! Somebody help me!!! Mark!!! My skin is on fire! Mark help me!!!" She was writhing on the ground scratching at her flesh. HELP M..." and her voice stopped instantly. The wind ceased. The darkness vanished. The quaking stopped. All was quiet. Daisy was gone.

"We've lost her!" Paramedics were scrambling around inside the bus. One of the rescue workers stuck their head out the window and called to another worker.

"What!? No!!!" Brianna screamed and attempted to stand. Her legs gave out and she hit the ground. "Who is it!?" She cried. "Jesus, NO!!!" She watched as another paramedic brought a large blue plastic bag over. At first Brianna's brain wondered why they were getting a trash bag. Were they going to start cleaning up? Then, when he handed it in to the other paramedic, it hit her. "NO!!!" Rhonda attempted to comfort her as she sobbed.

Traffic had stopped in both directions as the Highway Patrol attempted to get things moving around the accident. All those people's day being interrupted with this inconvenience, with little concern for the lives that were being affected forever. One ambulance had already left with Yvette and Eddie. They had attempted to move Brianna, but she was determined to see if her friends were okay.

"Can you find out who died?" Brianna asked Rhonda. "Please, I have to know."

"Okay, baby," Rhonda said. "But I'm going to need you to go with these nice men here." She pointed to two paramedics that were standing close by. "They need to look at you and make sure you're okay." Brianna nodded. Rhonda got out of their way.

"Can you stand up?" The first paramedic knelt beside her and put his arm around her. The other one went around to her other side as Brianna nodded. Together they lifted her up. "We're going to get you over here and check you out, okay?" She nodded and tried to get a look as the workers at the bus lifted the body bag out...with one of her friends inside. She began to sob again.

"Can you please tell me who it is?" Brianna said through her crying.

"Don't you worry your pretty little self about that right now," Rhonda said from behind her.

"No!" Brianna said, attempting to resist the paramedics. "I have to know! What is she wearing?" One of the paramedics nodded to the other, who turned and walked toward the bus to find out which of Brianna's friends were dead.

"Come on now," the paramedic said, and Rhonda helped him lead Brianna to the ambulance. He had her sit down in the back while he checked her vitals. She looked up as the other guy approached.

"Who is it?" Brianna wiped her eyes and nose. "What did she have on?"

"Are you sure you can handle it?"

"Yes! Tell me! Please!" She began to cry again. The other paramedic removed the blood pressure cuff from her arm.

"Well, she was wearing blue jean shorts and a pink t-shirt that said 'Free Hugs'. Little blonde girl..." He lowered his eyes. "I'm so sorry."

"No!" Brianna shook her head. "Not Daisy! No!" She tried to stand but they held her down. "You don't understand! She wasn't ready!"

"Okay, let's get you on the stretcher," the paramedic that had been tending to her said. She didn't resist as they lay her back. She just lay there sobbing as they strapped her down and gave her something to relax her. In the midst of all the commotion, she sensed that they had loaded someone else in beside her. Because of all the activity beside her, she couldn't see who it was though. She closed her eyes for what felt like two seconds but when she opened them again, they were moving. She looked over to see Mr. Bret, covered in dirt and blood. He was lying there with his hands over his eyes, sobbing.

"No, God," he said. "Please no."

"What happened, Captain?" Adam asked, having just returned from the battle to find Daniel, Chaz, and Brandon surrounding the overturned bus.

"It was Anansi," Daniel replied. "He surprised us. He attacked from behind at the exact moment a tire blew out on a passing truck."

"We've lost Daisy," Brandon said to Adam.

Daniel put his hand on Brandon's shoulder. "Brandon was amazing! He caught Brianna as she was thrown from the bus."

"Chaz caught Yvette!" Brandon said, attempting to get the attention off himself.

"And the others?" Adam asked.

"Bret, Eddie, Yvette, and Brianna are conscious," Chaz answered.

Daniel bowed his head. "The others are in the valley." He looked at Adam, who nodded his understanding. "Their fight is His."

As soon as Larry had gotten off the phone with Pastor Eric, having told him all that he knew about the accident, his phone rang again. He didn't recognize the number but answered anyway. "Hello?"

"Yes, Larry?" It was the lady Rhonda again. "I took down your number to keep you informed. They just loaded Brianna and the man that had been driving the bus into another ambulance. They are also going to Savannah."

"Okay, thank you so much." Larry replied.

"They were both conscious," Rhonda said. "But that's not the reason I called you." She was trying not to get choked up. "There's a little girl named Daisy, well, she didn't make it."

"Oh wow," Larry said. "She must've been one of the guests. I don't know a Daisy."

"That's who Brianna said she was after the paramedic gave her a description," Rhonda replied. "There hasn't been any confirmation of that...I just thought you should know."

"Okay, thank you. I will let my pastor know. Is there any word on any of the others yet?"

"No, sir, but I will call you as soon as I hear something."

"Okay, thank you again. My wife and I are getting ready to head to Savannah." He hung up and prayed as he packed a bag.

Pastor Eric wrote the name of the hospital down after Larry told him about the accident. They would be taking them to Memorial Hospital in Savannah. It was apparently an hour away from where the accident happened. "Father, I pray your blessings over each of those kids. Keep them safely in your hands. Show us, oh Lord, your hands in this tragedy." He quickly called Mark's mom and told her the news. Though panicked, she agreed to call Scotty's parents and told him they would see him in Savannah. As soon as he hung up the phone, it rang. "Hello?"

"Hey, Pastor, me again." It was Larry. "I'm afraid I have some more bad news."

"What is it, brother?" He braced himself for the worst.

"The name hasn't been confirmed but Brianna said it was her from the description. A girl named Daisy?"

"Yes, Daisy Canard went with the group. Her parents made her go..."

"Pastor, she died," Larry said, interrupting him. "But like I said, it hasn't been confirmed. Not sure how you should handle that. Well, that lady Rhonda that I talked to earlier, is going to keep me informed."

"Okay, Larry," Pastor Eric said. "You guys be safe. I will see you in Savannah." He set down the phone and prayed for wisdom. He called Billy's mom and told her what he knew and suggested she get a ride with Mark or Scotty's parents. After that he called Andy's mom, who broke down sobbing on the phone. Eddie's mom acted as if he were disturbing her and threatened to sue the church if anything happened to Eddie. Shadow's dad answered and asked him to keep him informed. He worked long hours but would go up if necessary. Yvette's mom was in shock and started blaming herself for making her go. In the end, she said she would see him in Savannah. Maria's mom answered the phone with several explicit words as if he'd called her in the middle of the night. In the middle of telling her about the accident, she hung up on him. He quickly called Cathie Snyder and told her that Bret was at least conscious and on his way to the hospital. He then stood and gathered his things. Before heading to Savannah, he would have to stop by the Canard's house. Some news had to be delivered in person.

"We're in Florida!" Matt's dad said, smiling back at him in the mirror. "Are you excited about seeing your friends today?"

"Yes, sir," Matt replied. "It seems like I haven't seen them in forever."

"Do you know what time they're getting in?"

"Billy says a few hours after we get home. Hey, Mom, will you take me to the church to meet them?"

"We'll see, Matt," she replied in an overly sad voice. "Maybe you can ride up with Mark's parents."

"Okay, cool."

Matt's mom's phone began to ring, and she picked it up and looked at the screen. "Hmm, Billy's mom." She answered it, "Hello Cheryl…oh my…uh huh." She glanced at Matt, "It's okay, yes…what do you need me to do?"

Matt was already leaning forward in his seat. "What's going on, Mom?"

"Savannah Memorial? Okay, goodbye." He clicked to hang up and let out a sigh.

"What is it?" Matt asked. "Is something wrong with Billy's mom?"

"It's not his mom, Matt," his mother said, talking into her hands as she rubbed her face. "The church bus was hit by a truck. There's been a terrible accident."

"Oh my God!" Matt's dad moaned. "Not again! What's going on?!"

"Was anybody hurt, Mom?" Matt asked, terrified of the answer.

His mom took a deep breath. "All they know so far, is that four of them were definitely okay and were being taken to Savannah by ambulance."

"What about the others, are they going to be okay?" Matt asked in a panic.

"Cheryl said that Pastor Eric had just called her back to say that the others were being flown in." His parents shared a look.

"What does that mean?" Matt asked. "Is it bad?"

"It's not good, son," his dad replied.

"Okay, everybody!" Gabi said. "Just calm down!" Everyone was in a panic over what had just happened with Daisy. Once they'd realized the creatures had gone too, they'd started bickering amongst themselves over what was going on.

"Yeah, let's try and get through this without arguing or freaking out!" Mark added.

"We're not at camp anymore, McGee!" Andy said. "You and your little friends are no longer in charge!"

"Oh, and I guess you are!" Scotty said with a laugh. "That's a hoot!"

"Well, I am the biggest guy here," Andy replied and walked toward Scotty. "So, you got a problem with that, Morgan?"

"The biggest and the dumbest!" Scotty replied, not backing down. "Seriously, dude! If Todd and Rusty are your idea of good friends..." Mark stepped over and put his arm around Scotty.

"Unless you plan to take on Scotty, Billy, and me...I'd suggest you chill out, Andy," Mark said.

"Yeah, and me too," Gabi said, and everyone looked at her.

"Hey, I'm not fighting Gabi!" Andy said and threw his hands up.

"Well, maybe you are smart after all," Scotty said to Andy and then smiled at Gabi.

"Well, we clearly need a leader," Shadow said. "Why don't we all vote on who we think it should be? I vote Gabi!"

"I vote Mark," Gabi said. "I'm more of an advisor. Mark is a good leader."

"I vote Mark," Scotty said.

"Me too," Billy added. "That's three for him. What say you, Mark?"

"You have got to be kidding me!" Andy snapped.

Mark shrugged. "Me I guess, but Gabi is my co-leader."

"That's four!" Billy exclaimed. "It's unanimous."

"Maria?" Gabi said, looking over at her. Maria was still standing in the same spot she'd been in before Daisy had vanished and was still staring up at the sky. "What are you looking at?" Maria didn't move or answer.

"Maria, are you okay?" Mark asked. Nothing.

"Maria, honey?" Shadow walked over to her and put her hand gently on Maria's back. Maria startled and looked at her. "What is it?" Shadow asked in a sweet voice. Maria looked around as if just noticing the others were there.

"Hello," she said in an airy voice. "I'm...my name is...I mean." She appeared to be in deep thought.

"Great, she's lost her mind," Andy said.

"Maria," Shadow said, smiling at her. "Are you okay?" Maria looked at her curiously.

"Maria...my name is Maria," she said with a smile. "Yes, I suppose you're right...but we only just met. How do you know my name?"

"What's going on?" Scotty asked.

"I'm not sure," Mark said, walking over to Maria. "What do you think, Gabi?" He looked over to see that Gabi had walked away from the group. She was turning in a circle slowly, looking in every direction.

"Awesome! Now Gabi's lost her mind, too!" Andy said, throwing his hands up. "I suppose we're all going to go crazy!"

"I haven't gone crazy, Andy," Gabi replied.

"What is it, Gabi?" Mark asked. "Have you figured out where we are?"

"I think so," she replied, still turning in place. "But I didn't realize it was an actual place."

"Where then?" Andy asked impatiently. "Please share with the class!"

"That darkness we saw," she said, pointing to the sky. "I'm almost positive that was death."

"Death?" Andy laughed. "Wait! THAT was death?"

"I think so."

"So, Daisy is dead?" Shadow asked.

Gabi nodded. "If I'm right."

"I have a friend named Daisy," Maria said to Shadow. Shadow smiled at her and wiped away a tear.

"So..what?" Andy asked. "This is hell?"

"Really, dude?" Scotty replied. "Do you really think Gabi would be in hell?"

"Or US!?" Billy added, more to Scotty than Andy. "We're saved too."

"Yeah...but Gabi's REALLY saved," Scotty said, and Billy nodded his agreement.

"So where are we then, Gabi?" Mark asked.

"I'm only guessing, but I think this place is the Valley of the Shadow of Death."

"The place Pastor Eric preached about?" Mark asked.

"So, you were listening," Gabi said with a smile. "Yes, but even he didn't mention it being a place you actually went to."

"So, are WE dead?" Billy asked.

"No, I don't think so," Gabi replied. "Not if this is the shadow of death."

"Then what are we?!" Andy asked. "Spit it out!!"

"I don't know for sure, Andy," Gabi said with a shrug. "Unconscious? In a coma? I'm only guessing, of course."

"So, this is all in our heads?" Andy asked. "That's just stupid."

"She said she was guessing, Andy!" Mark said. "And it couldn't be in our heads if we're all together! It has to be an actual place."

"And stupid isn't a nice word!" Scotty added, making Gabi smile.

"I'm just trying to grasp how we're all together in the same place," Andy said. "And are our bodies still in the bus or on the side of the road?"

"Wow, I'm starting to freak out now," Shadow said. "Are you telling me this isn't my actual body?"

"Listen," Mark said in a calm voice. "Let's all just take a step back and relax. Nobody knows anything for sure, though Gabi's idea does seem to fit. All we really know for sure is that we are out in the middle of nowhere with absolutely no supplies."

"And a crazy girl," Andy added, pointing at Maria. She had sat down in the dirt and was drawing circles with her finger. "How does that figure into your theory, Gabi?"

Gabi shrugged. "Maybe she has a head injury...I don't know."

"Anyway," Mark continued. "My gut tells me that we need to get to those mountains." He pointed into the distance.

"Yes! I had the same feeling!" Scotty said. Billy and Shadow nodded in agreement.

"I feel it too," Gabi said. "Who knows, maybe the way out of our unconsciousness is at the top of those mountains."

"Which mountains, though?" Andy asked. "We're surrounded by mountains...and they're all just as far away!"

"I know!" Scotty added. "It's like we were plopped right into the exact center of this valley."

"I really don't think it matters which way we go," Gabi said, "so long as we get to the top of one of them." She looked at Mark. "Lead us on, Mr. McGee!"

"Maria, honey," Shadow tapped her on the shoulder. "It's time to go."

"I like this place," Maria said, smiling up at her. "May I please stay?"

CHAPTER 15

THE JOURNEY BEGINS

Brianna awoke to the annoying sounds of humming and beeping. She had a slight headache and didn't want to open her eyes. Hearing what sounded like a page turning in a book, caused her to peel them open, however. She saw Mr. Larry and Abi sitting beside her hospital bed, looking at a magazine. Abi looked over and saw that Brianna was awake and shouted, "She's up, Daddy!" Mr. Larry smiled over at her and leaned forward.

"Hello, Brianna," he said in a gentle voice. "How do you feel?"

"Okay, I guess. I have a headache." She attempted to sit up and Larry stopped her by placing his hand on her shoulder.

"Take it slow," he said. "Why don't we have a nurse come in and check you out while you're awake." He pressed the nurse button.

"You were snoring!" Abi said with a giggle. "It was funny."

"Abi, will you go let Mommy know that Brianna is awake?" Larry asked, and she quickly dashed from the room.

"Gabi?!" Brianna asked frantically. "How is she?!"

"She's...okay," Mr. Larry said.

"What?! Tell me!"

"She hasn't woken up yet, that's all. The doctors say she should be fine, though. Her injuries are somewhat minor. Her arm is broken, and she took a good blow to the head. In fact, most everyone did."

"Tell me everything! How is everybody? Is Mark okay? Shadow?" She tried to sit up again. "Is it true that Daisy is dead?"

"You need to stay calm, Brianna," Larry said, helping her to lay back down. "Try to relax." He slid her hair out of her eyes and smiled at her. "It's true about Daisy," he said in a calm voice. "Everyone else is alive...some worse off than others, but alive."

"Tell me..." The tears came. She couldn't believe that Daisy was dead. Happily singing one second and then...gone.

"Well, Yvette, Eddie, and Mr. Bret are already awake and doing fine. A few bumps and bruises, but fine. You seem to be fine, praise God." Larry teared up a bit and smiled at her. "We called your parents. They're on their way here."

"The others?" Brianna asked.

"Well, everybody got thrown around pretty good in that bus... no seatbelts and all. Mark, Scotty, Gabi, Maria, Shadow, Billy, and Andy are all in critical condition and being kept in ICU."

"What?!" Brianna tried to sit up again.

"Shhhhhh," Larry said, holding her down. "Brianna, you need to stay calm. God's got this."

She relaxed and nodded, looking up at him. "There was an angel," she said, having just remembered.

He smiled at her, not doubting it for a second. "Tell me about it."

"Apparently, I was thrown from the bus," she said, trying to remember. "I awoke to a very bright light and was floating gently to the ground. Then I heard a voice...it said, 'Do not be afraid, Brianna Bowers...for God is with you...beware though, of the evil one."

"Wow," Larry said. "That's so awesome." He smiled at her. "You see? God is with you."

"Oh! We saw Topher the other day!" Brianna said. "Thursday, I think." This got Larry's attention. "He said that the enemy was planning an attack..." She gasped. "Do you think this is what he meant?"

Larry nodded. "I would imagine."

Just then Mrs. Gae came in with Abi and gave Brianna a big hug. A doctor and two nurses followed them in and asked the

Motes to step out for a few minutes while they checked Brianna out. Mrs. Gae insisted on staying with her.

"God is with you!" Larry said, smiling at Brianna as he left the room.

Pastor Eric was presently standing with Mark's mom and stepdad next to Mark's bed in the ICU. He was unconscious and hooked up to several wires and tubes. They had already prayed together and were now discussing how each of the kids were doing.

"Maria concerns us the most right now," Pastor Eric said in a whisper. "She appears to have received the most head trauma. The doctors fear that she'll never come out of her coma."

"I heard that Bret and Cathie are by her side," Mark's mom said.

Pastor Eric nodded. "Ever since they wheeled her in and against doctor's orders, Bret hasn't let her out of his sight. Broken ribs and all, he even insisted on being in the observation room when she went into surgery." He smiled. "Apparently, they bonded on this trip." He had no intention of telling anyone about her attempted suicide. Maria would have to be the one to share that information.

"So, have all the parents arrived?" Mark's stepdad asked.

"Not all," Pastor Eric shook his head. "Some aren't actually coming."

"What!?" Mark's mom gasped. "Why on Earth not?!"

"Shadow's father is working and can't get away and well, have you met Eddie's mother?"

"Oh...I've heard," she said. "Mother of the Year."

"Actually, that award will go to Maria's mother." They both looked at him. "Yeah, she cussed me out for waking her up and hung up on me."

"Wow," Mark's stepdad said. "I can't even imagine."

"Bret said that Maria accepted Christ at camp," Pastor Eric said. "At least if she doesn't wake up...we have that hope. He also says Maria was quite terrified of going back home.

Apparently, her mother makes her bring home the money…any way she can." He paused to let that sink in. "Anyway, I think that has a lot to do with their bonding."

"The poor thing," Mark's mom said.

"Well, remember Daisy's parents in your prayers," Pastor Eric said as he walked to the door. "I can't even begin to comprehend what it would be like to have to identify your own child's body."

Matt's dad had not been able to get away and go to Savannah. He was desperately needed back at work after being gone for so long. His hope had been to be able to drive Billy's mother up, but thankfully her on again off again boyfriend, Harold, had been available to take her.

Matt, however, had not been allowed to go. He had been told by his parents that he would only be an unnecessary burden for people who were experiencing tragedy in their lives. He understood, of course. None of those parents needed a kid to worry about while their own were lying in a hospital. Pastor Eric would also be too busy to keep up with Matt, with all the counseling and praying he would be doing. Still, Matt wanted to be there with his friends.

He walked over and sat on his bed. "Father, once again I lift up my friends to you. I pray that you bless and heal each one of them. I pray that you give their doctors and surgeons wisdom. I pray that you comfort their families. Bless Pastor Eric to speak your words to them, in Jesus' name." He paused. "And God, I really would like to be able to be there with them. If there's any way you can make that happen…" Matt jumped as his cell phone began ringing. "Hello?"

"Matt? Is it true what I'm hearing about the church bus?" A woman asked.

Forgetting to look at the caller ID, Matt asked, "Who is this?"

"It's Christina, silly!" she said. "Christina Bulford."

"I'm just saying, she's kind of a downer most of the time!" Andy said, talking about Maria. "Losing her mind might not be a bad thing! Look at her, she's quite happy!"

"Well, I'm just saying that it didn't help you when you lost your mind!" Scotty replied.

"You know what, Morgan?" Andy said, turning to face Scotty as they walked along.

"Guys!" Gabi yelled. "Stop bickering! Mark, will you please separate those two?"

"Scotty!" Mark said. "Stop getting me in trouble and get over here!" He pointed to the side of him that Andy wasn't on. Scotty gave Andy a final glance and obeyed.

They had been walking now for what seemed like hours. The air in this place seemed as dry as the ground. The only things they had seen since setting off were boulders and dirt. The orange and black sky was no mood lifter either. Each of them seemed to be getting more aggravated as they walked.

Gabi and Shadow were walking with Maria, who was constantly losing her focus.

"Do you remember MY name?" Shadow asked.

"Of course, I do," Maria answered. "You're a girl!" She looked at Gabi. "And this is your friend."

"What's her name?" Shadow asked, trying to keep Maria's mind occupied. Otherwise she would either wander off or just sit down.

"Her name is pretty flower!" Maria said with a giggle.

"Close enough! I like it!" Gabi said with a smile. She rubbed her arm and rolled it around in the socket. For some strange reason, it had started hurting her.

"I am so thirsty!" Andy said.

"And we still don't have any water, Andy," Mark said calmly. "Same as when you complained fifteen minutes ago."

"So, where do you think all those creatures went?" Billy asked. "What are we going to do if they live in the mountains?"

"They probably went back to hell," Scotty said.

"Demons don't live in hell, Scotty," Gabi said. "Why does everybody think that?"

"Okay, but were all of those things demons?" Scotty asked. "Did you see them? It was like mixed breeds of creatures."

"Satan likes to pervert God's creation," Gabi said. "He tries to twist and distort whatever God does. He hates the things that God loves."

"That's why he especially hates Christians," Mark added.

"That and the fact that they're annoying," Andy mumbled.

"You're one to talk about somebody being annoying!" Scotty said.

"I'm serious!" Andy said. "Christians think they're so perfect! Always right! They're so closed minded, and always looking down their noses at everyone who disagrees with them!"

"True Christians don't think they're perfect, Andy," Mark said. "True Christians understand that the only thing that separates them from hell is the cross of Jesus. They didn't do anything to deserve God's grace."

"Well put, Mr. McGee!" Gabi said. "I couldn't have said it better myself."

"I'm sure you guys have learned tons of snappy comebacks in Sunday School," Andy said. "But that doesn't change the fact that you still look down your noses at the rest of us."

"If you feel like Christians are better than you, Andy," Scotty said. "Then maybe it's the Holy Spirit talking to you."

"Well, if the Holy Spirit is telling me that you are looking down your nose at me, then you should probably stop, Scotty!" Andy laughed.

"No, He's telling you that..."

"Just stop preaching at me, Morgan! I don't care!"

"Look at the big ball!" Maria said, pointing at a large boulder. She ran over and wrapped her arms around it as if giving it a big hug. "I love this place!"

"Wow!" Andy said, shaking his head. "Loopy much?"

"Come on, sweetie," Shadow said, giving Andy a bitter look. "Let's keep walking."

"There's more of them up ahead," Gabi said to Maria. "Look!" She pointed to the hundreds of large boulders that were between them and their destination. "See all the rocks!"

"They aren't rocks, silly!" Maria said with a child-like giggle. "They're balls! I bet we could kick them far!"

"Hey, Maria!" Scotty said, trying to get her mind off the rocks. "Do you remember MY name?"

"No way!" Maria replied. "You're a stranger!"

Andy laughed. "Yeah, Morgan! You're creeping her out!"

"Why are there shadows all around HIM?" Maria asked, pointing at Andy. "He should tell them to go away."

Everyone stopped and looked at Andy. "What?" Andy asked. "Aw, come on! She's insane! She just called Morgan a stranger and Gabi a pretty flower."

"Oooh, look at the clovers!" Maria said, looking down at the dirt.

"See!" Andy pointed at her. "Crazy!"

"Well, in her defense," Gabi said. "I am a pretty flower."

"Let's keep moving, guys!" Mark said. "We've still got a lot of ground to cover!"

"Andy, you need to consider something," Gabi said, still thinking about what Maria said concerning the shadows around Andy.

"And what, may I ask, is that?"

"If I'm right..." she began.

"And you know she is," Scotty said, interrupting her.

"If I'm right," she continued, cutting her eyes at Scotty. "And Daisy died. It didn't exactly sound like she was going to a happy place."

Andy looked at her with a serious face, as if he could still hear Daisy's screams. "Well, any place away from you guys sounds happy to me."

"Yeah! All that screaming about being on fire and burning up!" Scotty said as if just remembering it himself. "Dude, you know she never accepted Christ!"

"Whatever, Morgan!" Andy screamed. He stopped walking and looked at each of them. "Hear me right now! I don't NEED or WANT any of you to preach to me again! I'm sick to death of hearing about your God!"

Unable to take it any longer, Bret got out his phone to call Maria's mother. How could a mother be so cold toward a daughter that lay comatose in the hospital? She had not shown any sign of concern. Bret's wife, Cathie, sat in the ICU waiting room, reading a magazine as he walked in. Andy's mother was in there as well, along with some guy named Harold that had come in with Billy's mom.

Bret had told Cathie everything about his connection with Maria. How she had poured her heart out to him after her suicide attempt and how she had broken his heart in the process. Having had three tough sons, a teenage girl crying on his shoulder had brought out emotions that he'd never experienced. He wanted to protect this girl that lay broken and unconscious a few doors away. The only thing that he could do at this point though, was check in with her family.

He had her mother's contact number in his phone for emergencies on the trip. He silently prayed for wisdom as he dialed and waited.

"Hello?!" A woman shouted over loud music playing in the background.

"Hello? Mrs. Lewis?" Bret said, still unsure of where this would go.

"It's Ms. Lewis! Who is this?!" she shouted into the phone.

"My name is Bret Snyder and I'm here at the hospital in Savannah with Maria."

"Well, good for you!" she yelled with a cackle. She sounded as if she was already several beers into her party. "What do you want with me?"

"Ma'am, I was just wondering if you were planning to come up and see her? She's in a co..."

After a few loud expletives, she explained to Bret how she had no intention whatsoever of going to Savannah. "You tell that girl to get off her butt and get back home right now! You hear me?! She's already taken a week off and needs to get back to work! This rent ain't gonna pay itself!" She broke into a fit of laughing and coughing.

"Ma'am, Maria is in a coma!" Bret said while she was occupied with coughing.

There was a momentary pause and Bret was hoping that she was having a change of heart and would be jumping in the car any second to come see her baby. "Are you with that church she went with?"

"Yes, ma'am," Bret replied.

"Well, if you broke her...you buy her!" She said in a more serious tone, "I'm serious, I'll sue the Jesus out of your church!"

"Ma'am!" Bret was tired of this utter callousness. "Your daughter is in a coma...and the doctors are saying that there is a good chance she won't wake up! You need to come and see her!" Other than the music in the background and the sounds of laughter from party goers, the line went silent. "Hello?"

"Now you listen to me, you holier than thou piece of garbage!" she said with a bit of a slur. "Don't you ever tell me what I need to do! That girl ain't been nothin' but trouble to me ever since I had her daddy killed!"

"I'm sorry...you what!?" Bret asked, standing up.

"Ever since her daddy left her! Nothing but trouble..." The line went dead.

"What's wrong?" Cathie asked.

"I think I need to call Officer Ramsey," Bret replied.

Pastor Eric was sitting in the hospital chapel with Mr. and Mrs. Canard. Daisy's mom had fainted upon seeing her daughter's body lying on the cold, metal table. Mr. Canard had caught his wife and helped her into a chair. He then proceeded to sob uncontrollably over Daisy's lifeless body. After several minutes,

Pastor Eric had joined them. He had helped get them to the chapel, where they cried into each other's shoulders.

Pastor Eric prayed silently for God to give him the right words to say. The Canards did not attend his church, so he didn't know them at all. They had only heard about Camp Ricochet through an article in the local paper.

"She wasn't a bad kid," Mr. Canard said, wiping his nose with a tissue. Pastor Eric smiled at him. "It was just...she was always on the computer or cell phone. It was her only social outlet." He wiped his eyes and pulled away from his wife. "She would get so angry anytime we would try and make her socialize. We tried to get her to go out. Do things with kids her age." He took his wife's hand. "Then she began to go boy crazy. I guess it was her way of showing us that she could be social. Calling boys, having them over." He looked at Pastor Eric. "When we heard about Camp Ricochet, we knew it was exactly what she needed to find her focus."

"Bret tells me that she had a wonderful time," Pastor Eric said, knowing it would bring little comfort. "You did the right thing," he said, placing his hand on Mr. Canard's shoulder. "And for the right reason."

"Then why?" Mr. Canard sobbed. "Why did God take her?"

"I wish I knew," Pastor Eric replied calmly. "There just isn't an answer I can give you that will be what you need to hear."

"She was all we had!" Mrs. Canard said. "Our only baby!" She slid to the floor crying uncontrollably.

"I am so sorry," Pastor Eric said as Mr. Canard attempted to console his wife. "Is there anyone I can call for you? A pastor? Family?"

Mr. Canard shook his head. "We haven't been to church in years. All our family lives in Illinois."

"Well, I'm here if you need anything. May I pray for you?"

"Will it bring her back?!" Mrs. Canard asked, wiping her eyes with her balled up fists. "Will it bring my Daisy back to me?!" she shouted and attempted to stand. "Just GO!!! Take your God and your pity and GO!!!" She pointed toward the door.

Cruising up Interstate 95 just past the Florida-Georgia line, Christina listened as Matt continued to update her on the situation.

Christina had been a big part of the castle adventure. Being an investigative reporter, Matt and Billy had gone to her as a last-ditch effort to get someone to investigate Mark's disappearance. In fact, her investigation had gotten her cameraman killed and landed her right smack-dab in the middle of the castle herself. Along the way she had accepted Christ into her life. Somehow, having demons and other creatures chasing you through a castle, only to see them flee at the name of Jesus, would do that to a person. She had then taken the hope of Jesus to the airways at the end of her adventure, only to have the plug pulled. Thinking she was going to be fired, she faced her boss with a boldness that only the Holy Spirit could provide. Come to find out, her rant had gone viral and was the biggest thing to ever come out of Channel 6 Gateway News. She had then been given an anchor chair and was lead investigator on major stories.

Matt had started at the beginning. He told her the purpose of the trip to Camp Ricochet, the names of all who'd gone, the reason he'd had to leave along with a few details about his funeral trip, and then his notification of the accident. Christina was especially excited to hear that Matt had been visited by Topher. She turned off her recorder when he'd finished.

"Thanks for coming with me, Matt," Christina said, taking a sip from her mug of coffee.

"Are you kidding?" Matt replied. "You're a Godsend! I had just prayed for God to make a way for me to get to Savannah when you called."

"It seems like forever since I've seen you guys!" she said. "I've just been so busy."

"Are you still going to Pastor Joshua's church?" Matt asked.

"Yes! Gateway Community Church. I love it there! My parents have been going there for years, you know."

"That's awesome!" Matt replied. "I didn't know that. Pastor Joshua is amazing! He sometimes comes over to Billy's and attempts to skate the halfpipe." They both laughed. "Oh! Billy told me that Pastor Randy spoke at the last night of camp! He said it was so good."

"Awesome! That's exciting!" Christina replied. "What a small world!" She looked over and noticed that after mentioning Billy, Matt had a somber look on his face. "I'm sure he'll be fine." She put her hand on his arm.

"He's my best friend," Matt said, looking out the window. "He used to call me his bodyguard in grade school. I was bigger than the other kids our age and he was so small." He smiled at the thought. "Poor kid was a target for bullies."

"Isn't it funny how bullies always pick on the ones smaller than them? Like that makes them look tough." She squeezed his arm. "I'm sure you took good care of him."

Matt shrugged. "I was always shy and terrified of fighting, but I guess my size intimidated them because they never messed with him when we were together." They were quiet for several minutes. "If anything happens to him...to any of them. Scotty, Gabi, Mark...I don't think I could take it" He quickly wiped his eyes. "Not after Megan."

"Let's pray," Christina said, not sure of what else to say. "Let's take this problem to the problem solver."

"It honestly does not seem like those mountains are getting any closer," Billy said.

"Sure, it does," Gabi said. "Look how much further away the ones behind us are."

"Well, they're not much closer!" Andy added. "How long have we been walking?"

"A couple of hours at least," Mark said. "How's Maria?" he asked, looking back at Shadow, who was guiding her by the arm.

"She's doing just fine," Shadow replied, smiling over at Maria, who was mumbling quietly to herself.

"What is she saying?" Scotty asked.

"Nothing that makes sense. Just random words. I keep hearing the word smoke."

"Do you want someone else to walk with her?" Mark asked.

"We can take turns."

"No, I'm fine," Shadow replied. "Just try not to leave us behind."

"I am so thirsty!" Andy said. "My mouth has never been this dry!"

"Yeah, me too," Billy said. "And my head hurts like crazy." He massaged his temples.

"How good would a cheeseburger, fries, and a coke be right now?" Scotty asked.

"Really, Scotty?" Gabi said. "You're going to talk about food?"

"Sorry, I'm starving!"

"Yeah, thanks, Morgan," Andy said. "It isn't bad enough."

"A pizza!" Billy said. "And a chocolate milkshake! That's what I want!" Mark laughed.

"Mark?" Shadow said.

"Tacos!" Scotty said and he and Billy high-fived.

"Ooh, fried chicken!" Billy said. "From Gateway Barbecue!"

"Oh yeah!" Scotty replied. "They're the best!" Gabi was shaking her head.

"Mark!" Shadow screamed and everyone stopped walking and looked back. Maria had stopped walking and was staring into the sky muttering louder. "You guys need to hear what she's saying."

"What now?" Andy asked as they all walked back to where they stood. "She can't keep slowing us down!"

"Listen!" Shadow said.

"Smoke-fire-pain-run-smoke-fire-pain-run-smoke-fire-pain-run," Maria mumbled over and over.

"Maria, honey," Gabi said and touched Maria's arm.

Maria jumped back and screamed at the top of her lungs. They all backed away from Maria as she grabbed her own head as if it were about to explode. She looked right at Gabi and screamed, RUN!"

Just then, clicking sounds erupted from behind them.

"Scotty!" Mark yelled, and he and Scotty grabbed Maria's arms. "Let's go!" They all took off running as the clicking sounds grew louder. Mark looked over his shoulder but couldn't see anything but a thick cloud of dust that seemed to be spreading. "Stay together!" he screamed to them all. "No matter what!"

Billy was looking back. "I can't see anything!"

"Just run!" Gabi said.

"Fire-pain-smoke-fire-pain-smoke!" Maria continued to chant as they ran. "Fire-pain-smoke-delvvr-fire-pain-smoke-delivrr."

"What is she saying?" Scotty asked.

"I'm not sure," Mark said. "Deliver?"

"Maybe she wants pizza too!" Billy said, and shrugged as Mark gave him a look.

The clicking grew louder and sounded as if the creatures were right on top of them.

"Deliverer!" Maria screamed and dropped to the ground causing Mark and Scotty to topple over. Everyone came to a screeching halt. There, standing about fifteen feet in front of them, was a man in a robe holding a staff. Behind him a small campfire was burning with something delicious smelling cooking over it in a pot. There were several bowls and cups placed on a wooden table with seven chairs next to the fire. It was all so strange to see that they each just stared in disbelief.

"Come," the stranger said with a smile. "Eat."

The clicking had stopped.

CHAPTER 16

THE PUPPY

"Hey, Butler, didn't you investigate the Michael Lewis disappearance a few years back?" Officer Ramsey asked the older officer.

"Michael Lewis?" Officer Butler thought back. "Sounds vaguely familiar."

Typing in the information, Ramsey called back, "Never mind, I got it...and it WAS you. Supposedly, he abandoned his family. Reported missing by his employer."

"Yeah, I remember!" Butler said. "I found it strange that after being gone for three days, he was reported missing by his job and not his wife. Then I met her...piece of work."

"Betty?" Ramsey asked. "Betty Lewis, age twenty-two at the time. Daughter, Maria, was six."

"Why are you looking into that case? We could never prove foul play. He just vanished," Butler said.

"I just got a call from a friend who had a strange conversation with Betty," Ramsey replied. "Apparently, she was intoxicated, high, or both...but she actually told him that she had Maria's father killed."

"Really?!" Butler replied, looking up. "Wish I could say it surprised me. Pretty sure she was stoned when I questioned her."

"Supposedly," Ramsey said. "She's refusing to go and visit her daughter, who is lying in a coma in a Savannah hospital."

"Maria?"

"Yeah, she's fourteen now. She was one of the kids on that bus I told you about."

"That's sad," Butler said. "Pretty girl too; I arrested her about a year ago on shoplifting charges. She seemed to be heading down the same road as her mother."

"You okay with me looking into this?" Ramsey asked.

"Absolutely! Let me know if you need any help."

As Officer Ramsey read over the files on Michael Lewis, he saw that Betty had worked for Watson Plumbing at the time. Jack Watson had a bad reputation in those days. He was always getting into trouble for one thing or another. What ever happened to that guy?

Christina and Matt walked into the hospital and quickly found out where everyone was at.

Bret Snyder had already discharged himself. Brianna Bowers, Eddie Schumer, and Yvette Turner were each on the third floor being treated for minor injuries. They were supposed to be released tomorrow.

Mark McGee, Scotty Morgan, Gabriella Motes, Maria Lewis, Shadow Riley, Billy Mumpower, and Andy Cruz were each in ICU on the seventh floor. Only family and clergy were allowed beyond the waiting room up there.

Christina suggested they visit those on the third floor first. Matt barely knew Yvette and had no desire to see Eddie, so he suggested they visit Brianna first. Knocking on the door, they entered to find her sitting up with a Bible in her lap.

"Hey, girl!" Matt said. Brianna looked up and smiled big.

"Matt!" She held up her arms to hug him. "It's so good to see you!" They hugged. "How are you doing?"

"I'm fine, how are YOU doing?"

"Oh, I'm great!" Brianna said. "They just have me in here to check for internal damage."

"Well, thank God you're okay," Christina said from behind Matt. She held out her hand, "Christina Bulford."

"I'm sure Gabi told you all about her," Matt said. "She's the reporter lady from the castle."

"Yes!" Brianna exclaimed. "It's very nice to meet you!"

"It's nice to meet you as well, Brianna," Christina replied. "So, Matt tells me you're on vacation from California."

"I am!" Brianna said with a laugh. "And it has not been boring!" Christina smiled.

"Oh, I bet your parents are freaking out," Christina said. "Are they flying in?"

"Yes, they should be here sometime tonight."

"So, what happened, Brianna?" Matt asked. "The crash, I mean."

She shook her head and thought back. "We were all singing and laughing," she said with a smile. "The Wheels on the Bus!" Matt shook his head, remembering the song from the trip up. Suddenly there was a loud bang, like a gun. I later found out it was a tire blowing out on a passing semi-truck. The truck then slammed into us and caused the bus to go into a spin that led to it flipping over several times." She paused and Matt could see her breathing pick up. "Me, Yvette, and Eddie were thrown, which actually saved our lives." She looked at them with tears in her eyes. "I mean, we're the only ones not in ICU...or dead."

"Except Mr. Bret," Matt said. Brianna nodded.

"That's crazy," Christina said, placing a hand on Brianna's. "Thank God you're okay."

"Thank God, indeed," Brianna said. "An angel actually caught me and set me gently on the ground." She said it so softly they almost couldn't hear her. Matt and Christina leaned in closer. She told them what he'd done and said.

"Oh wow!" Matt said. "That is so cool!" Christina agreed.

"So, Matt," Brianna said. "How are you really doing? I'm so sorry about your cousin. And then to get home and receive this news."

"Yeah," Matt said. "It's all quite heavy. You know, Megan's boyfriend died too." Brianna nodded. "The saddest part for me...

neither one of them were saved. They were both so smart! They had every step of their lives planned out...except eternity."

"We are definitely not promised tomorrow," Christina said, patting his back. "Hey, I'll let you two talk. I'm going to try and find Pastor Eric."

"Okay, nice meeting you, Christina!" Brianna said. "Please let me know if there's any updates on the others."

"I will," Christina left.

Brianna saw the worried look on Matt's face. "Pull up a chair, Mr. Ramsey, we need to talk."

Chad was playing in the park at the front of his neighborhood in Gateway. Having finished his chores early, his mother had set him free with a stern warning not to leave the neighborhood. He had excitedly jumped on his bicycle and headed to the park, expecting to find other kids there. Instead, he'd found the park empty and extremely quiet.

For a seven-year old, Chad was small for his age. With his dark hair and pale skin, people often thought he was sick. His parents had opted to put him in private school, although his older sister had begged for public. He liked his school but had few friends from there that lived near him. His sister, however, made public school sound so cool. She had tons of friends that loved her and was so popular. Chad had never been popular. He had a handful of friends that he hung out with at school but mostly kept to himself. His parents kept trying to get him to play team sports, but he hadn't found anything that he was good at...or liked.

As he sat there swinging, bored out of his mind, he saw something move out of the corner of his eye. There, across the street from the entrance to the neighborhood, a little brown puppy was running down the side of the road as several cars whizzed by. Chad jumped from his swing and ran across the park. Looking both ways, he saw that the puppy was alone. It had apparently escaped from its home and was running away.

"Puppy!" Chad yelled and whistled. Now about fifty yards away, it stopped and looked back. Yelping, it ran out into the street and began running in the opposite direction. "No!" Chad looked around. Nobody was around. His mother had told him not to leave the neighborhood, but this was important. The little guy could get hit by a car. Chad ran back, grabbed his bicycle, and headed out of the park for the puppy. For the moment, there was no traffic, so he took off straight down the middle of the road. The puppy was running at full speed so Chad had to pedal as fast as he could to catch up. "Puppy!" he called. "Here boy!... or girl!" The little guy didn't even slow down. Chad attempted to whistle but the wind in his face prevented any sound from coming out. "Slow down little dude! What's your hurry?!" The puppy looked over his shoulder and ran even faster. Did he think Chad was going to hurt him? That's when Chad saw it. A big blue pickup truck was heading straight for them. "No! Get out of the road!" He would never make it to the puppy before the truck did. Hopefully the driver would see it. Moving off the road, Chad waved his arms at the driver, but the truck didn't seem to be slowing down. "Stop! Watch out for the puppy!" The guy honked his horn and seemed to speed up as he got closer. Chad squeezed his eyes shut and waited for the inevitable yelp of the puppy as the truck hit it. The truck roared past Chad and he eased his eyes open. No sign of a dead puppy anywhere. There was no way the little guy didn't get hit. He'd been heading straight for the truck. Just then, Chad saw him running up a driveway and crawling up under a large gate. Was it where he lived? The large, metal gate was hanging off its hinges and didn't seem like a place where anybody would presently live. The weeds were quite high all around it and there were vines growing up the gate. Chad crossed the street and rode up the driveway to the gate. The place looked super creepy with grass and weeds growing through the paved driveway and spider webs on the gate. "Puppy!" The little guy started barking ferociously at something. It was adorable to think of anything being afraid of that cute bark. Chad hopped off his bike and slid it behind some bushes. He might as well help the dumb dog out; he'd come this far. He squeezed through an opening in the gate and made his way down the overgrown driveway. He climbed over fallen trees and made his way around large spider webs. "Oh, I hate spiders," he said out loud. The puppy continued to bark but seemed further away now. Chad tried calling and whistling for it, but it just kept barking. The stone driveway led him into an open field where the weeds were almost as tall as Chad. To his right, he saw the remnants of an old shed that looked like it had been there for a thousand years. To his left, he could just make out what looked like piles of black stones placed randomly throughout the field. Straight ahead he noticed an old wooden bridge that seemed to have no purpose. There was nothing but forest on the other side... and a ferociously barking puppy. "Hold on! I'm coming!" He made his way to the bridge and found it to be sturdy enough to cross. Still, he walked cautiously over it, checking each board before stepping. The last thing Chad needed was to fall through and get hurt. Nobody would ever think to look in here for him. When he reached the top, he saw the puppy going into the woods. "No puppy! Come back! This is getting ridiculous!" He lost sight of him in the thick forest but could hear him rustling through the leaves and bushes. "I'm going to call you Jack! You're such a pirate, conquering the unknown! Unless, of course you're a girl! Then I'll call you Jack...alyn. Yeah! Jackalyn, I like it! I had a crush on a Jacalyn last year, you know!" When Chad reached the bottom of the bridge, he noticed a large duffle bag. "What have we here?" He sat down beside it and opened it, hoping to find some pirate treasures himself. "Cans of food, clothes, and OH, the smell!" He quickly closed it when the rancid smell of body odor and other things he didn't want to think about reached his nose. Just then, the puppy began barking again. It sounded like he was barking into a barrel or something now. "Jack! Where are you at buddy?" He made his way over to the forest where the puppy had entered. "This doesn't look fun at all!" He stepped into the thick brush and began making his way toward a large overturned tree that seemed to be where all the barking was coming from. "You are going to get me into so much trouble! Do you know that? OUCH!" A thorn caught his arm and scraped across it. He wiped the beads of blood on his shirt and kept going. "So much trouble," he mumbled as he drew closer to the large tree roots. "Where are you at, dude?!" Chad made his way around the mound of tree roots, whistling for the puppy. "Where are you boy...girl? Whatever you are." There was a small clearing next to the mound. The barking seemed to be in that direction, so Chad made his way over. "Jack! Where are y..." As he entered the small clearing, he saw it. A large round opening that looked like some kind of tunnel. The barking was coming from inside. Chad walked over and peeked inside. To his surprise there were stairs. There were actually stairs leading underground. Out here in the middle of the woods, under an overturned tree, there were stone steps leading down. Was this Narnia or what? Jack's barking turned even more fierce and he started growling. "Well, that's not promising. Jack! Come here, boy!" He whistled into the cave. "Come on, boy, I really can't go in there! Not to mention it's so dark!" The puppy stopped barking. "Jack?" Nothing. "Stupid dog." Just then Jack let out a loud yelp as if he'd been hurt. "Jack!!?" Chad screamed into the darkness. "Jack! Here, boy!" Nothing. Not a sound. Patting his pocket, Chad remembered his small flashlight that was on his keychain. He pulled it out and clicked the LED light on. "Perfect." He shined it into the dark cave and found it to be quite bright. "Okay, Jack! I'll come in just a little bit. You better show yourself though!" And Chad entered the darkness.

Daniel stood quietly at the end of the hospital corridor. He was watching the doctors and nurses come and go from the rooms of the seven kids in ICU. Adam stood stoically at the other end of the hall. There was an angel posted in each room as well. Brandon was four stories below watching over Brianna. Daniel had made him Brianna's keeper. He'd asked for the job after having caught her at the accident. Chaz was overlooking Mark, who Daniel felt was the main target of the dragon.

Most of the kids had family members there with them. Mark, Scotty, and Gabi had their parents. Billy and Andy had their mothers. Maria had Bret and Cathie praying for her in the waiting room. Shadow had nobody there, so Daniel had arranged for extra angels in her room. Every nurse and doctor that walked out of her room mentioned how peaceful it was in her room. It made it so they would visit her more often. Pastor Eric, of course, was there for all of them.

Daniel was there to make sure that there were no further attacks. Not on his watch. He still couldn't believe that Anansi had gotten the jump on him. He'd known without a doubt that the battle ahead on the interstate was a diversion, but somehow the dragon had still been able to surprise him. He had told his warriors that he accepted full responsibility.

Just then, an extremely bright light erupted in the middle of the hall. He and Adam drew their swords at the speed of light. An enormous angel in blue robes that were being stretched by his massive muscles, stood staring at Daniel. His hand was on the hilt of his giant golden sword that hung sheathed at his side.

"My General!" Both Daniel and Adam said together.

Michael smiled as the two warrior angels approached him. "Daniel! Adam! HE is worthy!"

"HE is worthy indeed!" they said in unison.

He placed a hand on the shoulder of each of them. "The Master has sent me to encourage you!" He smiled. "Though YOU were surprised by this demonic attack, Daniel...HE was not." They both nodded.

"Yes, General," Daniel said. "Still..."

"Daniel!" Michael said in a stern voice. "Do not question HIS methods! What you see as your failure, God sees as His opportunity. He is and always will be...in control."

"Yes, sir!" Daniel replied and held his head high. "I live to serve HIM!"

With a squeeze of Daniel's shoulder, Michael smiled at him. "Now, gather ALL of your men and come with me."

"Sir?"

"HIS orders." Michael said, pointing up.

"Not to question HIM, but…"

"No Greater Love!" Michael replied and Daniel understood.

"Who?" Daniel asked with sadness in his voice.

"Come, you shall see."

Pastor Eric had invited all the families together in the ICU waiting room to pray. Bret and Cathie, Larry and Gae, Harold and Cheryl, Mark's mom and stepdad, Scotty's parents, Yvette's parents, Christina, and even Andy's mom had all shown up. They got in a large circle and joined hands.

"First of all, I want to thank you all for coming and agreeing in prayer," Pastor Eric said. "We serve a God that is still in the healing business. I would like us all to remember Mr. and Mrs. Canard in our prayers. As you know, their daughter Daisy passed away in the accident." He paused for a few seconds. "My absolute hope and prayer is that nobody else in this room has to go through what they are going through."

"Amen," Larry said. "I can't even imagine having to identify a child like that."

"Are there any other specific requests, Pastor?" Martha, Scotty's mom, asked.

"Let's just pray for total healing for all these kids, and Bret as well…even though he won't admit it, he is still in pain."

"How is the truck driver that hit them?" Gae asked. "Was he okay?"

"I was told that he didn't even get a scratch," Bret said. "He helped the paramedics with getting the kids out."

"Was he even ticketed with the accident?" Andy's mom asked, quite emphatically.

"I'm not sure," Pastor Eric said. "I know his tire blew out, so his company will probably be accountable for that."

"As they should be," Andy's mother replied.

"Okay, let's go to the Lord in prayer," Pastor Eric said before she could continue. Everyone bowed their head. "Dear Heavenly Father, we stand before you this evening in awe. In awe of your authority, in awe of your power, in awe of your mercy, and in awe of your love. You are a mighty and loving God, and You have allowed us to bring our petitions before You. Father, I lift up the Canard family to You in Jesus' name. Bless them God. Bless them in their grief. Your word says that in ALL things You work for the good of those who love You and have been called according to Your purpose. Father, I cannot speak for the Canards; but I can say that we here before You tonight, love You with all our hearts. Bless them, we pray Father. Show them Your love in this horrible situation. And Lord, I lift up Bret, Brianna, Eddie, and Yvette. Thank you, Father, that they are not seriously injured. I also pray that You would continue to heal them. And Father, we lift up Mark, Andy, Scotty, Billy, Gabi, Maria, and Shadow before You. Heal their bodies, their minds, and awaken them from their sleep, God. They are young and still have their whole lives before them. Heal them, we pray, God. We stand in the faith that You are their healer. With that said, God...bless the hands of the doctors, nurses, and surgeons. Lord, I also lift up each family that is here in this room. Give them strength for what is before them. In Christ's name we pray. Amen."

They all said amen, just as the door opened and a nurse walked in and stopped as she saw that everyone was in a circle.

She scanned the room quickly and found Pastor Eric. "I'm sorry, Pastor, but I need to speak with you." The room went silent.

"Please come," the man in the robe said. He had shoulder length brown hair and a short, neatly trimmed beard. His eyes were brown and seemed to sparkle when he smiled. "I have prepared food for you."

"Because you knew we were coming?" Andy asked sarcastically.

The man smiled at him and Andy looked away. Pulling a chair out, he smiled and said, "for you, Andy."

"Whoa!" Billy exclaimed. "Dude, he knew your name!"

"Come Billy, Gabi, Mark, Scotty, Shadow, and..." He paused and walked up to Maria, who stood smiling insanely at him. "Hello, Maria."

"Del..." she started to say but he touched her arm. Her smile broadened, as if she had just received an amazing revelation. "Hello!"

"Please come," the man said. He led them each to the table and began serving them. He gave them water and poured what looked like chicken soup into their bowls.

"It smells delicious," Gabi said.

"Thank you, Gabi." He smiled at her. "I do hope you like it...please, eat."

"I'm sorry, I don't want to sound rude," Mark said. "But who are you?"

He filled Mark's bowl and smiled down at him. "My name is Tobiah."

"Wow! This is awesome!" Billy said, having just taken his first bite. "You guys have to try it!"

"Ooh, it IS!" Shadow said. "Thank you so much, Tobiah!"

"You are welcome, Shadow," he said with a big smile.

"So, Gabi!" Andy said. "If we are all unconscious and this is all in our head, then who exactly is Tobiah?"

Gabi looked up as Tobiah carried the pot back to the fire. "I'm not sure, Andy, why don't you ask HIM?"

"So, what gives, Tobiah?" Andy asked. "Where are we and who in the world are you?"

"In the world?" Tobiah asked with a chuckle. "No, my friend, we are not in the world."

"But..." Andy started to say.

"Why don't you just enjoy your food and water? Were you not just saying that you were hungry and thirsty?"

"Repeatedly," Scotty said. "So, chill out and eat, Andy!"

Over the next several minutes, the only sound being made was the sound of spoons scraping bowls. Tobiah sat stoking the fire with his back to the group.

"Seriously though," Andy whispered and leaned in close to Mark. "Is this guy trustworthy?"

Mark shrugged. "He's feeding us, isn't he?"

"Yeah, and farmers fatten the pigs before they slaughter them too," Andy replied. "That doesn't answer my question. Besides, what about how those creatures vanished when he showed up?

"Isn't that a good thing, Andy?" Gabi asked. "They WERE chasing us, you know."

"Yeah, I guess." He went back to eating his soup. "There's just something about him I don't trust."

"So, which is it, Andy?" Billy asked. "His pleasant hospitality or the protection from danger?"

Andy shot Billy a threatening look and was about to respond when…

"Hello there!" The voice of an old man came from behind them. They all, including Tobiah, turned to look. An old man in a long robe and sandals stood there supporting himself with a staff. He smiled and winked at Andy. "My name is Torheit."

"I know you!" Mark said, jumping up from his seat and causing his chair to fall back. "You were in the castle! You lied to Angel and me!"

"Lied is a strong word, son," Torheit said calmly.

"You deliberately led us in the wrong direction," Mark replied.

"Did I? Think back, Mark McGee. If I had not led you and your friend in that direction, do you really believe you would have been there to find Scotty when he arrived?"

Mark walked right up to him. "Did you plan Angel's death?"

Torheit smiled at Mark and glanced at Tobiah. "Why, Mark McGee, are you calling me God?"

"What can we do for you, Torheit?" Tobiah asked.

Torheit's smile slowly faded as Tobiah stared him down. He shrugged and waved his hand. "Hello…Tobiah." He smiled at Andy again and walked toward the table. "I was just wondering

if any of the children would like to go with me to the mountain."
His eyes sparkled as he looked at each of them.

"While I would not encourage it, they most certainly have
the freedom to go with you," Tobiah said.

"I'll go," Andy said, looking up at Torheit.

"Andy, no!" Mark said. "We have to stay together!"

"Then come with me, McGee!" Andy replied. "He's going to
the mountain! Isn't that where you said we needed to go anyway?"

"He's lying to you, Andy!" Mark said, trying to hold Andy
back. "Don't do it!"

Andy pulled away from him. "Yeah, I'm getting sick of you
guys bossing me around anyway."

"Let him go!" Billy said, and Gabi shot him a look. "I mean,
if it's what he wants."

"Oh, it's what I want!" Andy said. "And I don't need your
permission." He turned to Torheit and smiled at him. "After
you, sir."

"Would anyone else care to join me?" Torheit asked.

"No!" Mark said. "The rest of us have a brain. Come on,
Andy! His plan is to lead you astray!"

"The mountains are all around us, McGee!" Andy replied.
"Relax, I got this! Besides, your buddy Tobiah gives me
the creeps."

"He fed you, you moron!" Scotty said, jumping up.

"Be on your way, Torheit!" Tobiah said with authority.
Torheit smiled and turned away.

"Yes, good then," Torheit said. He placed his hand on Andy's
shoulder. "We have all chosen our paths."

"Andy!" Mark said. "Andy! Don't be stupid!"

"I'll see you on the other side, McGee!" Andy said without
looking back. "If you make it out alive!"

Tobiah walked up and stood beside Mark. They both watched
as Andy and Torheit slowly walked back in the direction they
had just come from. "He has made his choice, Mark. Come,
sit." He led Mark back over to the table and stood his chair up

for him. "Has everyone had enough to eat?" They all smiled and nodded.

"Thank you so much, Tobiah," Gabi said. "It was delicious."

"And exactly what we needed," Shadow added.

"Are you an angel, Tobiah?" Scotty asked. "We've met a few, you know. Well, Gabi, Mark, and I have."

Tobiah smiled. "No, Scotty. I am only a friend...though I too must confess to meeting a few angels."

"Oh, I would love to meet an angel!" Shadow said. "That would be so cool!"

Tobiah walked around the table to where Shadow sat and held out his hand to her. "Shadow Riley, any angel in heaven would be honored to meet you." She smiled and took his hand. He had her stand and face the others. He leaned close and said something into her ear. She smiled. And she vanished.

"Hey!" Mark jumped to his feet.

"Shadow!" Gabi screamed.

CHAPTER 17

NO GREATER LOVE

S tepping out into the hallway with the nurse, Pastor Eric braced himself for the worst. She turned and faced him, "I'm sorry to interrupt, Pastor," she whispered.

"Oh no," he replied. "You're perfectly fine. What's the news?"

"It's Shadow Riley," she continued softly. "She's awake."

"Praise God!" he said. "How is she doing?"

"The doctors are with her now, but she seemed fine. With no family here, I figured it would be best if you could be the one to… fill her in on what's happened."

"Absolutely," Pastor Eric said. "Let me give the news to the room, and I'll follow you over." He opened the door to the waiting room and all eyes were immediately on him. "Good news! Shadow is awake!"

They all clapped and praised God. "How is she doing, Pastor?" Gae asked.

"I'm about to go find out. If everyone would, continue to pray, please."

The nurse led Pastor Eric to Shadow's door. "Just let me check," she said and slipped inside. A couple of minutes later she opened the door. "Come on in, Pastor."

Pastor Eric stepped inside to find two doctors standing next to Shadow's bed. She lie there, eyes wide open, looking quite confused.

"It appears," one of the doctors began, "that Ms. Riley has had quite a dream." The other doctor laughed. "But other than that, she appears to be just fine."

"We'll be keeping an eye on her over the next 24 hours," the other doctor said, patting her shoulder. They nodded to Pastor Eric and excused themselves.

"Shadow," the nurse said. "Do you know who this is?" She pointed to Pastor Eric and Shadow shook her head no.

"We've never actually met, Shadow," he said. "I'm Pastor Eric, the pastor of…"

"Oh!" Shadow started and had to clear her throat. "Okay, yeah! Gabi talked about you!"

He smiled and walked over to place his hand on hers. "How do you feel?"

"A little groggy."

"I'll leave you guys," the nurse said as she opened the door. "Just hit the button if you need anything, sweetie."

"Thank you," Pastor Eric said, then turned his attention back to Shadow. "So…do you remember what happened?"

"Not really…I only remember the valley."

"The valley?"

"The doctors said it was only a dream, but I know it was real, Pastor!"

"Okay," he patted her hand. "Calm down. Tell me about it."

"It was a strange place, like a desert. We were all there… well…me, Gabi, Maria, Mark, Scotty, Billy, and Andy…oh, and Daisy was there at first for a few second…but then…" Shadow teared up. "Did…did she really die?"

Pastor Eric tried to contain his confusion about this knowledge. He nodded. "I'm afraid so." Shadow began crying and it took her a few minutes to collect herself. He thought it strange that she also named everyone that was still unconscious.

"What about Maria?" Shadow asked with concern. "Is she alright, Pastor?"

Before he answered, "Why do you ask?"

"It's just...she was acting...strange. Like something was wrong with her mind. She was almost childlike."

He stood up straight and thought for a second. "She's had a nasty blow to her head...but..."

"I think everyone will be okay though," Shadow whispered and looked out the window as if in deep thought. "Tobiah is with them"

"I'm sorry, Tobiah?" Pastor Eric was really confused now.

She nodded. "He's the one who sent me back here. He's so nice and everything seemed so peaceful in his presence...before he sent me, he told me he would always be there for me."

Quickly, Pastor Eric pulled out his cell phone and googled the name Tobiah. "A boy's name of Hebrew origin meaning the Lord is good." He looked at Shadow. "Tell me more about this valley."

"There was another man...he didn't seem to like Tobiah very much...but Andy really did like him."

"What was his name?"

"His name was..." she was trying to remember. "It was another t word...um...Tor something. Torheat, but I'm not sure how you would spell that. Yeah, it was definitely Torheat. Isn't that strange?"

He googled that also and found it to be a word and not a name. It was the German word for folly. Pastor Eric knew that the Bible represented folly as a woman, but wouldn't it be just like Satan to twist that.

"He took Andy and left," Shadow said. "They were heading towards the mountains and away from Tobiah."

"Shadow," Pastor Eric said, "have you accepted Jesus into your heart?"

"Yes sir!" She replied with a big smile.

He smiled back. "That's awesome," he said, that meant that Andy was the only one who hadn't. "Listen, I'm going to let you rest. I'll be back in a little while to check on you. Okay?" She nodded. He needed to discuss this with Bret. Make some sense of it. As he approached the waiting room, he saw that Bret was talking on his cell phone just outside the door.

He laughed as Pastor Eric approached. "Well, that's just about the craziest testimony I've ever heard! Listen, the pastor is back and hopefully he has some good news...okay, you guys need to get down to Gateway and see us soon. Love you, lady!" He hung up and looked at Pastor Eric. "Boy, have I got a story for you!"

Seeing his excitement, Pastor Eric decided to let Bret go first. "What happened?"

"Well, do you remember my pastor friend whose wife was in a car accident?"

"Yeah, you said she'd come out of her coma and was doing fine."

"Absolutely, well let me tell you what happened while she was in the coma!"

"Whoa!" Pastor Eric stepped back as the hair on his arms raised up.

"What?" Bret stopped when he saw the look on his friend's face.

"This story doesn't happen to involve a man named Tobiah, does it?"

Now it was Bret's turn to step back. "How in the world did you know that?"

"Shadow just told me about him," Pastor Eric said. "The others that are unconscious...they're with him now."

Bret had to prop himself up on the wall. "Whoa..."

"You need to be careful, Matt," Brianna said after he finished telling her everything. "You're in a very dangerous place, spiritually." He just stared at her. "Don't let bitterness creep in, because once it does, the devil will destroy you."

"Well, what am I supposed to do?"

"Trust God!" she exclaimed. "He knows what He's doing, even if you don't."

"But they weren't ready to die...Brianna, they're in hell! Is that what God wanted?"

"You know it isn't," she said gently. "I'm sure they had numerous opportunities to accept Him. None of us are promised tomorrow, Matt...ready or not."

Matt just sat there staring into space. "And then, if that isn't bad enough...I find out my best friend and pretty much everyone I hang out with, have been in an accident and may not live!"

"Matt!" Brianna said, sitting up in bed. "Once again, we have to trust..." Her cell phone rang. "Oh, it's my mom." She picked it up. "Excuse me, hey Mom!"

Matt nodded and stepped out. As he walked toward the drink machines, his cell phone buzzed. The number didn't look familiar but given everything going on, he decided to answer it. "Hello?"

"Matt?"

"Yeah, this is Matt," he responded. "Who..."

"Dude, this is Rusty! Where are you at?"

"Where am I at? Where are YOU at!?"

"I'm walking into the hospital right now, where are you?"

"You're what? What hospital? Are you in Savannah?"

"Yes! When I heard about the accident on the radio, a truck driver brought me and dropped me off."

"Oh wow," Matt told him that he was on the third floor and Rusty said he would be right up. Matt was waiting when the elevator doors opened.

"Dude, is everybody okay?" Rusty asked with true concern on his face.

"Some are," Matt said. "Mr. Bret, Brianna, Eddie, and Yvette. The others are unconscious, except..."

"Except who?" Rusty asked.

"Daisy died in the accident." Matt could've sworn he saw Rusty smile before he turned his head.

"Aw, man, no way," Rusty's hands covered his face. "She was so full of life. So young and pretty." He looked up at Matt. "What about Andy?"

"He's in ICU," Matt replied. "His mom's in the waiting room! You want to see her?"

"No, I want to see Andy! He's my boy! What floor are they on?" He headed back to the elevator.

"You can't, Rusty!" Matt exclaimed. "You have to be family!"

"I'll say I'm his brother."

"Yeah, because you look Spanish!" Matt said. "They won't let you in, they're quite strict here." The doors opened and both boys got in. Matt pushed the button for the seventh floor.

"What happened to Shadow!?" Gabi screamed at Tobiah. "What did you do!?"

"It's okay, Gabriella," Tobiah said and gently patted her shoulder. "She is just fine."

Mark walked over. "Which means what? She's awake?"

Tobiah smiled at Mark. "Yes, Mark McGee, that is what it means."

"Praise God," Mark said softly.

"Yes!" Tobiah said to them all. "Praise Him indeed! Let His praises always be on your lips!"

"So, can we go back also?" Scotty asked.

"In due time, Scotty Morgan," Tobiah replied. "You will reach your destination."

"As long as it's not our final destination!" Billy replied with a laugh. They all looked at him. "You know, the movie? Death? Wow, tough crowd."

"So, what now, Tobiah?" Mark asked.

"You have been quite busy over the past few days. Wouldn't you like to just rest?"

"I, for one," Scotty said. "Would love to get home to my family."

"So, what you are saying," Tobiah said, looking at each of them in turn. "Is that you are ready to be on with it?" They each nodded at him.

"Yes, sir," Gabi said. "Can we please just…"

He had vanished right before their eyes. The dishes, the fire, all of it was gone.

"Whoa!" Scotty said, looking around.

"He's gone!" Maria yelled and jumped up from her seat on the ground. "No more of him!"

"I couldn't have said it better myself," Billy replied.

"What now, Gabi?" Mark asked.

Gabi looked at each of them. "I guess we should continue our quest for the mountains."

"Yeah, that's what I was hoping you would say," Mark replied. "We can each take turns with Maria."

"Yeah, Shadow was so good with her," Scotty said.

Just then, there was a loud roar in the distance that caused the ground to shake. Suddenly, the sky began to darken. Maria began to scream and grabbed Mark's arm. He pulled her into a hug. "It's okay," he whispered into her ear and gave Gabi a concerned look.

"Guys," Billy said, looking behind Mark and Gabi. "I say we go in this direction." He pointed the opposite way. Everyone turned to see thousands of creatures heading their way. "And I say we get a move on!"

"But that's the direction Torheit took Andy!" Gabi said.

"Got a better plan?" Billy asked.

"Yeah, it seems like we're being led into a trap," Mark added. "But you're right, Billy. Right now, it's our only option." He knelt in front of Maria. "Maria, how do you feel about a race?"

She nodded and laughed. "I'm faster than you, Marky!"

"Are you sure about that?" He teased. "I'm pretty fast!"

"Then catch me if you can!" Before Mark could stop her, she bolted as fast as she could in the wrong direction. Maria was heading straight for the creatures.

"Maria! No!" Mark screamed before realizing that Billy had shot off after her like a lightning bolt.

She was about a hundred yards from the oncoming creatures when Billy grabbed her arm and pulled her in the opposite direction. "This way, Maria!" Billy yelled over the horrible noises of the beasts and the thundering sky. "The race is this way!"

"Look!" Maria said, looking over her shoulder. "Scary monsters!"

"Yeah, that's why the race is this way," Billy said, holding onto her wrist as they ran together. As they caught up to Mark, Scotty, and Gabi, something caught Billy's eye. "Um, Mark!?" Billy yelled. "What is that in the sky!?"

"Is that...?" Scotty began as they all stopped to watch the dragon soar towards them.

"What does he have in his claw?" Gabi asked.

One of the dragon's claws appeared to be clinched around something large. He hid it behind his large scaly body as he landed, facing the group. He chortled his ominous laugh. "Well, well, well... if it isn't Mark McGee and his wary band of disciples." His laugh actually shook the ground.

"Bad dragon!" Maria yelled.

Gabi stepped forward. "Be gone foul...!"

"Enough!" the dragon roared so loud that Gabi actually fell back. With one swift motion, he produced what he had been hiding.

"Hey!" Billy yelled. "Is that...

"Andy!" Mark exclaimed and stepped forward.

"Exactly!" the dragon said. "And one misuse of a certain name that nobody really wants to hear, and I will slice this idiot in half." He placed one of his razor-sharp claws just over Andy's body.

"Let him go, you...!" Gabi began and the dragon lowered his head to within inches of her face.

"I will personally escort his soul into hell, if you open your mouth one more time, little girl!"

Matt and Rusty exited the elevator on the seventh floor. Rusty pushed past him and moved down the hall at a fast trot.

"Dude, they aren't going to let you in his room!" Matt said, noting that it was quite odd that nobody was around to stop them from entering the ICU. Earlier, when he and Christina had come up, the floor was teeming with nurses and staff that had stopped them before they got two feet off the elevator.

"It's easier to ask forgiveness than permission," Rusty said as he checked the names on each door. Each room had a small window where you could look in, but most of them had the blinds closed. "Aha!" Rusty called out and entered the room.

"Dude, where are you going?" Matt called after him. "Andy's room is right here!"

Maria stepped up and took Gabi by the hand. "We should go home. I don't want to play here anymore."

Gabi smiled at her. "Yeah, me either."

"So, what's the plan here, Dragon?" Mark asked. "Are we just going to stand here and stare at each other?" The other creatures had gathered just behind the dragon and looked as if they were ready to feast.

The dragon laughed again. "No, Mark McGee, we are not! This, my boy, is the plan…your life for his." He nudged Andy's still body with his claw. "I kill you and Andy Cruz can live." The creatures roared at this new development.

Out of the corner of his eye, Mark noticed that Billy had quietly slid behind a boulder. The dragon didn't seem to notice.

"Isn't it true, Mark McGee, that you want to be more like your savior? Well, what better way than to lay down your life?" More laughter and cheering from the creatures.

"I would gladly lay down my life for Andy!" Mark said, taking a step forward. Scotty and Gabi shared a glance.

"Then come closer," the dragon said softly. "Do it, you coward."

Billy could see Andy's body lying there motionless. It would take him about three seconds to get to him, and about five more to grab him and slide him away. Hopefully Mark, Scotty, and

Gabi could keep the dragon from striking. Looking over, he nodded to Gabi and she looked back at the dragon.

"Do it, you coward!" the dragon said.

It was now or never. "I love you, Jesus," Billy said in a whisper. "Please help me to do this." He took off from behind the boulder like a rocket.

Matt walked over to the room where Rusty had entered. Just as he did, he noticed that Rusty had opened the blinds. Matt couldn't see who exactly it was that Rusty was standing over and just as he registered that his hands were over their chest, Rusty looked up at Matt and smiled. He then removed the long blade of a knife from the chest of...Matt read the name on the door... "Nooo!!! Billy!!!" Matt burst in screaming to the sound of Billy's heart monitor registering no pulse...and Rusty was gone.

CHAPTER 18

THE SHADOW OF DEATH

"Nooo!" Mark screamed. He thought he'd been doing a good job of distracting the dragon as Billy had gotten into place. Out of the corner of his eye he had seen Billy take off like a rocket. Ten feet…five…and just as he reached to grab Andy's arms, the dragon swung his claw out and punctured Billy's chest. He dropped like a rag doll. Mark ran to him, noticing the blood slowly saturating his shirt. Billy stared up with empty eyes. Just as Mark bent down to help him…Billy vanished. "Billy!"

Scotty ran up and grabbed Mark, pulling him away from the dragon, who had repositioned himself to face Mark. "Dude! He's gone! Back away!" Scotty said, watching the dragon. Shocked, Mark allowed Scotty to lead him away from danger. The dragon began laughing.

Gabi stepped up in front of Scotty and Mark to face the dragon. Just as she was about to say something, the ground shook with the sound of thunder and the sky went dark. It seemed that a major storm was coming.

An alarm went off and a light above Billy's door was flashing as Matt stood there in stunned silence. Several nurses came running down the hall and pushed past him into the room. Moments later a woman in a doctor's jacket emerged from the elevator and joined them. Matt couldn't see what they were doing.

Pastor Eric and Bret heard the commotion from where they stood in the hall. They shared a glance and headed in that direction. Pastor Eric attempted to stop a passing nurse, but she ignored him and pressed past. That's when he noticed Matt.

"Matt!?" Pastor Eric called and Matt looked his way.

"It was Rusty!" Matt exclaimed, heading towards them. "Pastor Eric, Rusty stabbed Billy with a knife.

"What!?" Bret replied. "Rusty is here!? How!?"

"Rusty Staggerbush!?" Pastor Eric asked. "That's not possible, Matt. How would he even know to come here."

"I saw him do it!" Matt yelled. "With my own eyes! He came to the hospital saying he wanted to see Andy and then he ran ahead of me into Billy's room and...he stabbed him!" Matt began crying. "Why would he do that?"

Pastor Eric put his arms around Matt and pulled him into a hug. "We'll figure this all out."

Just then they heard someone scream out as if in agony behind them. Turning around they realized it was coming from the waiting room. Bret began to head that way while Pastor Eric stayed back with Matt. "That's Billy's mom, oh God, is he dead!?" Matt cried out. Bret reached the door just as a doctor and the nurse who had passed them exited the room with their heads down. Billy's mom was clearly sobbing. "Not my baby!!!" Bret quickly closed the door and Pastor Eric went to be with her, leaving Matt there to stare after him. Bret walked toward him. "Come here, Matt. Let's go for a walk. We can pray."

"No!" Matt replied, pushing past him and heading toward the stairs. "Keep your prayers! And keep you God!" He slammed the door behind him. Bret could hear him yelling something as he headed downstairs.

"Billy," Daniel said to nobody in particular. He and the hosts of heaven were gathered thousands of feet above the hospital.

"Greater love has no one than this: to lay down one's life for one's friends." Adam said, placing his hand on Daniel's shoulder.

"Anansi will feel my blade," Daniel replied.

"Vengeance is not our responsibility, my Captain," Adam said. "It is only our pleasure...when the Master allows it." He smiled at Daniel."

"Then let us hope the Master will allow it," Daniel replied.

"Until then," Adam said, facing Daniel, "we need to prepare our troops for a battle our enemies will not soon forget." Daniel nodded.

"Daniel, my Captain!" it was the messenger angel, Topher. "I have come from the throne room with a message from the Holy One."

Daniel glanced at Adam and faced Topher. "What message do you bring? Are we to fight?"

"No," Topher replied. "Stand down. The Master has ordered all warriors to return to heaven for further instructions. You and Adam are to come with me." Daniel closed his eyes and accepted the disappointment of not being more involved in this fight. "He said to tell you, and these are His words...I've got this, Daniel."

"Mark McGee!" the dragon roared, as the sky grew dark and thunder rolled in the distance. "I am about to take everyone from you!" He laughed. "Every! Single! Person!"

"Mark," Gabi said from behind him. "Was Billy..."

"Dead? Yes." Mark replied without turning around.

Gabi put her hand over her mouth, in shock. She fought back the stinging tears as the dragon slammed his tail to the ground, shaking it beneath them.

"This game has gone on long enough!" He faced Mark. "Your family has been a thorn in my side for too long!" The dragon's eyes were blood red.

Gabi walked over and stood in front of Maria, who was staring intently at the sky. "Father!" Gabi began. "We come before you in the name..."

"There is only ONE god here!" The dragon raised up and appeared to be bigger than ever before. He spun around and looked Gabi in the eyes. "This is not a place where help will come to you, Gabi Motes! Now, bow and worship me, and perhaps your death will be swift and painless!"

Then it was Gabi's turn to laugh and she took a step forward. Scotty immediately took Maria by the hand. "Jesus said to him, 'Away from me, Satan! For it is written: Worship the Lord your God and serve him only."

Mark noticed the dragon flinch at the name of Jesus. He glanced back at Scotty, and that's when he noticed that thousands of demons and creatures had completely surrounded them.

"Enough!" the dragon roared. "It is time for you to meet the god of this land!"

The clouds above them began to swirl, and the rumbles of thunder almost sounded like laughter.

Suddenly, nurses and doctors began running down the hall and going into each of the kid's rooms. Lights were flashing and alarms going off over Mark, Scotty, Gabi, Maria, and Andy's doors. It seemed like the largest concentration of help was going to Andy.

"What's going on?" Pastor Eric, having come from the waiting room, asked Bret.

"Brother, I think we need to pray," Bret replied.

"I'm sorry, gentlemen, but I'm going to have to ask you to go to the waiting room," a nearby nurse said, prodding them in that direction.

"Is everything okay?" Pastor Eric asked. "What's going on?"

"We're not sure, Pastor," she said in a whisper. "It's strange, almost like they are under duress."

"All of them?" Bret asked. "At the same time?"

"I will send one of the doctors to answer your questions as soon as things settle down," she replied, once they were at the waiting room. "And oh, Pastor?" He turned back to her. "Pray."

Matt walked across the parking lot, his eyes stinging with tears. His best friend was dead, and he would never see him again. Billy...so full of life. He kicked a garbage can and knocked it over. "What are you doing here, God!? First you take Megan, then Caleb, and NOW Billy!? I feel like you're abandoning me here!" He yelled at the sky. "What's going on!? Huh!?" He looked over to see a young couple sitting in a car, staring at him. He headed across the street to an old abandoned gas station and noticed that his hands were shaking. "I can't take anymore, God." He said under his breath. "Is this why you wanted me to become a Christian? So, you could destroy my life? I am so done with this..." His phone vibrated. "Just leave me alone, God!" He screamed at the sky. "I'm done with YOU!" He sobbed as he pulled his phone out to check his message, half expecting it to be from Topher.

"NO MORE BFF...LOL!!!" It read...Rusty.

Matt was so angry that it was difficult for him to text. "Where r u? Show urself COWARD!!!"

"LOL, MATT!!! I'M ABOUT TO KILL THEM ALL!!!"

The dragon and all the foul creatures began to back away as the sky turned almost totally black. The clouds swirled and the thunder boomed above. It was as if a living force were controlling it.

Andy lie perfectly still several yards away from Mark. "What's the plan, Mark!?" Scotty yelled over the roaring thunder. Mark glanced back at Scotty and Gabi and took a step toward Andy.

"I wouldn't do that if I were you, Mark McGee!" The dragon roared with laughter, causing Mark to pause. "Then again, go ahead! Save your friend!" His laughter caused Maria to cry and cover her ears. "Go on!" He dared Mark. "Give it a try!" More laughter.

Gabi attempted to calm a very distressed Maria. She met Mark's eye as he looked back and they both looked up. It appeared that the clouds were taking shape.

"It sure would be nice to have a few warrior angels right about now!" Scotty yelled into the air, causing the dragon to laugh even louder.

"Scotty Morgan! There will be no help for you today! Even your angels aren't foolish enough to show themselves in this place!" More laughter and rumblings of thunder. "No, Scotty Morgan! You are alone…and I am about to introduce your friend Andy to a force more powerful than all the hosts of heaven!"

"Dear Heavenly Father!" Pastor Eric began as the entire group gathered in a circle. "We come before you this evening to lift up each of these young people, in Jesus' name. Gabi Motes, Mark McGee, Scotty Morgan, Maria Lewis, Andy Cruz…" He paused for a moment and glanced over at the corner where Harold sat with his arms around Billy's mom. She was in shock. "And Ms. Mumpower also, Father. Comfort her in this difficult time." He saw the concern on Larry's face and was brought back to the task at hand. "Father, I pray your protection over each of these kid's lives right now…"

Christina felt her phone vibrate in her pocket. She let go of Cathie and Gae's hands and stepped away. Pulling the phone from her pocket, she saw that it was Matt. "Hello?" she said softly, trying not to interrupt Pastor Eric's prayer.

"Christina, he's going to kill them all!" Matt yelled. He was out of breath and it sounded like he was running.

"Matt, what are you talking about? Who?"

"Rusty! He already killed Billy and now he's going to kill the rest of them!"

"Matt, the doctor said Billy died from cardiac arrest. He had a heart attack!" she said as she stepped out into the hall. "Wait, are you trying to tell me that Rusty is here?"

"Yes! Go to the ICU and see if you can find him!" Matt yelled. "I'm about to get on the elevator, I'll see you in a few." He disconnected.

Christina headed to the ICU rooms. As she drew closer, she saw where there seemed to be a lot of commotion going on in one of the rooms. A doctor was shouting orders and nurses were moving in and out of the room with different equipment.

"Ma'am, I'm sorry!" a nurse called to her. "You can't be down here! You need to wait in the..."

"What's going on?" Christina demanded. "Whose room is that?" She pointed to the room with all the commotion.

"One of the doctors will come down and speak with everyone in a moment. You'll need to..."

"Have you seen a boy?" Christina asked, grasping at straws. "One of our teens has wandered off. Tall, red headed?"

"No, ma'am, I'll send him your way if I see him." She pointed Christina toward the waiting room.

About that time, the elevator doors opened down the hall and Matt came running toward them.

Andy's vitals were not good, and the medical team couldn't figure out why. As one of the nurses worked over him, she saw something move in the corner of the room. She glanced over and didn't see anything, but a chill ran up her spine. When she looked back at Andy, he was smiling up at her with an evil grin. She jumped back and screamed.

"What is it, Jamie!?" another nurse asked, in a panic.

Jamie noticed that Andy's eyes were closed and decided not to mention it. "Sorry...I thought I saw something."

"You nearly gave me a heart attack!"

"Yeah," Jamie panted. "Me too. Sorry." The other nurse turned back around, and Jamie looked back at Andy, who was now completely covered in blood. With a blood curdling scream, Jamie jumped back against the wall.

The second nurse turned around quickly and saw a red headed boy standing right beside Jamie, with his hand on her head. "Hey! Who are you!? Get out of here!"

Jamie slid down the wall to the floor, crying. "It's me! Jamie!"

"Not you," she replied, as two doctors ran in. "Him! Who is he and how did he get in here!?"

"What are you talking about, nurse?" one of the doctors asked. "There is nobody there."

Both nurses seemed to snap out of it and look around. "There was a boy!" the one nurse said, looking around in confusion. "He was saying something..." She began to cry.

"Exactly what was this boy saying?" one of the doctors asked sarcastically, while grinning at the other doctor.

"That he's about to kill them all."

"For we wrestle not against flesh and blood!" Mark said, stepping forward to face the dragon.

The dragon laughed even louder. "Are you expecting to turn into your spiritual warfare body, Mark McGee!? Become some muscle-bound warrior for God? Not going to happen in this place! You're in the valley of the shadow of death now!" More laughter. "Here, Mark McGee, you fear evil! For it is evil's domain...housed at the entrance to death and hell!" He raised up larger than Mark had ever seen him before. "It's almost as terrifying as my own lair!" he said with a laugh. Thunder clapped and the clouds above them continued to roll. "Now, let me introduce you, to your host!"

They all looked up and the black clouds had taken the shape of a man towering over them all. He had red glowing eyes that seemed to peer straight through them.

"Behold..." the dragon continued "the end of each of man... the beginning of eternity! DEATH himself!!!" The thunder boomed ever louder and the ground shook.

Maria screamed and curled into a ball. Gabi dropped down beside her and tried to cover her. "It's okay, Maria! Jesus is always with us!"

"Mark, this can't be good!" Scotty said. He grabbed his friend's shoulder and squeezed. Looking around, he saw that the creatures had moved in closer and they were completely surrounded. "This can't be good at all!"

"What seems to be the problem here?" came a voice from behind Gabi. She looked up to see Tobiah standing there smiling. Maria also caught sight of him and jumped up. She reached out her hand to touch him. "Deliverer!" She vanished.

"Where is he!?" Matt screamed. "Where is Rusty!?"

"Young man!" a nurse stepped in front of Matt. "What seems to be the problem?"

"There's a boy...Rusty!" Matt was panting from running. "Tall, red hair..."

"We haven't seen him!" this nurse had clearly heard enough. "Now I need you..."

"Did you say red hair?" another nurse asked. "A boy?"

"Yes!" Matt and Christina both replied. "Have you seen him?"

"Nurse!" a doctor called from one of the rooms. "Get back in here this instant!"

"I...thought I did...but just for a moment," she replied, clearly flustered. "Then he vanished."

"Nurse Thompson!" the doctor called again.

"Where did you see him!?" Matt asked.

"Just there," she pointed to Andy's room as Matt rushed past them all. "But he's not there!"

"Matt, stop!" Christina yelled and went after him.

"He's going to kill them all!" Matt yelled as he burst into each room and looked around. "Show yourself, Rusty! You coward!"

Pastor Eric and Bret had heard the commotion and came running.

"What is going on out here!?" an older doctor had stepped out of Andy's room and grabbed Matt by the arm. Matt tried to pull away with no success. The doctor looked around at all the people. "This is a hospital! Not a circus!" He looked right at Pastor Eric. "Sir, I don't know what kind of cockamamie religious nuts you people are, but you are to leave this hospital immediately!" Matt pulled away from him. "Nurse! If they are still here in one minute, call the police!" He stormed back into Andy's room and closed the door.

"What's going on, Matt?" Pastor Eric asked.

"Rusty texted me and said he is going to kill them all!" Matt said, in a panic. "Show yourself, you chicken coward!!!" Matt screamed, spit flying.

Bret wrapped his arms around Matt, "Dude, you have to calm down. He's clearly not here." He led Matt down the hall.

"He's not like us, Mr. Bret," Matt said. "He's like…demonic. I saw him kill Billy…"

"Come on, let's go outside and discuss this," Bret said, and they all got on the elevator.

"He's not human, Pastor Eric…you have to believe me!" Matt pleaded.

Just as the elevator doors began to close, there was a loud scream from down the hall, and they all jumped. "The Deliverer is COMING!!!" they heard Maria say as the doors closed.

Brianna's parents had arrived and were in her room. Her dad stood beside her bed, holding her hand as she told him everything she could remember. Her mom was on the phone with Gae, who was in the waiting room on the seventh floor.

"Hey, Brianna," her mom said. "Ms. Gae wants me to put her on speaker. Something is going on up there." Brianna nodded.

"Hey, Brianna," Ms. Gae said.

"Hey, is everything okay?"

"I'm not sure," she paused, and Brianna could hear shouting.
"It seems like Matt is losing it. He's saying something about
Rusty. Isn't that the boy who went missing?"

"Yes ma'am, what is he saying?" Brianna asked.

"Oh my..." Brianna could tell Ms. Gae was walking.
"Something about Rusty killing people."

"What!?"

"Mr. Bret has him now and I think they are all being kicked
out of the hospital...I better get back in the waiting room."

"I need to get up there," Brianna said, sitting up.

"No way, young lady!" her father held up his hand. "There
are people to deal with this..."

"Dad, it's my friends!" she protested. "Gabi is up there!"

"And so are a lot of other people...some of which are being
kicked out of the hospital for being in the way."

"Listen to your dad, Brianna!" Gae said. "I'll keep you guys
informed." Just then they all heard a girl scream over the phone.

Brianna shot out of bed. "Come with me, Daddy!" she said
while slipping a robe on over her gown. Her dad followed her
out of the room as her mom continued to talk to Gae. Out in the
hall, she saw Yvette heading towards her.

"Brianna, what's the rush? Hey, is this your dad?" She
smiled at him.

"Something's going on in ICU," Brianna said, on her way
to the elevators.

"I'll come too," Yvette said, following them.

Brianna's dad knew better than to argue with teenage girls
who had made their minds up. He just went along to make sure
they didn't get hurt.

Once they reached the seventh floor, Brianna took off with
Yvette in tow before her dad could stop her. "Brianna! Hold on!"
She was already around the corner.

As Brianna rounded the corner, she slid to a stop. "Whoa!"
Her and Yvette stood there taking in the scene. It was total chaos.
Pastor Eric and everyone from the waiting room were trying
to get information while doctors and nurses scrambled around

trying to keep people at bay and take care of the patients. "Ms. Gae!" Brianna called. "Please tell me that nobody else has died."

"I don't think so, but Andy isn't doing good." Gae replied. "Matt says Rusty is going to kill the rest of them like he did Billy."

"What!?" Brianna gasped. "Rusty killed Billy? I thought they said he had a heart attack!?"

"He did," Gae said. "But Matt was there...and said that Rusty caused it. That Rusty is some kind of demon."

"Mark was right..." Brianna said, looking at Yvette. "All along he tried to tell us that Rusty..."

"That Rusty what?" Pastor Eric had walked over.

"Was the dragon...from before." She locked eyes with Pastor Eric. "Is it possible?"

"Well, Mark would know, wouldn't he?" Gae said.

"Wait, who was that I heard scream?" Brianna asked.

"Maria," Pastor Eric replied. "She's awake...Bret's in there with her...the doctors couldn't stop him."

"Is she okay?" Yvette asked.

"Perfectly fine!" Pastor Eric said. "They have to run some tests, but there doesn't seem to be any brain damage. Though she did wake up screaming that the Deliverer was coming."

"Well, that's not a bad thing," Brianna said with a smile.

Andy opened his eyes as the black clouds above him swirled and spun. It was like awakening inside a tornado. As he attempted to figure out what was going on, his eyes focused on something close by. Something large, black, and scaly. He let out an audible scream when he realized that it was a dragon standing over him. As he attempted to move away, a large claw slid him back to where he'd been.

"Andy!" Mark yelled, when he saw him moving around. "Are you alright?"

"Not exactly!" Andy yelled.

"I will start with this one," an extremely deep voice called from above.

"It talks!" Scotty yelled, pointing at the sky.

"What was that!?" Andy called out. "Can I get a little help here, McGee!?"

"Then…I will take the rest of you!" A low rumble of laughter like thunder. "One by one."

"Andy!" Mark called. "Listen to me…you need to accept Jesus into your heart! Make Him the…"

"Give it up, McGee!" Andy called out with the little bit of strength he had left. Just then he began to rise into the air. "Whaaat's happening!?"

Gabi and Scotty appeared at Mark's side; both had their eyes closed praying.

"Andy! Please! You're going to die!!!" Mark called out as Tobiah placed a hand on his shoulder.

"I'm afraid I'm going to have to insist that everyone move back to the waiting room!" a nurse called out.

"Come on," Gae said to Brianna and Yvette. "There's nothing we can do here." Just then, Brianna's mom rounded the corner and joined them. Her dad filled her in on the details.

As they were walking back, a man in a doctor's coat brushed past Brianna. "Excuse me," he said, looking back at her and smiling. She gasped when she saw who it was. He held his finger to his lips to shush her and motioned for her to follow him.

"What is it?" Yvette asked, having heard Brianna gasp.

"Oh, nothing…I just need to use the restroom," she replied and headed past the waiting room following the man in the lab coat.

When they reached the restrooms, he turned to go into the ladies' room and she followed, giving him a strange look.

"You told them you were going to the restroom…I couldn't let you lie," Topher said with a smile and hugged her.

"What's going on, Topher?" she couldn't stop herself from crying. "Why did Billy have to die?"

"God's will is not always what WE think is best," Topher replied, gripping her shoulders. "On a lighter note…I was there when Billy entered heaven…and he isn't too upset," he said with a wink. "Now, why aren't you praying?"

"I was before my parents arrived," she replied.

"Rusty is here and right now it's up to you to stop him," he looked around. "The angels are being held back."

"ME!?" she yelled, in a panic. "Wait! What exactly IS Rusty?"

"Anansi, the dragon," Topher whispered. "And he has led your friends into the shadow of death."

Just then the door swung open and Yvette gasped at the sight of a man standing there in front of Brianna. Brianna pulled her in and let the door close. "What's going on?" Yvette asked, looking suspiciously at Topher.

"Yvette, this is Topher," she patted his chest. "He's an…"

"Brianna!" Topher shouted. "You must fight!" With that, he smiled at Yvette, gave her a wink, and vanished.

"Angel," Brianna finished as Yvette gasped and jumped back. Brianna grabbed her hand and pulled her close. "You gave your heart to Jesus, right?" Yvette nodded. "Good, let's pray."

"Hello there!" Tobiah said, looking up into the red eyes of death.

"Wait your turn, old man!" came a rumbling of thunder.

The dragon stepped forward and took a closer look. "Who is this that dares to stand in the presence of darkness?" he hissed. "Prepare to meet your doom!"

Andy continued to rise, squirming like a worm on a hook. "Help!" he screamed. "Somebody help me!"

"I'm going to need you to put that boy down," Tobiah said.

"Father God," Brianna began, holding Yvette's hands in the middle of the bathroom on the seventh floor of Savannah Memorial Hospital in the ICU wing. "We come to you in the name of Jesus." Yvette nodded, still not sure what was going on. "Not exactly sure what we are supposed to do," Brianna continued. "Other than call on you for help in our time of need."

"Yes," Yvette said. "Thank you, Father."

"We lift up Gabi, Mark, Scotty, and Andy to you, right now! I pray that you would deliver them from the shadow of death!"

There was a low rumble of laughter from above. "Anansi! Deal with this fool!"

"With pleasure!" the dragon stepped forward and raised his claws to strike. Tobiah dropped his staff and let his cloak fall off his shoulders. Immediately a burst of light shot from his face, his hands, and his feet, piercing the darkness.

Mark, Scotty, and Gabi fell back and covered their eyes. "Gabi!?" Mark screamed.

"Yes!" Gabi called back with tears in her eyes. She too had seen that the light was beaming from the holes in Tobiah's hands and feet. "Yes, Mark!" she screamed at the top of her lungs. "It's JESUS!!!"

"Guys!" Scotty yelled. "Where'd the dragon go?"

At the far end of the hallway, on the seventh floor, a red-headed teenage boy appeared. He was sweating profusely and breathing heavily. "There's more than one way to skin a cat," he said to himself. "I'll just kill them all like I did Billy." He began walking with a purpose toward the ICU wing. As he rounded the first corner, he passed the open door of the waiting room and heard several people gasp. He smiled. "That's right," he thought. "You know why I'm here. I'm about to fill up this hospitals morgue." Then, as he rounded the final corner to enter the ICU, he slid to a stop and let out his own gasp.

There, standing before him, were two teenage girls...over ten feet tall and covered in armor. Swords of fire drawn and ready to strike. "Not my friends, you, slimy lizard!" Brianna shouted, and raised her sword to strike.

"Not tonight!" Yvette added, raising her sword as well. Together, they brought their swords down to slice through the middle of a shocked teenage boy-demon of hell. He vanished in an explosion of ash and smoke.

Immediately the hall filled with a thousand warrior angels, swords drawn and cheering for the two teenage girls that had just defeated the dragon. Daniel, Adam, Brandon, and Chaz were high fiving them and giving them hugs as they returned to their normal size.

Pastor Eric came around the corner at that moment, looking for Rusty, when he saw Brianna and Yvette holding hands in the middle of the hall, praying. He could've sworn he saw a flash of light just beyond them.

"No!" Death screamed and the smoke that composed him began to dissipate. Andy dropped to the ground like a sack of potatoes. He quickly scampered away from the man with the lights.

Mark jumped up and ran to him. "Andy! Are you okay?"

"Who is that!?" Andy yelled, pointing at Tobiah. "What's going on?"

Mark helped him up. "Dude, that was Death that was lifting you up. You were almost a goner."

Andy was still backing away. "And that?" he asked in a panic. "Who is that?"

"Andy…" Mark said, putting his hands on Andy's shoulders. "That's Jesus!"

Andy stopped moving. He was breathing heavy and covered in sweat. He couldn't stop looking at the man who had just saved him from death. The glowing light began to wane. The man smiled at him. "Jesus?" A tear rolled down his cheek. He covered his face. "Forgive me."

Jesus walked over to him and placed his nail scarred hand on Andy's head. "My blood covers you." Andy looked up through tear stained eyes. "You're forgiven." Andy blinked away the tears and Jesus was gone.

Pastor Eric had been told that Mark, Gabi, and Scotty were stable, but it wasn't looking good for Andy. He had gathered everyone into the waiting room to pray. Eddie had even been brought up to join them. They gathered in a circle and prayed for Andy. That God would let him live. That God would miraculously wake them all up and give them an AMAZING testimony.

No sooner had those words crossed his lips, when the door burst open and a nurse paused at the door to wait for them to finish. Pastor Eric peeked over at her and smiled.

"I'm sorry, Pastor," she began. "I just thought you would want to know that they're awake."

Stepping out of the circle, Larry asked, "who's awake???"

"All of them!" she yelled. "As God as my witness! It's a miracle!"

CHAPTER 19

THE WELCOME HOME

4 days later

After shutting off his computer and clearing all the junk from his desk, Officer Ramsey walked into the captain's office. "Hey, boss, I'm heading up to the church."

"Today's the day, huh?"

"Yeah," he checked his watch. "The caravan should be arriving in about fifteen minutes. Supposed to be a big crowd up there. You should come, it's a church thing, you know there'll be food."

"Well, thanks to you I have quite a bit of paperwork to do," the captain responded, smiling up at the officer. "By the way, how's Matt?" he asked, sounding genuinely concerned.

"Christina says he's basically shutdown. Won't talk to anyone. I wish I could've gone up, but with the investigation and everything…"

"He'll be fine, it'll just take some time."

"Those two were inseparable," Ramsey said. "Even I can't believe Billy is gone. He's the fourth chair at our table."

"Have you heard how Mrs. Mumpower is doing?" The captain asked.

"As can be expected. Harold says she's a basket case." He looked away. "They had the body brought in yesterday. The funeral will be the day after tomorrow. Daisy Canard's funeral is tomorrow."

"Such a terrible situation," the captain said. "Well, you better get going."

"You're right, see ya." Ramsey turned to go.

"Oh, Ramsey...are you taking care of the other thing today also?"

"Yes, sir," he held up the file. "I'll see you later."

The six-car caravan, led by Pastor Eric, pulled into the church parking lot to much cheering from family and church members. There were people everywhere, some smiling, some crying, some clapping, and some waiting patiently to hug their loved ones. There were even tables set up in the parking lot, with a potluck assortment of goodies.

"Wow," Mark commented from the seat next to Pastor Eric, having called shotgun a mere half second faster than Scotty. He, Scotty, Andy, and Eddie had ridden back with Pastor Eric. Their parents had left earlier because of work.

"It's like a parade," Andy said, taking in what appeared to be his new crowd to hang out with. "So cool."

"This is all for you guys," Pastor Eric said. "You're the talk of the town!"

"This is awesome!" Scotty added.

Mark saw all the parents, family members, business owners, church members from various churches, "Hey, there's Pastor Joshua!" There were even firemen and some of the police force. In fact, Matt's dad was just pulling up in his squad car. "It looks like everybody is here!"

"Except my mom," Eddie replied. "Which is probably for the best."

Maria was asleep between Bret and Cathie with her head on Bret's shoulder. "So, what are you planning to do about her mother?" Cathie asked in a whisper.

"Right now, it's in God's hands," Bret replied, glancing over at Maria. "This girl needs a stable home environment."

"Daddy!" Shadow jumped out of the car with Brianna and her parents and ran into her father's arms.

"I'm so sorry I couldn't get away, baby girl," he said, with tears in his eyes.

"It's okay, Daddy," she replied. "I have so much to tell you."

Everyone was getting out of their vehicles and being surrounded by friends and family.

"Andy!" his mom yelled across the parking lot from her car. "Let's go!"

"I'll get a ride home later, Mom! I have some things to do!" he responded. "I won't be late!" he waved to her. She drove off without a word.

"Remember, dude," Mark said, putting his arm around Andy. "Be an example to her. God will work on her heart...same with you, Eddie!" They both nodded.

"We got this, McGee!" Andy fist bumped him. "Don't you worry, I'm not going to let Billy's sacrifice for me be in vain... Jesus' either." He smiled and teared up.

Mark was proud of the strides Andy had taken already. He'd borrowed a bible and read most of the New Testament in two days, lying in a hospital bed. Pastor Eric had taught him how to pray and Andy had even said he may just want to grow up to become a pastor himself.

After talking to several family members and receiving an exorbitant number of hugs and kisses, Yvette saw Daisy's parents sitting at a table watching her. She instantly teared up. Her heart broke for them...she couldn't even imagine their pain. She broke through the crowd and went to Daisy's mom, kneeling down and wrapping her arms around her. No words were necessary...they both just sobbed.

Mark, Scotty, Gabi, and Brianna kind of made their way to each other, and stood next to Pastor Eric's car. "Where's Andy and Eddie?" Gabi asked.

"Free food," Mark replied with a smile and pointed toward the tables where the boys were being lavished with love...and fried chicken.

"How long are you staying, Brianna?" Scotty asked.

"We're flying back right after Billy's funeral," she replied, looking sad. They all looked over at Matt, still sitting in Christina's backseat staring out the window away from the festivities.

"What are we going to do about him?" Scotty asked.

"Matt needs time," Gabi replied. "And lots of love and support."

"I have a feeling that God has that situation under control," Mark said, glancing over at Andy and Eddie. Andy was laughing at one of the older church ladies pinching Eddie's cheek. "So... pretty crazy stuff huh? That whole valley of the shadow of death thing."

"What I can't wrap my brain around," Brianna said. "Is how you were all there...I mean, you were each unconscious, yet your minds were linked...or something."

"And we all remember it," Gabi added. "Except Maria, she doesn't remember anything."

"Yeah, I guess with the extent of her head injury and all... boy, was she loopy," Scotty said. "But thank God she's better."

"And what about Tobiah?" Mark said. "Just wow! I mean, he was with me in the castle...just wow." His eyes misted.

"So, Pastor Eric told me that the name Tobiah means the Lord is good," Gabi said.

"And He is!" Mark said. "Greater is He!" he fist bumped Scotty. "Isn't it amazing that when we were in a place where we couldn't defend ourselves, Christ himself showed up to fight our battle?"

"Yes, it is!" Scotty and Gabi said together.

"That is so awesome!" Brianna added. "I'm jealous! You guys got to see Jesus!"

"Gabi? Brianna?" They all turned around to see their friend from the park standing behind them with tears in her eyes.

"Donna!" Gabi yelled and her and Brianna gave her a big hug. Donna had recently given her heart to Jesus while at the park cleanup with the gang.

Mark noticed that Donna was holding flyers in her hand. He took one while she was hugging the girls. "Missing boy, Chad Stanley. Who is this, Donna?"

The girls released her from her hug, and she looked down at her stack of flyers. "My little brother. He's been missing for five days." She wiped her eyes.

"What!?" Gabi exclaimed and grabbed Mark's flyer to read it. "Seven years old, last seen by neighbors, riding his bike toward the park in his neighborhood."

"We found his bike behind some bushes near that big creepy iron gate on the main road," Donna said.

"Wait, what!?" Scotty shouted and they all looked at each other.

"Where the castle used to be?" Mark asked.

"Yeah!" Donna replied. "Whatever happened to that thing?"

"Did they look for him in there?" Gabi asked.

Donna nodded. "Of course, but there was no trace of him... all they found was some homeless guy's bag.

"This is crazy," Mark began. "We need to..."

"Maria!" Maria's mother was traipsing across the parking lot straight for her. She appeared to be under the influence of alcohol or drugs. Maria stiffened and Cathie wrapped her arm around her. "You don't look sick to me, young lady! Go get in the car while I talk with these fine people about how much I'm about to sue them for!" Everyone had gone quiet and watched as the drama played out.

"I'm not going anywhere with you, Mama!" Maria said.

"I knew these Bible thumpin' idiots would brainwash you, girl! Ain't it bad enough they tried to kill you!? Now get in my car right now! You got workin' to do!" She cackled a witch-like laugh out and then had a coughing fit. She grabbed Maria by the arm and snatched her away from Cathie. When she turned to walk away, she slammed right into Bret's chest and almost fell backwards. "Get outta my way!"

"You're an unfit mother," Bret said calmly. "Now, take your hands off her."

"I'm already suing this church...you want to join the fun, mister? What's your name?"

Bret grabbed her hand away from Maria with one quick snatch. She pulled away from him and was about to say something when he put his finger in her face. "Touch her again and I'll give you a reason to sue me."

"She's my daughter!" she screamed.

"Ms. Lewis?" Officer Ramsey had walked up.

"Finally!" she spit out. "A cop when you actually need one! Arrest this man...he assaulted me!" She put her finger in Bret's face now. "I'm suing you for every penny you have!"

"Ms. Betty Lewis," Officer Ramsey said. "I'm actually here to place YOU under arrest for the murder of Michael Lewis."

"What are you talking a..." Ms. Lewis began.

"EXCUSE ME!!!???" It was Maria's turn to shout now. She faced her mother and shoved her. "You killed my daddy!?"

"Shut up, girl! Don't you ever get in my face...I'll slap the Jesus outta you!" She raised her hand to hit Maria and Officer Ramsey grabbed it and put it behind her back, cuffing her and reading her rights to her.

"Get your filthy hands off me, you dirty pig!"

Maria slapped her mother across the face. "You did it! Didn't you!?" You were always cheating on him with your drug dealers and..."

"I didn't kill your daddy, baby," her mother said softly, and it gave Maria pause, making her feel guilty. Then her mother smiled. "But my boyfriend did!" She cackled out another cough-inducing laugh. "Mr. Perfect was always meddling into my business and threatening to take you away! I couldn't let that happen!" She laughed again. "We dumped his worthless body in the St. Johns River!" she coughed out.

Cathie wrapped her arms around a sobbing Maria. "It's okay, baby."

"A confession!" Officer Ramsey said. "Well, that makes my job easy." He led her away.

"Wait! I was just messing with her, getting her riled up. That girl abandoned me! How am I supposed to pay rent?"

"There's no rent where you're going," Officer Ramsey said, opening the back door of his squad car. When he looked back, Bret and Cathie were hugging a sobbing Maria.

"Wow," Scotty said. "That was harsh."

"Never a dull moment in Gateway," Mark said just as he looked over and spotted Topher standing near the corner of the church building. Topher held a finger to his lips and motioned for Mark to join him. He disappeared around the corner. "I'll be right back, guys." He headed in that direction while Scotty demonstrated that he could fit more marshmallows in his mouth than Brianna could. Gabi had gone to help Donna pass her flyers out. He rounded the corner just in time to see Topher and someone else head behind the church. He walked faster, trying to catch up. Topher had his back to him when he rounded the next corner and Mark couldn't see who he was with. "Dude, are you trying to act like a drug dealer? Being all secretive." Just then, Topher turned around and Mark froze when he saw who it was with him. "Charles?"

Charles, his friend from camp, gave him a big smile as Mark fist bumped him and gave him a hug. "Actually, it's Chaz," he said with a sheepish grin.

"Say what?" Mark said, thoroughly confused, especially when Charles and Topher shared a glance.

In an instant Charles transformed into a huge warrior angel, towering over Mark and causing him to fall back on his rear. "The name is Chaz."

"Whoa!" Mark exclaimed. "So, you really were our guardian angel!"

Chaz transformed back to Charles. "One of many that had your back on that trip…" He hung his head. "Except, you know."

"Dude, that was God's plan," Topher said. "You have to let it go." He smiled at Mark and they hugged. "We need to talk."

Matt sat in the backseat of Christina's car, refusing to get out and celebrate with everyone else. He had absolutely nothing to celebrate. He hadn't even wanted to talk to his dad. What was the point of it all, anyway? Happiness leads to sadness. Hope leads to disappointment. Life leads to death. God had taken his cousin, and then in his grief, God had taken his best friend. Gee, thanks God. Matt no longer wanted anything to do with Him. It wasn't that he didn't believe in God, he just outright hated Him. God was not who the Bible said He was. As far as Matt was concerned, He was no better than the devil. He couldn't care less about Matt or anyone else for that matter.

What Matt didn't realize was, that sitting right beside him in the car, was a large scaly creature with his claws buried deep into Matt's mind. "That's right...God is evil. He doesn't care about you. He killed your cousin and your best friend in the same week. What kind of GOOD God would allow that?" A deep-throated laugh.

Just then, the driver door and the other back door opened, and Andy and Eddie climbed in, both holding plates of food. Andy handed one back to Matt. "No thanks, man...listen guys..."

"Take the plate, dude," Andy said. "And listen to what I have to say." Matt took the plate begrudgingly. "Great, now listen," Andy continued. "I'm really sorry about your cousin dying, dude. I didn't know her, but I hear she was really nice." Matt looked out the window. "I'm also sorry about Billy. Dude was always so happy and crazy it was annoying." Matt gave him a look that said tread carefully. "But he was a good friend to everybody he knew...even me." Andy set his plate in the seat next to him and wiped his eyes.

"I'm sorry about Billy too, Matt," Eddie said. Matt glanced at him and looked back out the window.

"Listen, man," Andy continued. "I don't know if you heard about what went down in there when we were all unconscious… or if you even believe it. But the fact that we can all remember detail for detail tells me it was more than just our imagination…it happened. I was there. I was stupid, but like Pastor Eric said, I didn't have a relationship with Christ, so I didn't know any better. Anyway, your boy…Billy…he laid down his life for me." He paused again and Matt looked at him. "That crazy fool tried to rescue me from a dragon, man…who does that?" Andy sniffed and wiped his eyes again.

Matt actually smiled. "Billy does."

"Yeah," Andy nodded. "And he saved me from hell, bro… just like Jesus."

"Your best friend died saving my best friend," Eddie said.

"That's why we're here, Matt," Andy said. "In this car, bothering you…because we want to honor Billy, so to speak, by asking you, his best friend, to help us."

"Help you what?" Matt asked.

"Keep us in line…help us with this God stuff…be our friend and I guess our leader."

"We're idiots," Eddie said with a smile. "We have to have a leader…you know, Todd…Rusty."

"I don't know, guys," Matt said. "I'm kind of in a bad place right now."

"Yeah!" the demon-creature said in his ear. "Not to mention, God is a liar!" Just then an enormous blade sliced him in half, and he vanished in a puff of smoke.

"That's what I'm talking about," Adam said, smiling at Daniel, who was sliding his sword back into its sheath. They fist bumped and disappeared.

"That's why you need us," Andy said. Matt looked at them both and saw their sincerity. Andy held up his fist. "Pound it." Matt pounded it.

308

EPILOGUE

"**M**ark! Your princess is green!" Bethany giggled as her and Mark lay on her bed coloring. "She can't be green!"

"What!? Why not!?" Mark replied. "That isn't fair."

"Her dress can be green, her shoes can be green, even her hair can be green, but not her self!" Bethany said, with a laugh. "She just looks silly!"

"Well, I think she is the prettiest green princess of them all," Mark announced.

"That's because she's the ONLY green princess of them all," she said, rolling her eyes at him.

"Bethany! It's time for bed, sweetheart!" Mom called from downstairs.

"Yes, ma'am!" Bethany yelled. "Mark will tuck me in!"

"Okay, good night, I love you!"

"Good night, Mommy! I love you too!"

Mark got up from her bed and put the crayons and coloring books away. "Did you brush your teeth yet?"

"Yes, do you want to smell my breath?" she giggled, getting under the covers. "Mark, tell me again what happened when you were in a comma."

Mark sat down next to her and laughed. "It's called a coma and I was actually just unconscious, not really in a coma like Maria was."

"Did you REALLY get to see Jesus?" Bethany asked with excitement in her voice, and Mark nodded. "What did He look like?"

309

"Well, He was an old man named Tobiah," Mark replied.

"Why was He like that?" She had already asked these questions a dozen times over the past two days, but Mark knew her mind was soaking it all in.

"Because, at the time, that's who we needed Him to be." Mark thought back. "We were hungry and thirsty and tired...he took care of us."

"What about..." she began to ask but Mark tickled her side. She screamed and giggled.

"You've heard this story a hundred times," he said with a smile. "Now you need to go to sleep and dream about green princesses." He stood up and walked to the door.

"Nope, I'm gonna dream about normal colored princesses."

"What about dragons?" Mark asked.

"No dragons," Bethany said in a serious tone. "I don't want to dream about dragons."

"And that brings us to prayer time," Mark said. "Because how do we get rid of dragons?"

"By praying to Jesus," she replied and closed her eyes to pray.

When Mark got to his room, he sent Scotty a text. "Whatchu doin?"

"Watching Avengers with the fam." Scotty replied.

"Cool" Mark replied and sat down to play some video games. He slid on his headphones and hit start. The music began to play in his ears, but something didn't feel right. It was almost like he could hear the wind blowing behind the music. He hit the pause button and the wind sound continued. He removed his headphones and could still hear it from behind him. Jumping up really fast, he spun around ready for anything. Topher was standing there with a grim look on his face. "Dude, angels really shouldn't instill fear."

"Sorry," Topher said.

"I'm just saying...you should check into that. I think it's in the Bible."

"Mark," Topher said, and Mark sighed. "It's time."

"At least I got to go to both funerals," Mark said, as he walked over and grabbed an already prepared bag. "Thanks for that, by the way." Topher grabbed his arm and instantly they were in a dark, thick forest. Mark began searching his bag for his flashlight when Topher went full angel and lit up the night around them. They were standing next to a tree that had been knocked over. Mark saw a hole on the side, near all the roots and almost invisible. "Is that it?" Topher nodded and they just looked at each other.

"I want to tell you that you don't have to do this," Topher said.

"And you would be correct!" Came a voice from behind them. They both jumped. There among the trees stood Daniel, Adam, Brandon, and Chaz."

"Seriously, guys!" Mark said. "Read a Bible!"

"Topher is right, Mark," Daniel said. "You don't have to do this. In fact, I don't recommend it."

"Was he also right in saying that I was the only one who COULD do this?" Mark asked. They all nodded. "Then I have to."

"The chance is very slim that you will find Chad alive," Adam said.

"But there's still a chance," Mark replied. "Besides, that's not the only reason I'm going."

Daniel walked up to Mark and knelt down to his level. "We cannot come where you are going. Tobiah will not show up in your darkest hour. He will watch over you, Mark…but He will not interfere." He placed his giant hands on Mark's shoulders. "You will be completely alone."

"Yeah," Topher said. "There's not any cell service where you're going."

Mark smiled at them. "I left my phone anyway. I'll be fine guys…just, take care of my family…and Scotty, he'll probably fall apart without me. Oh, and Ga…"

At that moment the entire forest lit up like a football stadium. Thousands of angels had gathered all around them. Mark's eyes misted up and he quickly wiped them.

"Well, this is it." He picked up his bag and walked to the entrance. "Hey looky there...stairs." He turned around and faced them.

"Goodbye, Mark McGee," Topher said. "Greater is He!"

Mark smiled, "Greater is He!" With that, he turned around, closed his eyes, said a prayer, and stepped into the darkness.

Coming soon:

MARK MCGEE AND THE JOURNEY TO THE
DRAGON'S LAIR

#gr8risHE

CPSIA information can be obtained
at www.ICGtesting.com
Printed in the USA
FSHW020158040919
61671FS